"THE HERO GOES FROM THE FRYING PAN INTO THE FIRE and back with breathtaking agility. In the process he is never far from willing and nubile females. The heat generated from his escapades uses a carnal fuel."

—*The New York Times*

"FLASHMAN IS A THREE-DIMENSIONAL ANTIHERO —a coward, a scoundrel, a selfish, dishonest libertine . . . Flashman visits an African king who sells his countrymen to the slavers, masquerades as a Royal Navy 'spy,' hides out in a New Orleans brothel, smuggles a beautiful half-caste girl up the Mississippi, meets the young Abraham Lincoln . . . His engrossing escapades are pure entertainment." —*The Nashville Tennessean*

"A LITERARY EVENT . . . It is so much fun, with so much suspense, that you will be captured by it and will read till your eyes can literally stand no more!"

—*The Columbus Dispatch*

"THE VERY CREAM OF PARODY . . . Marvelous fun!"

—*The Cleveland Plain Dealer*

"OUTRAGEOUS ADVENTURES AND LUSTY WENCHING . . . The best Flashman yet!" —*The Buffalo News*

GEORGE MACDONALD FRASER was born in England, served in a Highland regiment in India, Africa, and the Middle East, and has worked as a journalist. He continues to work on the Flashman series, ten of which are available in Plume editions. He now lives on the Isle of Man with his family.

THE FLASHMAN PAPERS
(in chronological order)

FLASH FOR FREEDOM!

FLASH FOR FREEDOM!

GEORGE MacDONALD FRASER

A PLUME BOOK

PLUME
Published by the Penguin Group
Penguin Books USA Inc., 375 Hudson Street, New York, New York 10014,
U.S.A.
Penguin Books Ltd, 27 Wrights Lane, London W8 5TZ, England
Penguin Books Australia Ltd, Ringwood, Victoria, Australia
Penguin Books Canada Ltd, 10 Alcorn Avenue, Toronto, Ontario, Canada M4V
3B2
Penguin Books (N.Z.) Ltd, 182-190 Wairau Road, Auckland 10, New Zealand

Penguin Books Ltd, Registered Offices: Harmondsworth, Middlesex, England

Published by Plume, an imprint of New American Library, a division of Penguin
Books USA Inc.

PUBLISHER'S NOTE

This novel is a work of fiction. Names, characters, places, and incidents either
are the product of the author's imagination or, if real, used fictitiously.

Library of Congress Cataloging in Publication Data

Fraser, George MacDonald, 1925–
  Flash for freedom.

  I. Title.
[PR6056.R287F55   1985]   823'.914   8422721
ISBN 0-452-26089-2

 REG. TRADEMARK—MARCA REGISTRADA

First Plume Printing, August, 1985

30 29 28 27 26 25 24
PRINTED IN THE UNITED STATES OF AMERICA

For Kath, a memento of
the long Sunday

Explanatory Note

When the first two packets of the Flashman Papers were published, in 1969 and 1970, there was some controversy over their authenticity. It was asked whether the papers were, in fact, the true personal memoirs of Harry Flashman, the notorious bully of *Tom Brown's Schooldays* and later an eminent British soldier, or were simply an impudent fake.

This was not a controversy in which either Mr Paget Morrison, the owner of the papers, or I, his editor, thought fit to join. The matter was thoroughly discussed in various journals, and also on television, and if any doubters remain they are recommended to study the authoritative article which appeared in the *New York Times* of July 29, 1969, and which surely settles the question once and for all.

The first two packets of the papers contained Flashman's personal narrative of his expulsion from Rugby School by Dr Thomas Arnold, his early service in the British Army (1839–42), his decoration by Queen Victoria after the First Afghan War, and his involvement in the Schleswig-Holstein Question, in which he found himself pitted against the young Otto von Bismarck and the celebrated Countess of Landsfeld. The third packet, which is now presented to the public, continues his story in the year 1848 and the early months of 1849. It is remarkable as a first-hand account of an important social phenomenon of the early Victorian years—the Afro-American slave trade—and in its illumination of the characters of two of the most eminent statesmen of the century, one a future British Prime Minister and the other a future American President. Flashman's recollections cast interesting light on what may be called their formative years.

When the Flashman Papers were brought to light at Ashby, Leicestershire, in 1965, it was noted that while the great volume of manuscript had obviously been examined and re-arranged round about 1915, no alteration or amendment had been made to the text as set down by Flashman himself in 1903–1905. Closer examination of the third packet reveals, however, that an editorial hand has been lightly at work. I suspect that it belonged to Grizel de Rothschild, the youngest of Flashman's sisters-in-law, who with a fine Victorian delicacy has modified those blasphemies and improprieties with which the old soldier occasionally emphasised his narrative. She was by no means consistent in this, for while she paid close attention to oaths, she left untouched those passages in which Flashman retails his amorous adventures; possibly she did not understand what he was talking about. In any event, she gave up the task approximately half-way through the manuscript, but I have left her earlier editing as it stands, since it adds a certain period charm to the narrative.

For the rest, I have as usual inserted occasional explanatory notes.

G.M.F.

FLASH FOR FREEDOM!

I believe it was the sight of that old fool Gladstone, standing in the pouring rain holding his special constable's truncheon as though it were a bunch of lilies, and looking even more like an unemployed undertaker's mute than usual, that made me think seriously about going into politics. God knows I'm no Tory, and I never set eyes on a Whig yet without feeling the need of a bath, but I remember thinking as I looked at Gladstone that day: "Well, if *that's* one of the bright particular stars of English public life, Flashy my boy, you ought to be at Westminster yourself."

You wouldn't blame me; you must have thought the same, often. After all, they're a contemptible lot, and you'll agree that I had my full share of the qualities of character necessary in political life. I could lie and dissemble with the best, give short change with a hearty clap on the shoulder, slip out from under long before the blow fell, talk, toady, and turn tail as fast as a Yankee fakir selling patent pills. Mark you, I've never been given to interfering in other folks' affairs if I could help it, so I suppose that would have disqualified me. But for a little while I did think hard about bribing my way to a seat—and the result of it was that I came within an ace of being publicly disgraced, shanghaied, sold as a slave, and God knows what besides. I've never seriously considered politics since.

It was when I came home from Germany in the spring of '48, after my skirmish with Otto Bismarck and Lola Montez. I was in d----d bad shape, with a shaven skull, a couple of wounds, and the guts scared half out of me, and all I wanted was to go to ground in London until I was my own man once more. One thing I was sure of: nothing was going to drag me out of England again—which was ironic, when you consider that I've spent more than half of the last fifty years at the ends of the earth, in uniform as often as not, and doing most of my walking backwards.

Anyway, I came home across the Channel one jump ahead of half the monarchs and statesmen in Europe. The popular rebellion I'd seen in Munich was only one of a dozen that broke out that spring, and all the fellows who'd lost their thrones and chancellorships seemed to have decided, like me, that old England was the safest place. So it proved, but the joke was that for a few weeks after I came home it looked touch and go whether England didn't have a revolution of her own, which would have sold the fleeing monarchs properly, and serve 'em right.

Mind you, I thought it was all gammon myself; I'd just seen a real rebellion, with mobs chanting and smashing and looting, and I couldn't imagine it happening in St James's. But that crabbed old Scotch miser, Morrison, my abominable father-in-law, thought different, and poured out his fears to me on my first evening at home.

"It's thae bluidy Chartists," cries he, with his head in his hands. "The d - - - - d mob is loose aboot the toon, or soon will be. It's no' enough, their Ten Hoors Bill, they want tae slake their vengeance on honest fowk as well. Burn them a', the wicked rascals! And whit does the Government do, will ye tell me? Naethin'! Wi' rebellion in oor midst, an' the French chappin' at oor doors!"

"The French have too much on hand with their own rebels to mind about us," says I. "As to the Chartists, I recall you expressing the same fears, years ago, in Paisley, and nothing came of it. If you remember—"

"Naethin' came o't, d'ye say?" cries he, with his chops quivering. "I ken whit came o't! You, that should hae been at your post, were loupin' intae the bushes wi' my Elspeth. Oh, Goad," says he, groaning, "as if we hadnae tribulation enough. Wee Elspeth, in her . . . her condeetion."

That was another thing, of course. My beautiful Elspeth, after eight years of wedded bliss, had now conceived at last, and to hear her father, mother, and sisters you would have thought it was Judgement Day. Myself, I believe she'd done it just to be topsides with the Queen, who had recently produced yet another of her innumerable litter. But what concerned me most was the identity of the father; I knew my darling feather-head, you see, for the trollop she was—you would never have thought it, to look at her beguiling innocence, but it had long been an unspoken bargain between us that we let each other's private lives alone, and I could guess she had been in the woodshed with half a dozen during my absence. Mind you, I might have pupped her myself before I went to Germany, but who could tell? And if she gave birth to something with red hair and a pug nose there was liable to be talk, and God knows what might come of that.

You see, we were an odd family. Old Morrison was as rich as an Amsterdam Jew, and when my guv'nor went smash over railway stock, Morrison had paid the bills for Elspeth's sake. He had been paying ever since, keeping me and my guv'nor on a pittance while he used our house, and got what credit he could out of being related to the Flashman family. Not that that was much, in my opinion, but since we were half-way into Society, and Morrison had daughters to marry off, he was prepared to tolerate us. He *had* to tolerate *me*, anyway, since I was married to his daughter. But it was a d - - - - d tricky business, all round, for he could kick me out if he chose, and would do like a shot the moment Elspeth decided she'd had enough of me. As it was, we dealt well enough with each other, but with a child on the way things might, I suspected, be different. I'd no wish to be out in the street trying to scrape by on a captain's half pay.

So what with Elspeth pregnant and old Morrison expecting the Communist rabble at the door at any moment, it was a fairly cheerless homecoming. Elspeth seemed pleased enough to see me, all right, but when I tried to bundle her into bed she would have none of it, in case the child was harmed. So instead of bouncing her about that evening I had to listen fondly to her drivelling about what name we should give our Little Hero—for she was sure it must be a boy.

"He shall be Harry Albert Victor," says she, holding my hand and gazing at me with those imbecile blue eyes which never lost their power, somehow, to make my heart squeeze up inside me, God knows why. "After you, *my* dearest love, and our dear, dear Queen and *her* dearest love. Would you approve, my darling?"

"Capital choice," says I. "Couldn't be better." Not unless, I thought to myself, you called him Tom, or Dick, or William, or whatever the fellow's name was who was in the hay with you. (After all, we'd been married a long while and made the springs creak time without number, and devil a sign of our seed multiplying. It seemed odd, now. Still, there it was.)

"You make me so happy, Harry," says she, and do you know, I believed it. She was like that, you see; as immoral as I was, but without my intelligence. No conscience whatever, and a blissful habit of forgetting her own transgressions—or probably she never thought she had any to forget.

She leaned up and kissed me, and the smell and feel of her blonde plumpness set me off, and I made a grab at her tits, but she pushed me away again.

"We must be patient, my own," says she, composing herself. "We must think only of dear Harry Albert Victor."

(That, by the way, is what he is called. The bastard's a bishop, too. I can't believe he's mine.)

She cooed and maundered a little longer, and then said she must rest, so I left her sipping her white-wine whey and spent the rest of the evening listening to old Morrison groaning and snarling. It was the same old tune, more or less, that I'd grown used to on the rare occasions when we had shared each other's company over the past eight years—the villainy of the workers, the weakness of government, the rising cost of everything, my own folly and extravagance (although heaven knows he never gave me enough to be extravagant with), the vanity of his wife and daughters, and all the rest of it. It was pathetic, and monstrous, too, when you considered how much the old skinflint had raked together by sweating his mill-workers and cheating his associates. But I observed that the richer he got, the more he whined and raged, and if there was one thing I'll say for him, he got richer quicker than the only sober man in a poker game.

The truth was that, coward and skinflint though he was, he had a shrewd business head, no error. From being a prosperous Scotch mill owner when I married his daughter he had blossomed since coming south, and had his finger in a score of pies—all d----d dirty ones, no doubt. He had become known in the City, and in Tory circles too, for if he was a provincial nobody he had the golden passport, and it was getting fatter all the time. He was already angling for his title, although he didn't get it until some little time later, when Russell sold it to him—a Whig minister ennobling a Tory miser, which just goes to show. But with all these glittering prizes in front of him, the little swine was getting greedier by the hour, and the thought of it all dissolving in revolution had him nearly puking with fear.

"It's time tae tak' a stand," says he, goggling at me. "We have to defend our rights and our property"—and I almost burst out laughing as I remembered the time in Paisley when his mill-workers got out of hand, and he cringed behind his door, bawling for me to lead my troops against them. But this time he was really frightened; I gathered from his vapourings that there had been recent riots in Glasgow, and even in Trafalgar Square, and that in a few days there was to be a great rally of Chartists—"spawn of Beelzebub" he called them—on Kennington Common, and that it was feared they would invade London itself.

To my astonishment, when I went out next day to take my bearings, I discovered there was something in it. At Horse Guards there were rumours that regiments were being brought secretly to town, the homes of Ministers were to be guarded, and supplies of cutlasses and firearms were being got ready. Special constables were being recruited to oppose the mob, and the Royal Family were leaving town. It all sounded d - - - - d serious, but my Uncle Bindley, who was on the staff, told me that the Duke was confident nothing would come of it.

"So you'll win no more medals this time," says he, sniffing. "I take it, now that you have consented to honour us with your presence again, that you are looking to your family" (he meant the Pagets, my mother's tribe) "to find you employment again."

"I'm in no hurry, thank'ee," says I. "I'm sure you'd agree that in a time of civil peril a gentleman's place is in his home, defending his dear ones."

"If you mean the Morrisons," says he, "I cannot agree with you. Their rightful place is with the mob, from which they came."

"Careful, uncle," says I. "You never know—you might be in need of a Scotch pension yourself some day." And with that I left him, and sauntered home.

The place was in a ferment. Old Morrison, carried away by

terror for his strong-boxes, had actually plucked up courage to go to Marlborough Street and 'test as a special constable, and when I came home he was standing in the drawing-room looking at his truncheon as though it was a snake. Mrs Morrison, my Medusa-in-law, was lying on the sofa, with a maid dabbing her temples with eau-de-cologne, Elspeth's two sisters were weeping in a corner, and Elspeth herself was sitting, cool as you please, with a shawl round her shoulders, eating chocolates and looking beautiful. As always, she was the one member of the family who was quite unruffled.

Old Morrison looked at me and groaned, and looked at the truncheon again.

"It's a terrible thing to tak' human life," says he.

"Don't take it, then," says I. "Strike only to wound. Get your back against a brick wall and smash 'em across the knees and elbows."

The females set up a great howl at this, and old Morrison looked ready to faint.

"D'ye think ... it'll come tae ... tae bloodshed?"

"Shouldn't wonder," says I, very cool.

"Ye'll come with me," he yammered. "You're a soldier—a man of action—aye, ye've the Queen's Medal an' a'. Ye've seen service —aye—against the country's enemies! Ye're the very man tae stand up to this ... this trash. Ye'll come wi' me—or maybe tak' my place!"

Solemnly I informed him that the Duke had given it out that on no account were the military to be involved in any disturbance that might take place when the Chartists assembled. I was too well known; I should be recognised.

"I'm afraid it is for you civilians to do your duty," says I. "But I shall be here, at home, so you need have no fear. And if the worst befalls, you may be sure that my comrades and I shall take stern vengeance."

I left that drawing-room sounding like the Wailing Wall, but it was nothing to the scenes which ensued on the morning of the great Chartist meeting at Kennington. Old Morrison set off, amidst the lamentations of the womenfolk, truncheon in hand, to join the other specials, but was back in ten minutes having sprained his ankle, he said, and had to be helped to bed. I was sorry, because I'd been hoping he might get his head stove in, but it wouldn't have happened anyway. The Chartists did assemble, and the specials were mustered in force to guard the bridges—it was then that I saw Gladstone with the other specials, with his nose dripping, preparing to sell his life dearly for the sake of constitutional liberty and his own investments. But it poured down, everyone was soaked, the foreign agitators who were on hand got nowhere, and all the inflamed mob did was to send a monstrous petition across to the House of Commons. It had five million signatures, they said; I know it had four of mine, one in the name of Obadiah Snooks, and three others in the shape of X's beside which I wrote, "John Morrison, Arthur Wellesley, Henry John Temple Palmerston, their marks".

But the whole thing was a frost, and when one of the Frog agitators in Trafalgar Square got up and d - - - - d the whole lot of the Chartists for English cowards, a butcher's boy tore off his coat, squared up to the Frenchy, and gave the snail-chewing scoundrel the finest thrashing you could wish for. Then, of course, the whole crowd carried the butcher's boy shoulder high, and finished up singing "God Save the Queen" with tremendous gusto. A thoroughly English revolution, I dare say.[1]

You may wonder what all this had to do with my thinking about entering politics. Well, as I've said, it had lowered my opinion of asses like Gladstone still further, and caused me to speculate that if I were an M.P. I couldn't be any worse than that sorry pack of fellows, but this was just an idle thought. However, if my chief feeling about the demonstration was disappointment that so little mischief had been done, it had a great effect on my father-in-law, crouched at home with the bed-clothes over his head, waiting to be guillotined.

You'd hardly credit it, but in a way he'd had much the same thought as myself, although I don't claim to know by what amazing distortions of logic he arrived at it. But the upshot of his panic-stricken meditations on that day and the following night, when he was still expecting the mob to reassemble and run him out of town on a rail, was the amazing notion that I ought to go into Parliament.

"It's your duty," cries he, sitting there in his night-cap with his ankle all bandaged up, while the family chittered round him, offering gruel. He waved his spoon at me. "Ye should hiv a seat i' the Hoose."

I'm well aware that when a man has been terrified out of his wits, the most lunatic notions occur to him as sane and reasonable, but I couldn't follow this.

"Me, in Parliament?" I loosed a huge guffaw. "What the devil would I do there? D'ye think that would keep the Chartists at bay?"

At this he let loose a great tirade about the parlous state of the country, and the impending dissolution of constitutional government, and how it was everyone's duty to rally to the flag. Oddly enough, it reminded me of the kind of claptrap I'd heard from Bismarck—strong government, and lashing the workers—but I couldn't see how Flashy, M.P., was going to bring that about.

"If yesterday's nonsense has convinced you that we need a change at Westminster," says I, "—and I'd not disagree with you there—why don't you stand yourself?"

He glowered at me over his gruel-bowl. "I'm no' the Hero of Kabul," says he. "Forbye, I've business enough to attend to. But you—ye've nothing to hinder ye. Ye're never tired o' tellin' us whit a favourite ye are wi' the public. Here's your chance to make somethin' o't."

"You're out of your senses," says I. "Who would elect me?"

"Anybody," snaps he. "A pug ape frae the zoological gardens could win a seat in this country, if it was managed right." Buttering me up, I could see.

"But I'm not a politician," says I. "I know nothing about it, and care even less."

"Then ye're the very man, and ye'll find plenty o' kindred spirits at Westminster," says he, and when I hooted at him he flew into a tremendous passion that drove the females weeping from the room. I left him raging.

But when I came to think about it, do you know, it didn't seem quite so foolish after all. He was a sharp man, old Morrison, and he could see it would do no harm to have a Member in the family, what with his business interests and so on. Not that I'd be much use to him that I could see—I didn't know, then, that he had been maturing some notion of buying as many as a dozen seats. I'd no idea, you see, of just how wealthy the old rascal was, and how he was scheming to use that wealth for political ends. You won't find much in the history books about John Morrison, Lord Paisley, but you can take my word for it that it was men like him who pulled the strings in the old Queen's time, while the political puppets danced. They still do, and always will.

And from my side of the field, it didn't look a half bad idea. Flashy, M.P. Sir Harry Flashman, M.P., perhaps. Lord Flash of Lightning, Paymaster of the Forces, with a seat in the Cabinet, d - - n your eyes. God knows I could do *that* job as well as Thomas Babbling Macaulay. Even in my day dreaming I stopped short of Flashy, Prime Minister, but for the rest, the more I thought of it the better I liked it. Light work, plenty of spare time for as much depraved diversion as I could manage in safety, and the chance to ram my opinions down the public's throat whenever I felt inclined. I need never go out of London if I didn't want to—I would resign from the army, of course, and rest on my considerable if ill-gotten laurels—and old Morrison would be happy to foot the bills, no doubt, in return for slight services rendered.

The main thing was, it would be a quiet life. As you know, in spite of the published catalogue of my career—Victoria Cross, general rank, eleven campaigns, and all that mummery—I've always been an arrant coward and a peaceable soul. Bullying underlings and whipping trollops always excepted, I'm a gentle fellow—which means I'll never do harm to anyone if there's a chance he may harm me in return. The trouble is, no one would believe it to look at me; I've always been big and hearty and looked the kind of chap who'd go three rounds with the town tough if he so much as stepped on my shadow, and from what Tom Hughes has written of me you might imagine I was always ready for devilment. Aye, but as I've grown older I've learned that devilment usually has to be paid for. God knows I've done my share of paying, and even in '48, at the ripe old age of twenty-six, I'd seen enough sorrow, from the Khyber to German dungeons by way of the Borneo jungles and the torture-pits of Madagascar, to convince me that I must never go looking for trouble again.[²] Who'd have thought that old Morrison's plans to seat me at Westminster could have led to . . . well, ne'er mind. All in good time.

As to getting a suitable seat, that would be easy enough, with Morrison's gelt greasing the way. Which prompted the thought that I ought to have a word with him about issues of political importance.

"Two thousand a year at least," says I.

"Five hundred and no' a penny more," says he.

"Dammit, I've appearances to keep up," says I. "Elspeth's notions ain't cheap."

"I'll attend to that," says he. "As I always have done." The cunning old bastard wouldn't even let me have the administration of my own wife's household; he knew better.

"A thousand, then. Good God, my clothes'll cost that."

"Elspeth can see tae your wardrobe," says he, smirking. "Five hundred, my buckie; it's mair than your worth."

"I'll not do it, then," says I. "And that's flat."

"Aye, weel," says he, "that's a peety. I'll just have to get one that will. Ye'll find it a wee bit lean on your army half-pay, I'm thinkin'."

"Damn you," says I. "Seven-fifty."

And eventually I got it, but only because Elspeth told her father I should have it. She, of course, was delighted at the thought of my having a political career. "We shall have soirées, attended by Lord John and the Marquis of Lansdowne,"[³] she exclaimed. "People with *titles*, and their ladies, and—"

"They're Whigs," says I. "I've an idea your papa will expect me to be a Tory."

"It doesn't signify in the least," says she. "The Tories are a better class of people altogether, I believe. Why, the Duke is a Tory, is he not?"

"So the rumour runs," says I. "But political secrets of that kind must be kept quiet, you know."

"Oh, it is all quite wonderful," says she, paying me no heed at all. "You will be famous again, Harry—you are so clever, you are sure to be a success, and I—I will need at least four page boys with buttons, and footmen in proper uniform." She clapped her hands, her eyes sparkling, and pirouetted. "Why, Harry! We shall need a new house! I must have clothes—oh, but papa will see to it, he is so kind!"

It occurred to me that papa might decide he had bitten off more than he could chew, listening to her, although personally I thought her ideas were excellent. She was in tremendous spirits, and I took the opportunity to make another assault on her; she was so excited that I had her half out of her dress before she realised what I was about, and then the wicked little b - - - h teased me along until I was thoroughly randified, only to stop me in the very act of boarding her, because of her concern for dear little Harry Albert Victor, blast his impudence.

"To think," says she, "that he will have a great statesman for a father!" She had me in the Cabinet already, you see. "Oh, Harry, how proud we shall be!"

Which was small consolation to me just then, having to button myself up and restrain my carnal appetites. To be sure I eased them considerably in the next week or two, for I looked out some of the Haymarket tarts of my acquaintance, and although they were a poor substitute for Elspeth they helped me to settle in again to London life and regular whoring. So I was soon enjoying myself, speculating pleasantly about the future, taking my ease with the boys about the town, forgetting the recent horrors of Jotunberg and Rudi Starnberg's gang of assassins, and waiting for old Morrison to start the wheels of my political career turning.

He was helped, of course, by my own celebrity and the fact that my father—who was now happily settled down with his delirium tremens at a place in the country—had been an M.P. in his time, and a damned fine hand at the hustings; he had got in on a popular majority after horse-whipping his opponent on the eve of the poll and offering to fight bare-knuckle with any man the Whigs could put up, from Brougham down. He had a good deal more bottom than I, but they did for him at Reform, and if I didn't have his ardour I was certain I had a greater talent for survival, political and otherwise.

Anyway, it was some weeks before Morrison announced that I was to meet some "men in the know" as he called them, and that we were to go down to Wiltshire for a few days, to the house of a local big-wig, where some politicos would be among the guests. It sounded damned dull, and no doubt would have been, had it not been for my own lechery and vanity and the shockingest turn of ill luck. Apart from anything else, I missed the Derby.

We left Elspeth at home, working contentedly at her Berlins,[4] and took the train for Bristol, Morrison and I. He was the damndest travelling companion you ever saw, for apart from being a thundering bore he carped at everything, from the literature at the station book stalls, which he pronounced trash, to the new practice of having to pay a bob "attendance money" to railway servants.[5] I was glad to get to Devizes, I can tell you, whence we drove to Seend, a pretty little place where our host lived in a fairish establishment called Cleeve House.

He was the kind of friend you'd expect Morrison to have—a middle-aged moneybags of a banker called Locke, with reach-me-down whiskers and a face like a three-day corpse. He was warm enough, evidently, but as soon as I saw the females sitting about in chairs on the gravel with their bonnets on, reading improving books, I could see this was the kind of house-party that wasn't Flashy's style at all. I was used to hunting weeks where you dined any old how, with lots of brandy and singing, and chaps p - - - - - g in the corner and keeping all hours, and no females except the local bareback riders, as old Jack Mitton used to call them. But by '48 they were going out, you see, and it was as much as you dare do, at some of the houses, to produce the cards before midnight after the ladies had retired. I remember Speed telling me, round about this time, of one place he'd been to where they got him up at eight for morning prayers, and gave him a book of sermons to read after luncheon.

Cleeve House wasn't quite as raw as that, but it would have been damned dreary going if one of the girls present hadn't been quite out of the ordinary run. I fixed on her from the start—a willowy blonde piece with a swinging hip and a knowing eye. Strange, I met her at Cleeve, and didn't see her again till I came on her cooking breakfast for a picket of Campbell's Highlanders outside Balaclava six years later, the very morning of Cardigan's charge. Fanny Locke her name was;[6] she was the young sister of our host, a damned handsome eighteen with the shape of a well-developed matron. Like so many young girls whose body out-grows their years, she didn't know what to do with it—well, I could give her guidance there. As soon as I saw her swaying down the staircase at Cleeve, ho-ho, thinks I, hark forrard. You may be sure I was soon in attendance, and when I found she was a friendly little thing, and a keen horsewoman, I laid my plans accordingly, and engaged to go riding with her next day, when she would show me the local country—it was the long grass I had in mind, of course.

In the meantime, the first evening at Cleeve was quite as much fun as a Methodist service. Of course, all Tory gatherings are the same, and Locke had assembled as choice a collection of know-all prigs as you could look for. Bentinck I didn't mind, because he had some game in him and knew more about the turf than anyone I ever met, but he had in tow the cocky little sheeny D'Israeli, whom I never could stomach. He was pathetic, really, trying to behave like the Young Idea when he was well into greasy middle age, with his lovelock and fancy vest, like a Punjabi whoremaster. They were saying then that he had spent longer "arriving" at Westminster than a one-legged Irish peer with the gout; well, he "arrived" in the end, as we know, and if I'd been able to read the future I might have toadied him a good deal more, I dare say.[7]

Locke, our host, introduced us as we were going in to dinner, and I made political small talk, as old Morrison had told me I should.

"Bad work for your lot in the Lords, hey?" says I, and he lowered his lids at me in that smart-affected way he had. "You know," says I, "the Jewish Bill getting thrown out. Bellows to mend in Whitechapel, what? Bad luck all round," I went on, "what with Shylock running second at Epsom, too. I had twenty quid on him myself."[8]

I heard Locke mutter "Good God", but friend Codlingsby just put back his head and looked at me thoughtfully. "Indeed," says he. "How remarkable. And you aspire to politics, Mr Flashman?"

"That's my ticket," says I.

"Truly remarkable," says he. "Do you know, I shall watch your career with bated breath." And then Locke mumbled him away, and I pounced on Miss Fanny and took her in to dinner.

Of course, it was all politics at table, but I was too engaged with Fanny to pay much heed. When the ladies had gone and we'd all moved up, I heard more, but it didn't stick. I remember they were berating Russell's idleness, and the government's extravagance, on which D'Israeli made one of those sallies which you could see had been well polished beforehand.

"Lord John must not be underestimated," says he. "He understands the first principle, that the great strength of the British Constitution lies in the money it costs us. Make government cheap and you make it contemptible."

Everyone laughed except old Morrison, who glared over his glass. "That'll look well in one o' your nov-elles, sir, I don't doubt. But let me tell you, running a country is like running a mill, and waste'll ruin the baith o' them."

D'Israeli, being smart, affected to misunderstand. "I know nothing of running *mills*," says he. "Pugilism is not among my interests," which of course turned the laugh against old Morrison.

You may judge from this the kind of rare wit to be found at political gatherings; I was out of all patience after an hour of it, and by the time we joined the ladies Miss Fanny, to my disgust, had gone to bed.

Next day, however, she and I were off on our expedition soon after breakfast, with sandwiches and a bottle in my saddlebag, for we intended to ride as far as Roundway Down, a place which she was sure must interest me, since there had been a battle fought there long ago. On the way she showed me the house where she had once lived, and then we cantered on across the excellent riding country that lies north of Salisbury Plain. It was the jolliest day, with a blue sky, fleecy clouds, and a gentle breeze, and Fanny was in excellent trim. She looked mighty fetching in a plum-coloured habit with a tricorne hat and feather, and little black boots, and I never saw a female better in the saddle. She could keep up with *me* at a gallop, her fair hair flying and her pretty little lips parted as she scudded along, so to impress her I had to show her some of the riding tricks I'd picked up in Afghanistan, like running alongside my beast full tilt, with a hand on the mane, and swinging over the rump to land and run on t'other side. D----d showy stuff, and she clapped her hands and cried bravo, while the bumpkins we passed along the way hallooed and waved their hats.

All this put me in capital form, of course, and by the time we got to Roundway I was nicely primed to lure Miss Fanny into a thicket and get down to business. She was such a jolly little thing, with such easy chatter and a saucy glint in her blue eye, that I anticipated no difficulty. We dismounted near the hill, and we led our beasts while she told me about the battle, in which it seemed the Cavaliers had thoroughly chased the Roundheads.

"The people hereabouts call it Runaway Down," says she, laughing, "because the Roundheads fled so fast."

It was the best thing I'd ever heard about Cromwell's fellows; gave me a fellow-feeling for 'em, and I made some light remark to this effect.

"Oh, you may say so," says she. "You who have never run away." She gave me an odd little look. "Sometimes I wish I were a man, with the strength to be brave, like you."

Flashy knows a cue when he hears it. "I'm not always brave, Fanny," says I, pretty solemn, and stepping close. "Sometimes —I'm the veriest coward." By G - d, I never spoke a truer word.

"I can't believe—" says she, and got no further, for I kissed her hard on the lips; for a moment she bore it, and then to my delight she began teasing me with her tongue, but before I could press home my advantage she suddenly slipped away, laughing.

"No, no," cries she, very merry, "this is Runaway Down, remember," and like a fool I didn't pursue on the instant. If I had done, I don't doubt she'd have yielded, but I was content to play her game for the moment, and so we walked on, chatting and laughing.

You may think this trivial; the point is that if I'd mounted Miss Fanny that day I daresay I'd have lost interest in her—at all events I'd have been less concerned to please her later, and would have avoided a great deal of sorrow, and being chased and bullyragged halfway round the world.

As it was, it was the most d - - - ably bothersome day I remember. Half a dozen times I got to grips with her—over the luncheon sandwiches, during our walk down from the hill, even in the saddle on the way home—and each time she kissed like a novice

French whore and then broke off, teasing. And either because we met people on the way, or because she was as nimble as a fly-weight, I never had a chance to go to work properly. Of course, I'd known chits like this before, and experience told me it would come all right on the night, as the theatricals say, but by the time we were cantering up to Cleeve again I was as horny as the town bull, and not liking it overmuch.

And there was a nasty shock waiting, in the shape of two chaps who came out of the front door, both in Hussar rig, the first one hallo-ing and waving to Fanny and helping her down from her mare. She made him known to me, with a mischievous twinkle, as her fiancé, one Duberly, which would have been bad news at any other time, but all my attention was taken by his companion, who stood back eyeing me with a cool smile, very knowing: my heart checked for a second at the sight of him. It was Bryant.

If you know my memoirs, you know him. He and I had been subalterns in Cardigan's regiment, nine years before; on the occasion when I fought a memorable duel, he had agreed, for a consideration, to ensure that my opponent's pistol was loaded only with blank, so that I had survived the meeting with credit. I had cheated him out of his payment, to be sure, and there had been nothing he could do except make empty threats of vengeance. After that our ways had parted, and I'd forgotten him; and now here he was, like corpse at a christening. Of course, he still couldn't harm me, but it was a nasty turn to see him, just the same.

"Hollo, Flash," says he, sauntering up. "Still campaigning, I see." And he made his bow to Miss Fanny, while Duberly presented him.

"Most honoured to know you, sir," says this Duberly, shaking my hand as I dismounted. He was a fattish, whiskered creature, with muff written all over him. "Heard so much—distinguished officer—delighted to see you here, eh, Fan?" And she, cool piece that she was, having sensed in an instant that Bryant and I were at odds, chattered gaily about what a jolly picnic we had made, while Duberly humphed and grinned and was all over her. Presently he led her indoors, leaving Bryant and me by the horses.

"Spoiled the chase for you has he, Flash?" says he, with his spiteful little grin. "D - - - lish nuisance, these fiancés; sometimes as inconvenient as husbands, I dare say."

"I can't imagine you'd know about that," says I, looking him up and down. "When did Cardigan kick you out, then?" For he wasn't wearing Cherrypicker rig. He flushed at that, and I could see I'd touched him on the raw.

"I transferred to the Eighth Irish," says he. "We don't all leave regiments as you do, with our tails between our legs."

"My, my, it still rankles, Tommy, don't it?" says I, grinning at him. "Feeling the pinch, were we? I always thought the Eleventh was too expensive for you; well, if you can't come up to snuff in the Eighth you can always take up pimping again, you know."

That made his mouth work, all right; in the old days in Canterbury, when he was toadying me, I'd thrown a few guineas his way in return for his services as whoremonger and general creature. He fell back a step.

"D - - n you, Flashman," says he, "I'll bring you down yet!"

"Not to your own level, if you please," says I, and left him swearing under his breath.

Now, if I'd been as wise then as I am now, I'd have remembered that even as slimy a snake as Bryant still has fangs, but he was such a contemptible squirt, and I'd handled him so easily in the past, that I put him out of my mind. I was more concerned with the inconvenience of this fat fool Duberly, whose presence would make it all the more difficult for me to cock a leg athwart Miss Fanny—I was sure she was game for it, after that day's sparring, but of course Duberly quite cut me out now that he was here, squiring her at tea, and fetching her fan, clucking round her in the drawing-room, and taking her arm in to dinner. Locke and the rest of her family were all for him, I could see, so I couldn't put him down as I'd have done anywhere else. It was d - - - - d vexing, but where's the fun if it's all too easy, I told myself, and set to scheme how I might bring the lady to the sticking point, as we Shakespeare scholars say.

I was much distracted from these fine thoughts by old Morrison, who berated me privately for what he called "godless gallivanting after yon hussy"; it seemed I should have spent the day hanging on the lips of Bentinck and D'Israeli and Locke, who had been deep in affairs. I soothed him with a promise that I'd attend them after dinner, which I did, and steep work it was. Ireland was very much exciting them, I recall, and the sentencing and transportation of some rebel called Mitchel; old Morrison was positive he should have been hanged, and got into a great passion because when they shipped him off to the Indies they didn't send him in chains with a bread-and-water diet[9]

"If the d - - - d rascal had sailed on any vessel o' mine, it would hae been sawdust he got tae eat, and d - - - - d little o' that," says dear kind papa, and the rest of them cried "hear, hear," and agreed that it was this kind of soft treatment that encouraged sedition; they expected the Paddies to rise at any time, and there was talk of Dublin being besieged. All humbug, of course; you can't mount a rebellion on rotten potatoes.

After that there was fierce debate over whether the working class wanted reform, and one Hume was damned for a scoundrel, and D'Israeli discoursed on the folly of some measure to exclude M.P.s who couldn't pay their debts—no doubt he had a personal interest there—and I sat and listened, bored to death, until Bentinck suggested we join the ladies. Not that there was much sport there either, for Mrs Locke was reading aloud from the great new novel, *Jane Eyre*, and from the expression on the faces of Fanny and the other young misses, I guessed they'd have been happier with *Varney the Vampire* or *Sweeney Todd*.[10] In another corner the older folk were looking at picture books—German churches, probably—another pack of females were sewing and mumbling to each other, and in an adjoining salon some hysterical bitch was singing "Who will o'er the downs with me?" with a governess thrashing away at the pianoforte. A couple of wild old rakes were playing backgammon, and Duberly was explaining to whoever would listen that he would have been glad to serve in India, but his health wouldn't allow, don't ye know. I asked myself how long I could bear it.

I believe it was Bentinck who suggested cards—Locke looked like the kind who wouldn't have permitted such devices of the devil under his roof, but Bentinck was the lion, you see, and couldn't be gainsaid; besides, there was still a little leeway in those days which you'd never have got in the sixties or seventies. I wasn't in at the beginning of the game, having been ambushed by an old dragon in a lace cap who told me how her niece Priscilla had written to her with an envelope, instead of waxing her letter, and what did I think of that? I despaired of getting away, until who should appear but Fanny herself, sparkling and full of nonsense, to insist that I should come and show her how to make her wagers.

"I am quite at sea," says she, "and Henry"—this was Duberly —"vows that counting makes his head ache.[11] You will assist me, Captain Flashman, won't you, and Aunt Selina will not mind, will you, auntie dear?"

I should have told her to go straight to h - - l, and clung to Aunt Selina like a shipwrecked lascar—but you can't read the future. Ain't it odd to think, if I'd declined her invitation, I might have been in the Lords today—and a certain American might never have become President? Mind you, even now, if a fresh piece like Fanny Locke stooped in front of me, with those saucy eyes and silken hair, and pushed those pouting lips and white shoulders at me—ah, dry your whiskers, old Flash—you could keep your coronet for me, and I'd take her hand and hobble off to my ruin, whatever it was.

Aunt Selina sniffed, and told her she must not wager more than a pair of gloves—"and not your Houbigants, mind, you foolish little girl. Indeed, I don't know what the world is coming to, or Henry Duberly thinking of, to permit you wagering at cards. No doubt he will be one of these husbands who will allow you to waltz, and drink porter in company. It would not have done in my day. What are the stakes?"

"Oh, ever so little, aunt," says Fanny, tugging at my sleeve. "Farthings and sweets—and Lord George has the bank, and is ever such fun!"

"Is he, indeed?" says Aunt Selina, gathering up her reticule. "Then I shall come myself, to see you are not excessively silly."

There was quite a crowd round the table in the salon, where Bentinck was presiding over vingt-et-un, amid great merriment. He was playing the chef to perfection, calling the stakes and whipping round the pasteboards like a riverboat dude. Even Locke and Morrison were present, watching and being not too sour about it; Mrs Abigail Locke was among the players, with Bryant advising, toady-like, at her elbow; D'Israeli was making a great show of playing indulgently, like a great man who don't mind stooping to trivialities if it will amuse lesser minds, and half a dozen others, old and young, were putting up their counters and laughing with delight at Bentinck's sallies.

As Fanny and Aunt Selina took their seats, an old fellow with white whiskers leans across to me. "I must warn you," says he, "that Lord George has us playing very deep—plunging recklessly, you know." He held up some counters. "The green ones are—a farthing; the blue—a ha'penny; and the yellow—you must take care—are *a penny*! It is desperate work, you see!"

"I'm coming for you, Sir Michael!" cries Bentinck, slapping the pack. "Now, ladies, are you ready? Then, one for all, and all for the lucky winner!" And he flicked the cards round to the players.

It was silly, harmless stuff, you see, all good nature and playfulness—and as desperate a card game as I ever sat in on in my life. Not that you'd have guessed it at first, with Bentinck making everyone merry, and one of the players—a sulky-looking youth of about fourteen, of the kind whose arse I delighted to kick in happier days—protesting that he was cleaned out, and Bentinck solemnly offering to take his note of hand for two-pence. Fanny was all excitement, holding her card up close for me to see and asking how much she should go, which gave me the opportunity to huddle in and stroke her bare shoulder as I whispered in her ear. Next to her, old Aunt Selina was buying cards like a St James's shark, very precise and slow; she took four and paused at 17; Bentinck was watching her, his handsome face very intent, his thumb poised on the next card; she took it, and it was a trey, which meant that she had a five-card hand, at which there was great applause, and Bentinck laughed and cried "Well done, ma'am," as he paid her counters over.

"I never buy beyond 16, you know," Aunt Selina confided to Fanny, "unless it is for a five-card hand. I find it a very good rule."

So the game went round, and I found myself thinking that it doesn't take high stakes to show up who the real gamesters are.

You could sense the rapport there was between Bentinck and Aunt Selina—two folk with not a jot in common, mark you. He was one of the sportsmen of the day, used to playing for thousands, a grandee of the turf and the tables who could watch a fortune slip away in five seconds at Epsom and never bat an eyelid, and here he was, watching like a hawk as some dowager hesitated over a farthing stake, or frowning as the sullen Master Jerry lost his two-penny I.O.U. and promptly demanded further credit. Wasn't it Greville who said that the money Lord George Bentinck won was just so many paper counters to him—it was the game that mattered? And Aunt Selina was another of the same; she duelled with him like a good 'un, and won as often as not, and he liked her for it.

And then the bank passed round to Fanny, and I had to deal the cards for her. Bryant, who had raised a great laugh by coming round to touch Aunt Selina's mittened hand for luck, said we should have a fair deal at last, since I had been notoriously the worst vingt-et-un player in the whole Light Cavalry—there was more polite mirth at this, and I gave him a hard look as he went back to Mrs Locke, and wondered to myself just what he had meant by that. Then Fanny, all twittering as she handled the stakes, claimed my attention, and I dealt the cards.

If you know vingt-et-un—or poor man's baccarat, or blackjack, or pontoon, whichever you like to call it—you know that the object is not to go above 21 with the cards dealt to you. It's a gambler's game, in which you must decide whether to stay pat at 16 or 17, or risk another card which may break you or, if it's a small one, may give you a winning score of 20 or 21. I've played it from Sydney to Sacramento, and learned to stick at 17, like Aunt Selina. The odds are with the bank, since when the scores are level the banker takes the stakes.

Fanny and I had a good bank. I dealt her 19 the first round, which sank everyone except D'Israeli, who had two court cards for 20. The next time I gave Fanny an ace and a knave for vingt-et-un, which swamped the whole board, and she clapped her hands and squealed with delight. Then we ran two five-card hands in succession, and the punters groaned aloud and protested at our luck, and Bentinck jestingly asked Aunt Selina if she would stand good for him, and she cried "With you, Lord George!" and made great play of changing his silver for her coppers.

I was interested in the game by this time—it's a fact, Greville was right, it don't matter a d--n how small the stakes are—and Fanny was full of excitement and admiration for my luck. She shot me an adoring look over her shoulder, and I glanced down at her quivering bosoms and thought to myself, you'll be in rare trim for another kind of game later. Get 'em excited—a fight is best, with the claret flowing, but any kind of sport will do, if there's a hint of savagery in it—and they'll couple like monkeys. And then, as I pulled my eyes away and dealt the first cards of another hand, looking to see that all the stakes were placed, I saw that on Mrs Locke's card there was a pile of yellow counters —about two bob's worth. That meant they had an ace, for certain. And they had, but it did 'em no good; they draw a seven with it, bought a five, and then went broke with a king. But next time round they staked an even bigger pile of yellows, lost again, and came back with a still larger wager for the following hand.

I paused in the act of dealing the second cards. "You're playing double or quits, ma'am," says I to Mrs Locke. "Road to ruin."

But before she could speak, Bryant cut in: "Stakes too high for you, are they? Why, if you can't afford . . ."

"Not a bit," says I. "If my principal's content," and I looked down at Fanny, who was sitting with a splendid pile of counters before her.

"Oh, do go on, please!" cries she. "It is the greatest fun!" So I put round the second cards; if Bryant thought he was going to rattle *me* over a few shillings' worth of stake he was a bigger fool than I thought. But I knew he wasn't a fool, and that he was a d---d sharp hand at card tricks, so I kept my eye on Mrs Locke's place.

They lost again, and next time Mrs Locke would only put up a single yellow, on which they won. There was a good deal of heavy jesting at this, and I saw Bryant whispering busily in her ear. When I dealt the first card he pounced on it, they consulted together, and then they put their whole pile—yellows, blues, everything, on top of the card, and Bryant gave me a nasty grin and stood back waiting.

I couldn't follow this; it couldn't be better than an ace, and it was just a kindergarten game, anyway. Did he think he could score off me by breaking Miss Fanny's bank? I noticed Bentinck was smiling, in a half-puzzled way, and D'Israeli was fingering his card thoughtfully and shifting his lidded glance from Bryant to me. They were wondering, too, and suddenly I felt that cold touch at the nape of my neck that is the warning signal of danger.

It was ridiculous, of course: a ha'penny game in a country house, but I could sense Bryant was as worked up as if there'd been a thousand guineas riding on his partner's card. It wasn't healthy, and I wanted to be out of that game then and there, but I'd have looked a fool, and Aunt Selina was tapping for a second card and looking at me severely.

I put them round, and perhaps because I had that tiny unease I fumbled Master Jerry's second card, so that it fell face up. I should have taken it back, by rights, but it was an ace, and the little scoundrel, who should have been in his bed long before, insisted on keeping it. Bryant snapped up Mrs Locke's second card and showed it to her with a grin; D'Israeli displayed vingt-et-un by laying his second card, a queen, face up across the first one. The rest bought a third or stood pat.

I faced our cards—a knave and a three, which was bad. I faced a third, an ace, which gave us 14; nothing for it but to go on, and I turned up a four. We were at 18, and at least three players were sitting pat on three cards, which meant probably they had 18 or 19 or better. I whispered to Fanny, did she want to try for a five-card trick, which would beat everyone except Codlingsby's vingt-et-un.

"Oh, yes, please!" cries she. "We are in luck, I feel sure of it!"

I put my thumb on the top card, and stopped. Something was d - - - d far wrong, somewhere, and I knew it. Bentinck knew it, too, and Aunt Selina, who was staring over her spectacles at the pack in my hand. Others in the room sensed something; Locke and Morrison had broken off their conversation to watch. Bryant was smirking across at me.

I flicked over the top card. It was a deuce, giving us 20 and victory, Bentinck cried "Ha!", Aunt Selina muttered something under her breath, and Fanny gave an ecstatic squeal and began to rake in the stakes. I gathered in the cards while everyone chattered and laughed—Mrs Locke had an ace and a nine, I noticed, and I commiserated her on her bad luck. Bryant pipes up at once:

"Very bad luck indeed, I should say."

But I ignored him, and told Fanny we must now pass the bank to D'Israeli, since he had scored vingt-et-un.

"Oh, must we?" cries she, pouting. "And we were doing so well! What a shame it is!"

Aunt Selina exclaimed at her greed, there was more laughter, and D'Israeli took out his eye-glass and bowed to Fanny.

"I would not dream," says he, "of claiming the cards from such a *fair* banker," a pun which was greeted with polite applause.

"Oh, I daresay her partner is quite happy to pass the cards," cries Bryant. "The killing's made, eh, Flashy?"

Now, I daresay we must have won thirty shillings on that bank, most of it from Mrs Locke, and you could take what he'd said as a joke, but the jarring note in his voice, and the grin on his flushed face told me it wasn't. I stared at him, and Bentinck's head whipped round, and suddenly there was a silence, broken only by Miss Fanny's tinkling laughter as she exclaimed to Aunt Selina about her own good luck.

"I think it is your bank, Dizzy," says Bentinck quietly, at last, his eyes on Bryant. "Unless the ladies feel we have played enough."

The ladies protested against this, and then Bryant cut in again:

"I've played quite enough, thank'ee, and I daresay my partner has, too." Mrs Locke looked startled, and Bryant went on:

"I never thought to see—ah, but let it go!"

And he turned from the table, like a man trying to control himself.

There was a second's silence, and then they were babbling, "What did he say?" "What did he mean?" and Bentinck was flushed with anger and demanding to know what Bryant was implying. At this Bryant pointed to me, and says:

"It is really too bad! In a pleasant game, for the ladies, this fellow . . . I beg your pardon, Lord George, but it is too much! Ask him," cries he, "to turn out his pockets—his coat pockets!"

It hit me like a dash of icy water. In the shocked hush, I found my hand going to my left-hand coat pocket, while everyone gaped at me, Bentinck took a pace towards me saying, "No, stop. Not before the ladies..." and then my hand came out, and there were three playing cards in it. I was too horrified and bewildered to speak, there was a shriek from one of the females, and a general gasp, and someone muttered: "Cheat... oh!" I could only stare from the cards to Bentinck's horrified face, to Bryant's, flushed and exultant, and to Dizzy's, white with disbelief. Miss Fanny jumped up with a shriek, starting away from me, and then someone was shepherding the females from the room in a terrible silence, leaving me with the stern, disgusted faces and the exclamations of incredulity and amazement. They crowded forward while I stood there, gazing at the cards in my hand —I can see them yet: the king of clubs, the deuce of hearts, and the ace of diamonds.

Bentinck was speaking, and I forced myself to look round at him, with Bryant, D'Israeli, old Morrison, Locke and the others crowding at his back.

"Gentlemen," my voice was hoarse. "I... I can't imagine. I swear to God..."

"I thought I hadn't seen the ace of diamonds," says someone.

"I saw his hand go to his pocket, at the last deal." This was Bryant.

"Oh, my Goad, the shame o't... Ye wicked, deceitful..."

"The fellow's a damned sharp!"

"A cheat! In this house..."

"Remarkable," says D'Israeli, with an odd note in his voice. "For a few pence? You know, George, it's d----d unlikely."

"The amount never matters," says Bentinck, with a voice like steel. "It's winning. Now, sir, what have you to say?"

I was gathering my wits before this monstrous thing, trying to understand it. God knew I hadn't cheated—when I cheat, it's for something that matters, not sweets and ha'pence. And suddenly it hit me like a lightning flash—Bryant coming round to touch Aunt Selina's hand, standing shoulder to shoulder with me. So this was how he was taking his revenge!

Put me in that situation today, and I'd reason my way out of it, talking calmly. But I was twenty-six then, and panicked—

d--n it, if I *had* been cheating I'd have been ready for them, with my story cut and dried, but for once I was innocent, and couldn't think what to say. I dashed the cards down and faced them.

"It's a b----y lie!" I shouted. "I didn't cheat, I swear it! My God, why should I? Lord George, can you believe it? Mr D'Israeli, I appeal to you! Would I cheat for a few coppers?"

"How came the cards in your pocket, then?" demands Bentinck.

"That little viper!" I shouted, pointing at Bryant. "The jealous little b-----d placed them there, to disgrace me!"

That set up a tremendous uproar, and Bryant, blast his eyes, played it like a master. He took a step back, gritted his teeth, bowed to the company, and says:

"Lord George, I leave it to you to determine the worth of a foul slander from a proven cheat."

And then he turned, and strode from the room. I could only stand raging, and then as I saw how he had foxed me—my God, ruined me, and before the best in the land, I lost control altogether. I sprang for the door, bawling after him, someone caught my sleeve, but I threw him off, and then I had the door open and was plunging through in pursuit.

There was a hubbub behind me, and a sudden squeal of alarm ahead, for there were ladies at the head of the stairs, their white faces turned towards me. Bryant made off at the sight of me, and in blind passion I hurled myself after him. I had only one thought: to catch the undersized little squirt and pound him to death—sense, decency and the rest were forgotten. I got my hand on his collar at the top of the stairs, while the females screamed and shrank back; I wrenched him round, his face grey with fear, and shook him like a rat.

"You foul vermin!" I roared. "Try to dishonour me, would you, you scum of ... of the Eighth Hussars!" And as I swung him left-handed before me, I drew back my right fist and with all my strength, smashed it into his face.

Nowadays, when I'm day-dreaming over the better moments of my misspent life—galloping Lola Montez and Elspeth and Queen Ranavalona and little Renee the Creole and the fat dancing-wench I bought in India whose name escapes me, and having old Colin

Campbell pinning the V.C. to my unworthy breast, and receiving my knighthood from Queen Victoria (and she in tears, maudlin little woman), and breaking into the Ranee's treasure-cellar and seeing all that splendid loot laid out for the taking—when I think back on these fine things, the recollection of hitting Tommy Bryant invariably comes back to me. God knows it was a nightmare at the time, but in retrospect I can't think of inflicting a hurt that I enjoyed more. My fist caught him full on the mouth and nose so hard that his collar was jerked clean out of my hand, and he went hurtling head foremost down that staircase like an arrow, bouncing once before crashing to rest in the hall, his limbs all a-sprawl.

There were shrieks of hysterical females in my ears, and hands seizing my coat, and men scampering down to lift him up, but all I remember is seeing Fanny's face turned towards me in terror, and Bentinck's voice drifting up the staircase:

"My God, I believe he's killed him!"

As it turned out, Bentinck was wrong, thank God; the little louse didn't die, but it was a near-run thing. Apart from a broken nose, his skull was fractured in the fall, and for a couple of days he hung on the edge, with a Bristol horse-leech working like fury to save him from going over. Once he regained consciousness, and had the impertinence to say, "Tell Flashman I forgive him with all my heart," which cheered me up, because it indicated he was going to live, and wanted to appear a forgiving Christian; if he'd thought he was dying he'd have d - - - - d me to hell and beyond.

But after that he lost consciousness again, and I went through the tortures of the pit. They had confined me to my room—Locke was a justice of the peace—and kept me there with the muff Duberly sitting outside the door like a blasted water-bailiff. I was in a fearful sweat, for if Bryant kicked the bucket it would be a hanging matter, no error, and at the thought of it I could only lie on my bed and quake. I'd seen men swing, and thought it excellent fun, but the thought of the rope rasping on my neck, and the blind being pulled over my brows, and the fearful plunge and sickening snap and blackness—my God, it had me vomiting in the corner. Well, I've had the noose under my chin since then, and waited blubbering for them to launch me off, and even the real thing seems no worse, looking back, than those few days of waiting in that bedroom, with the yellow primroses on the wall-paper, and the blue and red carpet on the floor with little green tigers woven into it, and the print of Harlaxton Manor, near Grantham, Lincolnshire, the seat of one John Longden, Esq., which hung above the bed—I can still recite the whole caption.

With the thought of the gallows driving everything else from my mind, it was small consolation to learn from Duberly—who seemed to be in a mortal funk himself over the whole business—that there was by no means complete agreement that I had been caught cheating. D'Israeli—he was clever, I'll say that for him—had sensibly pointed out that a detected cheat wouldn't have hauled the evidence out of his pocket publicly as soon as he was challenged. He maintained I would have protested, and refused to be searched—he was quite right, of course, but most of the other pious hypocrites disagreed with him, and the general feeling was that I was a fraud and a dangerous maniac who would be well served if I finished up in the prison lime-pit. Whatever happened, it was a hideous scandal; the house had emptied as if by magic next day, Mrs Locke was in a decline, and her husband was apparently only waiting to see how Bryant fared before turning me over to the police.

I don't know, even now, what was determined, or who determined it, in those few days, except that old Morrison was obviously up to the neck in it. Whatever happened to Bryant, my political career was obviously over before it had begun; at best I was probably disgraced as a cheat, and liable to sentence for assault—that was if Bryant lived. In any event, I was a liability to Morrison henceforth, and whether he decided to try to get rid of me permanently, or planned simply to get me out of harm's way for a time, is something on which I've never made up my mind. In fact, I don't suppose he cared above half whether I lived or died, so long as his own interests weren't harmed.

He came to see me on the fifth day, and told me that Bryant was out of danger, and I was so relieved that I was almost happy as I listened to him denouncing me for a wastrel, a fornicator, a cheat, a liar, a brute, and all the rest of it—I couldn't fault a word of it, anyway. When he was done, he plumped down, breathing like a bellows, and says:

"My certie, but ye're easier oot o' this than ye deserve. It's no' your fault the mark o' Cain isnae on yer broo this day—a beast, that's whit ye are, Flashman, a ragin', evil beast!" And he mopped his face. "Weel, Locke isnae goin' tae press charges—ye have me tae thank for that—and this fellow Bryant'll keep mum. Huh! A few hundred'll tak' care of him—he's anither 'officer and gentleman' like yersel'. I could buy the lot o' ye! Jist trash." He snarled away under his breath, and shot me a look. "But we'll no' hush up the scandal, for a' that. Ye cannae come home—ye're aware o' that, I suppose?"

I didn't argue; I couldn't, but I was ill-advised enough to mutter something about Elspeth, and for a moment I thought he would strike me. His face went purple, and his teeth chattered.

"Mention her name tae me again—jist once again, and as Goad's my witness I'll see ye transported for this week's work! Ye'll rue the day ye ever set eyes on her—aye, as I have done, most bitterly. Goad alone knows what I and mine have done tae be punished by . . . you!"

Well, at least he didn't pray over me, like Arnold; he was a different kind of hypocrite, was Morrison, and as a man of business he didn't waste overmuch holy vituperation before getting down to cases.

"Ye'll be best oot o' England for a spell, until this d--- able business has blown by—if it ever does. Your fine relatives can mak' your peace wi' the Horse Guards—this kind o' scandal'll be naethin' new there, I dare say. For the rest, I've been at work tae arrange matters—and whether ye like it or no:, my buckie, ye'll jump as I whistle, D'ye see?"

"I suppose I've no choice," says I, and then, deciding it would be politic to grovel to the old b-----d, I added: "Believe me, sir, I feel nothing but gratitude for what you are doing, and—"

"Hold your tongue," says he. "Ye're a liar. There's no more tae be said. Now, ye'll pack yer valise, and go at once tae Poole, and there take a room at the 'Admiral' and wait until ye hear from me. Not a word to a soul, and never stir out—or ye'll find my protection and Locke's is withdrawn, and that'll be a felon's cell for ye, and beggary tae follow. There's money," says he, and dropping a purse on the table he turned on his heel and stamped out.

I made no protest; he had me by the neck, and I didn't waste time reflecting on the eagerness with which my relatives and friends have always striven to banish me from England whenever opportunity offered—my own father, Lord Cardigan, and now old Morrison. They could never get shot of me fast enough. And, as on previous occasions, there was no room for argument; I would just have to go, and see what the Lord and John Morrison provided.

I slipped away from the house at noon, and was in Poole by nightfall. And there I waited a whole week, fretting at first, but gradually getting my spirits back. At least I was free, when I might have been going to the condemned hold; whatever lay in front of me, I'd come back to England eventually—it might be no more than a year, and by that time the trouble would be half-forgotten. Curiously enough, the assault on Bryant would be far less to live down than the business over the cards, but the more I thought about that, the more it seemed that no sensible men would take Bryant's word against mine—he was known for a toady and a dirty little hound, whereas I, quite aside from my popular fame, was bluff, honest Harry to everyone who thought they knew me. Indeed, I even toyed with the notion of going back to town and brazening the thing then and there, but I hadn't the gall for that. It was all too fresh, and Morrison would have thrown me into the gutter for certain. No, I would just have to take my medicine, whatever it was; I've learned that there's no sense in kicking against the prick—a phrase which fits old Morrison like a glove. I would just have to make the best of whatever he had in store for me.

What that was I discovered on the eighth day, when a man called to see me just as I was finishing breakfast. In fact, I had finished, and was just chivvying after the servant lass who had come to clear away the dishes from my room; I had chased her into a corner, and she was bleating that she was a good girl, which I'll swear she wasn't, when the knock sounded; she took advantage of it to escape, admitting the visitor while she straightened her cap and snapped her indignation at me.

"Sauce!" says she. "I never—"

"Get out," says the newcomer, and she took one look at him and fled.

He kicked the door to with his heel and stood looking at me, and there was something in that look that made me bite back the d - - n-your-eyes I'd been going to give him for issuing orders in my room. At first glance he was ordinary looking enough; square built, middle height, plain trousers and tight-buttoned jacket with his hands thrust into the pockets, low-crowned round hat which he didn't trouble to remove, and stiff-trimmed beard and moustache which gave him a powerful, businesslike air. But it wasn't that that stopped me: it was the man's eyes. They were as pale as water in a china dish, bright and yet empty, and as cold as an ice floe. They were wide set in his brown, hook-nosed face, and they looked at you with a blind fathomless stare that told you here was a terrible man. Above them, on his brow, there was a puckered scar that ran from side and side and sometimes jerked as he talked; when he was enraged, as he often was, it turned red. Hollo, thinks I, here's another in my gallery of happy acquaintances.

"Mr Flashman?" says he. He had an odd, husky voice with what sounded like a trace of North Country. "My name is John Charity Spring."

It seemed d----d inappropriate to me, but he was evidently well enough pleased with it, for he sat himself down in a chair and nodded me to another. "We'll waste no time, if you please," says he. "I'm under instructions from my owner to take you aboard my vessel as supercargo. You don't know what that means, I daresay, and it's not necessary that you should. I know why you're shipping with me; you'll perform such duties as I suppose to be within your power. Am I clear?"

"Well," says I, "I don't know about that. I don't think I care for your tone, Mr Spring, and—"

"Captain Spring," says he, and sat forward. "Now see here, Mr Flashman, I don't beat about. You're nothing to me; I gather you've half-killed someone and that you're a short leap ahead of the law. I'm to give you passage out, on the instructions of Mr Morrison." Suddenly his voice rose to a shout, and he crashed his hand on the table. "Well, I don't give a d--n! You can stay or run, d'ye see? It's all one to me! But you don't waste my time!" The scar on his head was crimson, and then it faded and his voice dropped. "Well?"

I didn't like the look of this one, I can tell you. But what could I do?

"Well," says I, "you say Mr Morrison is your ship's owner —I didn't know he had ships."

"Part owner," says he. "One of my directors."

"I see. And where is your ship bound, Captain Spring, and

— 34

where are you to take me?"

The pale eyes flickered. "We're going foreign," says he. "America, and home again. The voyage may last six months, so by Christmas you'll be back in England. As supercargo you take a share of profit—a small share—so your voyage won't be wasted."

"What's the cargo?" says I, interested, because I remembered hearing that these short-haul traders on the Atlantic run did quite well.

"General stuffs on the way out—Brummagem, cloths, some machinery. Cotton, sugar, molasses and so forth on the trip home." He snapped the words out. "You ask too d - - - - d many questions, Mr Flashman, for a runner."

"I'm not all that much of a runner," says I. It didn't sound too bad a way of putting by the time till the Bryant business was past. "Well, in that case, I suppose—"

"Good," says he. "Now then: I know you're an Army officer, and it's in deference to that I'm making you supercargo, which means you mess aft. You've been in India, for what that's worth —what d'you know of the sea?"

"Little enough," says I. "I've voyaged out and home, but I sailed in Borneo waters with Rajah Brooke, and can handle a small boat."

"Did you now?" The pale eyes gleamed. "That means you've been part-pirate, I daresay. You look like it—hold your tongue, sir, it doesn't matter to me! I'll only tell you this: on my ship there is no free-and-easy sky-larking! I saw that slut in here just now—well, henceforth you'll fornicate when I give you leave! By God, I'll not have it otherwise!" He was shouting again; this fellow's half-mad, thinks I. Then he was quiet. "You have languages, I understand?"

"Why, yes. French and German, Hindoostani, Pushtu—which is a tongue..."

"... of Northern India," says he impatiently. "I know. Get on."

"Well, a little Malay, a little Danish. I learn languages easily."

"Aye. You were educated at Rugby—you have the classics?"

"Well," says I, "I've forgotten a good deal..."

"Hah! *Hiatus maxime deflendus*,'* says this amazing fellow.

* A want greatly to be deplored.

35 -

"Or if you prefer it, *Hiatus valde deflendus*." He glared at me. "Well?"

I gaped at the man. "You mean?—oh, let's see. Great—er, letting down? Great—"

"Christ's salvation!" says he. "No wonder Arnold died young. The priceless gift of education, thrown away on brute minds! You speak living languages without difficulty, it seems—had you not the grace to pay heed, d - - n your skin, to the only languages that matter?" He jumped up and strode about.

I was getting tired of Mr Charity Spring. "They may matter to you," says I, "but in my experience it's precious little good quoting Virgil to a head-hunter. And what the d - - - l has this to do with anything?"

He stood lowering at me, and then sneered: "There's your educated Englishman, right enough. Gentlemen! Bah! Why do I waste breath on you? *Quidquid praecipies, esto brevis,** by God! Well, if you'll pack your precious traps, Mr Flashman, we'll be off. There's a tide to catch." And he was away, bawling for my account at the stairhead.

It was obvious to me that I had fallen in with a lunatic, and possibly a dangerous one, but since in my experience a great many seamen are wanting in the head I wasn't over-concerned. He paid not the slightest heed to anything I said as we made our way down to the jetty with my valise behind on a hand-cart, but occasionally he would bark a question at me, and it was this that eventually prodded me into recollecting one of the few Latin tags which has stuck in my mind—mainly because it was flogged into me at school as a punishment for talking in class. He had been demanding information about my Indian service, mighty offensively, too, so I snapped at him:

"*Percunctatorem fugitus nam garrulus idem est*",† which I thought was pretty fair, and he stopped dead in his tracks.

"Horace, by G - d!" he shouted. "We'll make something of you yet. But it is *fugito*, d'ye see, not *fugitus*. Come on, man, make haste."

He got little opportunity to catechise me after this, for the first

* When you moralise, keep it short.
† Avoid the inquisitive man, for he is a talker.

– 36

stage of our journey was in a cockly little fishing boat that took us out into the Channel, and since it was h - - lish rough I was in no condition for conversation. I'm an experienced sailor, which is to say I've heaved my guts over the rail into all the Seven Seas, and before we were ten minutes out I was sprawled in the scuppers wishing to God I'd gone back to London and faced the music. This spewing empty misery continued, as it always does, for hours, and I was still green and wobbly-kneed when at evening we came into a bay on the French coast, and sighted Mr Spring's vessel riding at anchor. Gazing blearily at it as we approached, I was astonished at its size; it was long and lean and black, with three masts, not unlike the clippers of later years. As we came under her counter, I saw the lettering on her side: it read *Balliol College*.

"Ah," says I to Spring, who was by me just then. "You were at Balliol, were you?"

"No," says he, mighty short. "I am an Oriel man myself."

"Then why is your ship called *Balliol College*?"

I saw his teeth clench and his scar darkened up. "Because I hate the b - - - - y place!" he cried in passion. He took a turn about and came back to me. "My father and brothers were Balliol men, d'you see? Does that answer you, Mr Flashman?"

Well, it didn't, but at that moment my belly revolted again, and when we came aboard I had to be helped up the ladder, retching and groaning and falling a-sprawl on the deck. I heard a voice say, "Christ, it's Nelson", and then I was half-carried away, and dropped on a bunk somewhere, alone in my misery while in the distance I heard the hateful voice of John Charity Spring bawling orders. I vowed then, as I've vowed fifty times since, that this was the last time I'd permit myself to be lured aboard a ship, but my mind must still have been working a little, because as I dropped off to sleep I remember wondering: why does a British ship have to sail from the French coast? But I was too tired and ill to worry just then.

Sometime later someone brought me broth, and having spewed it on to the floor I felt well enough to get up and stagger on deck. It was half-dark, but the stars were out, and to port there were lights twinkling on the French coast. I looked north, towards

England, but there was nothing to be seen but grey sea, and suddenly I thought, my G - d, what am I doing here? Where the deuce am I going? Who is this man Spring? Here I was, who only a couple of weeks before had been rolling down to Wiltshire like a lord, with the intention of going into politics, and now I was shivering with sea-sickness on an ocean-going barque commanded by some kind of mad Oxford don—it was too much, and I found I was babbling to myself by the rail.

It's always the way, of course. You're coasting along, and then the current grips you, and you're swept into events and places that you couldn't even have dreamed about. It seemed to have happened so quickly, but as I looked miserably back over the past fortnight there wasn't, that I could see, anything I could have done that would have prevented what was now happening to me. I couldn't have resisted Morrison, or refused Spring—I'd had to do what I was told, and here I was. I found myself blubbering as I gazed over the rail at the empty waste of sea—if only I hadn't got lusty after that little b - - - h Fanny, and played cards with her, and hit that swine Bryant—ah, but what was the use? It was done, and I was going God knew where, and leaving Elspeth and my life of ease and drinking and guzzling and mounting women behind. But it was too bad, and I was full of self-pity and rage as I watched the water slipping past.

Of course, if I'd been like Jack Merry or Dick Champion, or any of the other plucky little prigs that Tom Brown and his cronies used to read about, setting off to seek my fortune on the bounding wave, I'd have brushed aside a manly tear and faced the future with the stout heart of youth, while old Bosun McHearty clapped me on the shoulder and held me enthralled with tales of the South Seas, and I would have gone to bed at last thinking of my mother and resolving to prove worthy of my resolute and Christian commander, Captain Freeman. (God knows how many young idiots have gone to sea after being fed that kind of lying pap in their nursery books.) Perhaps at twenty-six I was too old and hard-used, for instead of a manly tear I did another manly vomit, and in place of Bosun McHearty there came a rush of seamen tailing on a rope across the deck, hurling me aside with a cry of "Stand from under, you - - - - farmer!", while from the dark above me my

Christian commander bellowed at me to get below and not hinder work. So I went, and fell asleep thinking not of my mother, or of the credit I'd bring my family, but of the chance I'd missed in not rogering Fanny Locke that afternoon at Roundway Down. Aye, the vain regrets of youth.

You will judge from this that I wasn't cut out for the life on the ocean wave. I can't deny it; if Captain Marryat had had to write about me he'd have burned his pen, signed on a Cardiff tramp, and been buried at sea. For one thing, in my first few days aboard I did not thrash the ship's bully, make friends with the nigger cook, or learn how to gammon a bosprit from a leathery old salt who called me a likely lad. No, I spent those days in my bunk, feeling d - - - - d ill, and only crawling on deck occasionally to take the air and quickly scurry below again to my berth. I was a sea-green and corruptible Flashy in those days.

Nor did I make friends, for I saw only four people and disliked all of them. The first was the ship's doctor, a big-bellied lout of an Irishman who looked as though he'd be more at home with a bottle than a lancet, and had cold, clammy hands. He gave me a draught for my sea-sickness which made it worse, and then staggered away to be ill himself. He was followed by a queer, old-young creature with wispy hair who shuffled in carrying a bowl from which he slopped some evil-looking muck; when I asked him who the d - - - l he was he jerked his head in a nervous tic and stammered:

"Please, sir, I'm Sammy."

"Sammy what?"

"Nossir, please sir, Sammy Snivels, cap'n calls me. But they calls me Looney, mostly."

"And what's that?"

"Please sir, it's gruel. The doctor sez for you to eat it, please, sir," and he lumbered forward and spilled half of it over my cot.

"D - - n you!" cries I, and weak and all as I was I caught him a back-handed swipe on the face that sent him half across the cabin. "Take your filth and get out!"

He mowed at me, and tried to scrape some of the stuff off the floor back into the bowl. "Doctor'll thump me if you don't take it, please, sir," says he, pushing it at me again. "Please, sir, it's nice tack, an' all—please, sir," and then he squealed as I lunged out at him, dropped the bowl, and fairly ran for it. I was too weak to do more than curse after him, but I promised myself that when I was better I would put myself in a better frame of mind by giving the blundering half-wit a thumping on my own account, to keep the doctor's company.

Next man in was no half-wit, but a nimble little ferret of a ship's boy with a loose lip and a cast in one eye. He gave me a shifty grin and sniffed at the spilled gruel.

"Looney didn't 'ave no luck, did 'e?" says he. "I told 'im gruel wouldn't go down, no'ow."

I told him to go to blazes and leave me alone.

"Feelin' groggy, eh?" says he, moving towards the bunk. "Grub's no good ter you, mate. Tell yer wot; I'll get in bed wiv yer for a shillin'."

"Get out, you dirty little b - - - - - d," says I, for I knew his kind; Rugby had been crawling with 'em. "I'd sooner have your great-grandmother."

"Snooks!" says he, putting out his tongue. "You'll sing a different tune after three months at sea an' not a wench in sight. It'll be two bob then!"

I flung a pot at him, but missed, and he let fly a stream of the richest filth I've ever listened to. "I'll get Mister Comber ter you, yer big black swine!" he finished up. "'E'll give you what for! Ta-ta!" And with that he slipped out, thumbing his nose.

Mr Comber was the fourth of my new acquaintances. He was third mate, and shared the cabin with me, and I couldn't make him out. He was civil, although he said little enough, but the odd thing was, he was a gentleman, and had obviously been to a good school. What a playing-field beauty like this was doing on a merchantman I couldn't see, but I held my tongue and watched him. He was about my age, tall and fair haired, and too sure of himself for me to get on the wrong side of. I guessed he was as puzzled about me as I was about him, but I was feeling too poorly at first to give much heed to him. He didn't champion the cabin boy, by the way, so that worthy's threat had obviously been bluff.

It was four or five days before I got my sea legs, and by then I was heartily sick of the *Balliol College*. Nowadays you have no notion of what a sailing-ship was like in the forties; people who travel P.O.S.H. in a steam packet can't imagine, for one thing, the h - - - ish continual din of a wooden vessel—the incessant creaking and groaning of timber and cordage, like a fiend's orchestra playing the same discordant notes, regular as clockwork, each time she rolled. And, by G - d, they rolled, far worse than iron boats, bucketing up and down, and stinking, too, with the musty stale smell of a floating cathedral, and the bilges plashing like a giant's innards. Oh, it was the life for a roaring boy, all right, and that was only the start of it. I didn't know it, but I was seeing the *Balliol College* at her best.

One morning, when I was sufficiently recovered to hold down the gruel that Looney brought me, and strong enough to kick his backside into the bargain, comes Captain Spring to tell me I'd lain long enough, and it was time for me to learn my duties.

"You'll stand your watch like everyone else," says he, "and in the meantime you can start on the work you're paid for—which is to go through every scrap of that cargo, *privatim et seriatim*, and see that those long-shore thieves haven't bilked me. So get up, and come along with me."

I followed him out on deck; we were scudding along like a flying duck with great billows of canvas spread, and a wind on the quarter deck fit to lift your hair off. There was plenty of shipping in sight, but no land, and I knew we must be well out of the Channel by now. Looking forward from the poop rail along the narrow flush deck, it seemed to me the *Balliol College* didn't carry much of a crew, for all her size, but I didn't have time to stop and stare, with Spring barking at me. He led me down the poop ladder, and then dropped through a scuttle by the mizzen mast.

"There you are," says he. "Take a good look."

Although I've done a deal more sailing than I care to remember, I'm no canvas-back, and while I know enough not to call the deck the floor, I'm no hand at nautical terms. We were in what seemed to be an enormous room stretching away forward to the foremast, where there was a bulkhead; this room ran obviously the full breadth of the ship, and was well lighted by gratings in the deck about fifteen feet above our heads. But it was unlike the interior of any ship I'd ever seen, it was so big and roomy; on either side, about four feet above the deck on which we stood, there was a kind of half-deck, perhaps seven feet deep, like a gigantic shelf, and above that yet another shelf of the same size. The space down the centre of the deck, between the shelves, was piled high with cargo in a great mound—it must have been a good seventy feet long by twelve high.

"I'll send my clerk to you with the manifest," says Spring, "and a couple of hands to help shift and stow." I became aware that the pale eyes were watching me closely. "Well?"

"Is this the hold?" says I. "It's an odd-looking place for cargo."

"Aye," says he. "Ain't it, though?"

Something in his voice, and in the dank feel of that great, half empty deck, set the worms stirring inside me. I moved forward with the great heap of cargo, bales and boxes, on one side of me, and the starboard shelves on the other. It was all clean and holy-stoned, but there was a strange, heavy smell about it that I couldn't place. Looking about, I noticed something in the shadows at the back of the lower shelf—I reached in, and drew out a long length of light chain, garnished here and there with large bracelets. I stood staring at them, and then dropped them with a clatter as the truth rushed in on me. Now I saw why the *Balliol College* had sailed from France, why her deck was this strange shape, why she was only half-full of cargo.

"My G - d!" cries I. "You're a slaver!"

"Good for you, Mr Flashman!" says Spring. "And what then?"

"What then?" says I. "Well, you can turn your b - - - - - d boat about, this minute, and let me ashore from her! By G - d, if I'd guessed what you were, I'd have seen you d - - - - d, and old Morrison with you, before I set foot on your lousy packet!"

"Dear me," says he softly. "You're not an abolitionist, surely?"

"D - - n abolition, and you too!" cries I. "I know that slaving's piracy, and for that they stretch your neck below high-water mark! You—you tricked me into this—you and that old swine! But I won't have it, d'ye hear? You'll set me ashore, and—"

I was striding past him towards the ladder, as he stood with his hands thrust deep in his pockets, eyeing me under the brim of his hat. Suddenly he shot out a hand, and with surprising strength swung me round in front of him. The pale eyes gazed into mine, and then his fist drove into my belly, doubling me up with pain; I reeled back, and he came after me, smashing me left and right to the head and sending me sprawling against the cargo.

"D - - n you!" I shouted, and tried to crawl away, but he pinned me with his foot, glaring down at me.

"Now, see here, *Mister* Flashman," says he. "I didn't want you, but I've got you, and you'll understand, here and now, that while you're on this ship, you're mine, d'ye see? You're not going ashore until this voyage is finished—Middle Passage, Indies, homeward run and all. If you don't like slaving—well, that's too bad, isn't it? You shouldn't have signed aboard, should you?"

"I didn't sign! I never—"

"Your signature will be on the articles that are in my cabin this minute," says he. "Oh, it'll be there, sure enough—you'll put it there."

"You're kidnapping me!" I yelled. "My G - d, you can't do it! Captain Spring, I beg you—set me ashore, let me get off—I'll pay you—I'll—"

"What, and lose my new supercargo?" says this devil, grinning at me. "No, no. John Charity Spring obeys his owner's orders—and mine are crystal clear, *Mister* Flashman. And he sees to it that those aboard his ship obey *his* orders, too, ye hear me?" He stirred me with his foot. "Now, get up. You're wasting my time again. You're here; you'll do your duty. I won't tell you twice." And those terrible pale eyes looked into mine again. "D'ye understand me?"

"I understand you," I muttered.

"Sir," says he.

"Sir."

"Come," says he, "that's better. Now, cheer up, man; I won't have sulks, by G - d. This is a happy ship, d'ye hear? It should be, the wages we pay. There's a thought for you, Flashman—you'll be a d - - - - d sight richer by the end of this voyage than you would be on a merchantman. What d'ye say to that?"

My mind was in a maze over all this, and real terror at what the consequences might be. Again I pleaded with him to be set ashore, and he slapped me across the mouth.

"Shut your trap," says he. "You're like an old woman. Scared are you? What of?"

"It's a capital crime," I whimpered.

"Don't be a fool," says he. "Britain doesn't hang slavers, nor do the Yankees, for all their laws say. Look about you—this ship's built for slaving, ain't she? Slavers who run the risk of getting caught aren't built so, with chains in view and slave decks and all. No, indeed, *qui male agit odit lucem**—they pose as honest merchantmen, so if the patrols nab 'em they won't be impounded under the equipment regulations. The *Balliol College* needs no disguises—for the simple reason we're too fast and handy for any d - - - - d patrol ship, English or American. What I'm telling you, *Mister* Flashman, is that *we* don't get caught, so you won't either. Does that set your mind at rest?"

It didn't, of course, but I knew better than to protest again. All I could think of was how the h - - l I was going to get out of this. He took my silence for assent.

"Well enough," growls he. "You'll begin on this lot, then"— and he jerked a thumb at the cargo. "And for Christ's sake, liven up, man! I'll not have you glooming up this ship with a long face, d'ye see? At eight bells you'll leave off and come to my cabin— Mrs Spring will be serving tea for the officers, and will wish to meet you."

I didn't believe my ears. "Mrs Spring?"

"My wife," he snapped, and seeing my bewilderment: "Who the d - - - l else would Mrs Spring be? You don't think I'd ship my mother aboard a slaver, do you?"

And with that he strode off, leaving me in a fine sweat. Thanks to an instant's folly, and the evil of that rotten little toad, my father-in-law, I was a member of the crew of a pirate ship, and nothing to be done about it. It took some digesting, but there it was; I suppose that after all the shocks I'd had in my young life this should have been nothing out of the way, but I found myself shuddering at the thought. Not that I'd any qualms about slaving, mark you, from the holy-holy point of view; they could have transported every nigger in Africa to the moon in chains for all I cared, but I knew it was a d - - - - d chancy business—aye, and old Morrison had known that, too. So the old swine had his fin-

* The evil-doer hates the light.

- 44

gers in the blackbird pie—and I'll lay my life *that* was a well concealed ledger in his countinghouse—and had taken advantage of the Bryant affair to shanghai me into this. He had wanted me out of the way, and here was a golden chance of making sure that I would be away for good; no doubt Spring was right, and the *Balliol College* would come through her voyage safe, as most slavers did, but there was always the chance of being caught, and rotting your life away in jail, even if they didn't top you. And there was the risk of getting killed by niggers on the Slave Coast, or catching yellow jack or some foul native disease, as so many slaving crews did—oh, it was the perfect ocean cruise for an unwanted son-in-law. And Elspeth would be a widow, I would never see her, or England, again, for even if I survived the trip, word of it might get home, and I'd be an outlaw, a felon . . .

I sat down on the cargo with my head in my hands, and wept, and raged inwardly against that little Scotch scoundrel. G - d, if ever I had the chance to pay him back—but what was the use of thinking that way in my present plight? In the end, as usual, one thought came uppermost in my mind—survive, Flashy, and let the rest wait. But I resolved to keep my spite warm in the meantime.

In the circumstances it was as well that I had work to do; going through that cargo, as I did when a couple of hands and the ship's clerk came down presently, at least occupied part of my thoughts, and kept me from working myself into a terror about the future. After all, thinks I, men like these didn't sign on in the expectation of dying; they seemed handy, sober fellows who knew their business—very different from the usual tarry-john. One of them, an oldish man named Kirk, had been a slaver all his days, and had served on the notorious *Black Joke*;[12] he wouldn't have shipped on any other kind of vessel.

"What," says he, "at £15 a month? I'd be a fool. D'ye know, I've four thousand quid put by, in Liverpool and Charleston banks—how many sailormen have the tenth of that? Risk? I've been impounded once, on the *Joke*, shipwrecked once, and seen two cargoes of black ivory slung overside—which meant a dead loss for the owners, but I drew me pay, didn't I? Oh, aye, I've been chased a score o' times, and been yard-arm to yard-arm in running fights wi' Limey an' Yankee patter-rollers, but no harm done. An' for sickness, ye've more chance of that from some poxed-up yellow tart in Havana than on the coast these days. You've been east—well, you know to keep yourself clean an' boil your water, then."

He made it sound not half bad, apart from the stuff about fighting the patrols, but I understood that this was a rare event— the *Balliol College* had never been touched in five trips that he knew of, although she had been sighted and chased times without number.

"She's built light, see, like all the Baltimore brigs an' clippers," says Kirk. "Save a patch o' calm, she'll show her heels to anything, even steam-ships. West o' Saint Tommy, even wi' a full load o' black cattle, she could snap her fingers at the whole Navy, and wi' the fair winds coming south, like we are now, she's gone before they see her. Only risky time is on the coast itself, afore we load up. If they was to catch us there, wi' the Government wind pinning us on the coast, they could impound us, empty an' all, 'cos o' the law as lays down that if you're rigged and fitted for slavin', like we are, they can pinch you even wi'out a black aboard. Used to be that even then they couldn't touch ye, if ye had the right papers—Greek, say, or Braziliano." He laughed. "Why, I've sailed on a ship that had Yankee, Gyppo, Portugee, an' even Rooshian papers all ready for inspection, as might serve. But it's different now—ye don't talk, ye run."[18]

He and the clerk and the other man—I think he was a Norwegian—harked back a good deal to the old days, when the slave-ships had waited in turn at the great African barracoons to ship their cargoes, and how the Navy had spoiled the trade by bribing the native chiefs not to deal with slavers, so that all the best stretches of coast nowadays were out of court, and no niggers to be had.

"Mind you," says Kirk, winking, "show 'em the kind o' goods we got here, an' they'll spring you a likely cargo o' Yorubas or Mandingos, treaty or not—an' if sometimes you have to fight for 'em, as we did two trips back, well, it comes cheaper, don't it? An' Cap'n Spring, he's got a grand nose for a tribal war, or a chief that's got too many young bucks of his own people on his hands. He's a caution, he is, an' worth every penny the owners pay him. Like to guess 'ow much?"

I said I had no idea.

"Twenty thousand pound a trip," says Kirk. "There now! An' you wonder I ship on a slaver!"

I knew slavers made huge profits, of course, but this staggered me. No wonder old Morrison had an interest in the trade—and no doubt paid a subscription to the Anti-Slavery Society and thought it well worthwhile. And he wasn't laying out overmuch in trade goods, by the look of this cargo—you never saw so much junk, although just the kind of stuff to make a nigger chief happy, no doubt. There were old Brown Bess muskets that probably hadn't been fired in fifty years, sackfuls of condemned powder and shot, rusty bayonets and cheap cutlasses and knives, mirrors and looking glasses by the dozen, feathered hats and check trousers, iron pots and plates and cauldrons, and most amazing of all, a gross of Army red coats, 34th Foot; one of 'em had a bullet-hole and a rusty stain on the right breast, and I remember thinking, bad luck for someone. There was a packet of letters in the pocket, which I meant to keep, but didn't.

And there was case after case of liquor, in brown glass bottles; gin, I suppose you'ld call it, but even to sniff the stuff shrivelled the hairs off your arse. The blacks wouldn't know the difference, of course.

We were searching through all this trash, I counting and calling out to the clerk, who ticked the manifest, and Kirk and his fellow stowing back, when Looney, the idiot steward, came down to gape at us. He squatted down, dribbling out of the corner of his mouth, making stupid observations, till Kirk, who was bundling the red coats, sings out to him to come over. Kirk had taken two of the brass gorgets off the officers' coats—they must have been d----d old uniforms—and winking at us he laid the gorgets on the deck, and says:

"Now, Looney, you're a sharp 'un. Which is the biggest? If you can tell, I'll give you my spirits tomorrow. If you can't, you give me yours, see?"

I saw what he was after: the gorgets were shaped like half-moons, and whichever was laid uppermost looked bigger—children

amuse themselves with such things, cut out of paper. Looney
squinted at them, giggling, and pointing to the top gorget, says:

"That 'un."

"Ye're sure?" says Kirk, and taking the gorget which Looney
had indicated, placed it *beneath* the other one—which now looked
bigger, of course. Looney stared at it, and then said:

"That un's bigger now."

Kirk changed them again, while his mates laughed, and Looney
was bewildered. He gaped round helplessly, and then kicking the
gorgets aside, he shouted:

"You make 'em bigger an'—an' littler!"

And he started to cry, calling Kirk a dirty b - - - - - d, which
made us laugh all the more, so he shouted obscenities at us and
stamped, and then ran over to a pile of bags stowed beyond the
cargo and began to urinate on them, still swearing at us over his
shoulder.

"Hold on!" cries Kirk, when he could contain his mirth. "That's
the niggers' gruel you're p - - - - - g on!"

I was holding my sides, guffawing, and the clerk cries out:

"That'll make the dish all the tastier for 'em! Oh, my stars!"

Looney, seeing us amused, began to laugh himself, as such idiots
will, and p - - - - d all the harder, and then suddenly I heard the
others' laughter cut off, and there was a step on the ladder, and
there stood John Charity Spring, staring at us with a face like the
demon king. Those pale eyes were blazing, and Looney gave a
little whimper and fumbled with his britches, while the piddle ran
across the tilting deck towards Spring's feet.

Spring stood there in a silence you could feel, while we
scrambled up. His hands clenched and unclenched, and the scar
on his head was blazing crimson. His mouth worked, and then he
leaped at Looney and knocked the cowering wretch down with
one smashing blow. For a moment I thought he would set about
the half-wit with his boots, but he mastered himself, and wheeled
on us.

"Bring that—that vermin on deck!" he bawled, and stamped
up the ladder, and I was well ahead of the seamen in rushing to
Looney and dragging him to the scuttle. He yelled and struggled,
but we forced him up on deck, where Spring was stamping about

in a spitting rage, and the hands were doubling aft in response to the roars of the Yankee first mate.

"Seize him up there," orders Spring, and with me holding Looney's thrashing legs, Kirk very deftly tied his wrists up to the port shrouds and ripped his shirt off. Spring was calling for the cat, but someone says there wasn't one.

"Then make one, d - - n you!" he shouted, and paced up and down, casting dreadful glances at the imploring Looney, who was babbling in his bonds.

"Don't hit us, cap'n! Please don't hit us! It was them other b - - - - - ds, changin' things!"

"Silence!" says Spring, and Looney's cries subsided to a whisper, while the crew crowded about to see the sport. I kept back, but made sure I had a good view.

They gave Spring a hastily made cat, and he buttoned his jacket tight and pulled his hat down.

"Now, you b - - - - r, I'll make you dance!" cries he, and laid in for all he was worth. Looney screamed and struggled; each time the lashes hit him he shrieked, and between each stroke Spring cursed him for all he was worth.

"Foul my ship, will you?" Whack! "Ruin the food for my cargo, by G - d!" Whack! "Spread pestilence with your filth, will you?" Whack! "Yes, pray, you wharfside son-of-a-b - - - h, I'm listening!" Whack! "I'll cut your b - - - - y soul out, if you have one!" Whack! If it had been a regulation Army cat, I think he'd have killed him; as it was, the hastily spliced yarn cut the idiot's back to bits and the blood ran over his ragged trousers. His screams became moans, and then silence, and then Spring flung the cat overboard.

" Souse him and let him hang there to dry!" says he, and then he addressed the unconscious victim. "And let me catch you at your filthy tricks again, you scum, so help me G - d I'll hang you —d'ye hear!"

He glared at us with his madman's eyes, and my heart was in my mouth for a moment. Then his scar faded, and he said in his normal bark:

"Dismiss the hands, Mr Comber. Mr Sullivan, and you, supercargo, come aft. Mrs Spring is serving tea."

There were a few curious glances at me as I followed Spring and the Yankee mate—I was new to the crew, of course—and as we went down the ladder to his cabin, Spring looked me over. "Go and put on a jacket," he growled. "G-d d--n you, don't you know anything?" so I scudded off smartly, and when I came back they were still waiting. He examined me—and in a flash of memory I thought of waiting with Wellington to see the Queen, and being fussed over by flunkeys—and then he threw open the door.

"I trust we don't intrude, my dear," says he. "I have brought Mr Sullivan to tea, and our new supercargo, Mr Flashman."

I don't know what I expected—the Queen of Sheba wouldn't have surprised me, aboard the *Balliol College*—but it wasn't the mild-looking, middle-aged woman sitting behind a table, picking at a sampler, who turned to beam at us pleasantly, murmured something in greeting, and then set to pouring tea. Presently Comber came in, smoothing his hair, and the grizzled old second mate, Kinnie, who ducked his head to me when Spring made us known to each other. Mrs Spring handed over cups, and we stood round sipping, and nibbling at her biscuits, while she beamed and Spring talked—she had little to say for herself, but he paid her as much respect as though it had been a London drawing-room. I had to pinch myself to believe it was real: a tea-party aboard a slaver, with this comfortable woman adding hot water to the pot while a flogged man was bleeding all over the deck above our heads, and Spring, his cuff specked with the victim's gore, was laying it off about Thucydides and Horace.

"Mr Flashman has had the beginning of an education, my dear," says he. "He was with Dr Arnold at Rugby School."

She turned a placid face in my direction. "Mr Spring is a classical scholar," says she. "His father was a Senior Fellow."

"Senior Tutor, if you please, my dear," says Spring. "And it's my belief he achieved that position by stealing the work of better men. Scholarship is merely a means to an end these days, and *paucis carior est fides quam pecunia.** You remember Sallust, Mr Comber? No? There seems to be little to choose between the ignorance of Rugby and that of Winchester College." (Oho, thinks

* Few do not set a higher value on money than on good faith.

I, Winchester, that accounts for a lot.) "However, if we have some leisure on this voyage, we may repair these things, may we not, Mr Flashman?"

I mumbled something about being always eager to learn.

"Aye," says he, "*pars sanitatis velle sanari fuit,** we may hope. But I imagine Seneca is yet another among the many authors with whom you are not acquainted." He munched on a biscuit, the pale blue eyes considering me. "Tell me, sir, what do you know?"

I stole a glance at the others; Kinnie had his head down over his cup, and Sullivan, the big, raw-boned Yankee, was gazing bleakly before him. Comber was looking nervous.

"Well, sir," says I, "not very much . . ." And then, like a fool, I added, toady-like: "Not as much as a Fellow of Oriel College, I'm sure."

Comber's cup clattered suddenly. Spring says, very soft: "I am not a Fellow, Mr Flashman. I was dismissed."

Well, it didn't surprise me. "I'm very sorry, sir," says I.

"You well may be," says he. "You well may be. You may come to wish that I was in my rightful place, sir, instead of here!" His voice was rising, and his scar going crimson. He set his cup down with a force that rattled the table. "Herding with the carrion of the sea, sir, instead of . . . of . . . d - - n your eyes, man, look at me! You think it a matter for contempt, don't you, that a man of my intellect should be brought to this! You think it a jest that I was flung into the gutter by jealous liars! You do! I see it in your . . ."

"No, no indeed, sir!" cries I, quaking. "I was expelled myself . . . I don't . . ."

"Hold your confounded tongue!" he bawled. "You can't do right for doing wrong, can you? No, by G - d! Well, I warn you, *Mister* Flashman—I'll remind you of another text from Seneca, whom you don't b - - - - y well read, d - - n your ignorance! *Gravis ira regum sempert* Mr Comber will construe it for you—he's heard it before, and digested it! He'll tell you that a captain is to be feared as much as a king!" He thumped the table. "Mrs

---

* The wish to be cured is itself a step towards health.
† The anger of kings is always severe.

Spring, you'll excuse me!" And he burst past me, slamming the door behind him.

He left me shaking, and then we heard his voice on deck, bawling at the man at the wheel, and his feet stamping overhead. I felt the sweat starting on my forehead.

"May I give you some more tea, Mr Sullivan?" says Mrs Spring. "Mr Comber, a little more?" She poured for them in silence. "Have you been to sea before, Mr Flashman?"

God knows what I said; it was too much for me, and it's quite likely I answered nothing at all. I know we stood about a little longer, and then Sullivan said we must be about our duties, and we thanked Mrs Spring, and she inclined her head gravely, and we filed out.

Outside, Sullivan turned to me, glanced up the ladder, sighed, and rubbed his jaw. He was a youngish, hard-case sailor, this one, with a New England figurehead and a slantendicular way of looking at you. At last he says:

"He's mad. So's she." He thought for a moment. "It don't matter, though. Much. Sane or silly, drunk or dry, he's the best d----d skipper on this coast, or any other. You follow me?"

I stood there, nodding.

"Well and good," says he. "You'll be in Mr Comber's watch —just tail on to the rope and keep your eyes open. And when the skipper starts talkin' Latin, or whatever it is, just shut up, d'ye hear?"

That was one piece of advice which I didn't need. If I'd learned one thing about the *Balliol College*, it was that I had no wish to bandy scholarship with John Charity Spring—or anything else, for that matter.

By now you will have some idea of what life at sea was like when Uncle Harry was a boy. I don't claim that it was typical—I've sailed on many ships since the *Balliol College*, and never struck one like it, thank G-d—but although it was often like cruising in an asylum, I'll say one thing: that ship and crew were d---d good at their work, which was kidnapping niggers and selling them in the Americas.

I can say this now, looking back; I was hardly in a position to appreciate their qualities after that first day of flogging and tea parties. All I could think of then was that I was at the mercy of a dangerous maniac who was h--l bent on a dangerous criminal expedition, and I didn't know which to be more scared of—him and his Latin lectures or the business ahead. But as usual, after a day or two I settled down, and if I didn't enjoy the first weeks of that voyage, well, I've known worse.

At least I had an idea of what I was in for—or thought I had —and could hope to see the end of it. For the moment I must take care, and so I studied to do my duties well—which was easy enough—and to avoid awakening the wrath of Captain J. C. Spring. This last wasn't too difficult, as it proved: all I had to do in his presence was listen to his interminable prosing about Thucydides and Lucan, and Seneca, whom he particularly admired, for he dearly loved to display his learning. (In fact, I heard later that he had been a considerable scholar in his youth, and would have gone far had he not assaulted some dignitary at Oxford and been kicked out. Who knows? he might have become something like Head at Rugby—which prompts the thought that Arnold would have made a handy skipper for an Ivory Coast pirate.)

At any rate, he lost no opportunity of airing his Latinity to Comber and me, usually at tea in his cabin, with the placid Mrs Spring sitting by, nodding. Sullivan was right, of course; they were both mad. You had only to see them at the divine service which

Spring insisted on holding on Sundays, with the whole ship's company drawn up, and Mrs Spring pumping away at her German accordion while we sang "Hark! the wild billow", and afterwards Spring would blast up prayers to the Almighty, demanding his blessing on our voyage, and guidance in the tasks which our hands should find to do, world without end, amen. I don't know what Wilberforce would have made of that, or my old friend John Brown, but the ship's company took it straight-faced—mind you, they knew better than to do anything else.

They were as steady a crowd as I've ever seen afloat—hard men, and sober, who didn't say much but did their work with a speed and efficiency that would have shamed an Indiaman. They were professionals, of course, and a good cut above your ordinary shellback. They respected Spring, and he them—although when one of them, a huge Dago, talked back to him, Spring smashed him senseless with his bare fists inside a minute—a man twice his size and weight. And another, who stole spirits, he flogged nearly to death, blaspheming at every stroke—yet a couple of hours later he was reading aloud to us from the *Aeneid*.

Mind you, if it was a tolerable life, it was damned dull, and I found my thoughts turning increasingly to Elspeth—and other women—as the days grew longer. But it was Elspeth, mostly; I found myself dreaming about her soft nakedness, and that silky golden hair spilling down over my face, and the perfume of her breath—it was rough work, I tell you, knowing there wasn't a wench in a hundred miles, nor likely to be. And from that my thoughts would turn to Morrison, and how I might get my own back when the time came: that at least was a more profitable field of speculation.

So we ran south, and then south by east, day after day, and the weather got warmer, and I shed my coat for a red striped jersey and white duck trousers, with a big belt and a sheath knife, as like Ralph Rover as ever was, and the galley stopped serving duff and the cask-water got staler by the day, and then one morning the wind had a new smell—a heavy, rotten air that comes from centuries of mangrove growing and decaying—and that afternoon we sighted the low green bank far away to port that is the coast of Africa.

We sighted sails, too, every now and then, but never for long. The *Balliol College*, as Kirk told me, drew wind like no other ship on the ocean—the best fun was stand up in her forechains as she lay over, one gunwale just above the crests, thrashing along like billy-be-damned, with mountains of canvas billowing above you —Dick Dauntless would have loved it, I'll be bound, and I enjoyed it myself—or at night, when you could lean over and watch the green fire round her bows, and look up at that African sky that is purple and soft like no other in the world, with the stars twinkling. G-d knows I'm no romantic adventurer, but sometimes I remember—and I'd like to run south again down Africa with a fair wind. In a private yacht, with my youth, half a dozen assorted Parisian whores, the finest of food and drink, and perhaps a German band. Aye, it's a man's life.

That land we had sighted was the Guinea Coast, which was of no interest to us, because as Kirk assured me it was played out for slaving. The growing sentiment for abolition at home, the increasing number of nations who joined with England in fighting the trade, the close blockade of the coast by British and Yankee patrol ships, who burned the slave stations and pounced on the ships— all these things were making life more difficult in the blackbird trade in the '40s. In the old days, the slavers had been able to put in openly, and pick up their cargoes, which had been collected by the native chiefs and herded into the great pens, or barracoons, at the river mouths. Now it wasn't so easy, and speed and secrecy were the thing, which was why fast ships like the *Balliol College* were at an advantage.

And of course clever slavers like Spring knew exactly where to go for the best blacks and which chiefs to deal with—this was the great thing. Your slaver might easily dodge the patrols on the way in and out—for it was a huge coast, and the Navy couldn't hope to watch it all—but unless he had a good agent ashore, and a native king who could keep up a supply of prime nigs, he was sunk. It's always amused me to listen to the psalm-smiting hypocrisy of nigger-lovers at home and in the States who talk about white savages raping the Coast and carrying poor black innocents into bondage—why, without the help of the blacks themselves we'd not have been able to lift a single slave out of

Africa. But I saw the Coast with my own eyes, you see, which the Holy Henriettas didn't, and I know that this old wives' tale of a handful of white pirates mastering the country and kidnapping as they chose, is all my eye. We couldn't have stayed there five minutes if the nigger kings and warrior tribes hadn't been all for it, and traded their captured enemies—aye, and their own folk, too—for guns and booze and Brummagem rubbish.

Why my pious acquaintances won't believe this, I can't fathom. *They* enslaved *their* own kind, in mills and factories and mines, and made 'em live in kennels that an Alabama planter wouldn't have dreamed of putting a black into. Aye, and our dear dead St William Wilberforce cheered 'em on, too—weeping his pious old eyes out over niggers he had never seen, and d - - ning the soul of anyone who suggested it was a bit hard to make white infants pull coal sledges for twelve hours a day. Of course, he knew where his living came from, I don't doubt. My point is: if he and his kind did it to their people, why should they suppose the black rulers were any different where their kinsfolk were concerned? They make me sick, with their pious humbug.

But it's all by the way; the main thing is that Spring had a good black king to work with, a horrible old creature named Gezo, who lorded it over the back country of Dahomey. Now that the Windward Coast wasn't the place any more, and the slavers were concentrating round the corner in the White Man's Grave, stretches like Dahomey and Benin and the Oil rivers were where the real high jinks were to be found. The Navy lay in all the time at places like Whydah and Lagos, and your sharp captains like Spring were as likely as not to use the lonelier rivers and lagoons, where they could load up at their leisure, provided no one spotted 'em coming in.[14]

After our first landfall we bore away south, and came eastabout to Cape Palmas, where you could see the palm trees that gave it its name down by the water's edge, and so along the Ivory Coast and Gold Coast past Three Points to Whydah, where we put into the open roads. Spring had the Stars and Stripes at the masthead, and was safe enough, for there wasn't a Yankee in port. There were two British naval sloops, but they wouldn't come near us —this was where the slavers scored, Kirk told me; the Yanks wouldn't let any but their own navy search an American ship, so our blue-jackets would interfere only with Portuguese and Spaniards and so on.

We lay off, looking at the long yellow beach with the factories and barracoons behind it, and the huge rollers crashing on the sand, and it was as hot as hell's kitchen. I watched the kites diving and snatching among the hundreds of small craft plying about between ships and shore, and the great Kroo canoes riding the surf, and tried to fan away the stench that rose from all the filth rotting on the oily water. I remembered what Kinnie had said:

"Oh, sailor, beware of the Bight o' Benin.

There's one as comes out for a hundred goes in."

You could smell the sickness on the wind, and I wondered why Spring, who was talking at the rail with Sullivan and scanning the shore with his glass, had put in here. But presently out comes a big Kroo canoe, with half a dozen niggers on board, who hailed us, and for the first time I heard that queer Coast lingo which passes for a language from Gambia to the Cape.

"Hollo, Tommy Rot," cries Spring, "where Pedro Blanco?"[15]

"Hollo, sah," sings out one of the Kroos. "He lib for Bonny; no catch two, three week."

"Why he no lib for come? Him sabby me make palaver, plenty plenty nigras. Come me plenty good stuff, what can do, him lib Bonny?"

"Him say Spagnole fella, Sanchez, lib for Dahomey ribber. Him make strong palaver, no goddam bobbery. You take Tommy Rot, sah, catch Rum Punch, Tiny Tim, plenty good fella, all way ribber. Make good nigra palaver wid Spagnole fella, no Inglish Yankee gunboat."

Spring cursed a bit at all this; it seemed he had been hoping to meet one Pedro Blanco at Whydah, but the Krooboy Tommy Rot was telling him instead he should make for a river where a Spaniard named Sanchez would supply him with slaves. Spring didn't like it too much.

"Blanco bobbery b------d," says he. "Me want him make palaver King Gezo one time."

"Palaver sawa sawa," bawls the Kroo. "Sanchez lib for Gezo,

lib for you, all for true."

"He'd better," growls Spring. "All right, Tommy Rot, come aboard, catch Tiny Tim, ten fella, lib for ship, sabby?"

We took on a dozen of the Kroos, grinning, lively blacks who were great favourites among the Coast skippers. They were prime seamen, but full of tricks, and went by ridiculous names like Rum Punch, Blunderbuss, Jumping Jack, Pot Belly and Mainsail. Each one had his forehead tattooed blue, and his front teeth filed to points; I thought they were cannibals, but it seems they carried these marks so that they would be recognised as Kroos and therefore wouldn't be taken as slaves.

With them aboard, the *Balliol College* stood out from Whydah, and after two days sniffing about out of sight of land we put in again farther east, on to a long low rotting coast-line of mangrove crawling out into the sea among the sunken sandbars. It looked d----d unpleasant to me, but Spring at the wheel brought her through into a lagoon, beyond which lay a great delta of jungle-covered islands, and through these we came to what looked like a river mouth. We inched through the shoals, with everyone hauling and sweating at the sweeps, and the Kroos out ahead in canoes, while three men either side swung the lead incessantly, chanting "Three fathom, two and a half, two and Jesus saves, two and a half, two and Jesus saves, three fathom!"

And then, round the first bend, was a clearing, and huge stockades between river and jungle, and huts, and presently a fat Dago in a striped shirt with a hankie round his head and rings in his ears comes out in a small boat, all smiles, to meet a great storm of abuse from Spring.

"You're Sanchez, are you? And where the h--l's my cargo? Your barracoons are empty, you infernal scoundrel! Five hundred blacks I signed for with that thieving blackguard, Pedro Blanco, and look yonder!" He flung out an arm towards the empty stockades, in which the only sign of life was a few figures idling round a cooking-fire. "D---l a black hide in sight apart from your own! Well, sir?"

The dago was full of squealing apologies, waving his arms and sweating. "My dear Captain Spring! Your fears are groundless. Within two days there will be a thousand head in the barracoons.

Pedro Blanco has taken order. King Gezo himself has come down country—especially on your behalf, my good sir. He is at Dogba, with his people; there has been much fighting, I understand, but all quiet now. And many, many nigras in his slave train—strong young men, hardy young women—all the best, for you, captain!" He beamed around greasily.

"You're sure?" says Spring. "Two days? I want to be out of here in three—and I want to see King Gezo, d'you hear?"

Sanchez spread his sticky hands. "There is no difficulty. He will be coming west from Dogba to Apokoto tomorrow."

"Well..." growls Spring, quieting down. "We'll see. What's he got for us. Sombas?"

"Sombas, Fulani, Adja, Aiza, Yoruba, Egbo—whatever the captain requires."

"Is that so? Well, I'll have six hundred, then, 'stead of five. And no sickly niggers, see? They're not going to be auctioned off with their arses stuffed with tar, mind that! I want sound stock."[16]

Sanchez took his leave, full of good wishes, and the *Balliol College* was made fast, as close to the bank as she could be warped. Men were sent aloft to hang her topmasts with leaves and creepers, so that no patrol vessel out at sea might spot us, and Sanchez sent men aboard to unload the cargo. This meant work for me, making sure they pinched nothing, and by the time the last bale was out and under the guard of Sanchez's native soldiers, I was running with sweat. It was a hellish place; green jungle all around, and steam coming off the brown oily surface of the water as though it were a bath; clouds of midges descended as soon as the sun dropped, and the heat pressed in on you like a blanket, so that all you could do was lie stifling, with your chest heaving and the perspiration pouring off you. Three days, Spring had said; it was a wonder to me that we had survived three hours.

That night Spring called a council in his cabin, of all his officers; I was there, as supercargo, but you can be sure I was well out of the running. I don't suppose I've listened to a more interesting discussion in my life, though, unless it was Grant and Lee meeting in the farmhouse, or Lucan and my old pal Cardigan clawing at each other like female cousins at Balaclava. Certainly, for technical knowledge, Spring's little circle was an eye-opener.

"Six hundred," says Spring. "More than I'd bargained for; it'll mean fifteen inches for the bucks, and I want two bucks for every female, and no d - - - - d calves."

"That's an inch under the old measure, cap'n," says Kinnie. "Might do for your Guineas, but it's tight for Dahomeys. Why, they're near as big as Mandingos, some of 'em, an' Mandingos take your sixteen inches, easy."

"I've seen the Portugoosers carry Mande's in less than that," says Sullivan.

"An' had twenty in the hundred die on 'em, likely."

"No fear. They put bucks in with wenches—reckon they spend all their time on top of each other, an' save space that way."

Spring didn't join in their laughter. "I'll have no mixing of male and female," he growled. "That's the surest way to trouble I know. I'm surprised at you, Mr Sullivan."

"Just a joke, sir. But I reckon sixteen inches, if we dance 'em regular."

"I'm obliged to you for your opinion. Dance or not, they get fifteen inches, and the women twelve."[17]

Kinnie shook his head. "That won't do, sir. These Dahomey b - - - - - s takes as much as the men, any day. Sideways packin's no use either, the way they're shaped."

"Put 'em head to toe, they'll fit," says Sullivan.

"You'll lose ten, mebbe more, in the hundred," says Kinnie. "That's a ten thousand dollar loss, easy, these days."

"I'll have no loss!" cries Spring. "I'll not, by G - d! We'll ship nothing that's not A1, and the b - - - - - s will have fresh fruit with their pulse each day, and be danced night and morning, d'ye hear?"

"Even so, sir," insisted Kinnie. "Twelve inches won't. . . ."

Comber spoke up for the first time. He was pale, and sweating heavily—mind you, we all were—but he looked seedier than the others. "Perhaps Mr Kinnie is right, sir. Another inch for the women. . . ."

"When I want your advice, Mr Comber, I'll seek it," snaps Spring. "Given your way, you'd give 'em two feet, or fill the b - - - - y ship with pygmies."

"I was thinking of the possible cost, sir. . . ."

"Mr Comber, you lie." Spring's scar was going pink. "I know you, sir—you're tender of black sheep."

"I don't like unnecessary suffering, and death, sir, it's true . . ."

"Then, by G-d, you shouldn't have shipped on a slaver!" roars Spring. "D--nation, d'you want to give 'em a berth apiece? You think I'm cruising 'em round the b----y lighthouse for a lark? Forty pieces a pound, Mr Comber—that's what an ordinary buck will fetch in Havana these days—perhaps more. A thousand dollars a head! Now, take note, Mr Comber, of what your extra inch can mean—a forty thousand dollar loss for your owner! Have you thought of that, sir?"

"I know, sir," says Comber, sticking to his guns nervously. "But forty dead gives you the same loss, and. . . ."

"D--nation take you, will you dispute with me?" Spring's eyes were blazing. "I was shipping black pigs while you were hanging at your mother's teat—where you ought to be this minute! D'ye think I don't take as much thought to have 'em hale and happy as you, you impudent pup! And for a better reason— I don't get paid for flinging corpses overboard. It's dollars I'm saving, not souls, Mr Comber! Heaven help me, I don't know why you're in this business—you ought to be in the b----y Board of Trade!" He sat glaring at Comber, who was silent, and then turned to the others. "Fifteen and twelve, gentlemen, is that clear?"

Kinnie sighed. "Very good, cap'n. You know my views, and . . . ."

"I do, Mr Kinnie, and I respect them. They are grounded in experience and commercial sense, not in humanitarian claptrap picked up from scoundrels like Tappan and Garrison. *The Genius of Universal Emancipation*, eh, Mr Comber?[18] You'll be quoting to me in a moment. Genius of Ill-digested Crap! Don't contradict me, sir; I know your views—which is why I'm at a loss to understand your following this calling, you d----d hypocrite, you!"

Comber sat silent, and Spring went on: "You will take personal responsibility for the welfare of the females, Mr Comber. And they won't die, sir! We shall see to that. No, they won't die, because like you—and Mr Flashman yonder—they haven't read Seneca, so they don't know that *qui mori didicit servire dedidicit.** If they did, we'd be out of business in a week."

I must say it sounded good sense to me, and Comber sat mumchance. He was obviously thankful when the discussion turned to more immediate matters, like the arrival of King Gezo the next day at Apokoto, which lay some miles up river; Spring wanted to meet him for a palaver, and said that Kinnie and Comber and I should come along, with a dozen of the hands, while Sullivan began packing the first slaves who would be arriving at the barracoons.

I was all in favour of getting off the *Balliol College* for a few hours, but when we boarded the Kroos' big canoe at the bank next day, I wasn't so sure. Kinnie was distributing arms to the hands, a carbine and cutlass for each man, and Spring himself took me aside and presented me with a very long-barrelled pistol.

"You know these?" says he, and I told him I did—it was one of the early Colt revolvers, the type you loaded with powder and ball down the muzzle. Very crude they'd look today, but they were the wonder of the world then.

"I picked up a dozen of these last winter in Baltimore," says he. "American army guns—Gezo would give his very throne for 'em, and I intend to use them in driving a very special bargain with him. Are you a good shot? Well, then, you can demonstrate them for him. Get Kinnie to give you a needle gun and cutlass as well."[19]

"D'you think ... we'll need them?" says I.

He turned the pale eyes on me. "Would you rather go unarmed —into the presence of the most bloodthirsty savage in West Africa?" says he. "No, Mr Flashman—I don't expect we shall need to use our weapons; not for a moment. But I fear the Greeks even when I'm bearing gifts to 'em, sir, d'you see?"

Well, that was sense, no doubt of it, so I took my needle carbine and bandolier, buckled on the cutlass and stuck the Colt in my belt, and stood forth like Pirate Bill; as we took our places in the canoe, it looked like something from a pantomime, every man with his hankie knotted round his head, armed to the teeth, some of 'em with rings in their ears, and one even with a patch over his eye. It struck me—what would Arnold say if he could

* Who has learned to die, has learned how not to be a slave.

look down now from his place at the right hand of God? Why, there, he would say, is that worthy lad, Tom Brown, with his milk-and-water wife in the West Country, giving bread and blankets to needy villagers who knuckle their heads and call him "squire": good for you, Brown. And there, too, that noble boy Scud East, lording it over the sepoys for the glory of God and the profit of John Company—how eminently satisfactory! And young Brooke, too, a fearless lieutenant aboard his uncle's frigate *Unspeakable*—what a credit to his old school! Aye, as the twigs are bent so doth the trees grow. But who is this, consorting with pirates and preparing to ship hapless niggers into slavery, with oaths on his lips? I might have known—it is the degraded Flashman! Unhappy youth! But just what I might have expected!

Aye, he would have rejoiced at the sight—if there's one thing he and his hypocritical kind loved better than seeing virtue rewarded, it was watching a black sheep going to the bad. The worst of it is, I wasn't there of my own free will—not that you ever get credit for that.

These philosophical musings were disturbed by the tender scene between Mr and Mrs Spring as he prepared to board the canoe. Unlike the rest of us, he was dressed as usual—dark jacket, round hat, neck-cloth all trim—how the devil he stood it, in that steaming heat, I can't figure. Well, at the last minute, Mrs Spring leans over the ship's side crying to him to take his comforter "against the chill of the night". This in a country where the nights are boiling hot, mark you.

"D - - nation!" mutters Spring, but out he climbed, and took the muffler, crying good-bye, my dear, good-bye, while the men in the canoe grinned and looked the other way. He was in a fine temper as we shoved off, kicking the backside of the cabin boy —who had been ordered to come along—and d - - ning the eyes of the man at the tiller.

Just as we pushed out into mid-stream came another diversion —from the jungle on the landward side of the stockade came a distant murmuring and confused sound. As it grew nearer you could hear that it was a great shuffling and moaning, with the occasional shout and crack of a whip, and a dull chanting in cadence behind it.

"It's the slave train!" bawls Spring, and sure enough, presently out of the jungle came the head of a long line of niggers, yoked two by two with long poles, shuffling along between their guards. They were a startling sight, for there were hundreds of 'em, all naked, their black bodies gleaming in the sunshine and their legs covered with splashes of mud up to the thigh. They moaned and chanted as they walked, big stalwart bucks with woolly heads, jerking and stumbling, for the yokes were at their necks, and if a man checked or broke his stride he brought his yoke-fellow up short. The sound they made was like a huge swarm of bees, except when one of the guards, big niggers in kilts and blouses carrying muskets, brought his whip into play, and the crack would be followed by a yelp of pain.

"Easy with those kurbashes, d - - n you!" yelled Spring. "That's money you're cutting at!" He leaned eagerly over the thwart, surveying the caravan. "Prime stuff, 'pon my soul, Mr Kinnie; no refuse there. Somba and Egbo, unless I'm mistaken."

"Aye, sir, good cattle, all of 'em," says Kinnie.

Spring rubbed his hands, and with many a last glance, gave the order to give way. The men at the sweeps hauled, and the big canoe pushed forward up river, Mrs Spring fluttering her handkerchief after us from the *Balliol College*'s rail.

Once round the first bend, we were in another world. On either side and overhead the jungle penned us in like a huge green tent, muffling the cries and shrieks of the beasts and birds beyond it. The heat was stifling, and the oily brown water itself was so still that the plash of the sweeps and the dripping of moisture from the foliage sounded unnaturally loud. The men pulling were drenched in sweat; it was a labour to breathe the heavy damp air, and Kirk was panting under his breath as he accompanied the rowers with "Rock an' roll, rock an' roll, Shenandoah sail-or! hoist her high, hoist her dry, rock an' roll me ov-er!"

It must have been three or four hours, with only a few brief rests, before Spring ordered a halt at a small clearing on the water's edge. He consulted his watch, and then his compass, and announced:

"Very good, Mr Kinnie, we'll march from here. No sense in risking our craft any nearer these gentlemen than we have to.

Cover her up and fall in ashore."

We all piled out, and the huge canoe was manhandled in under the mangroves which hung far out from the water's edge. When she was hidden to Spring's satisfaction, with a guard posted, and he had ensured that every man was properly armed and equipped, he led the way along a track that seemed to me to run parallel with the river—although the jungle was so thick you couldn't see a yard either side. The air was alive with mosquitoes, and in the shadows of that little green tunnel we stumbled along, slapping and cursing; it was a poor trail, and when Spring asked me what I thought of it, I answered, h - - lish. He barked a laugh and says:

"Truer than you know. It's made of corpses—some of the thousands that result from the Dahomeyans' yearly festival of human sacrifice.[20] They build up the path with 'em, bound together with vines and cemented with mud." He pointed to the dense thickets either side. "You wouldn't make a mile a day in there—nothing but ooze and roots and rotting rubbish. Sodden wet, but never a drop of water to be had—you can die of thirst in that stuff."

You may guess how this cheered up the journey, but there was worse ahead. We smelled Apokoto long before we saw it; a rank wave of corruption that had us cursing and gagging. It was a stink of death—animal and vegetable—that hit you like a hot fog and clung in your throat. "Filthy black animals," says Spring.

The town itself was bigger than I had imagined, a huge stockaded place crammed with those round grass lodges which are beehive shaped with an onion topknot. All of it was filthy and ooze-ridden, except for the central square which had been stamped flat and hard; the whole population, thousands of 'em, were gathered round it, stinking fit to knock you flat. The worst of the reek came from a great building like a cottage at the far side, which puzzled me at first because it seemed to be built of shiny brown stones which seemed impossible in this swampy jungle country. Kirk put me wise about that: "Skulls," says he, and that is what they were, thousands upon thousands of human skulls cemented together to make the death-house, the ghastly place where the human sacrifices—prisoners, slaves, criminals, and the like—were herded before execution. Even the ground directly before it was paved with skulls, and the evil of the place hung over that great square like an invisible mist.

"I seen as many as a hundred chopped up at one time before that death-house," says Kirk. "Men, women, an' kids, all cut up together. It's like a Mayday fair to these black heathen."

"They seem amiable enough just now," says I, wishing to God I were back at the ship, and he agreed that as a rule the Apokoto folk were friendly to white traders—provided they had trade goods, and looked as though they could defend themselves. It was plain to see now why Spring had us heavily armed; I'd have been happier with a park of artillery as well.

"Aye, they're savage swine if you don't mind your eye," says Kirk, rolling his quid, "an' Gezo's the most fearsome b - - - - - d of the lot. He's the man to set upon your landlord, by G - d! An' wait till you see his warriors—you're a military man, ain't you?— well, you never seen nothin' like his bodyguard, not nowheres. You just watch out for 'em. Best fighters in Africa, they reckon, an' probably the on'y nigger troops anywhere that march in step —an' they can move in dead silence when they wants to, which most niggers can't. Oh, they're the beauties, they are!"

We had to wait near an hour before Gezo put in an appearance, in which time the sun got hotter, the reek fouler, and my mind uneasier. I've stood before the face of savage kings often enough, and hated every minute of it, but Gezo's little home-from-home, with its stench of death and corruption, and its death house, and its thousands of big, ugly niggers to our little party, was as nasty a hole as I've struck; I found myself shivering in spite of the heat haze, but took heart from the fact that all our fellows seemed quite composed, leaning on their muskets, chewing and spitting and winking at the niggers. Only Spring seemed agitated, but not with fear; he fidgeted eagerly from time to time, snorting with impatience at the delay, and took a turn up and down. Then he would stop, standing four square with his hands in his pockets, head tilted back, and you could feel he was working to contain himself as he waited.

Suddenly everything went dead quiet; the chatter of the crowd stopped, everyone held their breaths, and our fellows stiffened and shifted together. Utter silence lay over that vast place, broken only by the distant jungle noises. Spring shrugged and muttered: "High time, too. Come on, you black b - - - - - d."

The silence lasted perhaps a minute, and then out of the street beside the death house scampered a score of little figures, either dwarves or boys, but you couldn't tell, because they were grotesquely masked. They swung rattles as they ran, filling the air with their clatter, and crying out a confused jumble of words in which I managed to pick out "Gezo! Gezo!" They scattered about the square, prancing and rattling and questing, and Spring says to me:

"Chasing away bad spirits, and finding the most propitious place for his majesty to plant his fat posterior. Aye, as usual, on the platform. Look yonder."

Two warriors were carrying forward a great carved stool, its feet shaped like massive human legs, which they planked down on the dais of skulls before the death house. The masked dancers closed in, whisking away round the stool, and then scattered back to the edge of the square. As they fell silent a drum began to beat from beyond the death house, a steady, marching thump that grew louder and louder, and the crowd began to take it up, stamping and clapping in unison, and emitting a wordless grunt of "Ay-uh! ay-uh!" while they swayed to the rhythm.

"Now you'll open your eyes," says Kirk in my ear, and as he said it I saw emerging from the street by the death house a double file of warriors, swinging along in time to the steady cadence of the drum, while the chanting grew louder. "Ha!" cries Spring, eagerly. "At last!"

They marched out either side of the square in two long lines, lithe, splendid figures, swaying as they marched, and it was something in the manner of that swaying that struck me as odd; I stared harder, and got the surprise of my life. The warriors were all women.

And such women. They must have been close on a man's height, fine strapping creatures, black as night and smart as guardsmen. I gaped at the leading one on the right as she approached; she came sashaying along, looking straight before her, a great ebony Juno naked to the little blue kilt at her waist, with a long stabbing spear in one hand and a huge cleaver in her belt. The only other things she wore were a broad collar of beadwork tight round her throat, and a white turban over her hair, and as she passed in front of us I noticed that at her girdle there hung two skulls and a collection of what looked like lion's claws. The others who followed her were the same, save that instead of turbans they wore their hair coiled together and tied with ropes of beads, but each one carried a spear, some had bows and quivers of arrows, and one or two even had muskets. Not all were as tall as the leader, but I never saw anything on Horse Guards that looked as well-drilled and handsome—or as frighteningly dangerous.

"None o' your sogers could throw chests like them," says Kirk, licking his lips, and then I felt Spring's hand grip my wrist. To my surprise his pale eyes were shining with excitement, and I thought, well, you old lecher, no wonder you left Mrs Spring at home this trip. He pointed at the black, glistening line as they marched past.

"D'you realise what you're seeing, Flashman?" says he. "Do you? Women warriors—Amazons! The kind of whom Herodotus wrote, but he knew nothing of the reality. Look at them, man —did you ever see such a sight?"

Well, they were likely big wenches, certainly, and they bounced along very jolly, but when I watch a wobbling buttock I prefer it to be unobscured by a dangling skull. And I'm no hand with women who look as though they'd rather kill and eat me than grapple in the grass. But Spring was all for 'em; his voice was husky as he watched.

"D'you know what they call themselves? Mazangu—the fair ones. You see how every company leader wears a spotless turban —they call 'em Amodozo. Doesn't that name bring back an echo from your school-days—think, man! Who was the leader of the Amazons in Africa—Medusa! Amodozo, Medusa. Mazangu, Amazons." His face was alive with a delight I'd never seen before. "These are the cream of the Dahomeyan army—the picked bodyguard of the king. Every voyage I've made, I vowed I'd bring back half a dozen of them, but I've never been able to make this black Satan part with even one. He'll part this time, though." He rounded on me. "You've a gift of languages, have you not? On this voyage we'll learn it—we'll find out everything there is to know about 'em, study them, their history, their customs.

The real Amazons! By the holy, I'll make those smug half-educated Balliol sons-of-b - - - - -s sit up, won't I though? They'll find out what real scholarship is!"

I suppose I've been in some queer places, with some d - - - - d odd fellows, but nothing queerer than watching those big black fighting sluts march by while a classically-educated slaver skipper babbled to me about anthropological research. I thought it had been lust that excited him, at the sight of all those black boobies quivering, and it was lust, at that—but it was scholarly, not carnal. Well, if he thought I was going to huddle up with those female baboons, studying present infinitives, he was dead wrong.

"They've got both tits," I said. "Thought Amazons only had one."

He snarled his contempt. "Even Walter Raleigh knew better than that. But he was wrong about what mattered—so was Lopez Vaz, so was Herodotus. Not South America, not Scythia—here! Africa! I shall make a name—a great name, with my work on these women. Despise John Charity Spring, will they?" He was shouting again, not that anyone could hear much, above that drumming. "I'll show them, by G-d, I will! We'll keep one, perhaps two. The others will fetch a handy price in Havana—what? Think of the money they'll pay for black fighting women in New Orleans! I could get two—no, three thousand dollars a head for creatures like those!"

I never interrupt an enthusiast, especially one with a temper like a wild dog's. Presently he fell silent, but he never took his eyes off those women, who were halted now in a great circle round the square. Two other companies of them had filed in and taken station close to the death house, and now in their wake came a gross black figure, under a striped umbrella, at the sight of whom they raised their spears in salute and stamped, while the mob round the square roared a welcome.[21]

King Gezo of Dahomey was bitter ugly, even by nigger standards. He must have weighed twenty stone, with a massive belly hanging over his kilt of animal tails, and huge shoulders inside his scarlet cape. He had a kind of wicker hat on his head, and under it was a face that would have shamed a gorilla—huge flat nose, pocked cheeks, little yellow eyes and big yellow teeth.

He waddled to his stool, plumped down, and opened the palaver in a croaking voice that carried harshly all over the square.

At first we were ignored, although he could be seen squinting our way every now and then. He palavered with elders of the town, and then with several folk who were summoned forward from the crowd; one of them evidently displeased him, because he suddenly screamed an order, and two of the Amazons beside his throne stepped forward, drawing their cleavers, and without ceremony laid into the victim right and left, and literally slashed him to pieces. The crowd hollo'ed like mad, Gezo surged about on his stool, and those two harpies hacked away at the dismembered corpse, spattering the skull platform with blood. When they were done, slaves came forward to clear up—they had to sweep what was left of the body off the stage.

No doubt this was for our benefit, for we were now beckoned forward. Gezo was even more horrifying at close range, with those yellow eyeballs rolling at you, but he was civil enough to Spring, laughing hoarsely and chattering at him through one of his officials, who spoke fair Coast English.

They palavered for a while about the slaves who had been sent down to our ship, and then Gezo in high good humour ordered stools to be set for all our party, and we squatted down at the edge of the dais, while servants brought dishes of food—I expected it would turn my stomach, but it was not bad: stew, and fruit, and native bread, and a beer that was powerful and not unlike a German lager. Gezo gorged and talked, spluttering out food as he squealed and barked at Spring, and occasionally drinking beer from a gaudy china mug on which was inscribed, of all things, "A Present for a Good Boy from Scarborough". I remember thinking how odd it was that this shoddy article should obviously be a prized possession, while the local cups from which we drank were really fine pieces, of metal beautifully carved.

All told it was as pleasant a meal as one could have in the presence of a terrifying ogre, with the blood still sticky before his feet, and the foul stench of the death house all around. Another distraction was the Amazons, who ringed the dais; one of the white-turbanned leaders stood close by me and I took close stock of her. She had the flat face, broad nose, and thick lips usual on this part of the Coast, but with that splendid shape, and a fine black satin thigh thrust out and almost touching me as I sat, I thought, by gum, one could do worse. They had men only once a year, Spring had said, and I decided that being the man would be interesting work, if you survived it. I gave her a wink, and the sullen face never altered, but a moment later she raised the fly whisk that dangled from her wrist and brushed away an insect buzzing round my head. I could see she fancied me; black or white, savage or duchess, they're all alike.

Meanwhile the meal finished, and presently Gezo beckoned Spring to draw his stool closer; they grunted away at each other through the interpreter, and I heard Spring suggest the purchase of six of the Amazon women. This threw Gezo into a great passion, but Spring let it rage, and then whispered to the interpreter again. There was much conferring, and Gezo barked and screamed, but less loud each time, I thought, and at last Spring turned to me.

"Show him your pistol," says he, and I handed it over. Gezo pawed over it excitedly, rasping questions at Spring, and finally it was given back to me, and Spring says:

"Fire it for him—all five shots as fast as you can. Into the side of the death house will do."

I stood up, all eyes on me, Gezo chattering and bouncing up and down on his stool. I drew a bead on one of the skull bricks and fired; it kicked like blazes, but I thumbed back the hammer smartly and loosed off the next four shots in quick time. Five gaping holes were smashed in the wall, with splinters flying all over the place, the mob roared, Gezo beat his fists on his knees with excitement, and even the Amazons put up their knuckles to their mouths; my own pipsey-popsey with the white turban stared at me round-eyed.

Then Spring called up one of our seamen, who carried a case, and when he opened it there were the five other Colt pistols; Gezo slobbered and squealed at the sight of them, but Spring wouldn't hand them over—he had more guts than I'd have had with that blood-stained maniac mowing and yelling at me. They whispered away again, and then Gezo rolled his eyes shifty-like at the Amazons, summoned my girl, and mumbled orders to her. She didn't bat an eyelid, but snapped a command to six of her wenches. They grounded their spears like guardsmen, put by their cleavers, and then stood forward. Gezo yammered at them, one of them said something back, Gezo yelled at them, and from the ranks of all the other Amazons there was something like a gasp and a murmur, which rose to a growl; they didn't like what was happening, and Gezo had to stand up and bawl at them until they were quiet.

I didn't like the look of this; you could feel the anger and hatred welling up all round us. But Spring just snapped shut the case, handed it to Gezo, and then turned to us.

"Mr Kinnie," says he, "the palaver is finished. Form up round these six women; we're getting out of here." Then he tipped his hat to Gezo, who was sitting back on his stool, looking d----d peevish, and clutching his case. Our fellows had turned to face the crowd, who were milling closer beyond the ranks of the Amazons; it was beginning to look ugly, but Spring just marched ahead, bulldog fashion, the Amazons stepped back smartly to let him go, and with our six black beauties in our midst we followed after. Two of the girls hesitated, looking round over their shoulders, but my Amazon lady, standing beside Gezo's throne, shouted to them, and they dropped their heads meekly and marched on with us.

By jove, it was a long minute's walk to the gate of the stockade, through the double file of those black Amazon furies, their faces sullen with anger and grief at the sale of their fellows, while the great crowd of townsfolk roared in protest behind them. But the discipline of those women warriors was like iron; the king had said, and that was that—mind you, if Gezo had run for president at that moment, he wouldn't have had my money on him, but even so, no one in that whole town was bold enough to gainsay him.

We were moving d----d smartly by the time we reached the stockade, a tight knot of men with our needle guns at the ready, and the women being jostled along in the middle. Spring was first at the gate, where he stopped and hurried us through, I stood close by him; his jaw was tight and he was as near scared as I ever saw him.

"Hurry, b---t you!" he shouted. "D--n that Gezo, to haggle

so long, and d - - n those women—I didn't think they'd raise such a bother about the business. Straight ahead, Mr Kinnie, and keep those six sluts close, d'you hear?" Then to me: "Come on!"

"Wait!" say I—it was instinctive, believe me; I'd no wish to linger, not with that growling mob behind me. But I'd noticed the little ferrety cabin boy was missing. "Where the h - - l is he?"

"Back there!" snaps Spring. "He's senseless with nigger beer—Gezo wanted him—wanted a white slave! Come on, d - - n you, will you stand there all day?"

I'm not shocked easy, but that took me flat aback—for about the tenth part of an instant. If Spring wanted to trade his cabin boy to a nigger king, it was all one to me; I was into the fringe of the jungle a yard ahead of him, and then we were running, with the others in front of us, the Amazons being driven along, one of 'em wailing already. Behind us the hubbub of the town was cut off by the dense foliage; we hustled down the path, but you don't run far in that climate, and soon we had to slow down to a trot.

"Well enough, I think," says Spring. He stopped for a moment to listen, but there was nothing except the jungle noises and the sobbing of our own breathing. "I didn't like that," says he, addressing no one in particular. "By G - d, I didn't! If I'd known they were so d - - - - d jealous of their fighting wenches ... Phew! It's the last time I deal with Gezo, though. *Quid violentius aure tyranni?** For a moment I'd a notion he would change his mind —and keep the pistols, which would have been short shrift for us." He laughed, and the mad pale eyes blinked. "On, there, Mr Kinnie! Mr Comber, keep a sharp eye on the prisoners! Back to that boat in double time, my lads, before his majesty thinks better of his bargain!"

We pushed on down the narrow trail, and we must have been half-way to the river when Spring stopped again, listening. I strained my ears; nothing. Just the chickering of the forest beasts and birds. Spring called to the fellows to be quiet, and we all listened. Spring turned his head from side to side, and then I heard Kirk say: "Wot the h - - l we standing here for? If there's anything to hear, then the sooner we're in that boat the better."

"There's nuthin' behind us," says another, uneasily.

* What is more dangerous than having the ear of a tyrant?—Juvenal.

"Silence!" snaps Spring. He was peering through the foliage at the side of the path. I found my heart racing, and not just with exertion—if we were pursued, they couldn't have outflanked us, through that swamp and jungle, surely. We would have heard them—and then I remembered Kirk saying: "They can move in dead silence when they wants to."

"For G - d's sake!" I whispered to Spring. "Let's get on!"

He ignored me. "Mr Kinnie," he called softly. "D'you hear anything to port?"

"No, cap'n," sings back Kinnie, "there's noth—"

The end of that word was a horrid scream; in terror I stared down the path, and saw Kinnie stagger, clawing at the shaft in his throat before tumbling headlong into the mangrove. Someone yelled, a musket banged, and then Spring was thrusting forward, bawling:

"Run for it! Keep on the path for your lives. Run like h - - l!"

His order was wasted on me—I was running before he had started thinking, even; someone screamed in front of me, and a black shadow leaped on to the path—it was an Amazon, swinging a machete; one of the seamen caught it on his musket, and dashed the butt into her face. She went down, shrieking, and as I leaped over her my foot landed on her bare flesh; I stumbled, but went careering on. The vision of those two naked black fiends slashing a man to death was before my eyes, and the crash of shots and yelling behind me urged me on. I fairly flew along that trail.

And by gum, I wasn't alone. They say sailors are poor runners, but that landing party from the *Balliol College* could move when they wanted to; we stampeded along that twisting path, elbowing each other aside in our panic to get away from the horror in the jungle on either side. They were screaming their war cries now, those terrible black sows; once a spear flashed past in front of my face, and I believe a couple of arrows buzzed above our heads, and then I tripped and fell headlong, with the others trampling over me.

I thought I was done for, but when I scrambled to my feet I saw we were on the edge of the clearing by the river. The fleetest of our party was tearing aside the branches where our canoe was hidden, the man who had been left on guard was on one knee, aiming his musket; it banged, and I turned to see an Amazon fall shrieking not ten yards from me, her cleaver bouncing along to land at my feet. Instinctively I grabbed it, and then a flying body knocked me sideways. Some of our fellows were firing from the water's edge; as I scrambled up I saw an Amazon on her knees, clutching her side with one hand as she tried vainly to hurl her spear with the other. Close by me was Spring, bawling like a madman; he had his pepper-pot revolver in one hand, firing back towards the path, and by G - d, with the other he was trying to drag along one of the Amazons he'd bought. The man's dedication to scholarly research was incredible.

They were leaping through the edge of the jungle now, howling black devils, and if you believe that even the worst of young women has charms, you are in error. As I fled for the boat, I saw the man who had been on guard spin round with an arrow in his shoulder; before he could regain his feet three of them were on him, and while two held him down, throat and ankle, the third carefully pulled up his shirt, and with the utmost delicacy disembowelled him with her machete. Then I was at the boat, a needle gun was in my hands, and I was firing at another who was leaping across the clearing; she went cartwheeling into the river, and then Spring was beside me, dashing down his empty gun and drawing his cutlass.

"Shove off!" he bawled, and I made a leap for the thwart, missed, and came down in the shallows. Spring jumped over me, and I felt someone drag me upright; it was Comber. For a moment we were shoulder to shoulder, and then an Amazon was on us. Her spear was back to thrust into my breast, and in that split second I saw it was my white-turbanned wench of the fly whisk, her teeth bared in a ghastly grin. And you may think me fanciful, but I'll swear she recognised me, for she hesitated an instant, swung her point away from me, and drove it to the haft into Comber's side. And as I threw myself headlong over the gunwale the ridiculous thought flashed through my mind: bonny black cavalry whiskers, they can't resist 'em.

"D - - nation!" Spring was roaring. "I lost that confounded slut!" And as the boat shot away from the bank he seized a needle gun, almost crying with rage, and blazed away. I pulled myself up by the thwart, and the first thing I saw was a bloody hand gripping the edge of the boat. It was Comber, clinging on for dear life as we wallowed out into the stream, with the dark red blood staining the water around him. For a second I wondered whether I should try to haul him in or bash his fingers loose, for he was encumbering our way, but then Spring had leaned over and with one titanic heave had dragged him over the thwart.

We were ten yards from the bank, and it was lined with shrieking black women, hurling their spears, bending their bows, leaping up and down in a frenzy of rage. Why none of them took to the water after us I don't know, unless it was fear of crocodiles; we cowered down to escape their missiles, and then a voice was screaming from the bank:

"Help, cap'n! Cap'n, don't leave me—for Jesus' sake, cap'n! Save me!"

It was Kirk; he was in the shallows, being dragged back by half a dozen of those black witches. They hauled him on to the bank, screaming and laughing, while we drifted out into midstream. Some bold idiot had seized a sweep, and Comber, bleeding like a butchered calf, was crying:

"Help him, sir! We must turn back! We must save him!"

Spring thrust him away, threw himself on to the sweep with the sailor, and in spite of the arrows that whistled over the boat, the two of them managed to drive us still farther away towards the opposite mangrove shore. We were beyond the spears now, and presently the arrows began to fall short, although one of the last to reach the boat struck clean through the hand of the seaman at the oar, pinning him to the timber. Spring wrenched it clear and the fellow writhed away, clutching his wound. And then Holy Joe Comber was at it again:

"Turn back, sir! We can't leave Kirk behind!"

"Can't we, by G-d?" growls Spring. "You just watch me, mister. If the b - - - - - d can't run, that's his look-out!"

Spoken like a man, captain, thinks I; give me a leader you can trust, any day. And even Comber, his face contorted with pain, could see it was no go; they were swarming on the bank, and had Kirk spreadeagled; we could see them wrenching his clothes off, squealing with laughter, while close by a couple of them had even started kindling a fire. They were smart house-wifely lasses those, all right.

Kirk was yelling blue murder, and as we watched, my girl in the white turban knelt down beside him, and suddenly his voice rose into a horrible, blood-chilling shriek. Several of the Amazons prancing on the bank indicated to us, by obscene gestures, what she was doing to him; Comber groaned, and began to spew, and Spring, swearing like a lunatic, was fumbling to load one of the needle guns. He bawled to the rest of us to follow suit, and we banged away at them for a moment, but it was too dangerous to linger, and with Kirk's screams, and the gloating shrieks of those she-d - - - ls, drifting downstream after us, we manned the sweeps and rowed for all we were worth. With the current to help us we drove along hard, and I was finally able to choke down my panic and thank my stars for another delivery. Of the half dozen of us in the boat, I was the only one without even a scratch; Spring had a machete cut on his left arm, but not a deep one, and the others' wounds were mild enough, except for Comber's. But if Spring was only slightly injured in the flesh, his ambition had taken a nasty jar. He d - - - - d Gezo's eyes for a treacherous hound, and called the Amazons things that would have made a marine blush, but his chief fury, voiced over and over again as we rowed downstream was:

"I lost that black slut. All these years, and I lost the sow! Even that single one—she would have done! My G - d, I could have used that woman!"

I was pondering that I could have used my white-turbanned Hebe, for a different and less academic purpose—but then I thought of Kirk, and discovered that any *tendre* I might have cherished for the lady had died. And as I think back now, strap-ping lass though she was, I can't say that the old flame rekindles. She was a shrew if ever I saw one.

With the danger safely past, I was soon in good fettle again. As I've said before, there's nothing so cheering as surviving a peril in which companions have perished, and our losses had been heavy. Five men had died in our hasty retreat from Apokoto; apart from Kinnie, Kirk, and the guard on the boat, two others had been cut down by Amazons on the path, and of course the cabin boy had been left behind deliberately by Spring, not that he was any great loss. (It will give you some notion of the kind of men who manned the Coast slavers, when I tell you that not a word of protest was said about this; nobody had liked the little sneak anyway.)

For the rest, it looked as though Comber was a goner. My wench had shovelled her spear well in under his short ribs, leaving a hole like a hatchway; Murphy the surgeon, when he had sobered up, announced that there was nothing he could do but clean and stitch it, which he did, "but for what may have come adrift inside," says he, "I can't answer." So they put Comber in his berth, half-dead, with Mrs Spring to nurse him—"that'll carry the poor s - d off, even if his wound doesn't," says Murphy.

Then we went to work. There were upwards of a thousand niggers in the barracoons on the morning after our Apokoto exploit, and Spring was in a sweat to get our cargo loaded and away. It was the possibility of naval patrols sniffing us out that worried him; Sullivan's suggestion, that Gezo might take it into his head to come down and make a clean sweep of us, he dismissed out of hand. As Spring saw it, the Amazons and not Gezo had been responsible for the attack; now they had rescued their six wenches, and Gezo still had his pistols, he wouldn't want to offend us further. He was right; Sanchez, who was an astonishing good plucked 'un, for a Dago, actually went up to talk to Gezo a day later, to see that all was well, and found the black rascal full of alarm in case Spring was going to wash his hands of the Dahomey trade. Sanchez reassured him, and dropped a hint that if Gezo would even now part with an Amazon it would make for friendly relations, but Gezo was too windy of provoking his bodyguard. He just clutched his case of pistols and begged Sanchez to tell Spring that he was still his friend, *sawa sawa*, and hoped they would continue to do good business together—all this, mark you, while Kirk and one of the men who'd been caught on the path were strung up in front of the death house, with those black she-fiends working on them before a cheering crowd. They were still alive, Sanchez said, but you wouldn't have known they were human beings.

So honour was satisfied, both sides, but Spring and Sanchez took no chances. The *Balliol College*'s nets were rigged, and her twelve and nine-pounders shotted, while Sanchez's pickets guarded the jungle trails and the river. All remained peaceful, however, and the business of loading the slaves went ahead undisturbed.

With our second mate dead and our third apparently dying, I found myself having to work for a living. Even with men who knew their business as well as these, it's no easy matter to pack six hundred terrified, stupid niggers into a slave deck; it's worse than putting Irish infantry into a troopship.

First Spring and Murphy went through the barracoons, picking out the likeliest bucks and wenches. They were penned up in batches of a hundred, men and women separate, a great mass of smelling, heaving black bodies, all stark naked, squatting and lying and moaning; the sound was like a great wailing hum, and it never stopped, day or night, except when the tubs of burgoo were shoved into the pens, and they shut up long enough to empty the gourds which were passed round among them. What astonished me was that Spring and Murphy were able to walk in among them as though they were tame beasts; just the two of them in that mass of cowed, miserable humanity, with a couple of black guards jerking out the ones selected. If they'd had a spark of spirit the niggers could have torn them limb from limb, but they just sat, helpless and mumbling. I thought of the Amazons, and wondered what changed people from brave, reckless savages into dumb re-signed animals; apparently it's always the way on the Coast. Sullivan told me he reckoned it was the knowledge that they were going to be slaves, but that being brainless brutes they never thought of doing anything about it.

Those who were selected were herded out of the barracoons into a long railed place like a sheep pen, all jammed together with three black guards either side, armed with whips and pistols. There was a narrow gate at the other end, just wide enough to let one slave through at a time, and the two biggest guards were stationed there. As each nigger emerged they seized him and flung him face down beside an iron brazier full of glowing coals, and two of Sanchez's Dago pals clapped a branding iron on his shoulder. He would squeal like blazes, and the niggers in the pen would try to crowd back out the other end, but the guards lashed them on, and another would be hauled out and branded the same way. The screaming and weeping in the pen was something to hear; everyone who could was on hand to watch, and there was much merriment at the antics of the niggers, blubbering before they were burned, and hopping and squealing afterwards.

Spring was there for the branding of the wenches, to see that it was done lightly, just below the ankle on the inside, in the case of the better-looking ones. "Who the d - - - l wants a young wench with scars on her backside?" he growled. "Even if we ain't selling fancies, the less marking the better; the Legrees tell me the Southern ladies don't want even their field women burned these days.[22] So have a care with those irons, you two, and you, doctor, slap on that grease with a will."

This was to Murphy, who sat beyond the brazier with a huge tub of lard between his feet. As each branded nigger was pulled forward one of the black guards would thrust the burned shoulder or ankle under Murphy's nose; he would take a good look at it and then slap a handful of the lard on the wound, crying either, "There's for you, Sambo", or "That'll pretty you up, acushla"; he was half full of booze, as usual, and from time to time would apply himself to his bottle and then cry encouragement to the niggers as they came through, or break into a snatch of raucous song. I can see him now, swaying on his stool, red face glistening, shirt hanging open over the red furze on his chest, plastering on the grease with his great freckled hand and chanting:

"Al-though with lav-ish kind-ness
The gifts of Go-od are strewn,
The heath-en in his blind-ness
Bows down to wood and sto-one."

When he was done with them the heathen were pushed through
a series of wooden frames set up close by the *Balliol College's*
gangplanks. One was six feet by two, another slightly smaller, and
a third smaller still. By means of these the slaves were sized, and
sent up one of three gangplanks accordingly; the biggest ones
were for the bottom of the slave deck, the middle-sized for the
first tier of shelves, and the smallest for the top tier, but care was
taken to separate men and women—a tall wench or a little chap
could have got in among the wrong sex, and Spring wouldn't have
that. He insisted that the women should be berthed forward of the
first bulkhead and the men all aft of it, and since they would be
chained up they wouldn't be able to get up to high jinks—I didn't
see why they shouldn't, myself, but Spring had his own reasons,
no doubt.

Once up the planks, though, the really hard work began. I
didn't know much about it, but I had to work with the hands who
stowed the slaves, and I soon picked up the hang of it. As each
slave was pushed down the hatch, he was seized by a waiting
seaman and forced to lie down on the deck in his allotted place,
head towards the side of the ship, feet towards the centre, until
both sides of the deck were lined with them. Each man had to go
in a space six feet by fifteen inches, and now I saw why there had
been so much argument over that extra inch; if they were jammed
up tight, or made to lie on their right sides, you could get ever so
many more in.

This was the hard part, for the slaves were terrified, stupid, and
in pain from their branding; they wriggled and squirmed on the
deck and wouldn't be still, and the hands had to knock them about
or lay into the most unruly ones with a rope's end. One huge buck,
bawling and with tears streaming down his face, made a dash for
the hatch, but Sullivan knocked him flat with a hand-spike, threw
him into place, and terrified the others by shaking a cat-o'-nine-
tails at them, to let them see what they might hope to get if they

misbehaved.

When they were placed, a shackle was clapped round each right ankle, and a long chain threaded through it, until they were all stowed, when the chain was made fast to the bulkheads at either end. Soon there were four lines of niggers flat on the deck, with a space up the middle between them, so that the seamen could stand there to pack the later arrivals into the shelves.

It's not that I'm an abolitionist by any means, but by the end of that day I'd had my bellyful of slaving. The reek of those musky bodies in that deck was abominable; the heat and stench grew by the hour, until you'd have wondered that anything could survive down there. They howled and blubbered, and we were fagged out with grabbing brown limbs and tugging and shoving and mudging them up with our feet to get the brutes to lie close. They fouled themselves where they lay, and before the job was half done the filth was indescribable. We had to escape to the deck every half hour to souse ourselves with salt water and drink great draughts of orange juice, before descending into that fearful pit again, and wrestle again with wriggling black bodies that stunk and sweated and went everywhere but where you wanted them. When it was finally done, and Sullivan ordered all hands on deck, we climbed out dead beat, ready to flop down anywhere and go to sleep.

But not with John Charity Spring about. He must go down to inspect, and count the rows, and kick a black body into place here and tug another one there, before he was satisfied. He d----d our eyes for letting 'em soil the deck, and ordered the whole place hosed down, niggers and all; they dried where they lay in no time, of course, and the steam came out of the hatches like smoke.

I looked down at it just before the hatch gratings went on, and it was an indiscribable sight. Row upon row of black bodies, packed like cigars in a box, naked and gleaming, the dark mass striped with glittering dots of light where the eyes rolled in the sooty faces. The crying and moaning and whimpering blended into a miserable anthem that I'll never forget, with the clanking of the chains and the rustle of hundreds of incessantly stirring bodies, and the horrible smell of musk and foulness and burned flesh.

My stomach doesn't turn easy, but I was sickened. If it had been left to me, then and there, I'd have let 'em go, the whole boiling of them, back to their lousy jungle. No doubt it's a deplorable weakness in my character, but this kind of raw work was a thought too much for me. Mind you, sit me down in my club, or at home, and say, "Here, Flash, there's twenty thou for you if you'll say 'aye' to a cargo of black ivory going over the Middle Passage", and I ain't saying I'ld turn you down. Nor do I flinch when someone whips a black behind or claps on a brand—but enough's enough, and when you've looked into the hold of a new-laden slaver for the first time, you know what hell is like.[28]

I mentioned this to Sullivan, and he spat. "You think that's hell, do you? First blackbird voyage I made, as a young hand, we took three hundred coons from the Gallinas, and we were setting out for Rio when a Limey sloop tacks on to us. It was a Portuguese flag we carried, with a yaller-black Dago skipper in command; he saw sure enough they were going to take us." He looked at me with his head on one side. "Can you guess what that Christian Angolese son-of-a-b - - - h did? G'wan, have a guess."

I said I had heard of slave cargoes being thrown overboard, so that when the Navy came up all the evidence had gone. Sullivan laughed.

"There wasn't time for that, our skipper figures. But we were carryin' palm oil as well as slaves, and had a good deal of trade powder left over. So he set the ship on fire, an' we took to the boats. Navy couldn't get near her, so she just burned out an' sank—with three hundred niggers aboard. I wouldn't care to guess how many of 'em were lucky enough to drown." He laughed again, without any mirth at all. "And you think *that's* hell, down *there*? I guess you also think that Mr J. C. Spring is a real tough skipper!"

Well, I did, and if there were bigger swine afloat in the earlies I'm only glad I never met them. But Sullivan's story gave me the shudders all right, for it reminded me that the next stage of our voyage was the notorious Middle Passage, with all the dangers of pursuit and capture, to say nothing of hurricane and shipwreck.

"D'you think there's any chance of . . . of that happening with us?" says I, and Sullivan snorted.

"I'll say this for Spring—he don't lose ships, or cargoes. He believes in keeping the sharks hungry. Any Navy coaster that comes up with us is in for a h--l of a chase—less'n she's a steamer an' catches us in a flat calm."

Here was a fearful thought. "What then?" says I.

"Then—why, we fight her," says he, and left me prey to a nausea that had nothing to do with the heat or the slave-stench or my weariness. Having lately been at grips with fighting nigger women, I could see myself shortly assisting in a running-sea-battle against the Royal Navy—just what was needed to liven up the cruise. And by jove, it nearly came to that, too, and on our very first hour out from that abominable coast.

We dropped down river early the next morning, to catch the ebb tide, I believe, and it seemed a piece of lunacy to me to try those shoals and islands in the half light. However, Spring knew his business; he took the wheel himself, and with only the fore-topsail spread we drifted slowly between the green banks, the leadsmen chanting quietly, and the first hint of dawn beginning to lighten the sky over the black jungle mass astern. It was a queer, eery business, gliding so silently along, with only the mumble of the slaves, the creak of rope and timber, and the gurgle of water to break the stillness, and then we were clear of the last banks and the sun shot a great beam of light ahead of us across the placid surface of the sea.

It was all very beautiful, in its way, but just as Sullivan was roaring the watch up to set more sail the idyll was marred by the appearance round the southern headland of a small, waspish-looking vessel, standing slowly out on a course parallel to our own. It happened that I saw her first, and drew my commander's attention to her with a sailor-like hail of: "Jesus! Look at that!"

Spring just stared for a moment, and then says: "Foresail and main-tops'l, Mr Sullivan," before getting his glass out for a look.

"White ens'n," says he presently, without any emotion. "Take a look, mister. Twenty-gun sloop, I'd say."

Sullivan agreed, and while my bowels did the polka the two of them just stood and watched her as though she'd been a pleasure steamer. I didn't know much about sailing, as you're aware, but even I could see that she was moving more briskly than we were, that there was nothing but light airs stirring the surface, and that she wasn't more than two miles away. It looked to me as though the *Balliol College's* voyage was over before it had rightly begun, which merely shows how ignorant I was.

For an hour, while my gorge rose steadily, we watched her; we were doing no more than creep out from the coast, and the sloop did the same, only a little faster, and converging gradually all the time on our course. I could see that eventually we would be bound to meet, if we held our courses, and I had an idea that in light wind the sailing advantage would be all with the smaller vessel. But Spring seemed unconcerned; from time to time he would turn and survey the coast behind us, and the sky, converse shortly with Sullivan, and then go back to watching the sloop, with his hands stuck deep in his pockets.

He was waiting confidently, I now know, for a wind, and he got it just when I had finally given up all hope. The sails flapped, Spring barked an order, and at a shout from Sullivan the hands were racing aloft; in the same moment the boom of a shot sounded over the water, and a pillar of spray rose out of the sea a few hundred yards from our port bow.

"Burn your powder, you useless son of a Geordie coaster skipper, you!" bawls Spring from the wheel. "Look alive, Mr Sullivan!" And he sent out a perfect volley of orders as the *Balliol College* heeled gently and lifted to the first puffs of wind, and then I found myself tailing on a rope with the others, hauling for dear life and wondering what the d - - - l would happen next.

If I were a nautical man, no doubt I could tell you, but I'm not, thank God; the mysteries of ship handling are as obscure to me today as they were fifty years ago. If I were Bosun McHearty I daresay I could describe how we jibed with our futtock gans'ls clewed up to the orlop bitts, and weathered her, d'ye see, with a lee helm and all plain sail in the bilges, burn me buttocks. As it was, I just stuck like a shadow to a big Portugal nigger of the deck watch, called Lord Peabody, and tailed on behind him with the pulley-hauley, while Spring and Sullivan bawled their jargon, the men aloft threw themselves about like acrobats, and the *Balliol College* began to surge forward at greater speed. There was another shot from the sloop, and an ironic cheer from our fellows —why I couldn't imagine, for our pursuer was soon cracking along famously, and I could make out her ensign plainly, and the figures on her deck, all far too close for comfort. I saw, in the intervals of scampering about after Peabody, and hauling on the ropes, that she would be able to fire in earnest soon, and I was just commending my soul to God and wondering if I could turn Queen's Evidence, when Spring let loose another volley of orders, there was a tremendous cracking and bellying of sails overhead, and the *Balliol College* seemed to spin round on her heel, plunge over with a lurch that brought my breakfast up, and then go bowling away across the track of the sloop.

I don't understand it, of course, but in the next hour Spring executed a similar manoeuvre half a dozen times, while the wind freshened, and although the sloop copied our movements, so far as I could see, she always somehow finished up farther away—no doubt any yachtsman could explain it. The hands cheered and laughed, although you could hardly hear them for the fearful howling that was coming from below decks, where the slaves were spewing and yelling in terror at the bucketing of the ship. And then we were standing out to sea again, and the sloop was away off our quarter, still flying along, but making no headway at all.

Only then did Spring hand over the wheel and come to the stern rail, where he delivered a catechism to the distant Navy vessel, calling them lubberly sons of dogs and shaking his fist at them.

"There's where the tax-payer's money goes!" he roared. "That's what's supposed to defend us against the French! Look at them! I could sail rings round 'em in a Blackwall coal lighter! *Quo, quo, scelesti ruitis,** eh? I tell you, Mr Sullivan, a crew of All Souls dons could do better on a raft! What the blazes are they letting into the Navy these days? He'll be some rum-soaked short-haul pensioner, no doubt—either that or a beardless brat with a father in the Lords and some ladylike Mama whoring round the Admiralty. My stars, wouldn't I like to put them all to sea under Bully Waterman,[24] or let 'em learn their trade in an opium clipper with a Down East Yankee skipper and a Scotch owner—you hear that, you Port Mahon bumboatman, you? You ought to be on the beach!"

It was fine stuff, but wasted since the sloop was miles away; by

* Where are you hastening, fools?

afternoon she was just a speck on the horizon, and the coast of Africa had vanished behind us. The ease of our escape, I was told, all came of Spring knowing his weather, for standing away from the Slave coast was evidently a most unchancy business, and many slavers had been caught in the calms that so often beset them there. But some of the deltas and river mouths could be relied on to give you wind, and Spring knew all about this; it was also true that he was a first-rate seaman with a prime crew, and together they were probably a match for anything. We did sight another patrol vessel on the following day, but we were tearing along at such a rate that she never came near us, and Spring didn't even interrupt his dinner.

It was blowing fairly stiffish now, and the slaves had an abominable time. For the first few days they just lay howling and weeping in their sea-sickness, but Spring insisted that the huge coppers and tubs in which their pulse porridge was made should be kept at work, and by flogging one of the bucks down on the slave deck in the sight of his fellows he terrified them into eating, ill as they were. Murphy was constantly at work, especially among the women, to make sure that none died, and twice a day the hoses were turned on to scour out the filth which would otherwise have bred an epidemic in no time.

About the fourth day, the wind dropped, the slaves stopped spewing, and the cooks who tended the mess tubs became the hardest-worked men on the ship. One thing the *Balliol College* didn't stint to its human cargo, and that was food—which was good business, of course. Spring also insisted that lime juice be issued, and the slaves forced to drink it—they hated it, but when they saw it was that or the cat they swilled it down fast enough. They were still in a fearful funk, of course, since they had no idea of what the ocean was like, and couldn't seem to get used to the rolling of the ship; when they weren't eating or sleeping they just lay there in their long black rows, wailing and rolling their eyes like frightened sheep. There was no spirit in them at all, and I began to see why the slavers thought of them not as humans, but as animals.

Every day they went through a curious exercise which was called dancing. They were brought up on deck in batches, and forced to caper about for half an hour, leaping up and down and trotting round the deck. This of course was just to keep them in trim; they didn't like that, either, at first, and we had to smarten them with rope's ends to get them moving. But after the first few times they began to enjoy it, and it was the most ludicrous sight to see them skipping and shuffling round the deck, clapping their hands and even crooning to themselves, the bolder spirits grinning and rolling their eyes—they were just like children, forgetting the misery of their condition, and sky-larking about, quite delighted if the hands cried encouragement to them. One of the fellows had a fiddle, on which he would play jigs and reels, and the niggers would try to out-do each other in capering to the music.

The men got over their fears faster than the women, who danced with much less jollity, although everyone on the ship was always on hand to watch them. You couldn't have called any of 'em pretty, with their pug faces and great woolly mops of hair, but they had fine shapely bodies, and none of us had seen a proper woman for near on six weeks. The sight of those naked black bodies shuffling and swaying got me into a fever the first time I saw it, and the others were the same, licking their lips and muttering when was Murphy the surgeon going to set about his business?

I understood what this meant when we were all ordered to report and strip down for Murphy in his berth, where he examined us carefully to see that none of us had pox or crabs or yaws or any of the interesting diseases that wicked sailormen are prone to. When we were pronounced clean Spring had us each pick out a black wench—I thought this was by way of seaman's comforts, but it turned out that the more black wenches who could be got pregnant by white men, the better the traders liked it, for they would produce mulatto children, who being half-white were smarter and more valuable than pure blacks. The Cuban dealers trusted Spring, and if he could guarantee that all his female slaves had been bulled by his crew, it would add to their price.

"I want all these wenches pupped," says he, "but you'll do it decently, d'you hear, *salvo pudore*.* in your quarters. I'll not have Mrs Spring offended."

* Without offending modesty.

It may sound like just the kind of holiday for a fellow like me, but it was no great fun as it turned out. I picked out a likely enough big wench, jet black and the liveliest dancer of the lot, but she knew nothing, and she reeked of jungle even when she was scrubbed down. I tried to coax some spirit into her, first by kindness and then by rope's end, but she was no more use than a bishop's maiden aunt. However, one has to make do, and in the intervals of our laborious grappling I tried to indulge my interest in foreign languages, which apart from horses is the only talent I can boast. I can usually make good use of a native pillow partner in this way, provided she speaks English, but of course this one didn't, and was as stupid as a Berkshire hog into the bargain. So it was no go as far as learning anything was concerned, but I did succeed in teaching her a few useful English words and phrases like:

"Me Lady Caroline Lamb. Me best rattle in *Balliol College*."

The hands thought this a great joke, and just for devilment I also taught her a tag from Horace, and with immense work got her perfect in it, so that when you pinched her backside she would squeak out:

"*Civis Romanus sum. Odi profanum vulgus.*"

Spring almost leaped out of his skin when he heard it, and was not at all amused. He took the opportunity to upbraid me for not having sent her back to the slave-deck and taken another wench, for he wanted them all covered; I said I didn't want to break in any more of 'em, and suggested that if this one learned a little English it might add to her value; he raised his voice and d - - - - d my impudence, not realising that Mrs Spring had come up the companion and could hear us. She startled him by suddenly remarking:

"Mr Flashman is a constant heart. I knew it the moment I first saw him."

She was mad, of course, but Spring was much put out, because she wasn't meant to know what was going on with the black women. But he let me keep Lady Caroline Lamb.

So it was a pleasant enough cruise to begin with, for the weather blew just enough to give us a good passage without being too

* I am a Roman citizen. I hate vulgar profane persons.

rough for the niggers; their health remained good, with no deaths in the first week, which greatly pleased Spring; the work was light above deck, as it always is in a fast ship with a favourable wind, and there was time to sit about watching the flying fish and listening to the hands swapping yarns—my respect for them had increased mightily over our encounter with the British sloop, which had confirmed my earlier impression that these were no ordinary packet rats with the points knocked off their knives, but prime hands. And I've learned that no time is wasted which is spent listening to men who really know their work.

However, as always when I feel I can loaf for a spell, something happened which drove all other thoughts out of my head— even my daydreams about Elspeth, and how I might contrive to come home respectably before too long, and scupper old Morrison, too, if possible. What happened was little enough, and not unexpected, but in the long run it certainly saved my liberty, and probably my life.

On the seventh day out from Dahomey, Murphy came to me and said I must go directly to Comber, who was dying. Since we sailed he'd been stowed away in a little cubby off the main cabin aft, where there was a window and Mrs Spring could tend to him. "It's all up with him, poor lad," says Murphy, fuming with liquor. "His bowels is mortified, I'm thinkin'; maybe that jezebel's spear wuz pizened. Any roads, he wants to see you."

I couldn't think why, but I went along, and as soon as I clapped eyes on him I could see it was the Union Jack for this one, no error. His face was wasted and yellow, with big purple blotches beneath the eyes, and he was breathing like a bellows. He was lying on the berth with just a blanket over him, and the hand on top of it was like a bird's claw. He signed feebly to me to shut the door, and I squatted down on a stool beside his cot.

He lay for a few moments, gazing blankly at the sunbeams from the open window, and then says, in a very weak voice:

"Flashman, do you believe in God?"

Well, I'd expected this, of course; his wasn't the first deathbed I'd sat by, and they usually get religious sooner or later. There's nothing for it but to squat down on your hunkers and let them babble. Dying people love to talk—I know I do, and I've been in extremis more often than most. So to humour him I said certainly there was a God, not a doubt about it, and he chewed this over a bit and says:

"And if there is a God, and a Heaven—there must be a Devil, and a Hell? Must there not?"

I'd heard that before, too, so playing up to my part as the Rev. Flashy, B.D., I told him opinion was divided on the point. In any event, says I, if there was a Hell it couldn't be much worse than life on this earth—which I don't believe for a minute, by the way.

"But there is a Hell!" cries he, turning on me with his eyes shining feverishly. "I know it—a terrible, flaming Hell in which the damned burn through all Eternity! I know it, Flashman, I tell you!"

I could have told him this was what came of looking at the pictures in Bunyan's *Holy War*, which had blighted my young life for a spell when I first struck it. But I soothed him by pointing out that if there was a Hell, it was reserved for prime sinners only, and he probably wasn't up to that touch.

He rolled his head about on the pillow, biting his lip with distress and the pain of his wound.

"But I am a sinner," he gasped. "A fearful sinner. Oh, I do fear I am beyond redemption! The Saviour will turn from me, I know."

"Oh, I'm not sure, now," says I. "Slaving ain't that bad, you know."

He groaned and closed his eyes. "There is no such sin on my conscience," says he fretfully, which I didn't understand. "It is my weak flesh that has betrayed me. I have so many sins—I have broken the seventh commandment..."

I couldn't be sure about this; I had a suspicion it was the one about oxen and other livestock, which seemed unlikely, but with a man who's half-delirious you can never tell.

"What is it that's troubling you?" I asked.

"In that—that village..." he said, speaking with effort "Those ... those women. Oh, God ... pity me ... I lusted after them ... in my mind ... I looked on them ... as David looked on Bathsheeba. I desired them, carnally, sinfully ... oh, Flashman ... I am guilty . . . in His sight . . . I . . ."

"Now, look here," says I, for I was getting tired of this. "You won't go to Hell for that. Leastways, if you do, it'll be a mighty crowded place. You'll have the entire human race there, including the College of Cardinals, I shouldn't wonder."

But he babbled on about the sin of lechery for a bit, and then, as repentant sinners always do, he decided I was right, and took my hand—his was as dry as a bundle of sticks.

"You are a good fellow, Flashman," says he. "You have eased my mind." Why he'd been worried beat me; if I thought that when I go I'll have nothing worse on my conscience than slavering over a buxom bum, well, I'll die happy, that's all. But this poor devil had obviously been Bible-reared, and fretted according.

"You truly believe I shall be saved?" says he. "There is forgiveness, is there not? We are taught so—that we may be washed clean in the blood of the Lamb."

"Clean as a whistle," says I. "It's in the book. Now, then, old fellow . . ."

"Don't go," says he, gripping my hand. "Not yet. I'm . . . I'm dying, you know, Flashman . . . there isn't much time . . ."

I said wouldn't he like Mrs Spring to look in, but he shook his head.

"There is something . . . I must do . . . first. Be patient a moment, my dear friend."

So I waited, wishing to blazes I was out of there. He was breathing harder than ever, wheezing like an old pump, but he must have been gathering strength, for when he opened his eyes again they were clear and sane, and looked directly at mine.

"Flashman," says he, earnestly, "how came you aboard this ship?"

It took me aback, but I started to tell him (a revised version, of course), and he cut me off.

"It was against your will?" He was almost pleading.

"Of course. I wouldn't have . . ."

"Then you too . . . oh, in God's name tell me truthfully . . . you detest this abomination of slavery?"

Hollo, thinks I, what's here? Very smartly I said, yes, I detested it. I wanted to see where he was going.

"Thank God!" says he. "Thank God!" And then: "You will swear to me that what I tell you will be breathed to no one on this accursed vessel?"

I swore it, solemnly, and he heaved a great sigh of relief.

"My belt," says he. "On the chest yonder. Yes, take it . . . and cut it open . . . there, near the buckle."

Mystified, I examined it. It was a broad, heavy article, double welted. I picked out the stitches as he indicated, with my knife, and the two welts came apart. Between them, folded very tight, was a slender oilskin packet. I unfolded it—and suddenly thought, I've been here before: then I remembered slitting open the lining of my own coat by the Jotunschlucht, with de Gautet lying beside me, groaning at the pain of his broken toes. Was that only a few months ago? It seemed an eternity . . . and then the packet was open, and I was unfolding the two papers within it. I spread the first one out, and found myself gaping at a letterhead design which showed an anchor, and beneath it the words:

"To Lieutenant Beauchamp Millward Comber, R.N. You are hereby required and directed . . ."

"Good G - d!" says I, staring. "You're a naval officer!"

He tried to nod, but his wound must have caught him, for he groaned and gasped. Then: "Read on," says he.

". . . to report yourself immediately to the Secretary of the Board of Trade, and receive from him, or such subordinate official as he may appoint, instructions and directions whereby you shall assist, in whatsoever capacity the Secretary shall deem most fitting, against those persons engaged in the illicit and illegal traffic in human slaves between the Guinea, Ivory, Grain, Togo, Dahomey, Niger and Angola Coasts and the Americas. You are most strictly enjoined to obey and carry out all such instructions and directions as though they had proceeded from Their Lordships of the Admiralty or others your superior officers in Her Majesty's service." It was signed "Auckland".

The other paper, which was from the Board of Trade, was really no more than a sort of passport, requesting that all officials, officers, and other persons in H.M. service, and of foreign governments, should render to Lieutenant Comber all assistance of which he might stand in need, etc., etc., but in its way it was equally impressive, for it was signed not only by the President, Labouchere, but also countersigned by my old pal T. B. Macaulay, as Paymaster, and some Frog or other for the French merchant marine.

I goggled at these things, hardly understanding, and then looked at Comber; he was lying with his eyes shut, and his face working.

"You're a spy," says I. "A spy on the slavers!"

He opened his eyes. "You . . . may call it that. If it is spying to help to deliver these poor creatures . . . then I am proud to be a spy." He made a great effort, gasping with pain, and turned on his side towards me. "Flashman . . . hear me . . . I'm going . . . soon. Even if you don't . . . see this as I do . . . as God's work . . . still, you are a gentleman . . . an Army officer. Why, you are one of Arnold's people . . . the paladins. For God's sake, say you will help! Don't let all my work . . . my death . . . be in vain!"

He was in a desperate sweat, straining a hand out towards me, his eyes glittering. "You must . . . in honour . . . and, oh, for these poor lost black souls! If you'd seen what I've seen . . . aye, and had to help in, God forgive me . . . but I had to, you see, until I had done my work. You must help them, Flashman; they cannot help themselves. Their minds are not as ours . . . they are weak and foolish and an easy prey to scoundrels like Spring . . . but they have souls . . . and this slavery is an abomination in God's sight!" He struggled to get farther up. "Say you will help . . . for pity's sake!"

"What do you want me to do?"

"Take those letters." His voice was weakening, and I could see blood seeping through his blanket; he must have opened his wound in his exertion. "Then . . . my chest . . . there under the canvas shirt . . . packet. Copy of Spring's accounts . . . last voyage. I took some of them . . . completed them this trip. Letters, too . . . evidence against him . . . and others. For God's sake get them to the Admiralty . . . or the American Navy people . . . oh, dear God!"

He fell back, moaning, but by then I was ferreting through his chest, snatching out a slender packet sewn in an oilskin cover. I slipped it and the letters quickly out of sight in my pocket, and bent over his cot.

"Go on, man! What more? Are there any others like yourself —agents, officers, or what?"

But he just lay there, coughing weakly and breathing in little moaning gasps. I closed the chest and sat down to see if he would revive again, and after a moment he began to mumble; I leaned close, but it was a moment before I could make out what he was saying—in fact, he was singing, in a little whisper at the back of his throat; it was that sad little song, "The Lass so good and true", that they call "Danny Boy" nowadays. I knew at once, without telling, that it was the song his mother had used to sing him to sleep, for he began to smile a little, with his eyes closed. I could have kicked the brute; if he'd spent less time making his soul and belly-aching to me about hell fire, and minded his duty, he would have had time to tell me more about his mission. Not that I cared a button for that, but all knowledge is useful when you're in the grip of folk like Spring. But he was going to slip his cable with all the good scandal untold, by the looks of it.

Sure enough, when his whispered song died away, he began muttering, "Mother . . . Sally . . . yes, Mother . . . cold . . ." but nothing to make sense. It was maddening. Of course, my generation were preoccupied with their mothers, which sets me apart; mine died when I was little, you see, and I never really knew her, which may account for a deal. It crossed my mind, in that moment, what will I have to say in the last few seconds before I slip over the edge of life? Whose name will be on my repentant lips? My father's?—now there would be a cheery vision to carry over to the other side, all boozy face and rasping voice. Elspeth's? I doubt it. Some of the other ladies?—Lola, or Natasha or Takes-Away-Clouds-Woman or Leonie or Lady White Willow or . . . no, there wouldn't be time. I'll have to wait and see. Which reminds me, young Harry East, when they pulled what was left of him into the dooli at Cawnpore, muttered, "Tell the doctor", and everyone thought he meant the surgeon—but I knew different. He meant Arnold, which as a dying thought has one advantage, that the Devil, if you meet him later, will be an improvement.

So I speculated, as Comber's breathing slackened, and then I saw the shadow of death cross his wasted face (there is such a shadow, down from the temple and across to the chin, seen it scores of times) and he was gone. I pulled the blanket over his head, went through his jacket pockets and chest, but found nothing worth while except a pencil case and a good clasp knife, which I appropriated, and then went topsides to tell Spring.

"He's gone at last, is he?" was his charitable comment. "Aye, *omne capax movet urna nomen.** We need not pretend he is a great loss. Blackwall fashion was about his style[25]—a sound enough seaman, but better fitted for an Indiaman than our trade. Very good, you can tell the sailmaker to bundle him up; we'll bury him tomorrow." And he continued to survey the horizon through his glass, while I slipped away to think over the momentous news I'd learned from the dying Comber. Obviously the fact that he had been an Admiralty man working against the slavers was of the first importance, but for the life of me I couldn't see what use it might be to me. For all that I'd soothed his passing moments out of an uncommon civility, I didn't mind a snap whether his precious evidence ever reached government hands or not. In fact, it seemed to me that if an information was laid against the *Balliol College* and her master, those who had sailed with him would land in the dock as well, and they included H. Flashman, albeit he wasn't aboard willingly. Yet my knowledge, and Comber's, might be valuable somehow, provided I kept them safe from prying eyes.

So it seemed to me at the time anyway, so I took a leaf out of Comber's book, and in the privacy of my berth sewed his two letters into my belt. I hesitated a long while over the packet, for I knew the secrets it contained would be fatally dangerous to whoever shared them; if Spring ever found out it would be a slit throat and a watery grave for me. But curiosity got the better of me in the end; I opened it carefully so that it could be re-sealed, and was presently goggling my way through the contents.

It was prime stuff, no question: all Spring's accounts for 1847 copied out in minute writing—how many niggers shipped, how many sold at Roatan and how many at the Bay of Pigs, the names of buyers and traders; a full description of deals and prices and orders on British and American banks. There was enough to hang old John Charity ten times over, but that wasn't the best of it;

* Every name is shaken in death's great urn.

Comber had been at his letters, too, and while some of them were in cypher, quite a few were in English. They included one from the London firm which had supplied the trade goods for our present voyage; another from New York lawyers who seemed to represent American investors (for Comber had annotated it with a list of names marked "U.S. interests, owners") and—oh, b - - - - y rapture!—a document describing the transfer of the *Balliol College* from its American builders, Brown & Bell, to a concern in London among the names of whose directors was one J. Morrison. I almost whooped at the sight of it—what Spring was thinking of to keep such damaging evidence aboard his vessel I couldn't fathom, but there it was. I found Morrison mentioned in one other letter, and a score of names besides; it might not be enough to hang him, or them, but I was certain sure he would sell his rotten little soul to keep these papers from the public gaze.

I had him! The knowledge was like a warm bath—with these papers at my command I could, when I got home again, turn the screw on the little shark until he hollered uncle. No longer would I be the poor relation; I would have evidence that could ruin him, commercially and socially, and perhaps put him in the dock as well, and the price of my silence would be a free run through his moneybags. By gad, I'd be set for life. A seat in the House? It would be a seat on the board, at least, and grovelling civility from him to me for a change. He'd rue the day he shanghaied me aboard his lousy slave ship.

Chuckling happily, I sewed it all up again in its oilskin, and stitched this carefully into the lining of my coat. There it would stay until I got home and it could be employed in safety to my enrichment and Morrison's confusion. I reflected, as I went back on deck later, that it all came from my act of Christian kindness in listening by Comber's deathbed and comforting his last moments. There's no doubt about it; virtue isn't always just its own reward.

Comber wasn't buried the next day, because one of the slaves died during the night, and when the watch found him at dawn they naturally heaved the body overside to the sharks. For some reason this sent Spring into a passion; he wasn't having a white man buried at sea on the same day as a black had been slung over, which seemed to be stretching it a bit, but a lot of the older hands agreed with him. It beats me; when I go they can plant me in with the whole population of Timbuctoo, but others see things differently. Spring, now, was mad about little things like that, and when eventually we did come to bury Comber on the morning after, and his body had been laid out on a plank by the rail, all neatly stitched up in sail-cloth, our fastidious commander played merry h - - l because no one had thought to cover it with a flag. This on a Dahomey slaver, mark you. So we all had to wait with our hats off while Looney was despatched to get a colour from the flag locker, and Spring stamped up and down with his Prayer Book under his arm, cursing the delay, and Mrs Spring sat by with her accordion. She was wearing a floral bonnet in honour of the occasion, secured with a black scarf for mourning, and her face wore its usual expression of vacant amiability.

Looney came back presently, and you wouldn't believe it, he was carrying the Brazilian colours. We were wearing them at the moment, this being the Middle Passage,[26] so I suppose he thought he'd done right, but Spring flew into a towering passion.

"D - - n your lousy eyes!" cries he. "Take that infernal Dago duster out of my sight—would you bury an Englishman under that?" And he knocked Looney sprawling and then kicked him into the scuppers. He cursed him something fearful, the scar on his head bright crimson, until one of the hands brought a Union Jack, and then we got on with the service. Spring rattled through it, the shotted corpse went over with a splash, Mrs Spring struck up, we all sang "Rock af Ages", and the "amen" hadn't died away before Spring had strode to the unfortunate Looney and kicked his backside again so hard that he went clean down the booby hatch to the main deck. I've often thought how instructive it would have been for our divinity students to see how the offices for the dead were conducted aboard the *Balliol College*.

However, this was just another incident which I relate to show you what kind of a lunatic Spring was; I suppose it stands out in my mind because the next few weeks were so uneventful—that may seem an extraordinary thing to say about a slave voyage on the Middle Passage, but once you are used to conditions, however remarkable, you start to twiddle your thumbs and find life a bore. I had little to do beyond stand my watches, help dance the slaves, and continue the instruction of Lady Caroline Lamb. She took to following me about, and had to be made to wear a cotton dress that the sailmaker ran up, in case Mrs Spring caught sight of her—as though she'd never seen naked black wenches before, by the hundred. Lady Caroline Lamb didn't care for this, and whenever she was in my berth she used to haul the dress off, and sit stark by the foot of my cot, like a black statue, waiting to be educated, one way or the other.

One other thing I should mention, because it turned out to be important, was the behaviour of Looney. Whether Spring's hammering had driven him even more barmy I can't say, but he was a changed man after Comber died. He'd been a willing, happy idiot, but now he became sullen, and started if anyone spoke to him, and took to muttering to himself in corners. I cuffed him smartly to make him stop it, but he wouldn't; he just blubbered and mowed and shuddered if Spring's name was even mentioned. "He's the Devil!" he whined. "The b----y Devil! He bashed us, for nowt. He did, the -----." And he would crawl away, whimpering obscenities, to find a place to hide. Even Sullivan, who was softer with him than most, couldn't prevail on him to do his duties aft as steward, and the cook's Chinese mate had to serve in Spring's cabin.

So we ran westward, and then north-west, for about a month if I remember rightly, until one morning I learned that we were out of the Atlantic and into the Caribbean. It all looked alike to me, for the weather had continued fine the whole way and I'd never worn more than my jersey, but now a change came over the ship. Each day there was gun drill at the long nines and twelves, which struck me as ominous, and you could sense a growing restlessness among the hands: where men off watch had been content to loaf before, they now kept watching the horizon and sniffing the wind; either Spring or Sullivan was always at the after rail with the glass; whenever a large sail was sighted Spring would have the guns shotted and their crews standing by. As the weather grew even hotter, tempers got shorter; the stench from the slave-deck was choking in its foulness, and even the constant murmuring and moaning of the cargo seemed to me to have taken on a deeper, more sinister note. This was the time, I learned, when slave mutinies sometimes broke out, as more of them died—although only five perished all told in our ship—and the others became sullen and desperate. You'd been able to feel the misery and fear down on the slave-deck, but now you could feel the brooding hatred; it was in the way they shuffled sulkily round when they were danced, heads sunk and eyes shifting, while the hands stood guard with the needle-guns, and the light swivel pieces were kept armed and trained to sweep the decks if need be. I kept as well away from those glowering black brutes as I could; even the sharks which followed the ship didn't look more dangerous—and there were always half a dozen of them, dark sinuous shapes gliding through the blue water a couple of fathoms down, hoping for another corpse to come overside.

I wasn't the only one in a fine state of nerves on the last week's run along the old Spanish Main; apparently even Spring was apprehensive, for instead of running up north-west to the Windward Passage and our intended destination—which was somewhere on the north side of Cuba—he held almost due west for the Mosquito Coast, which if anything is a more God-forsaken shore than the one we had left in Africa. I saw it only as a far distant line on our port beam, but its heavy air lay on the ship like a blanket; the pitch bubbled between the planks, and even the wind seemed to have come from a blast furnace door. By the time we stood into the bay at Roatan, which you'll find on the map in the Islas de la Bahia, off the Honduras Coast, we were a jittery, sun-dried ship, and only thankful that we'd come safe through with never a Yankee patroller or garda costa in sight.[27]

We dropped anchor in that great clearing-house of the African slavers, where Ivory Coast brigs and schooners, the Baltimore clippers and Angola barques, the Gulf free-traders and Braziliano pirates all rode at their moorings in the broad bay, with the bumboats and shorecraft plying among them like water-beetles, and even the stench of our own slave-deck was beaten all to nothing by the immense reek of the huge barracoons and pens that lined the shore and even ran out into the sludgy green waters of the bay on great wooden piers. One never dreams that such places exist until one sees and hears and smells them, with their amazing variety of the scum of the earth—blacks and half-breeds of every description, Rio traders with curling mustachios and pistols in their belts and rings in their ears, like buccaneers from a story-book; Down Easter Yankees in stove-pipe hats with cigars sticking out of faces like flinty cliffs; sun-reddened English tars, some still wearing the wide straw hats of the Navy; packet rats in canvas shirts and frayed trousers; Scowegians with leathery faces and knives hanging on lanyards round their necks; Frog and Dago skippers in embroidered weskits with scarves round their heads, and niggers by the hundred, of every conceivable shape and shade —everyone babbling and arguing in half the tongues on earth, and all with one thing in common: they lived by and on the slave trade.

But best of all I remember a big fellow all in dirty white calicos and a broad-brimmed Panama, holding on to a stay in one of the shore-boats that came under our counter, and bawling up red-faced in reply to some one who had asked what was the news:

"Ain't ye heard, then? They found gold, over to the Pacific coast! That's right—gold! Reckon they're pickin' it up fast as they can shovel! Why, they say it's in lumps big as your fist—more gold'n anyone's ever seen before! Gold—in California!"[28]

We landed all our slaves at Roatan, herding them down into the big lighters where the Dago overseers packed them in like sheep, while Spring conducted business aft of the mizzen-mast with half a dozen brokers who had come aboard. A big awning had been rigged up, and Mrs Spring dispensed tea and biscuits to those who wanted it—which meant to Spring himself and to a wizened little Frenchman in a long taffeta coat and wideawake hat, who perched on a stool sipping daintily from his cup while a nigger boy stood behind fanning the flies off him. The other brokers were three greasy Dagoes in dirty finery who drank rum, a big Dutchman with a face like a suet pudding who drank gin punch, and a swarthy little Yankee who drank nothing at all.

They had all made a quick tour of the slave-deck before it was cleared, and when they bickered and bid with Spring, the Dagoes jabbering and getting excited, the other three mighty calm and business-like. In the end they divided the six hundred among them, at an average price of nine dollars a pound—which came to somewhere between seven and eight hundred thousand dollars for the cargo. No money changed hands; nothing was signed; no receipts were sought or given. Spring simply jotted details down in a note-book—and I daresay that after that the only transactions that took place would be the transfer of bills and orders in perfectly respectable banks in Charlestown, New York, Rio and London.

The niggers we landed would be resold, some to plantation owners along the Main, but most of them into the United States, when smugglers could be found to beat the American blockade and sell them in Mobile and New Orleans at three times what we had been paid for them. When you calculate that the trade cargo we'd given to King Gezo, through Sanchez, had been worth maybe a couple of thousand pounds—well, no wonder the slave trade throve in the forties.[29]

I said we sold all our slaves, but in fact we kept Lady Caroline Lamb. Spring had decided that if I persevered with her instruction in English, she would be worth keeping as an interpreter for later voyages—such slaves were immensely valuable, and we had actually made our last trip without one. I didn't mind; it would help pass the time, and I felt somehow that it was a feather in my cap.

To her Spring also added about a dozen mustee and quadroon girls sent aboard by the brokers, who wanted them shipped to America where they were destined for the New Orleans brothels. Spring agreed for a consideration to take them as far as Havana, where we were to load cargo for our homeward trip. These yellow wenches were quite different from the blacks we had carried, being graceful, delicate creatures of the kind they called "fancy pieces", for use as domestic slaves. I'd have traded twenty Lady Caroline Lamb's for any one of them, but there was no chance of that. They weren't chained, being so few and not the kind who would make trouble anyway.

We didn't linger in Roatan. Slaves from the barracoons came aboard with a load of lime and scoured out the slave-deck, and then we warped out of the bay to cleaner water, and the pumps and hoses washed out the shelves for twenty-four hours before Spring was satisfied. As one of the hands remarked, you could have eaten your dinner off it—not that I'd have cared to, myself. After that we made sail, due north for the Yucatan Passage, and for the first time, I think, since I'd first set foot on that d----d ship, I began to feel easy in my mind. It was no longer a slaver, I felt—well, give or take the few yellows we were carrying— we had turned the corner, and now there was only Havana and the run home. Why, in two or three months, or perhaps even less, I would be in England again, the Bryant affair—how trivial it seemed now!—would be blown over, I would be able to see Elspeth—by jove, I would be a father by then! Somebody would be, anyway—but I'd get the credit, at least. Suddenly I began to feel excited, and the Dahomey Coast and the horrors of that jungle river were like a nightmare that had never truly happened. England, and Elspeth, and peace of mind, and—what else? Well, I'd see about that when the time came.

I should have known better, of course. Whenever I'm feeling up to the mark and congratulating myself, some fearful fate trips me headlong, and I find myself haring for cover with my guts churning and Nemesis in full cry after me. In this case Nemesis was a dandy little sloop flying the American colours that came up out of the south-west when we were three days out of Roatan and had Cuba clear on our starboard bow. That was nothing in itself; Spring put on more sail and we held our own, scudding north-east. And then, out from behind Cape San Antonio, a bare two miles ahead, comes a brig with the Stars and Stripes fluttering at her peak, and there we were, caught between them, unable to fly and —in my case, anyway—most unwilling to fight.

But not John Charity Spring. He turned the *Balliol College* on her heel and tried to race the sloop westward, but on this tack she came up hand over fist, and presently from her bow-gun comes a plume of smoke, and a shot kicked up the blue water off our port bow.

"Clear for action!" bawls he, and with Sullivan roaring about the deck they ran out the guns while the little sloop came tearing up and sends another shot across our bows.

Now, in my experience there is only one way to fight a ship, and that is to get below on the side opposite to the enemy and find a snug spot behind a stout bulkhead. I was down the main hatch before the first crash of our own guns, and found myself on the slave-deck with a dozen screaming yellow wenches cowering in the corners. I made great play ordering them to keep quiet and settle down, while overhead the guns thundered again, and there came a hideous crash and tearing somewhere forward where one of the Yankee's shots had gone home. The wenches shrieked and I roared at them and waved my sheath-knife; one of them ran screaming across the tilting deck, her hands over her face, and I grabbed hold of her—a fine lithe piece she was, too, and I was taking my time manhandling her back to her fellows when Sullivan stuck his head through the hatch crying:

"What the h - - l d'ye think you're about?"

"Preventing a slave mutiny!" says I.

"What? You skulking rascal!" He flourished a pistol at me. "You shift your d - - - d butt up here, directly, d'ye hear?" So reluctantly I dropped the wench and went cautiously up the ladder again, poking my head out to see what was what.

I'm no judge of naval warfare, but by the way the hands were serving the port guns we were in the thick of a d - - - - d hot running fight. The twelve-pounders were crashing and being reloaded and run out again like something at Trafalgar, and although from time to time there was the shuddering crack of a shot striking us, we seemed to be taking no great harm; the deck watch were tailing onto a line while Sullivan was yelling orders to the men aloft. He bawled at me, so I scrambled out and tailed on to the line, and out of the corner of my eye I saw the sloop running across our bows, her broadside popping away like fury, and the scream and crash of shot just overhead sent me diving for the scuppers. I fetched up against the rail with a crash, wondering why the blazes I'd been fool enough to come out from cover just because Sullivan told me to—instinct, I suppose—and then there was a rending crackle from overhead, something hit the deck with an almighty crash, and somebody fell on top of me. I pushed him off, and my hand came away sticky with blood. Horrified, I watched as the body rolled into the scuppers; it had no head, and blood was pouring out of the neck stump like a fountain.

All this had happened in a matter of minutes. I climbed unsteadily to my feet and looked around. A great tangle of cordage and splintered timber lay between the main and mizzen masts; looking up I saw that our main top mast had come away, and for a moment I felt the ship floundering and rolling helplessly. Someone was shrieking beneath the wreckage, and Sullivan was jumping forward with an axe and a dozen men at his heels to try to clear the tangle away. Beyond them Spring was at the wheel, hat jammed down as usual, but his orders were lost in the crash of one of our port guns.

What happened in the next five minutes I barely remember; I know that we were hit again, and for a time you could hardly see across the deck for acrid powder smoke. I crouched beside the rail, palpitating, until the clearing party came dragging their mass of wreckage and I had to jump away as they bundled it overside. Our guns had stopped firing, and presently I was aware the Yankee wasn't firing either, so I chanced a look.

Somehow, after that brief holocaust, a semblance of order had been restored. The gun crews were standing by their pieces, Sullivan was by the mizzen, volleying commands to the topmen, and Spring was at the wheel. The Yankee sloop was astern, limping, with her foresail all askew, but the brig was ploughing along like thunder; in our injured condition even I could see she would be with us in no time at all. And then, no doubt, she would batter us to pieces—or take us, with slaves aboard, and that would be prison, and possibly the gallows. I felt the bile coming up in my throat.

And then I heard Spring's voice, raised in a bellow of anger.

"You'll do as you're d----d well told, mister. Now, get those yellows up on deck, with their shackles on! Lively, d--n you, d'ye hear?"

Sullivan, his hat gone, seemed to be protesting, but Spring silenced him with another bellow, and presently the hands were driving up the yellow girls, fastening leg irons about their ankles and herding them together by the mizzen mast. Spring and Sullivan were by the wheel, the latter pointing to the brig, which was overhauling us fast.

"We'll have her shooting us up in five minutes!" he was shouting. "We can't run, skipper; we can't fight! We're crippled, d--n it!"

"We can fight, mister!" Spring's scar was flaming. "We've settled the sloop, haven't we? What's that but a measly brig? D'ye want me to strike to her?"

"Look at her!" cries Sullivan. "She's got thirty guns if she's got one!" I always knew he was a sensible chap.

"I'll fight her, though," says the idiot Spring. "I haven't made this cruise to be towed into New Orleans by that pack of longshore loafers! But we'll make that nigger rubbish safe first—and if we fight and fail there won't be a black hide aboard to show against us. Now—get the chain into 'em!"

Sullivan looked as though he would burst. "It won't do! They're too d----d close—they'll see 'm drop, won't they?"

"What if they do? No niggers, no felony—they can make what they like of the ship, with the d----d equipment law, but they can't lay a hand on you or me! Now, I'm telling you, mister—

get that chain rove through!"

I made nothing of this, until four of the hands came running aft, dragging a massive chain, which they laid by the starboard rail. Then they herded the wenches over, and began to pass the chain between their legs, above the shackles, so that it linked them all together. They made the chain fast with rope to the end slaves in the line, then forced the girls to lie flat with their feet up, and by main force lifted the chain until it lay along the rail.

"Steady, there!" bawls Spring. "Now—hold it, so, till I give the word."

I don't bilk at much: I watched them blowing sepoys from the ends of guns at Cawnpore with a keen interest, and I ate my dinner at Peking an hour after the massacre, but I confess that Spring's method of disposing of incriminating evidence made me gulp. The wenches screamed and writhed in terror; once that chain was pushed over they would be hurtled across the rail by its weight, and in the sea they would sink like stones. And then, if the *Balliol College* was taken—well, what slaves do you mean, captain? I'd heard of it being done,[30] and I remembered Sullivan's story of the Dago who set his ship on fire. But for all Spring's confidence, I couldn't believe it would wash; the Yankee brig must have half a dozen glasses trained on us; they could swear to murder done and seen to be done, and then it was the gallows for certain.

Funk-stricken though I was, I could think at least. Spring obviously hoped he could fight the Yankee off, and save his liberty and his slaves at the same time; he'd only push 'em over in the last extremity. I was sure Sullivan was right; we couldn't hope to fight the brig. Somehow that madman had to be stopped, or he'd have all our heads in the noose.

If there's one thing that will make my limbs work in a crisis, it is the thought of self-preservation. I'd no notion of what I intended, but I found myself, unheeded in the excitement, walking across to the chest of arms that had been broken out by the main mast. Two of the hands were loading and priming pistols and passing them out; I took a couple, one a double-barrelled piece, and thrust them into my belt. Then, seeing all eyes were fixed either on the pursuing brig or the line of squealing unfortunates shackled by the rail, I dropped down the main hatch on to the slave deck.

I still didn't know what I was going to do; I remember thinking, as I stood there in an agony of uncertainty, this is what comes of dabbling in politics and playing vingt-et-un with spinsters. I had some frenzied notion of making my way aft through the main bulkhead door, which was open now that the slave-deck was in a wholesome condition, finding Mrs Spring in the main cabin, and appealing to her; I knew it was a lunatic thought, but I found myself scampering through anyway, pulling up by the after companion, swithering this way and that, cursing feebly to myself and racking my brains over what to do next.

Spring's bellowing almost directly overhead had me jumping in alarm; squinting up the companion I could just see his head and shoulders, facing away from me, as he stood at the wheel. He was roaring to the gun crews, urging them to their stations, and by the sound of his voice he was having his work cut out. Like Sullivan, they were ready to strike, and then I heard the mate's voice, shouting at Spring, and suddenly cut off by the crack of a pistol shot.

"Take that, d - - n you!" shouts Spring. "Stand away from him, you there! Get to those tackles, or by G - d you'll get the next round!" His hand came into view, holding a smoking pistol, and thinks I, if he's daft enough to turn a gun on Sullivan there's no stopping him except by the same way.

That was it, of course, as I'd known all along. Here was I, armed, and there was the back of his head not fifteen feet away. And, by G - d, if ever a man needed a bullet in the skull it was J. C. Spring, Fellow of Oriel. But I daren't do it—oh, it wasn't that I shrank from the dirty deed for Christian reasons; I'd killed before, and anyone who stands between me and safety gets whatever I can give him, no holds barred. But only if it's safe—and this wasn't. Suppose I missed? Something told me that Spring wouldn't. Suppose the crew raised objections? Well, if they didn't the Yankee Navy would—they'd be just the kind of idiots to consider it murder. One way and another, I couldn't risk it, and I stood there sweating in panic, torn between my terrors.

Suddenly there was a patter of feet from the main bulkhead,

and here came the idiot Looney, trying to buckle on a cutlass as big as himself. And to my amazement he was grinning foolishly to himself as he hurried towards the companion.

"What the blazes are you doing?" cries I.

"I'm goin' to kill them b - - - - - ds!" cries he. "Them's is firin' on us!"

"You numskull!" And then suddenly a great light dawned, and I saw the safe way out. "You don't want to kill them! It's the captain that's doing this! That d - - - l Spring, up there!"

I pointed to the companion way, down which our skipper's dulcet voice could be clearly heard. "He's your man, Looney! He's the man to kill!"

He stood gaping at me. "Whaffor?" says he, bewildered.

"He's just killed Mr Sullivan!" I hissed at him. "He's gone mad! He's killed Sullivan, your friend!" And some guardian angel prompted my next words. "He's going to kill you next! I heard him say so! 'I'm going to settle that b - - - - - d Looney'; that's what he said!"

The loose idiot face just stared for a moment, while I shook his arm; from far astern came the boom of a gun, and from overhead there was a crash of breaking timber and shouts and running feet.

"It's *him* they're trying to kill! Not you! Not me! He's the Devil, remember! He just killed Sullivan! He'll kill you—and all of us"

Suddenly his face changed; I'll swear a light of understanding came into his eyes, and to my consternation he began to weep. He stared at me, choking:

" 'E killed Mr Sullivan? 'E done that?"

By gum, I know a cue when I hear one. "Shot him like a dog, Looney. In the back."

He gave a little whimper of rage. " 'E shouldn't 'ave! Why 'e done that?"

"Because he's the Devil—you know that!" I've done some fearful convincing in my time, but this topped everything. "That's why the Yankees are shooting at us! You've got to kill him, Looney, or we're all done for! If you don't, he'll kill you! He hates you—remember how he flogged you, for nothing! You've got to kill him, Looney—quickly!"

I was thrusting a pistol at him as though it had been red hot, and suddenly he grabbed it out of my hand, just as our own stern-chasers thundered overhead in reply. His face contorted with rage—wonderful, beatific sight—and he plunged past me to the ladder.

"'E killed Mr Sullivan! The b - - - - - d! I'll do for 'im!"

It was splendid. Thank God he was an idiot, and hated Spring like poison. I reckon it had taken me all of sixty seconds to turn him to murder, which was a considerable feat of persuasion; now all I had to do was make sure he didn't flinch from the act.

"Up you go, Looney! Good lad! It's him or you! Quick, man quick!" I thrust at his backside as he swung on to the ladder. "Jam it into his back and give him both barrels! He killed Sullivan! He's the Devil! Sick 'im, boy!"

I probably could have spared my breath; the thought of Sullivan —the only person Looney cared for—dead at Spring's hand, had probably completed the turning of that idiot brain. He fairly flung himself up the ladder, scrambled half-way through the hatch, mouthing hideous oaths; he thrust out the pistol, and with an incoherent scream let fly with both barrels together.

Before the echo of the shots had died I was tearing down to the main bulkhead, and up the main hatch. As my head came clear I looked aft; Spring was writhing on the deck beside the wheel, his hat gone, his hands beating at the planks. Looney was struggling in the grip of one of the hands, yelling that he'd killed the Devil. Sullivan was sprawled face down in the scuppers, and the after rail was a milling scene of men running every which way, while another shot from the brig's bow-chasers came whistling overhead to tear through the mainsail. She was close up now, and turning to port to show her starboard guns, like grinning teeth; there was a yell of alarm from the men aft, and then hands were hauling at the flag lanyard; with Spring gone, everyone knew what had to be done.

I was not backward, either. I strode over to the men at the rail who were still gripping the chain, and in my parade ground voice ordered them to bring it inboard, smartly. They obeyed without a second's pause, and when I ordered them to free the slaves' ankle-irons they did that, too, falling over each other in their hurry.

I lent a hand myself, patting the yellow sluts on the shoulder and assuring them that all was well now, and that I would see they came to no harm. I trusted this would go a little way to ensuring that I came to no harm myself, and as the Yankee brig ran up on our port beam I began to rehearse in my mind the scheme I had formed for getting old Flash safely out from under this time.

By and large I'm partial to Americans. They make a great affectation of disliking the English and asserting their equality with us, but I've discovered that underneath they dearly love a lord, and if you're civil and cool and don't play it with too high a hand you can impose on them quite easily. I'm not a lord, of course, but I've got the airs when I want 'em, and know how to use them in moderation. That's the secret, a nice blending of the plain, polite gentleman with just a hint of Norman blood, and they'll eat out of your hand and boast to their friends in Philadelphia that they know a man who's on terms with Queen Victoria and yet, by gosh, is as nice a fellow as they've ever struck.

When they came aboard the *Balliol College*, raging angry and full of zeal, I bided my time while they herded us all forward, and didn't say a word until the young lieutenant commanding them had ordered us all under hatches. They were pushing us to the companion, and being none to gentle about it, when I stepped smartly out of the line and said to him, very rapidly and civilly, that I wanted to see his commander on a most urgent matter.

He stared down his Yankee nose at me and snaps: "Goddam your impudence. You'll do your talking in New Orleans—much good may it do you. Now, git below!"

I gave him a cool stare. "Believe me, sir," says I, in my best Cherrypicker voice, "I am in most solemn earnest. Please—do nothing untoward." I tilted my head slightly towards the *Balliol College* hands who were being pushed below. "These people must not know," I said quietly, "but I am a British naval officer. I must see your commander without delay."

He stared at me, but he was sharp. He waited till our last man was down the companion, and then demanded an explanation. I told him I was Lieutenant Comber, Royal Navy, on special service from the Board of Admiralty—which, I assured him, I could prove with ease. That settled it, and when one of his men had collected my traps from below, I was hustled off under guard, the Yankee officer still eyeing me suspiciously. But he had other things to think about—there was Spring, shot through the back and unconscious, being taken down on a stretcher; Mrs Spring was under guard in the cabin; there were three corpses on our deck, including Sullivan's; Looney was below with the other prisoners, raving in a voice you could have heard in Aldershot; there was blood and wreckage on the deck, and a dozen weeping nigger girls huddled by the rail. I made the most of them, drawing the lieutenant's attention to them and saying:

"Take care of those poor people. They must suffer no more than they have done. Miserable souls, they have come through hell today."

I left him not knowing what to think, and allowed myself to be conducted aboard the *U.S.S. Cormorant* by my Leatherneck escort. And there it was plain sailing all the way, as I knew it must be. Captain Abraham Fairbrother, a very spry young gentleman, didn't believe a word I said, at first, but once I had slit open my belt and laid Comber's papers before his bulging eyes he hadn't a leg to stand on. It was all so impressively official, and my own bearing and manner, although I say it myself, were so overwhelming, that the poor soul took it all in like a hungry fish. Why shouldn't he? I would have done.

Of course I had to tell him a tremendous tale, but that sort of thing has never presented me with difficulty, and barring the fact that I wasn't Comber, the whole thing was gospel true, which always makes lying easier. He shook his fair young head in amazement, and vowed that it beat everything he had ever heard; he was full of venom against slavers, I discovered, and so naturally he was all admiration for me, and shook my hand as though it was a pump handle.

"I feel it an honour to welcome you aboard, sir," says he. "I had no notion that such a thing . . . that such people as yourself, sir, were engaged in this work. By George, it's wonderful! My congratulations, sir!" And believe it or not, he actually saluted.

Well, I fancy I can carry off this sort of situation pretty well, you know. Modest and manly, that's Flashy when the compliments are flying, with a touch of a frown to show that my mind is really on serious matters. Which it was, because I knew I hadn't got farther than the first fence so far, and would have to tread delicately. But Captain Fairbrother was all eager assistance: what could he do to serve me? I confess I may have given him the impression that the entire slave trade could expect its coup de grace when once I'd laid my report before the British and American governments, and he was itching to help oil the wheels.

Have you noticed, once you have succeeded in convincing a man of something incredible, he believes it with an enthusiasm that he wouldn't dream of showing for an obvious, simple fact? It had been like that with Looney; now it was so with Fairbrother. He simply was all over me; I just had to sit back and let him arrange matters. First, I must be delivered to Washington with all speed; the bigwigs would be in a positive lather to see me —I doubted that, myself, but didn't say so. Nothing would do but he must carry me to Baltimore in his own brig, while the sloop could take the *Balliol College* into New Orleans with a prize crew —there, observes Mr Fairbrother darkly, the miscreants would meet with condign punishment for slavery, piracy, and attempted murder. Of course, I would give evidence eventually, but that could wait until Washington had been thrown into transports by my advent there.

Washington, I could see, was going to present problems; they wouldn't be as easy to satisfy as Captain Fairbrother, who was your genuine Northern nigger-lover and violently prejudiced in my favour. He was one of these direct, virtuous souls, bursting with decency, whose very thought was written plainly on his fresh, handsome face. Arnold would have loved him—and young Chard could have used a few of him at Rorke's Drift, too. Brainless as a bat, of course, and just the man for my present needs.

I impressed on him the need for not letting any of the *Balliol College* crew know what I truly was, and hinted at dangerous secret work yet to come which might be prejudiced if my identity leaked out. (That was no lie, either.) He agreed solemnly to this, but thought it would be an excellent plan to take some of the freed slaves to Washington, just for effect; "tangible evidence, sir, of your noble and heroic endeavours in the great crusade against this vile traffic". I didn't object, and so about six yellows and

Lady Caroline Lamb were herded aboard and bedded down somewhere in the bowels of the brig. Fairbrother wondered about Mrs Spring, whose presence on the *College* shocked and amazed him; they had caught her hurling Spring's log, papers, and accounts out of the cabin window, whereby much valuable evidence had been lost (that's all you know, I thought). Still, she was a woman. . . .

"Take her to New Orleans, is my advice," says I. "There are not two more diabolical creatures afloat than she and her fiend of a husband. How is he, by the way?"

"In a coma," says Fairbrother. "One of his own pirates shot him through the back, sir—what creatures they are, to be sure! He will live, I dare say—which is no great matter, since the New Orleans hangman will, if the fellow survives, have the duty of breaking his neck for him."

Oh, the holy satisfaction of the godly—when it comes to delight in cruelty I'm just a child compared to them. His next remark didn't surprise me, either.

"But I am inconsiderate, Mr Comber—here have I been keeping you in talk over these matters, when your most urgent desire has surely been for a moment's privacy in which you might deliver up thanks to a merciful Heavenly Father for your delivery from all the dangers and tribulations you have undergone. Your pardon, sir."

My urgent need was in fact for an enormous brandy and a square meal, but I answered him with my wistful smile.

"I need hardly tell you, sir, that in my heart I have rendered that thanks already, not only for myself but for those poor souls whom your splendid action had liberated. Indeed," says I, looking sadly reflective, "there is hardly a moment in these past few months that I have not spent in prayer."

He gripped my hand again, looking moist, and then, thank God, he remembered at last that I had a belly, and gave orders for food and a glass of spirits while he went off, excusing himself, to splice the binnacle or clew up the heads, I shouldn't wonder.

Well, thinks I, so far so good, but we mustn't go too far. The sooner I could slip out of sight, the better, for while the *Balliol College* crew were alive and kicking there was always the risk that I would be given away. I didn't want to get the length of the British Embassy in Washington, for someone there might just know me, or worse still, they might know Comber. But for the moment, with the brig heading east by north, and the *Balliol College* making north under guard to Orleans, it was all sunshine for Harry—provided I didn't trip myself up. I was meant to be Navy, and Fairbrother and his officers were Navy also, so I must watch my tongue.

As it turned out, by playing the reserved Briton and steering the conversation as often as possible to India, about which they were curious, I passed the thing off very well. I had to talk some slavery, of course, and there was a nasty moment when I was almost drawn into a description of our encounter with the British sloop off Dahomey, but I managed to wriggle clear. It would have been easier, I think, with Englishmen, for Yankee bluebacks are deuced serious fellows, more concerned with their d - - - - d ratlines and bobstays than with interesting topics like drink, women and cash. But I was very pious and priggish that voyage, and they seemed to respect me for it.

However, there was a human side, I discovered, even to the worthy Bible-thumping Fairbrother. I had made a great thing, the second day, of visiting the freed slaves and giving them some fatherly comfort—husbandly comfort would have been more like it, but with those sharp Yankee eyes on me I daren't even squeeze a rump. Lady Caroline Lamb was there, eyeing me soulfully, but I patted her head sternly and told her to be a good girl. What she made of this I can only guess, but that evening, when I was settling down in the berth I had been allotted aft, I was startled by a rapping on my door. It was Fairbrother, in some consternation.

"Mr Comber," says he, "there's one of those black women in my berth!"

"Indeed?" says I, looking suitably startled.

"My G - d, Mr Comber!" cries he. "She's in there, now—and she's stark naked!"

I pondered this; it occurred to me that Lady Caroline Lamb, following her *Balliol College* training, had made her way aft and got into Fairbrother's cabin—which lay in the same place as my berth had done on the slaver. And being the kind of gently-reared fool that he was, Fairbrother was in a fine stew. He'd probably never seen a female form in his life.

"What shall I do?" says he. "What can she want? I spoke to her—she's the big, very black one—but she has hardly any English, and she just stays there! She's kneeling beside my cot, sir!"

"Have you tried praying with her?" says I.

He goggled at me. "Pray? Why, I . . . I don't know. She looks as though . . ." He broke off, going beetroot red. "My G-d! Do you suppose that slaver captain has been . . . using her as . . . as a *woman?*"

Humanity never ceases to amaze me. Here was this fine lad, old enough to vote, in command of a hundred men and a fighting ship which he could handle like a young Nelson, brave as a bull, I don't doubt—and quivering like a virgin's fan because a buxom tart had invaded his cabin. It's this New England upbringing, of course; even a young manhood spent in naval service hadn't obliterated the effect of all those sermons.

"Do you suppose she has been . . . degraded?" says he, in a hushed voice.

"I fear it is more than likely, Captain Fairbrother," says I. "There is no depth unplumbed by their depravity. This unfortunate young woman may well have been trained to concubinage."

He shuddered. "Monstrous . . . terrible. But what am I to do?"

"I find it difficult to know what to advise," says I. "The situation is . . . unique in my experience. Perhaps you should tell her to go back to the quarters she has been allotted."

"Yes, yes, of course. I must do that." He hesitated, pulling at his lip. "It is frightful to think of these ignorant young creatures being . . . misled . . . in that way."

"We must do what we can for them," says I.

"Indeed, indeed." He cleared his throat nervously. "I must apologise, Mr Comber, for disturbing you . . . I was startled, I confess . . . totally unexpected thing . . . yes. However, I shall do as you advise. My apologies again, sir. Thank you . . . er, and good night."

He fairly fled into his cabin, that good pious lad, and I listened in vain thereafter for the sound of his door re-opening. Not that I expected it. Next day he avoided my eye, and went red whenever the slaves were mentioned. He probably still does, but I'll wager his conscience has never been quite strong enough to make him regret his lost innocence.

We made capital speed to Baltimore, which is just another port at the far end of the uninviting Chesapeake Bay, and from there, after Fairbrother had reported to his commodore, and the importance of my presence had been duly emphasised, we were taken by train to Washington, about forty miles off. I was getting fairly apprehensive by now, and looking sharp for a chance to make myself scarce—although what I would do then, in a strange country without any means of support, I couldn't imagine. I knew the longer I kept up my imposture, the more chance there was of being detected, but what could I do? Fairbrother, who had wangled leave from his commander to be my personal convoy to the capital, stuck like a leech; he was looking for a share of the glory, of course. So I just had to sit back and see what came— at worst, I decided, I could make a bolt for it, but in the meantime I would carry the thing through with a wide eye and a bold bluff front.

Washington is an odd place. You could see the Jonathans had designed it with an eye to the future, when they envisaged it as the finest city in the world, and even then, in '48, there were signs of building on every hand, with scaffolding about even in the middle of the city, and the outer roads all churned mud with the autumn rain, but fringed with fine houses half-completed. I got got to know it well in the Civil War time, but I never liked it— sticky as Calcutta or Madras in summer, and yet its people dressed as though they'd been in New York or London. I could always smell fever in the air there, and why George Washington ever chose the site beats me. But that's your rich colonial Englishman all over—never thinks twice about other people's convenience.

But sticky or not, the officials who lived there were d----d sharp men, as I discovered. Fairbrother delivered me at the Department of the Navy, where a white-whiskered admiral heard my tale and d----d his stars at every turn; then he handed me on to a section much like our Board of Trade, where several hard-faced civilians took up the running and I went through the thing again. They didn't seem to know what to make of me at all, at first, or what precisely they ought to do; finally, one of them, a fat little fellow called Moultrie, asked me exactly what could I contribute to the anti-slave trade campaign apart from giving evidence against the crew of the *Balliol College*? In other words, what was so remarkable about me that Washington was being troubled with me at all? Where was the important report that had been talked about by Captain Fairbrother?

Since it didn't exist, I had to invent it. I explained that I had gathered an immense amount of detail not only about the slave-traders, but about those in Britain and America who were behind them, supplying them with funds and ships, and organising their abominable activities under the cover of legitimate commerce. All this, I explained, I had committed to paper as opportunity arose, with such documents as I had been able to obtain, and I had ear-marked useful witnesses along the way. I had consigned one report to a reliable agent at Whydah, and another to a second agent at Roatan—no, I dare not disclose their names except to my own chiefs in London. A third report I would certainly write out as soon as I could—a rueful smile here, and a reminder that life for me had been fairly busy of late.

"Yes, yes, sir," says he, "this is excellent, and very well, in its way. Your prudence about the disposal of your earlier reports is commendable. But from what you say you are obviously in possession of information which must be of the first importance to the United States Government—information which Her Majesty's ministers would obviously communicate to us. You have names, you say, of Americans who are behind the slave trade—who, at least, are involved in it at a safe remove from slaving operations. Now, sir, here we have the root of the thing—these are the men we must bring to book. Who are those men?"

I took a deep breath, and tried to look like a man in mental struggle, while he and his two fellow-inquisitors waited, and the secretary sat with his pen poised.

"Mr Moultrie," says I, "I can't tell you. Please, sir—let me explain." I solemnly checked his outburst. "I have many names

—both in my mind and in my reports. I don't know much about American public affairs, sir, but even I recognise some of them as —well, not insignificant names. Now if I were to name them to you—now—what would they be but names? The mass of evidence that would—that will—lead to their proven involvement in the traffic in black souls, is already on its way to England, as I trust. Obviously it will be communicated to you, and these people can be proceeded against. But if I were to name names now, sir" —I stabbed a finger on the table—"you could do nothing; you would have to wait on the evidence which has been assembled. And while I trust your discretion perfectly, gentlemen—it would be an impertinence to do otherwise—we all know how a word once spoken takes wings. Premature disclosure, and consequent warning, might enable some of these birds to escape the net. And believe me, gentlemen..." I gritted my teeth and forced moisture into my eyes "... believe me, I have not gone through the hell of those Dahomey raids, and watched the torture of those poor black creatures on the Middle Passage—I have not risked death and worse—in order to see those butchers escape!"

Well, it wasn't a bad performance, and it took them pretty well aback. Moultrie looked d - - - - d solemn, and his pals wore the alarmed expression of men in the presence of a portent they didn't understand. Then Moultrie says:

"Yes...I see. You are in no doubt, sir...of the consequence ...that is, the importance, of some of those implicated? Do you suggest that...when all is known...their would be a, er, a political scandal, perhaps?"

I gave my mirthless laugh. "I may indicate that best, sir, by assuring you that among the Britons whom I know to be involved in the traffic—and whose complicity can be proved, sir—are two peers of the realm and one whose name was, until lately, to be found among Her Majesty's Ministers. And I believe, sir, that the American names include men of comparable stature. The profits of the slave trade, sir, are immense enough to tempt the highest. Judge whether a scandal may be expected."

He was regarding me round-eyed. "Mr Comber," says he, "your knowledge makes you a very dangerous young man."

"And therefore," says I, smiling keenly, "you would say—a

very endangered young man? I am used to risk, sir. It is my trade."

I was almost believing it myself by now, so I wasn't surprised that they took it in. So much so, that being Yankees, and no fools, they made me go through my whole yarn again—from the Channel to Whydah, Gezo's village, our escape, the voyage west, Roatan, and all the rest—in the hope of my slipping out some information unawares. But since I didn't have any they were wasting their time. Finally they conferred while I cooled my heels, and announced that they would discuss matters with the British Ambassador, and in the meantime I would hold myself ready to go to New Orleans to testify against the *Balliol College*.

I didn't fancy this, at all, but again there was nothing to be done at the moment. So I bowed, and later that day I was hailed to the Ambassador's house—a very decent old stick, and a pleasant change from those yapping Jonathan voices. I was a shade wary in case he, or any of his people, might by a chance in a thousand be acquainted with the real Comber, but all was well. I told my story for a fourth time, and that evening, when he bade me to dinner with him, I went through it yet again for the entertainment of his guests. And I'll swear I didn't put a foot wrong—but there was one man at that table with as keen a nose for a faker as I have myself. How or when he saw through me I shall never understand, but he did, and gave me one of the many nasty moments in my life.

There were about a dozen at the dinner, and I didn't even notice him until the ladies had withdrawn, and Charterfield, our host, had invited me to regale the gentlemen with my adventures on the Slave Coast. But he seemed to take an even closer interest in my story than the others. He was an unusually tall man, with the ugliest face you ever saw, deep dark eye sockets and a chin like a coffin, and a black cow's lick of hair smeared across his forehead. When he spoke it was with the slow, deliberate drawl of the American back-countryman, which was explained by the fact that he was new to the capital; in fact, he was a very junior Congressman, invited at the last moment because he had some anti-slavery bill in preparation, and so would be interested in meeting me. His name will be familiar to you: Mr Lincoln.[81]

Let me say at once that in spite of all the trouble he caused me at various times, and the slight differences which may be detectable in our characters, I liked Abe Lincoln from the moment I first noticed him, leaning back in his chair with that hidden smile at the back of his eyes, gently cracking his knuckles. Just why I liked him I can't say; I suppose in his way he had the makings of as big a scoundrel as I am myself, but his appetites were different, and his talents infinitely greater. I can't think of him as a good man, yet as history measures these things I suppose he did great good. Not that that excites my admiration unduly, nor do I put my liking down to the fact that he had a sardonic humour akin to my own. I think I liked him because, for some reason which God alone knows, he liked me. And not many men who knew me as well as he did, have done that.

I remember only a few of his observations round that table. Once, when I was describing our fight with the Amazons, one of the company exclaimed:

"You mean to say the women fight and torture and slay on behalf of their menfolk? There can be no other country in the world where this happens."

And Lincoln, very droll, inquires of him: "Have you attended many political tea parties in Washington lately, sir?"

They all laughed, and the fellow replied that even in Washington society he hadn't seen anything quite to match what I had described.

"Be patient, sir," says Lincoln. "We're a young country, after all. Doubtless in time we will achieve a civilisation comparable with that of Day-homey."

I spoke about Spring, and Charterfield expressed amazement and disgust that a man of such obvious parts should be so great a villain.

"Well, now," says Lincoln, "why not? Some of the greatest villains in history have been educated men. Without that education they might have been honest citizens. A few years at college won't make a bad man virtuous; it will merely put the polish on his wickedness."

"Oh, come, now," says Charterfield, "that may be true, but you must admit that virtue more often goes hand in hand with learning than with ignorance. You know very well that a nation's criminal class is invariably composed of those who lack the benefits of education."

"And being uneducated, they get caught," says Lincoln. "Your learned rascal usually goes undetected."

"Why, at this rate, you will equate learning with evildoing," cries someone. "What must your view be of our leading justices and politicians? Are they not virtuous men?"

"Oh, virtuous enough," says Lincoln. "But what they would be like if they had been educated is another matter."

When I had finished my tale, and had heard much congratulation and expressions of flattering astonishment, it was Lincoln who remarked that it must have been a taxing business to act my part among the slavers for so long. Had I not found it a great burden? I said it had been, but fortunately I was a good dissembler.

"You must be," says he. "And I speak as a politician, who knows how difficult it is to fool people."

"Well," says I, "my own experience is that you can fool some people all the time—and all the people some times. But I concede that it's difficult to fool all the people all the time."

"That is so," says he, and that great grin lit up his ugly face. "Yes, sir, Mr Comber, that is indeed so."

I also carried away from that table an impression of Mr Lincoln's views on slaves and slavery which must seem strange in the twentieth century since it varies somewhat from popular belief. I recall, for example, that at one point he described the negroes as "the most confounded nuisance on this continent, not excepting the Democrats".

"Oh, come," says someone, "that is a little hard. It is not their fault."

"It was not my fault when I caught the chicken pox," says Lincoln, "but I can assure you that while I was infected I was a most unconscionable nuisance—although I believe my family loved me as dearly as ever."

"Come, that's better," laughs the other. "You may call the nigras a nuisance provided you love them, too—that will satisfy even the sternest abolitionist."

"Yes, I believe it would," says Lincoln. "And like so many

satisfactory political statements, it would not be true. I try to love my fellow man, with varying success, the poor slaves among the rest. But the truth is I neither like nor dislike them more than any other creatures. Now your stern abolitionist, because he detests slavery, feels he must love its victims, and so he insists on detecting in them qualities deserving unusual love. But in fact those qualities are not to be found in them, any more than in other people. Your extreme anti-slaver mistakes compassion for love, and this leads him into a kind of nigra-worship which, on a rational examination, is by no means justified."

"Surely the victim of a misfortune as grievous as slavery does deserve special consideration, though."

"Indeed," says Lincoln, "special consideration, special compassion, by all means, just such as I received when I had the chicken pox. But having the chicken pox did not make me a worthier or better person, as some people seem to suppose is the case with victims of slavery. I tell you, sir, to listen to some of our friends, I could believe that every plantation and barracoon from Florida to the river is peopled by the disciples of Jesus. Reason tells me this is false; the slave being God's creature and a human soul, is no better than the rest of us. But if I said as much to Cassius Clay[32] he would try to prove me wrong at the point of his bowie knife."

"You have worked too long on your anti-slavery bill," laughs Charterfield. "You are suffering from a surfeit."

"Why, sir, that is probably so," says Lincoln. "I wish I had ten dollars for every time I have fought a client's case, never doubting its justice and rightness, pursuing it to a successful verdict with all my powers—and finished the trial feeling heartily sick with that same worthy client. I would not confess it outside this room, but you may believe me, gentlemen, there are moments, God forgive me, when I become just a little tired of nigras."

"Your conscience is troubling you," says someone.

"By thunder, there is no lack of people determined to make my conscience trouble me," says Lincoln. "As though I can't tend to my own conscience, they must forever be running pins into it. There was a gentleman the other day, a worthy man, too, and I was ill-advised enough to say to him much what I've said tonight: that nigras, while deserving our uttermost compassion and assistance, were nevertheless, a nuisance. I said they were the rock on which our nation had been splitting for years, and that they could well assume the proportions of a national catastrophe—through no fault of their own, of course. I believe I concluded by wishing the whole parcel of them back in Africa. He was shocked: 'Strange talk, this', says he, 'from the sponsor of a bill against slavery'. 'I'd sponsor a bill to improve bad drains', says I. 'They're a confounded nuisance, too.' A thoughtless remark, no doubt, and a faulty analogy, but I paid for it. 'Good God,' cries he, 'you'll not compare human souls with bad drains, surely.' 'Not invariably,' says I, but I got no further, because he stalked off in a rage, having misunderstood me completely."

"You can hardly blame him," says the other, smiling.

"No," says Lincoln. "He was a man of principle and conscience. His only fault lay in his inability to perceive that I have both commodities also, but I didn't buy mine ready-made from Cincinnati, and I don't permit either to blind me to reality, I hope. And that reality is that the slave question is much too serious a matter for emotion, yet I very much fear that emotion will override reason in its settlement. In the meantime, I pray to God I am wrong, and continue to fight it in my own way, which I believe to be as worthy as polemical journalism and the underground railroad."

After that the talk turned to the great California gold strike that I had first heard of at Roatan, and which was obsessing everyone. The first rumours had spoken of fabulous wealth for the taking; then word had spread that the first reports had been greatly exaggerated, and now it was being said that the first reports had been true enough, and it was the rumours of disappointment that were false. Thousands were already heading west, braving the seas round Cape Horn or the perils of starvation, weather and Indian savages on the overland trails. Most of the men at that dinner agreed that there was obviously gold in quantity along the Pacific streams, but doubted if many of the enthusiastic seekers would find quite as much as they expected.

"You are the cynic, Abraham," says one. "What will the Tennessee wiseacres say of the New Eldorado?"

When the laugh died down, Lincoln shook his head. "If they are real Tennessee wiseacres, Senator, they won't 'say nuthin'.' But what they'll *do*—if they're *real* wiseacres—is buy themselves up every nail, every barrel-stave, every axe-handle, and every shovel they can lay hold on, put 'em all in a cart with as many barrels of molasses as may be convenient, haul 'em all up to Independence or the Kanzas, and *sell* them to the fortunate emigrants at ten times their value. That's how to make gold out of a gold strike."

"Well, you can handle a team, surely?" cries the merry Senator. "Why not make your fortune out of axe-handles?"

"Well, sir, I'll tell you," says Lincoln, and everyone listened, grinning. "I've just put the return on axe-handles at one thousand per centum. But I'm a politician, and sometime lawyer. Axe-handles aren't my style; my stock-in-trade is spoken words. You may believe me, words can be obtained wholesale a powerful sight cheaper'n axe-handles—and if you take 'em to the right market, you'll get a far richer return for 'em than a thousand per centum. If you doubt me—ask President Polk."

They guffawed uproariously at this, and presently we went to join the ladies for the usual ghastly entertainment which, I discovered, differed not one whit from our English variety. There was singing, and reading from the poetic works of Sir Walter Scott, and during this Lincoln drew me aside into a window alcove, very pleasant, and began asking me various questions about my African voyage. He listened very attentively to my replies, and then suddenly said:

"I tell you what—you can enlighten me. A phrase puzzled me the other day—in an English novel, as a matter of fact. You're a naval man—what does it mean: to club-haul a ship?"

For a moments my innards froze, but I don't believe I showed it. This was the kind of thing I had dreaded: a question on nautical knowledge which I, the supposed naval man, couldn't have answered in a thousand years.

"Why," says I, "let's see now—club-hauling. Well, to tell you the truth, Mr Lincoln, it's difficult to explain to a landsman, don't ye know? It involves ... well, quite complicated manoeuvres, you see ..."

"Yes," says he, "I thought it might. But in general terms, now ... what happens?"

I laughed, pleasantly perplexed. "If I had you aboard I could easily tell you. Or if we had a ship model, you know ..."

He nodded, smiling at me. "Surely. It's of no consequence. I just have an interest in the sea, Mr Comber, and must be indulging it at the expense of every sailor who is unlucky enough to—lay alongside me, as you'd call it." He laughed. "That's another thing, now, I recall. Forgive my curiosity, but what, precisely, is long-splicing?"

I knew then he was after me, in spite of the pleasant, almost sleepy expression in the dark eyes. His canny yokel style didn't fool me. I gave him back some of his own banter, while my heart began to hammer with alarm.

"It's akin to splicing the mainbrace, Mr Lincoln," says I, "and is a term which anyone who is truly interested in the sea would have found out from a nautical almanac long ago."

He gave a little snorting laugh. "Forgive me. Of course I wasn't really interested—just testing a little theory of mine."

"What theory is that, sir?" asks I, my knees shaking.

"Oh—just that you, Mr Comber—if that is your name—might not be quite so naval as you appear. No, don't alarm yourself. It's no business of mine at all. Blame my legal training, which has turned a harmless enough fellow into a confounded busybody. I've spent too long in court-rooms perhaps, seeking after truth and seldom finding it. Maybe I'm of an unusually suspicious nature, Mr Comber, but I confess I am downright interested when I meet an English Navy man who *doesn't* smother his food with salt, who *doesn't*, out of instinct, tap his bread on the table before he bites it, and who *doesn't* even hesitate before jumping up like a jack-rabbit when his Queen's health is proposed. Just a fraction of a moment's pause would seem more natural in a gentleman who is accustomed to drinking that particular toast sitting down." He grinned with his head on one side. "But all these things are trivial; they amount to nothing—until the ill-mannered busybody also finds out that this same English Navy man *doesn't* know what club-hauling and long-splicing are, either. Even then, I could still be entirely mistaken. I frequently am."

"Sir," says I, trying to sound furious, with my legs on the point of giving way, "I fail to understand you. I am a British officer and, I hope, a gentleman . . ."

"Oh, I don't doubt it," says he, "but even that isn't *conclusive* proof that you're a rascal. You see, Mr Comber, I can't be sure. I just suspect that you're a humbug—but I couldn't for the life of me prove it." He scratched his ear, grinning like a gargoyle. "And anyway, it's just none of my business. I guess the truth is I'm a bit of a humbug myself, and feel a kind of duty to other humbugs. Anyway, I'm certainly not fool enough to pass on my ridiculous observations and suspicions to anyone else. I just thought you might be interested to hear about the salt, and the bread, and so forth," said this amazing fellow. "Shall we go and listen to them laying it off about the Last Minstrel?"

It was touch and go at this point whether I launched myself head first through the open window or not; for a moment it seemed that the wiser course might well be headlong flight. But then I steadied. I cannot impress too strongly on young fellows that the whole secret of the noble art of survival, for a single man, lies in knowing exactly when to make your break for safety. I considered this now, with Lincoln smiling down at me sardonically, and decided ít was better to brazen things through than to bolt. He knew I was an impostor, but he could hardly prove it, and for some whimsical reason of his own he seemed to regard the whole thing as a joke. So I gave him my blandest smile, and said: "I confess, sir, that I have no idea what you're talkng about. Let us by all means rejoin the company."

I think it puzzled him, but he said nothing more, and we turned back into the room. I kept a bold front, but I was appalled at being discovered, and the rest of that evening passed in a confused panic for me. I recall that I was dragooned into singing the bass part in a group song—I believe it was "'Tis of a sailor bold, but lately come ashore", which no doubt caused Mr Lincoln some ironic amusement—but beyond that I can remember little except that eventually we all took our leave, and Fairbrother carried me off to quarters at the Navy Department, where I spent a sleepless night wondering how I could get out of this latest fix.

They would send me back to New Orleans, assuming that the

prying bumpkin Lincoln kept his suspicions to himself—which seemed likely—and it was imperative that I should take french leave before there was any risk of my confronting the *Balliol College* crew at their trial. Washington was no place to try to decamp, so that left Baltimore or New Orleans. I favoured the former, but as it turned out there was no opportunity, for when the Navy Department finally finished with me on the following morning, I was sent back with Fairbrother to his brig, and he took me straight aboard. We sailed within a few hours, so there was nothing to do but resign myself to sitting out the voyage, and make plans for escaping when we reached Louisiana. What I would do when I slipped away, I didn't know; if my own mother wit couldn't get me back to England hale and sound, I wasn't the man I thought I was. When you've come safe through an Afghan rising and a German revolution, with all manner of cut-throats on your tail, you regard evasion from the United States as a pretty smooth course, even if they set the traps after you for slave-running and impersonation, as Fairbrother and his superiors eventually would do. I fancied I could manage passably well, if I minded my step—oh, the optimism of youth. If I'd known what lay along the path to England, home and beauty, I'd have surrendered then and there, told Fairbrother the whole truth, and taken my chance in a slavery trial any day. Thank God I've never had the gift of second sight.

The closer we got to New Orleans, the worse my prospects of successful desertion looked, and by the time we dropped anchor at the big bend in the Mississippi River off Customs House levee, I was well in the dumps. Having nothing to unload, you see, except me, the brig stood well out in midstream, so my notion of slipping down a gangplank to the quay was quite out of court. We hove to at night, with the whole splendid panorama of lights twinkling on either bank, the glow of Algiers to port and the French Quarter to starboard, but it was lost on me. Fairbrother was to take me ashore personally in the morning, so my only hope must be to give him the slip when we landed.

I already had a good idea of what my first moves would be when I had won free, so I set about my preparations. First I went through the clothes which I hadn't worn since I first boarded the *Balliol College*, and which had been bundled up in my valise. There was a superb coat by Gregg of Bond Street, in fine plum broadcloth, now foully creased, but I borrowed an iron from the steward, waved away his offers of help, and working secretly in my cabin, soon put it to rights and sponged out the stains it had taken. I had two good pairs of trousers, excellent boots from Todd, a smart grey embroidered waistcoat, several shirts which were beyond redemption, and a fine neckercher of black China silk. That was my wardrobe; the coat and neckercher at least could be counted on for what I had in mind.

My other valuables consisted of a ruby pin and an old-fashioned gold and silver chain with seals which had belonged to my grandfather Paget. They could pawn for a tidy sum, but I hoped this would be unnecessary, as I had a more immediate use for them. For the rest, I had eleven gold sovereigns, which would tide me over the beginning at least.

Having completed my inventory, I packed everything carefully in my valise, and next morning when Fairbrother took me ashore I stood forth in the clothes he had lent me; since I should be staying ashore when he had presented me to the proper authorities it was natural that my valise should go with me in the boat.

We were rowed to the Algiers side by four bluejackets, Fairbrother sweating in full fig, and as we neared the bank my spirits rose. The levee and wharves were positively teeming with people, there was a forest of shipping along the bank, with small craft scudding about everywhere, half-naked negroes toiling at the derricks as cargo was swung ashore, folk bustling about every which way on the jettys, nigger children playing and squealing among the piles, ship's officers and cargo bosses bawling above the hubbub—a tremendous confusion of thousands of busy people, which was just what I wanted.

At need I had been prepared to bolt for it, but I didn't have to. While I was handed ashore at the levee, and one of the men swung up my valise, Fairbrother stopped a moment to give orders to the coxswain. I picked up my baggage, took three steps, and in that moment I was lost in the throng, jostling my way quickly along the wharf. I didn't even hear a shout from the boat; in two minutes I was striding along through the heaps of cargo and cotton bales, and when I glanced back there wasn't a glimpse of Fairbrother and his men to be seen. They would be gaping around, no doubt, swearing at my carelessness at having got lost, and would start a hunt for me, but it would be an hour or so before they began to suspicion that my disappearance wasn't accidental. Then the fun would begin in earnest.

Now, I had considered carefully the possibility of trying to board an outgoing ship immediately, and had dismissed the notion. When Fairbrother and his navy friends eventually decided I had slipped my cable, there would be a tremendous hue and cry, and the first places they would look for me would be on departing ships. I couldn't be sure of finding a vessel that would be out and away before that happened; anyway, I hadn't much passage money. So I had determined to lie low in New Orleans until I could see what was best to be done, and then carefully pick my best passage home, perhaps from another port altogether.

So now, when I had put a quarter of a mile between myself and the spot where the boat touched, I halted on the levee, waited till I spotted a likely-looking craft among the hundreds that were putting in and out along the bank, and asked its rower to carry me over to the north shore. He was a big, grinning nigger with brass rings in his ears who chattered unceasingly in a queer mixture of French and English, and in no time at all he set me down on the levee from which you walked up to the Vieux Carré, the old French Quarter which is the very heart of New Orleans. I paid him in English shillings, which didn't bother him at all; provided it's gold or silver, the Orleanais don't care whose head is on it.

There is no city quite like New Orleans ("Awlins" as its inhabitants called it then; outsiders called it "Nawlins"). I loved it at first sight, and I believe that setting aside London, which is my home, and Calcutta, which has a magic that I cannot hope to explain, I still think more kindly of it than of any other place on earth. It was busy and gay and bawdy and full of music and drink and pleasure; nowhere else did eyes sparkle so bright, voices sound so happy, colours look so vivid, food taste so rich, or the very air throb with so much excitement. In the unlikely event that there is a heaven for scoundrels like me, it will be built on the model of the Vieux Carré, with its smiling women, brilliant clothes, and atmosphere of easy indulgence. The architecture is also very fine, spires and gracious buildings and what not, with plenty of shade and places to lounge and sit about while you watch the ivory girls sauntering by in their gorgeous dresses. Indeed, it was sometimes not unlike a kind of tropical Paris, but without those bloody Frogs. New Orleans, of course, is where they civilised the French.

The first thing I did was to find a barber, and let him remove the fine black beard which I had sprouted in the past two or three months. I kept my whiskers, of course—where would Flash be without his tart-catchers?—but had my hair trimmed fairly short to suit the role I intended to play. Then I passed on to a good tailor, and laid out most of my cash on a new finely-frilled shirt, in the Southern style, a silver-topped cane, and a curly-brimmed white stove-pipe hat.

Finally, I sought out a printer, in one of the back streets, spun him a tale, and placed an order for a gross of cards in the name of Count Rudi von Starnberg, which was my new identity. It warmed me to think of how Rudi would have delighted in this, evil throat-cutting b - - - - - d that he was. I had the printer, who was all eagerness to oblige such a distinguished gentleman, run me off half a dozen of the cards then and there for immediate use, and promising to send round for the remainder next day, when they would be ready, bade him good morning. I had no intention of collecting them, of course, and doubtless they are still there. It occurred to me that if Rudi ever visited America he might find himself billed for them, which would have been most satisfactory.

Now I was ready to face the United States in all my glory—an immaculately dressed Austrian nobleman, speaking French and English with the accent of Vienna, and as different as you could wish from some English scoundrel calling himself Comber who had vanished, bearded and nautically attired, some hours before. True, I had little cash and no place of abode, but you would never have imagined that from a glance at the splendid gentleman who now strolled at ease through the Vieux Carré, stopping to refresh himself with wine and water at one of the wayside cafés, glancing over a newspaper, and generally spying out the land. I spent a few hours getting the sense of the place, dined extremely well at a Creole eating place where they had the good sense not to smother everying in garlic, and then went to work.

What I did, in my quest for quarters for the night, was to test a theory suggested to me years before by old Avitabile, the Italian soldier of fortune who had been governor of Peshawar. "When you're like-a light in the pocket, boy, in a strange town, you got to find a whore-house, see, an' wheedle-wheedle your way roun' the madame, you know? Do I got to tell you? No, sir. Your shoulders an' moustaches—jus' like-a mine—it's like-a fall under a log. You charm, you talk, you tell any goddam lies—but you get that madame into bed, boom-boom-boom—why, she's glad to lodge you for a week, ne' mind for a night! Didn't Avitabile travel clear from Lisbon to Paris, an' I didn't pay one night's lodging, not-a one, you bet. Goddam it, does a gentleman got to stay in hotels?"

Well, if he could do it, so could I, and towards evening I set out to find a likely bawdy house. This, in New Orleans, was child's play; there may have been establishments in the Vieux Carré which were not bordellos, but precious few. All I had to do was find one with a susceptible madame, and take my ease for a few days.

It took me all evening, and four false starts. What I did in each case was to select a good-class house, send my card up to the proprietress by the nigger porter, and then address myself to the arch-harpy herself. I had a story all ready, and even now I must say it sounds not half bad. I explained that I was an Austrian gentleman in search of his sister, who had eloped with a profligate Englishman and been abandoned by him during a visit to the United States. Since then we had heard nothing of her, except an unconfirmed report that she had somehow found her way into ... into, er, an establishment such as madame was conducting. We were beside ourselves with grief and horror, and here was I, the son of the family, on a tragic quest to find the erring creature and bring her back to the bosom of her distracted but unforgiving parents. Her name was Charlotte, she was a mere eighteen, blonde and of exquisite beauty ... could madame render me any assistance in tracing her? Money, of course, was of no object, if only I could rescue my dear wilful sister from the dreadful plight into which she had fallen.

This, of course, was purely introductory, to let me sum up the madame and see if she was likely game. The first four weren't —beaky, sharp-eyed old harridans whom I wouldn't have galloped for a pension, anyway. But they swallowed the story—no doubt it sounded well, coming from six-foot Harry with his curly whiskers and melancholy brown eyes, to say nothing of his well-cut clobber and light cavalry airs. Three of them even went the length of making fruitless inquiries among their staffs; the fourth, I'm afraid, didn't fully understand me—she said she had never heard of my sister, but she would undertake to procure her for me for seventy-five dollars. As with the others, I bade her a courtly good-night, thanked her profusely, and withdrew.

At the fifth knocking-shop, I struck pure gold. It was a splendid establishment, all plush and crystal, with a nigger band playing wild music, and in the saloons off the main hall the finest of trollops on view, willowy creatures of every colour from cream to jet black, with beautiful gowns cut away so that their breasts were bare, and strutting like duchesses. It was plain to see that outside New Orleans, fornication was still in its infancy.

However, I had no time for these distractions. My business was with the madame, and as soon as I was ushered upstairs into her private apartment, I knew I was home. She was nearing fifty, a stately buxom piece who must have been a rare beauty and was still handsome, running to fat but well laced up in a green velvet gown which looked as though it must burst asunder at any moment. She was painted and powdered and jewelled like a May Day cuddy, with an ostrich plume in her red-dyed hair, and a big peacock fan which she used to disclose her fine bust and shoulders; it was this, and the quizzy gleam in her eye as she sized me up and down, that convinced me I need look no farther. Here was one who fancied Flashy, no error. The fact that she appeared to have been at the bottle already that evening may have helped; she swayed a mite too much as she walked, even for a retired strumpet. She was all affability—and to my astonishment, when she invited me to take a seat and state my requirements, her voice was purest Bow Bells. "Honnered to 'ave a gentleman of the nobility calling at hower little hestablish'nt," says she, simpering and pressing my hand warmly. "'Ow may we be of service, pray?" Well, thinks I, if I can't charm this one flat on her back, I've lost my way with women.

It took me exactly three-quarters of an hour by her fine grandfather clock, which I thought quite smart work on first acquaintance. Ten minutes disposed of my mythical sister, of whom my plump hostess had naturally never heard, although she expressed touching dismay ("Why, the wicked villain!" and "Ow, yore pore mama!"). Another ten were spent in idle gossip, after which she suggested some refreshment, and I sipped a very reasonable Moselle while she fluttered her eyelids and shoved her tits at me. After half an hour we were quite intimate, and I was murmuring in her ear and tweaking her bottom while she giggled and called me a great sauce; with forty minutes gone I was unbuttoning her dress at the back—I have uncanny skill at this —and in a trice I had her standing in her corset. Before she could turn round I had impaled her, and was subsiding into a chair with her on my lap. She gave one protesting squeal of "Oh, Lor' ", and then lay back against me—God, what a weight she was! I thought my thigh-bones would crack, but I bulled away for all I was worth, and the baggage revelled in it, plunging and writhing until I thought we must go over, chair and all. The clock chimed the three-quarters, I remember, just as we finished.

This broke the ice splendidly, of course, and to cut a longish and damned tiring story short, I didn't spend only the night at Mrs Susie Willinck's establishment, but the best part of a week. Avitabile was absolutely right, you see; if you manage to get round a madame, you're made. But I must say in honesty that I doubt if many madames are as susceptible as Susie was. She proved to be one of those rare creatures who are even jollier and nicer —and randier—than they look, give her a man who was handsome and impudent and made her laugh and was a good mount, and she would do anything for him—so it followed naturally that she took to me from the start. Of course, the fact that I was English helped —she found that out smartly enough, on the first night, the shrewd old strumpet, but instead of being furious at the way I'd imposed on her, she just shook with laughter and called me a bonny young rascal and hauled me on to the sofa again. I had to tell her my name was Comber, and that I was on the run from the American Navy—which was true, in its way, although she naturally took it that I was a deserter. She didn't care; I was something new, and a lusty rogue, and that was enough for her.

Mind you, I earned my keep. I've always been able to keep pace with most women, but this one, when roused, was like a succubus gone berserk. She had a knack of getting astride of me, pinning me down with her weight, and going to work in her own way; it was fearful, for the randy trollop would tease and plague me for close on an hour, until I was nearly bursting, and by the time she was done I would be ecstatically ruined, and certain sure I'd never be able to present arms again. On the other hand, she could be as soft as mush, and cry over me afterwards, which was rather disturbing. At first I put it down to her fondness for port, but in fact it was just that she was a genuinely sentimental soul—where lively young men were concerned, anyway.

Mind you, I wasn't complaining, either way; I realised I was uncommon lucky to have found just the billet I was looking for, and I'll say this for Susie, although she was like a wild beast in bed, she was damned good to me during my stay with her. I soon recognised that it wasn't just that she was unusually partial to Adam's arsenal; she was one of these large-hearted females who can't go to bed with a man without conceiving an affection for him, and wanting to cherish and own him, even. She was as soft in that way as any woman I can remember, which was remarkable, for she knew men, and was far too worldly-wise to have any illusions about me. She must have seen I was a wrong 'un from the minute she laid eyes on me, and especially when she realised I was only romping her for the sake of a few nights' lodging. But although she knew I was the kind of heartless scoundrel who would use her shamelessly and then slide out when it suited me, she couldn't help liking me, apparently. She knew after the first couple of days that she was growing too fond of me, and it frightened her, so that she wished me away at the same time as she wanted me to stay.

This ain't Flashy's vanity, by the way; she admitted it herself, when I'd been there about four days and spoke about moving on.

"I orter be thankful," says she. "You're as big a villain as the rest—worse, prob'ly. I know you'll just break my heart in the end, if you stay."

Thinking back to the previous night, it struck me that whatever was in danger of breaking belonged to me, and it wasn't my heart. "Oh, come, now, it's short acquaintance to be talking like that," says I.

"You would, though," says she, smiling kind of wry. "I know your sort, an' what's worse, I know me. I was a fool even to let you in the 'ouse. You'd think, with all I've seen, an' the rotten swine I've known, that I'd 'ave more sense; I've been 'ere before. You men—you don't care a button; it's just another rattle to you, an' thanks ever so, dearie, an' good-night. But I like you too much as it is, an' I know what comes of that. Another two days an' you'd be bored, an' a flabby ol' faggot like me can't 'old a man against the kind of merchandise there is in this 'ouse—little yellow sluts with hard titties—humph!" She shook her head. "The trouble is—it'd hurt. I spose you think that's funny, from an' ol' bag like me."

"No," says I, "but since I'm not staying anyway, you needn't worry. I'll tell you this much—I may not love you, Susie, but I like you, and you're a damned sight better in bed than any of your fellow girls would be."

"Gammon!" says she, hitting me with her fan, but she looked pleased. She didn't believe me for a moment, of course, but for once I wasn't buttering her. It's one of the great truths, that young pieces aren't in it where love-making is concerned, compared with their mothers and aunts who have been about long enough to enjoy it. For the real thing, give me a well-fleshed matron every time, with her eyes wide open and a mind of her own. But women, of course, will never credit this.

The difficulty about my leaving, of course, was that the best way to get out of New Orleans was by the river, and that meant running the gauntlet of the Navy people who might be looking for me. Thanks to Susie, whose acquaintances were legion, there was no trouble about getting a passage to England, and it was arranged that I should go two days later, on a packet bound for Liverpool. One advantage to it was that she would weigh anchor at night, when I'd have a good chance of slipping aboard unnoticed.

There was the question of my fare, and here Susie turned up trumps. She would advance me the cash—not, she said, that she expected it back. I protested at this, and she laughed and chucked me under the chin.

"I've heard that, an' all," says she. "If I'd a guinea for every dollar I've given to stake a man out of town, I'd be a rich woman, an' never once did I see a penny of it back. Oh, I know—you're full o' good intentions now, when you need the cash, but come next week you'll 'ave forgotten all about it."

"I'll pay it back, Susie," says I. "I promise."

"Ducky," says she, "I'd rather not—honest. I don't want to hear from you no more—really, I don't."

"Why ever not?"

"Oh, hold your tongue!" snaps she, and turned away, dabbing at herself. "There—now! Me face'll be all to do up again. Go on, let me alone!" And she went off, sniffing. Which, I must admit, I found very gratifying.

You may think I've dwelt on my meeting with Susie at some length, but there's reason for it. For one thing, it may be a valuable pointer to young men who come after, and who find themselves adrift in a strange town. Secondly, it had a bearing on my life many years on, as my later memoirs will show. And she was unique, too: among all the women I've known she must be about the only one that I never had hard feelings with, on either side. And she could touch me, somehow—at least I remember thinking, the night I left, that in all the journeys I'd set off on before, never a woman had been at such pains to see I had everything packed and ready, and that my clothes were brushed, and my money safe, and the rest of it. She fussed over me in a way that none of the others—wife, aunts, mistresses, whores, legions of them—had ever done. It's strange, and no doubt significant, that the warmest leave-taking I remember should be from a bawdy-house.

I set out about ten, with a nigger carrying my valise, and Susie hustled me away. "Give us a kiss, dearie. Now, be off with you. 'Ave a glass in the Cider Cellars for me." She was absolutely crying, the soft old slut. "An' take care of yourself you—you big scallawag, you!"

We slipped out of the side gate into the alley. It was one of those lazy, warm nights, with many stars, and above the hum of the town I could hear a distant steamboat whistle on the river, where my ship, the *Anglesey Queen*, would be lying. We set off down the dark lane together, and just as we reached its end a dark shadow loomed up before us and I was aware of others suddenly coming in at my back. I stopped dead, and the figure in front of me, a tall man in a broad-brimmed hat, said:

"Hold it right there, mister. Hands away from your sides. Now, don't make a move, because you're covered front and rear!"

I must have heard the same sort of thing barked at me in a dozen different languages, and it has never failed to paralyse me on the spot. My first thought was that these must be American Navy men, and my heart froze inside me. How the devil had they traced me? Could I bolt?—but there wasn't a hope. They knew their business too well—one a couple of yards dead ahead, and two others on my flanks, slightly behind me. But if I couldn't bolt I could bluff.

"*Wer ruft mich?*" I demanded, trying to sound angry. "*Was wollen sie?*"

"Don't come your Dutch on me, Mr Comber," says the big one, and that settled it. They were Navy men, and I was done for.

"You, nigger, gimme that bag," he went on. "Billy, take him down to the levee and let him go. And now, mister, you step ahead right lively. Do as you're told and you won't get hurt; try to run and you're a dead man."

Sick with fear I started forward, with the big man and his mate right behind me, down a side-street and then, at their direction, into a maze of alleys until I had no earthly idea where I was. Why were they taking me out of the main ways, and why had they taken the nigger to the levee before letting him go? My G - d, were they going to murder me?—and at that instant the big fellow growls:

"Stop right there," and came up beside me.

At this my nerve broke. "What d'you want with me? What are you going to do? In God's name, if you're the Navy, I can explain, I can—"

"We ain't the Navy," says he, shortly. "And we ain't gonna hurt you." And amazingly he added: "You're the last man on God's earth I'd want to hurt."

I gaped at him, trying to make out the shadowy face beneath the hat brim, but he went on:

"I've got a black bag here, and I'm gonna put it over your head, so you don't see where you're goin'. Now, don't fret ye'self; do as you're told an' you'll come to no harm."

He slipped the bag over my head, and I choked in its coarse muffled folds, panicking, but he took my arm and said:

"Straight ahead now. Easy does it."

We walked for three hundred and sixty eight paces through innumerable turns, and then stopped. I heard a gate creak, and when we went forward there was gravel beneath my feet. Then up stone steps, and a door opened, and we were in a house. Forward up stairs—thickly carpeted, too. I was suffocating with dread and astonishment by the time we had passed down a well-carpeted corridor, and I heard knuckles knock on a door and a voice call: "Enter!" I was pushed forward, the bag was whipped from my head, and as the door closed behind me I found myself blinking in the light of a great, well-furnished library. Behind a big oak desk a little bald-headed man was standing eyeing me benevolently over his spectacles, and waving a hand to an empty chair.

"Pray be seated, Mr Comber. And before you assail me with angry protests—which you're perfectly entitled to do, I confess—allow me to extend my most sincere and heartfelt apologies for the rather ... er ... cavalier manner of my invitation. Now, won't you be seated, sir, please? No one intends you the least harm—quite the contrary, I assure you. Sit down, sir, do."

"Who the blazes are you?" I demanded. He was obviously friendly, and a kindly-looking little fellow in his old-fashioned neckercher and breeches, with bright grey eyes that peered eagerly at me. "And what's the meaning of this?" Now that I was half-past fear I was prepared to be angry.

"There, now, that's exactly what I mean to tell you, if you'll only be seated," says he soothingly. "That's better. A glass of port?—no, perhaps brandy would be better. Settling for the nerves, eh?—though I don't think yours are nerves that need much settling, young man, from all I've heard."

Well, I'll always take brandy when it's kindly offered, so I fastened on the glass and gulped a mouthful down. And as he went back to his desk I took stock of the richly-furnished room, with its fine carpet and dark panelling, and found myself reassured, if bewildered.

"Now, then," says he, "that feels better, eh? Well, Mr Comber, I owe you an explanation as well as an apology, so you shall have it." He was American, but well-educated, and when you took a closer view of him you saw that he wasn't quite such an old Cheeryble as he looked. "Let me begin by astonishing you. I have been waiting to make your acquaintance this past few days. Indeed, if you hadn't left tonight to board the *Anglesey Queen* —there, there, sir, all shall be made plain presently—I was preparing to come and call on you. Oh, yes, I much wanted to meet you. We have kept a very close eye on you indeed, sir, since you arrived in Washington, although I confess we lost you for a moment when you gave the good Captain Fairbrother the slip." He chuckled. "Very neat, that. Of course, we quite understood. Quite understood. Didn't we?"

This was bewildering, but I had my nerve back. "Did you? If you understand so much, you won't mind enlightening me. Who or what are you—are you American government?"

He smiled. "No—not exactly. Although we have great influence, and many highly-placed friends, in that same government —that government which, I'm afraid, has been rather embarrassing you lately with insistent questions. Naturally—you're in possession of what I believe one senior official called dangerous information, and Washington wants it. But you want to take it straight home to England—perfectly right, sir. So you gave them the slip, and behold you tonight preparing to set sail secretly for Liverpool."

He hadn't quite got hold of the wrong end of the stick, you see, but very nearly. His only mistake lay in believing that I was Comber, and in deducing the wrong reason for my attempted flight from New Orleans. A flight which, rot him, he was putting in severe jeopardy.

"Then would you kindly tell me," says I, "why you have hauled me here at gun-point, instead of letting me catch my ship? In heaven's name, sir, I must get aboard her—"

"You would never have got aboard her," says he. "The Navy Department want you, Mr Comber, as a witness against those slaver friends of yours, and the U.S. Government, I know, wish to question you further about—those certain names you have in your head. Slave-trade names, I believe." And suddenly he wasn't a genial little buffer any more; his mouth was like a rat-trap. "Believe me, Mr Comber, the levee is well-watched; they know which way you'll try to go."

"And by what right would they try to stop me?" says I, brazening. By George, if they ever found out I wasn't Comber, they'd have right enough. Maybe they *had* found out—but if they had my omniscient little friend evidently hadn't.

"Oh, no right at all," says he. "But governments can generally arrange diplomatic reasons for delaying departures. I suppose they might hold on to you for a few weeks—until your ambassador pressed them into letting you go home. By then, Washington would hope, you might have let slip those names they want to know about."

I saw I must play Comber's part for all I was worth, so I smiled grimly. "They have no hope of that; those names are for my chiefs in London, and no one else. And if you think—whoever you are—that you can get them out of me—"

"My dear Mr Comber." He held up a hand. "I'm not interested. My concern with the slave trade lies in quite another direction —the same direction, I believe, as your own. That is why you are here. That is why my agents have traced you, even into the house of ill fame where you took refuge." Well, thinks I, I hope they didn't trace too close, or they must have got an eyeful. "Thus we knew of the passage home its proprietress arranged for you—I take it she is an English anti-slavery agent ... but there, the less said, the better. Thus we were able to intercept you tonight."

"You know a lot," says I. "Now, look here; I've heard everything but what I want to know. Who are you, and what d'you want with me?"

He looked at me steadily. "You have heard, I am sure, of the underground railroad."

Six months earlier I wouldn't have known what he meant, but when you've been in the company of slavers, as I had been, you recognise the phrase. Spring had mentioned it; I'd heard it spoken about, low-voiced, in Susie's brothel.

"It's a secret society for stealing slaves, and helping them to escape, isn't it? To Canada."

"It is an organisation for saving souls!" snaps he, and once again he didn't look half amiable. "It is an army that fights the most horrible tyranny of our time—the blasphemous iniquity of black slavery! It is an army without colours, or ranks, or pay— an army of dedicated men and women who labour secretly to release their black brethren from bondage and give them liberty. Yes, we steal slaves! Yes, we run them to free soil. Yes, we die for doing it—like them we are hunted with dogs, and tortured and hanged and shot if we are caught by the brutes who own and trade in human flesh. But we do it gladly, because we are marching in Christ's army, sir, and we will not lay down our weapons until the last shackle is broken, the last branding iron smashed, the last raw-hide whip burned, and the last slave free!"**

I gathered he was an abolitionist. By gad, he was in a fine sweat about it, too, but now he sat back and spoke in a normal voice.

"Forgive me. As though I need to say such things to you. Why, you take a thousand risks for our one, you put your life in the hazard in the nethermost hell of this foul traffic. Oh, we know all about you, Mr Comber—as you yourself said in a certain Washington office, 'Walls have ears.' The underground railroad has ears, certainly, and it heard your name in Washington, and the heroic work you did in bringing the *Balliol College* and that scoundrel Spring to book. Which reminds me of a privilege I had promised myself tonight, but have overlooked." He got to his feet. "Mr Comber, may I have the honour to shake your hand?"

And blow me, he seized my fist and pumped it hard enough to start water out of me. I didn't mind, but the thought occurred to me, here I was again being congratulated on my dauntless devotion, when all the time it had been frantic poltroonery. But it had done the trick, which just goes to show: we also serve who only turn and run.

"Thank you, sir, thank you," says he. "You have made me a happy man. Now, may I tell you how you may make me happier still?"

I wasn't sure about this, but I sat down again and listened.

I couldn't decide whether this little blighter was going to turn out well for me or not.

"As you know, we of the underground railroad rescue slaves wherever we can—from plantations, markets, pens, wherever they may be—and send them north secretly to the free states beyond the Ohio river and the Mason–Dixon line. Alone, they could never hope to make the journey, so we send with them our agents, who pose as slave-owners and slave-dealers, and convoy the unfortunates to safety. It is perilous work, as I have said, and our roll of martyrs grows longer every day. This is a savage country, sir, and while there are many in government who love and assist our work, government itself cannot condone or protect us, because we break the law—man's law, not God's. We are criminals, sir, in the eyes of our country, but we are proud of our crimes."

He was almost away again, but checked himself.

"Now, all slaves are important to us, however lowly, but some are more important than others. Such a one is George Randolph. Have you heard of him? No, well you shall. You have heard of Nat Turner, the slave who led a great rebellion in Virginia, and was barbarously executed by his tormentors? Well, Randolph is such another—but a greater man, better educated, more intelligent, with a greater vision. Twice he has tried to organise insurrection, twice he has failed; three times he has escaped; twice he has been recaptured. He is a fugitive at this moment—but we have him safe, and God willing they shall never take him again."

Comber would have applauded, so I said, "Oh, bravo!" and looked pleased.

"Bravo indeed," says he, and then looked solemn. "But all is not done. Randolph must be taken in safety to Canada—what a blow that will be in our cause! Why, sir, think of what such a man can do, when he is on free soil. He can talk, he can write, he can go abroad, not only in Canada but in England, in our own free states—I tell you, sir, the burning words of such a man, striking the ears of the civilised world, will do more to rekindle the fire against slavery than all our white journalists and orators can accomplish. The world will see a man like themselves, and yet greater—a man fit for a chair in our finest universities, or to sit in the highest councils of a nation—but a black man, sir, with the whip-marks on his back and the shackle-scars on his legs! They will understand, as they have never understood, what slavery is! They will feel the whip and shackles on their own bodies, and they will cry out: 'This infamy shall not be!' "

Well, it seemed to call for something, so I said:

"Capital. First-rate. This news will be welcomed with joy in England, I'm sure, and as soon as I am home again you may rely..."

"But Mr Comber," says he, "this is still to be achieved. George Randolph is not in Canada yet—he is still here, a hunted runaway. The journey to freedom lies ahead of him."

"But is that difficult? For your splendid organisation? I mean, you have shown me, tonight, how far-reaching it is. Why, you know as much about me as I do myself—almost. Your agents..."

"Oh, we have many agents; our intelligence system is extensive. We have an eye at every window in this land, sir, and an ear at every door; information is no difficulty. But most of our spies are black; most are still slaves. Collecting intelligence is one thing, but running slaves to Canada is quite another. Here we need white agents, dedicated, resolute, and bold, and these are pitifully few. Many are willing, but only a handful are able. And even then, they have become too well known. Of the gallant young men who ran our last three convoys one is dead, one in jail, and the third in Canada, unable to return because he would certainly be arrested. I have not one that I can send with Randolph, sir, not one that I could trust. For with a cargo of such importance, I cannot risk sending any but the hardiest, the bravest, the least suspected. Do you see my plight, sir? Every day that Randolph hides in New Orleans his danger grows—the enemy has spies also. I must get him out, and quickly. Can you understand?"

I understood all right, but ass that I was, I didn't see what it had to do with me. I suggested sending him by sea.

"Impossible. The risk is too great. Ironically, his safest route is the one that would appear most dangerous—up the Mississippi to the free states. One slave in a coffle may pass unnoticed— my one fearful problem is the white agent to go with him. I tell you, Mr Comber, I was at my wits' end—and then, in answer to my prayers, I had word of you from Washington, and that you would be coming to Orleans."

I absolutely said: "Christ!" but he was in full spate.

"I saw then that God had sent you. Not only are you a man dedicated to fighting the abomination of slavery, but you are one who scorns danger, who has come unscathed through perils ten times greater than this, who has the experience, the intelligence —nay, the brilliance—and the cold courage such an enterprise requires. And, above all this, you are not known!" He smacked his fist on the table excitedly. "If I had all the world to choose from, I should have asked for such a man as you. You, who I had never heard of ten days ago. Mr Comber, will you do this for me —and strike yet another, greater blow above all those you have surely struck already?"

Well, of all the appalling nonsense I had ever heard, this beat everything, even Bismarck. By George, they were two of a kind— the same fanatic gleam in the eye, the same fierce determination to thrust a hapless fellow-human into the stew, head first, to further their own lunatic schemes. But Bismarck had had a pistol to my head; this idiot hadn't. I was on the point of telling him straight what I thought of his revolting suggestion, laughing right in his eager little face, and I suddenly checked—I was Comber. How would *he* have refused—my God, he probably wouldn't, the reckless fool. I had to go very canny.

"Well, sir? Well—is this not such a crusade as your heart desires?"

There was a fine, short answer to that, but I daren't give it. "Sir," says I, "this is a startling proposal. Oh, you honour me, indeed you do. But sir, my duty is to my country—I must return at once—"

He laughed exultantly. "But of course, and you shall! You may do this thing and be in England *faster* than if you wait here to catch a packet home. Listen, sir—you would go upriver by steamboat, as a slave-trader, with a coffle for—Kentucky, let us say. But you sail straight on to Cincinnati—why, you will be there in six days, pass Randolph to our agent there, and continue to Pittsburgh. You may be in New York in a week or a little more from now, sir, and a sailing there will have you home far more speedily than a boat from Orleans—if you could even get one here. Remember, the Navy are watching for you."

"But, sir," I protested, cudgelling fearfully for excuses, "consider the danger, not to me, but to my own mission—the information I hold, if I went astray, would be lost to my own government, and yours—"

"I have thought of it," cries he. Of course, he would, rot his measly little soul. "You may commit it to paper here, sir, this very night, under seal, and I swear upon my honour it shall go straight to London. No one in Washington, no one at all, shall see it. You have my word. But, Mr Comber," he went on earnestly, "there is no risk of that. You will come through without the slightest danger—no slave-catcher will give *you* a second glance. They know *us*, sir, but not you. And you will be serving the cause dear to your heart; I implore you, sir, say you will aid us in this."

Well, I knew the cause dear to my heart, if he didn't. "Sir," says I. "I am sorry. Believe me, I would aid you if I could, but my duty must come above my personal inclination."

"But you will be doing that duty, don't you see? Better than if you refuse—for if you do, why then, I could only apologise for bringing you here, and—send you back to the Navy Department. I should be reluctant—it would delay you still further, for they would keep you here for the trial of Spring and his pirates. But that would plainly be my only course."

So there it was. Blackmail, the pious little scoundrel. Oh, he was twinkling solemnly; he thought, you see, that all I had to fear from being delivered back to the clutches of the Navy and the U.S. Government was delay and more inconvenient questioning. He didn't know that if I appeared at the *Balliol College* trial my true identity must appear, and it would be into the dock for Flashy with the rest of the crew. Then it would be prison—my God, they might even hang us. Against that, the risk—which he said was no risk—of running a fugitive nigger to Ohio. He had me, the little serpent, but he didn't know *how* he had me, and he mustn't find out.

Well, if I refused him, I was done for, that was sure. So presumably, I must accept. I tried to think straight, tried to reason, tried to see a way out, but couldn't. My innards quailed at what he had proposed, but it was only a risk against a certainty. And *he* didn't think the risk was much at all—not that I put any faith in that. What could I do, though? I've been trapped so often, between two loathsome choices, and it's in my coward's nature to choose what seems the less dangerous. That was all I could do now, at this moment, and see what turned up. Yes, that was it: I must accept, and be ready to fly at the first hint of danger. If I must take this lout Randolph north, well, there it was. If things went adrift, I'd slide out somehow. I'd deny him, if I had to. But if all went well—and the chances were they would —why, I'd be half way home, with Spring and the U.S. Navy and the rest far astern. Looking back, I can only say it seemed the lesser of two evils. Well, I've been wrong before.

When you have to bow the knee, do it with grace.

"Very well, sir," says I, looking solemn, "I must accept. I must combine duty—" and I forced myself to look him in the eye "—with the desire of my heart, which is to assist you and your worthy cause."

Comber couldn't have said it better, and the little monster was all over me. He wrung my hand, and called me a saviour, and then he got business-like again. He called in another chap, a long-faced zealot, this one, and introduced me "—our own names," he added to me, "I think it wiser not to divulge to you, Mr Comber. I choose to be known as Mr Crixus, which you will no doubt consider appropriate, ha-ha."[34]

And then it was all joy and good fellowship and be damned, they were so delighted, and my mind was in a turmoil, but I couldn't for the life of me see a way clear. Crixus bustled about, calling in two other chaps who I suspected were the men who had brought me, and told them the glad news, and they shook hands, too, and blessed me, full of solemn delight. Yes, they said, all was ready, and the sooner things were started the better. Crixus nodded eagerly, rubbing his hands, and then beamed at me:

"And now I promise myself another little pleasure. I told you, Mr Comber, that George Randolph was in hiding. He is—in this house, and it shall now be my privilege to present to each other two of the greatest champions of our cause. Come, gentlemen."

So we filed out, downstairs, and came to the back of the house, and into a plain room where a young nigger was sitting at a table, writing by the light of an oil lamp. He looked up, but didn't rise, and one sight of his face told me that here was a fellow I didn't like above half.

He was about my age, slim but tall, and a quadroon. He had a white man's face, bar the thickish lips, with fine brows and a most arrogant, damn-you-me-lad expression. He sat while Crixus poured out the tale, turning his pencil in his hand, and when he had been told that here was the man who would pilot him to the promised land, and Crixus had got round to presenting me, he got up languidly and held out a fine brown hand. I took it, and it was like a woman's, and then he dropped it and turned to Crixus.

"You are in no doubt?" says he. His voice was cold, and very precise. A right uppity white nigger, this one was. "We cannot afford a mistake this time. There have been too many in the past."

Well, this took me flat aback; for a moment I almost forgot my own fears. And Crixus, to my astonishment, was all eagerness to reassure him.

"None, George, none. As I have told you, Mr Comber is a proved fighter on our side; you could not be in better hands."

"Ah," says Randolph, and sat down again. "That is very well, then. He understands the importance of my reaching Canada. Now, tell me, exactly how do we proceed from here? I take it the *modus operandi* is as we have already discussed it, and that Mr Comber is capable of falling in with it precisely."

I just gaped. I don't know what I had expected—one of your woolly-headed darkies, I suppose, massa-ing everyone, and pathetically grateful that someone was going to risk his neck to help him to freedom. But not your Lord George Bloody Randolph, no indeed. You'd have thought he was doing Crixus a favour, as the old fellow went through the plan, and our runaway sat, nodding and occasionally frowning, putting in his points and pursing his lips, like a judge on the bench. Finally he says:

"Very well. It should answer satisfactorily. I cannot pretend that I welcome some of the ... er ... details. To be chained in a gang of blacks—that is a degradation which I had hoped was behind me. But since it must be—" he gave Crixus a pained little smile "—why, it must be endured. I suppose it is a small price to pay. My spirit can sustain it, I hope."

"It can, George, it can," cries Crixus. "After all you have suffered, it is a little thing, the last little thing."

"Ah, yes—always the last little thing!" says Randolph. "We know about the camel, do we not, and the final feather. Do you know, when I look back, I ask myself how I have borne it? And this, as you say, is a trifle—why should it seem so bitter a trifle? But there." He shrugged, and then turned in his chair to look at me—I was still standing, too.

"And you, sir? You know the gravity of what lies before us. Your task should not be hard—merely to ride on a steamboat, in rather greater comfort than I shall be. Are you confident of . . ."

"Yes, yes, George," says Crixus. "Mr Comber knows; I talked to to him in the library."

"Ah," says Randolph. "In the library." He looked about him, with a little, crooked smile. "In the library."

"Oh, now, George," cries Crixus, "you know we agreed it was safer here. . . ."

"I know." Randolph held up a slim hand. "It is of no importance. However, I was speaking to Mr Comber—yes, you will have been told, sir, how vitally important is this journey of ours. So I ask again, do you trust yourself entirely to carry it through—simple though it should be?"

I could have kicked the black bastard off his chair. But caught as I was, in the trap Crixus had sprung on me, what was there to do but cram down my resentment on top of my fears—I was an overloaded man, believe me—and say:

"No, I've no doubts. Play your part on the lower deck, and I'll play mine in the saloon—George."

He stiffened just a little. "You know, I believe I prefer Mr Randolph, on first acquaintance."

I nearly hit him, but I held it in. "D'you want me to call you Mr Randolph on the steamboat?" says I. "People might talk—don't ye think?"

"We shall be on the steamboat soon enough," says he, and there our discussion ended, with Crixus fidgetting nervously as he ushered me out, and telling Randolph to get some sleep, because we must soon be off. But when the door had closed I let out my breath with a whoosh, and Crixus says hurriedly:

"Please, Mr Comber—well, I know what you may be thinking. George can be . . . difficult, I guess, but—well, we have not endured what he has endured. You saw his sensitivity, the delicacy of his nature. Oh, he is a genius, sir—he is three parts white, you know. Think what slavery must do to such a spirit! I know he is very different from the negroes with whom you are used to dealing. Dear me, I sometimes myself find it . . . but there. I remember what he means to our cause—and to all those poor, black people." He blinked at me. "Compassionate him, sir, as you compassionate them. I know, in your own loving heart, you will do so."

"Compassion, Mr Crixus, is the last thing he wants from me," says I, and I added privately: and it's the last thing he'll get, too. Indeed, as later I tried unsuccessfully to sleep under that strange roof, I found myself thinking that I'd find Master Randolph's company just a little more than I could stomach—not that I need see him much. My God, thinks I, what am I doing? How the devil did I get into this? But even as my fears reawoke, it came back to the same thing: almost any risk was preferable to letting the U.S. authorities get me, unmask me, and—. After all, this would be the quicker way home, and if things went adrift, well, Master Randolph could shift for himself while Flashy took to the timber. He would be all right; he was a genius.

If ever you have to run slaves—which seems unlikely nowadays, although you never can tell what may happen if we have the Liberals back—the way to do it is by steamboat. The *Sultana*, bound for Cincinnati by way of Baton Rouge, Vicksburg, Memphis and Cairo, beat the old *Balliol College* all to nothing. It was like cruising upriver in a fine hotel, with the niggers out of sight, mind and smell, no pitching or rolling to disturb the stomach, and above all, no John Charity Spring.

The speed and sureness with which Crixus and his minions organised our departure had almost banished my first fears. I had woken on a resolve to run from the house and take my chance with the Navy, but they kept far too close a watch on things for that, and by the afternoon I was glad of it. Crixus spent four hours drilling me in the minutest details of the journey, about cash, and passage tickets, and how the slaves would be fed en route, how I might answer casual inquiries and take part in river gossip without appearing too out of place, and by the end of it I realised how little chance I would have stood as a fugitive on my own account. The main thing was to talk as little as possible; there were enough Englishmen on the river in those days to make an extra one nothing out of the ordinary, but since I was meant to be a new-fledged slave trader it was important that I shouldn't make any foolish slips. My story would be that I had recently forsaken African blackbirding in favour of river dealing—I had all the expert knowledge for that, at any rate.

Really, it was astonishing how easy it was. In mid-afternoon, with a broad-brimmed planter's hat, my long-tailed coat, and half-boots, I joined my coffle in the cellars of Crixus's house. There were six of them, in light ankle irons, with Randolph in the middle, looking damned miffed, which cheered me considerably. The other five, by the way, were free niggers in Crixus's employ, and like him devoted to the underground railroad. There was much hand-shaking and God-blessing, and then we were conducted through what seemed like miles of cellars to a deserted yard, from which it was a short step to the levee.

I had my heart in my mouth as I strode along, trying to look like Simon Legree, with my gang of coons shuffling behind; I had protested to Crixus that if the Navy were on the look-out for me the waterfront would be a deuced dangerous place, but he said not at the steamboat wharves, and he was right. We pushed through the crowds of niggers, stevedores, boatmen, passengers and bummarees without anyone giving us a glance; there were coffles by the score, with fellows dressed like me shepherding and spitting and cursing, bawling to each other and chewing on big black cigars; old ladies with hat-boxes and parasols and men with carpet-bags and stove-pipe hats were hurrying for their boats; niggers with carts were loading piles of luggage; the big twin smoke-stacks were belching and the whistles squealing; it was like the Tower of Babel with the scaffolding about to give way. I pushed ahead until I found the *Sultana*, and within an hour we were thrashing upstream, close inshore, on the slow bend past what is now called Gretna—and with the great jam of ships and rafts and scuttling small boats along its levee, anything less like the real Gretna you never saw. My niggers were stowed down on the main deck at water-level, where the baggage and steerage people go, and I was reclining in my state-room up on the texas deck, smoking a cigar and deciding that things had turned out not so badly after all.

You see, it had gone so well and naturally in the first hour that I was beginning to believe Crixus. The purser fellow had accepted my ticket, in the name of James K. Prescott, without a blink, and bawled to one of his niggers to come an' take the gennelman's coffle and see 'em disposed forrard, thankee sir, straight ahead there to the stairway, an' mind your head. And with the boat so crowded with passengers I felt security returning; this looked like an easy trip to the point where one Caleb Cape, trader and auctioneer, would meet me at Cincinnati and take my coffle, and I would steam on up the Ohio, free as a bird.

In the meantime I set out to enjoy the trip as far as possible. The *Sultana* was a big fast boat, and held the New Orleans–

Louisville record of five and a half days; she had three decks from the texas to the water-line, with the boiler deck in the middle.[35] This was where the main saloon and state-rooms were, all crystal chandeliers and gilding and plush, with carved furniture and fine carpets; my own cabin had an oil painting on the door, and there were huge pictures in the main rooms. All very fine, in a vulgar way, and the passengers matched it; you may have heard a great deal about Southern charm and grace, and there's something in it where Virginia and Kentucky are concerned—Robert Lee, for instance, was as genteel an old prig as you'd meet on Pall Mall —but it don't hold for the Mississippi valley. There they were rotten with cotton money in those days, with gold watch-chains and walking-sticks, loud raucous laughter, and manners that would have disgraced a sty. They spat their "terbacker" juice on the carpets, gorged noisily in the dining saloon—the sight of jellied quail being shovelled down with a spoon and two fingers, and falling on a shirt-front with a diamond the size of a shilling in it, is a sight that dwells with me still, and I ain't fastidious as a rule. They hawked and belched and picked their teeth and swilled great quantities of brandy and punch, and roared to each other in their hideous plantation voices.

Theirs weren't the only manners to cause me concern, either. That first evening I went down to the main deck to see that my slaves were being properly housed and fed, as a good owner should, and to enjoy the sight of the precious Master Randolph regaling himself on pulse and pone. A slave's life didn't suit him one little bit; he had taken his place in the coffle that afternoon with a very ill grace, and much self-pitying nobility for Crixus's benefit. When he and his fellows were herded off to their passage quarters he had still been damned peaked and sulky, and now he was sitting with a bowl of hash from the communal copper, sniffing at it with disgust.

"How d'ye like it, George?" says I. "You and the other niggers feeding well?"

He gave me a glance of sheer hate, and seeing there was no one else at hand, he hissed:

"This filth is inedible! Look at it—smell it, if you can bear the nauseating stuff!"

I sniffed the bowl; it would have sickened a dog. "Capital stew!" says I. "Eat it down, heartily now, or I shall begin to fear I have been spoiling you, my boy. Now, you other niggers, are you all pitching into your vittles, hey? That's the spirit."

The other five all cried: "Yes, massa, shore 'nuff, mighty fine, massa." Either they had more acting gumption than Randolph or else they liked the awful muck. But he, all a-quiver with indignation, whispers fiercely:

"Capital stew, indeed! Could you bear to eat this foulness?"

"Probably not," says I, "but I'm not a nigger, d'ye see." And without another glance at him I strolled off to my own dinner, resolving to describe it to him later. I never believe in neglecting the education of my inferiors.

It was worth describing, too. Mississippi food, once you get outside Orleans, tends to be robust and rich, and I wolfed my stewed chicken, prime steak and creamed chocolate with all the more relish for the thought of Randolph squatting on the main deck grubbing at his gristle. I had champagne with it, too, and a very passable brandy, and finally topped the whole thing off with a buxom little cracker girl in my cabin. Her name was Penny or Jenny, I forget which; she had dyed gold hair which went vilely with her yellow satin dress, and she was one of your squealing hoydens, but she had tremendous energy and high pointed breasts of which she was immensely proud, which made up for a lot. Most of the women on the boat were noisy, by the way; the respectable ones clacked and squawked to each other interminably, and the mistresses and whores, of whom there seemed to be a great number, were brassy enough to be heard in San Francisco. Penny (or Jenny) was one of the quieter ones; she didn't scream with laughter above once a minute.

I was lying there, drowsy and well satisfied, listening to her prattling, when a nigger waiter comes up with a message that I was wanted on the main deck—something to do with my coffle, he said. Wondering what the devil was what, I went down, and to my rage and concern discovered that it was that confounded George up to his nonsense again.

The overseer was swearing and stamping over in the corner where my slaves were, with Randolph standing in front of him looking as arrogant as Caesar.

"What's the matter with it, damn ye?" the overseer was shouting, and then, seeing me:

"Say, look here, Mist' Prescott—here's this jim-dandy nigger o' yours don' like this yere 'commodation. No suh, 'pears like 'taint good enough for him. Now, then!"

"What's this I hear, George?" says I, pushing forward. "What are you about, my boy? Turning up your nose at the quarters —what's wrong with them, sir?"

He looked me straight in the eye, with as much side as old Lord Cardigan.

"We have been given no straw to make beds for ourselves. We are entitled to this; it is covered in the money you have paid for our passage."

"Well, — me drunk, will ye hear that, now?" cries the overseer. "Entye—entitt—ent-what-the-hell-you-say! Don' you give me none o' your shines, ye black rascal! Beds, by thunder! You'll lay right down where you're told, or by cracky you'll be *knocked* down! Who're you, that you gotta have straw to keep yore tender carcase offen the floor? 'Tother hands is layin' on it, ain't they? Now, you git right down there, d'ye hear?"

"My master has paid for us to have straw," says Randolph, looking at me. "The other slaves over yonder have it; only our coffle goes without."

"Well, there *ain't* no more goddamed straw, you no-good impident son-of-a-bitch!" cries the overseer. "So now! I never heerd the like—"

I could have felled that bloody ass Randolph on the spot— perhaps I should have done. Couldn't the fool understand that he must behave as a slave, even if he didn't feel like one? How the devil he ever existed on a plantation was beyond me—it must have taken a saint or a lunatic to put up with his insolent airs. All I could do was play the just master, kindly but firm.

"Come, come, George," I said sternly. "Let us have no more of this. Lie down where you are told directly—what, is this how you repay my kind usuage, by impertinence? Have you forgotten yourself altogether, that you speak back to a white man? Lie down at once, sir, this instant!"

He stared at me; I was urging him with my eyes, and he had just wit enough to obey, but with no great humility, plumping down on the deck and folding his arms stubbornly round his knees. The overseer growled.

"I'd take the starch outer *that* jackanapes right smart, if he was mine. You be 'vised, Mist' Prescott, an' give that uppity yaller bastard a good dressin' down, or he'll have the whole passel on 'em as bad as hisself. Beds, by Christ! An' sassin' back to me! That's the trouble with all these fancy house-niggers, with bein' roun' white folks they start thinkin' *they* white, too. Peacocky high-an'-mighties, every last dam' one of them. He'll have bin brought up 'mong white ladies, I don't doubt; too much dam' pettin' when he's young. You trim him up smart, Mist' Prescott, like I say, or he'll be a heap o' trouble to ye."

He stumped off, muttering to himself, and Randolph sneered softly to himself.

"The gentleman is not without perception," says he. "He, at least, was not brought up among white ladies; white sows, perhaps." He glared up at me. "We are entitled to straw to lie on —why did you not insist that he provides it? Isn't it enough that I am chained up like a beast in this verminous place, fed on nauseating slops? Aren't you meant to protect me—you, who neglect me to the mercies of that uncouth white scum?"

I wondered if the fellow was insane—not for the way he spoke to me, but for the purblind stupidity with which he overlooked the position he was in, the role he was meant to be playing. He was five days away from freedom, and yet the idiot insisted on drawing attention to himself and provoking trouble. Ordinarily I'd have taken my boot to him, but he so mystified me that I was alarmed. I glanced round; the overseer was out of sight.

"Come over by the rail," says I, and when we were standing apart:

"Look—haven't you got sense enough to keep your mouth shut and your head down? Where the hell do you think you are— the House of Lords? D'ye think it matters whether you get straw or not—or whether I've paid for it or not? D'ye expect me to take your side against a white man—it'd be the talk of the boat in five minutes, you fool. Just you forget your lofty opinion of yourself for once, and talk humble, and don't be so damned particular, or you'll never see Ohio this trip!"

"I need no advice from you!" he flashed back. "You would be better remembering the duty you have promised to do, which is to take me north in safety, than to spend your time in gorging with white-trash sluts."

It took my breath away—not just the insolence, but the discovery of how fast news travels among niggers. And there was just a note in his indignation that made me decide to put my anger aside and be amused instead.

"What's the matter, Sambo?" says I. "Jealous?"

If looks could kill there'd have been a corpse at his feet.

"I have no words to express my contempt of you, or of the slatterns you . . . you associate with," says he, and his voice was shaking. "But I will not have you endanger my freedom, do you hear? What kind of guardian are you? That swine of an overseer might have provoked me beyond endurance—while you were at your beastliness. It is your task to see me to Canada—that is all that matters."

There was no piercing this one's arrogance, I saw, not by reason or taunts. So I put my hands on my hips and stuck my face into his.

"All that matters, you black mongrel! I'll tell you what matters —and that is that you keep your aping airs to yourself, touch your forelock, and say 'Yes, massa' whenever I or any white man talks to you. That way you might get to Canada—you just might."
I shook my fist at him. "If you haven't the brain in that ape skull of yours to see that kicking up the kind of shines you've been at today is the surest way of setting us all adrift—if you can't see that, I'll teach it to you, by God! I'll follow that overseer's advice, Mr Randolph, and I'll have you triced up, Mr Randolph, and they'll take a couple of stone of meat off you with a raw-hide, Mr Randolph! Then maybe you'll learn sense."

If you think a quadroon can't go red with rage, you're wrong.

"You wouldn't dare!" he choked furiously. "To me! Why, you . . . you . . ."

"Wouldn't I, though? Don't wager your big black arse on that, George, or you'll find you've only half of it left. And what would you do about it, eh? Holler 'I'm a runaway nigger, and this man is smuggling me to Canada?' Think that over, George, and be wise."

"You . . . you scoundrel!" He mouthed at me. "This shall be reported, when I reach Cincinnati—the underground railroad shall hear of it—what manner of creature they entrust with—"

"Oh, shut up, can't you? I don't give a fig for the railroad—and if you weren't a born bloody fool you wouldn't even mention their name. 'When you reach Cincinnati,' no less. You won't reach Cincinnati unless I please—so if you can't be grateful, Randolph, just be careful. Now, then, take off your airs, close your mouth, and get back there among your brothers—lively now! Cross me or that overseer again, and I'll have the cat to you—I swear it. Jump to it, nigger!"

He stood there, sweat running down his face, his chest heaving with passion. For a moment I thought he would leap at me, but he changed his mind.

"Some day," says he, "some day you shall repent this most bitterly. You heap indignities on me, when my hands are tied; you insult me; you mock my degradation. As God is my witness you will pay for it."

There was no dealing with him, you see. It was on the tip of my tongue to yell for the overseer, and have him string Master George up and raw-hide the innards out of him, just for the fun of hearing him howl, but with this kind of quivering violet you couldn't be certain what folly he mightn't commit if he was pushed too far. There was a spite and conceit in that man that passed anything I've ever struck, so I lit a cigar while considering how to catch him properly on the raw.

"I doubt if I'll pay for it," says I. "But supposing I did—it's something *you* can never hope to emulate." I blew smoke at him. "*You'll* never be able to pay for this trip, will you?"

I turned on my heel before he had a chance to reply and strode off, leaving him to digest the truth which I guess he hated more than anything else. That would boil his bile for him, but I wasn't so certain that my threats would have the desired effect on his conduct. Well, if they didn't, I'd carry them out, by God, and he could get to Canada with a new set of weals to show on his lectures to the Anti-Slavery Society.

What beats me, looking back, is the stupidity of his ingratitude. Here was the railroad—and for all he knew, myself—in a sweat to save his black hide for him, but would he show a spark of thanks, or abate his uppity pride one jot? Not he. He thought he had a *right* to be assisted and cosseted, and that we had a *duty* to put up with his airs and ill humour and childishness, and still help him for his own sweet sake. Well, he'd picked the wrong man in me; I was ready to drop the bastard overboard just to teach him the error of his ways—indeed, I paused on the ladder going up to reflect whether I could get away with selling him to a trader or in one of the marts on the way north. He would fetch a handy sum to help me on my way home—but I saw it wouldn't do. He'd find a way to drag me down, and even if he didn't, the underground railroad would hear of it, and I'd developed too healthy a respect for Mr Crixus and his legions to wish them on my tail with a vengeance. No, I'd just have to carry on with the plan, and hope to God that Randolph wouldn't get us into some fearful fix with his wilful white-niggerishness.

It's an interesting thought, though, that within a few short weeks I'd found myself engaged in running niggers *into* slavery, and running 'em *out* again, and all the hundreds of black animals on the *Balliol College*, with every reason to resist and mutiny and raise cain, hadn't given a tenth of the trouble I was getting from this single quadroon, who should have been on his knees in gratitude to me and Crixus and the others. Of course, he was civilised, and educated, and full of his own importance. Lincoln was right; they're a damned nuisance.

One consolation I had on that first night was that it didn't look as though our trip would be a long one, and I could look forward to being shot of Master George Randolph within a week. We thrashed up and down the river in fine style—I say up and down because the Mississippi is the twistiest watercourse you ever saw, doubling back and forth, and half the time you are steaming south-east or south-west round a bend to go north again. It's a huge river, too, up to a mile across in places, and unlike any other I know, in that it gets wider as you go up it. There was nothing to see as far as the banks were concerned except mud flats and undergrowth and here and there a town or a landing place, but the river itself was thick with steamboats and smaller vessels, and great lumber rafts piled high with bales and floating lazily down the muddy brown waters towards the gulf.

It's a slow, ugly river, and the ugliness isn't in what you can see, but what you can feel. There's a palling closeness, and a sense of rot and corruption; it's cruel river, to my mind at any rate, both in itself and its people. Mind you, I may be prejudiced by what it did to me, but even years later, when I came booming down it with the Union Army—well, they boomed, and I coasted along with them—I still felt the same oppressive dread of it. I remember what Sam Grant said about it: "Too thick to drink and too thin to plough. It stinks." Not that he'd have drunk it anyway, unless it had been pure corn liquor from Cairo down.

She's a treacherous river, too, as I realised on the morning after we had boarded the *Sultana*, and she ran aground on a mud bank on the Bryaro bend, not far below Natchez. The channels and banks are always shifting, you see, and the pilots have to know every twist and stump and current; ours didn't, we stuck fast, and a special pilot, the celebrated Bixby, had to be brought down from Natchez to get us afloat again.[36] All of which consumed several hours, with the great man strutting about the pilot house and making occasional dashes out to the texas rail to peer down at the churning wheel, and scampering back to roar down his tube: "Snatch her! Hard down! Let her go, go, go!" while the Mississippi mud churned up in huge billows alongside and you could feel the boat shuddering and heaving to be off. And when she finally "snatched", and reared off the shoal into the water, Bixby was half over the rail again, yelling to the nigger leadsman, and the scream of the whistles all but drowned their great bass voices singing out: "Eight feet—eight and a half—nine feet—quarter-less-twain!" And then as she surged out; "Mark twai-ai-ain!" and the whole ship roared and cheered and stamped and Bixby clapped his tall hat on his head and resumed his kid gloves while they pressed cigars on him and offered him drinks from their flasks. It was quite fun, really, and I'd have enjoyed it if I hadn't been so anxious to get ahead, for I like to see a man who's *good* at something, *doing* it, and throwing on a bit of extra side, just for show. As I've said, I don't have many kindly memories of the Mississippi, but the best are of the steamboats riding tall, and the swaggering pilots, and the booming voices ringing "De-eep four!" and "Quarter-twa-ain!" across the brown waters. I'll never hear them again—but they wouldn't sound the same today anyway.

However, after Mr Bixby's performance we steamed on to Natchez, and there any slight enjoyment I'd been getting from our cruise came to an abrupt end. From now life on the Mississippi was to be one horror after another, and I was to regret most bitterly the day I'd clapped eyes on her dirty waters.

I had no inkling of anything wrong until we were away and steaming up river again, and I sauntered down to see my coffle getting their evening meal—and no doubt, I thought, to discuss the menu with Black Beauty himself. I was considering a few taunts to add sauce to his diet, and wondering if it was wise to stir up his hysteria again, but the sight of his face drove them clear out of my mind. He looked strained and ugly, and quite deaf to the sneering abuse that the overseer gave him as he received his hash from the copper. He shuffled off with his bowl, glancing round at me, and I followed him out of eyeshot round the bales to the rail, where we could be alone.

"What's the matter?" says I, for I knew something had shaken him badly. He looked left and right up the rail.

"Something dreadful has happened," says he in a low voice. "Something unforeseen—my God, it can undo us utterly. It is the most terrible chance—a chance in a thousand—but Crixus should have anticipated it!" He beat his fist on the rail. "He should have seen it, I tell you! The fool! The blind, incompetent blunderer! To send me into this peril, to—"

"What the hell is it?" I demanded, now thoroughly terrified. "Spit it out, in God's name!"

"A man came aboard at Natchez. I was watching, when the passengers came up the plank, and by God's grace he did not see me. He knows me! He is a trader from Georgia—the very man who sold me to my first master! The first time I escaped, he was among those who brought me back! Don't you see, imbecile— if he should catch sight of me here, we are finished! Oh, he knows all about George Randolph—he will know me on the instant.

He will denounce me, I will be dragged back to—oh, my God!" And he put his head in his hands and sobbed with rage and fear.

He wasn't the only one to be emotionally disturbed, I can tell you. *He* would be dragged back—by George, he would have company, unless I looked alive. I stood appalled—this was what my very first instinct had told me might happen, when Crixus had proposed this folly to me. But he had been so sure it would all be plain sailing, and in my cowardice I had allowed myself to be persuaded. I could have torn my hair at my own stupidity —but it was too late now. The damage was done, and I must try to think, and see a way out, and quieten this babbling clown before panic got the better of him.

"Who could have thought that it would happen?" he was chattering. "Not a soul in Mississippi or Louisiana knows me —not a soul—and this fiend from Georgia has to cross my path! What is he doing here? Why didn't Crixus *see* that this could happen? Why did I let myself be driven into this calamity?" He jerked up his head, glaring through his tears. "What are you going to do?"

"Shut up!" says I. "Keep your voice down! He hasn't seen you yet, has he?" I was trying to weigh the chances, to plan ahead in case we were discovered. "Perhaps he won't—there's no reason why he should, is there? He'll be travelling on the boiler deck or the texas—there's no reason why he should come down here, unless he has niggers with him, by God! Has he?"

"No—no, there were no new coffles came aboard at Natchez. But if he should, if—"

"He won't, then. Even if he did, why should he see you, if you lie low and keep out of sight? He's not going to go peering into the face of every nigger just for fun. Look, what's his name?"

"Omohundro—Peter Omohundro of Savannah. He is a terrible creature, I tell you—"

"Look, there's nothing to do but sit tight," says I. It was a nasty shaker, no error, but common sense told me it wasn't as bad as he made out it was. I don't need any encouragement to terror, as a rule, but I can count chances, and there wasn't a damned thing to be done except watch out and hope. The odds were heavy that Omohundro wouldn't come anywhere near him; if he did, thinks I, then Master Randolph can look out for himself, but in the meantime the best thing to do is get some of his almighty cockiness back into him.

"You keep out of sight and keep quiet," says I. "That's all we can do—"

"All! You mean you intend to do nothing! To wait until he sees me?"

"He won't—unless your vapourings attract attention!" I snapped. "I'll watch out for him, never fear. At the first hint that he may come down here, I'll be on hand. You've got the key to your irons hidden, haven't you? Well, then, you stay behind the bales and keep your eyes open. There isn't a chance in a million of his seeing you, if you are careful."

That calmed him down a little; I believe that he had been more angry than frightened, really, which in itself was a relief to me. He blackguarded Crixus some more, and threw in a few withering remarks about my own shortcomings, and there I left him, with a promise to return later and report any developments. I won't deny I was rattled, but I've had a lot worse perils hanging over me, and when I considered the size of the boat, and the hordes of folk aboard, white and nigger, I told myself we should be all right.

The first thing was to get a sight of Omohundro, which wasn't difficult. By discreet inquiry I got him pointed out to me by a nigger waiter: a big, likely-looking bastard with a scarred face and heavy whiskers, one of your tough, wide-awake gentlemen who stared carefully at whoever was talking to him, spoke in a loud, steady way, and laughed easily. I also discovered that he was travelling only as far as Napoleon, which we ought to reach on the following evening. So that was all to the good, as I told Randolph later; he wasn't going to have much time for prying about the boat. But I didn't sleep much that night; even the outside risk of catastrophe is enough to keep me hopping to the water closet, and reaching for the brandy bottle.

Next day passed all too slowly; we lost time at Vicksburg, and I became fretful at the realisation that we wouldn't reach Napoleon and get rid of Omohundro before midnight. The man himself did nothing to set my bowels a-gallop; he spent the morning loafing about the rail, and sat long after luncheon with a group of Arkansas planters, gossiping. But he never stirred off the boiler deck, and I became hopeful again. With evening and darkness coming, it looked as though we were past the most dangerous time.

I kept an eye on him at dinner, though, and afterwards, when he went into the saloon and settled himself with the planters to booze and smoke the evening away, I was glad of a chance offered me to stay on hand. Through Penny-Jenny I had made the acquaintance of two or three fellows on the boat, and one of them, a red-faced old Kentuckian called Colonel Potter, invited me to make up a game of poker. He was one of your noisy, boozy sports, full of heavy humour and hearty guffaws; he fumbled at Penny's thighs under table, slapped backs, twitted me about the Battle of New Orleans, and generally played Bacchus. With him there was a pot-bellied planter named Bradlee, with a great fund of filthy jokes, and a young Arkansan called Harney Shepherdson, who had a yellow whore in tow. Just the kind of company I like, and I was able to watch Omohundro at the same time.

He left his friends after a while, and during a pause in our game he approached our table. Potter welcomed him boisterously, pressed him to sit down, introduced us all round, called for another bottle, and said would Omohundro take a hand.

"No, thankee, colonel," says he. "Matter of fact, I'm taking the liberty of intrudin' on your little party in the hope I can kindly have a little word with your friend here—" he indicated Bradlee, to my relief "—on a matter of business. If the ladies will forgive, that is; I'm due off at Napoleon in an hour or two, so hopin' you won't mind."

"Feel free, suh; help y'self," cries Potter, and Omohundro turns to Bradlee.

"Understand you have some niggers below, suh," says he, and my innards froze at the words. "Couple of Mande's 'mong 'em, accordin' to my friends yonder. Now, while I'm not on a buyin' trip, you understand, I never miss a Mande if I can help it. Wonder if you feel inclined to talk business, suh, an' if so, I might take a look at 'em."

I leaned back, hoping no one would notice how the sweat was beginning to pump off me, as I waited for Bradlee's answer.

"Always talk business, anytime," says he. "Got to warn you though, suh, my niggers don't come cheap. Could be askin' a right nice price."

"Could be payin' one, for the right kind of cattle," says Omohundro. "Be deeply 'bliged to you, suh, if I might take a look at 'em for myself; be much beholden to you."

Bradlee said it was fine with him, and heaved himself up, with his apologies to the table. I was shuddering by this time; I must get down to the main deck before them, and get Randolph out of sight somehow. I was on the point of jumping to my feet and making my excuses, when Potter, the interfering oaf, sings out:

"Say, why'nt you take a look at Mr Prescott's coffle while you about it, suh? He got some right prime stock there, ain't you, though? Purtiest set o' niggers I seen in a while—it's so, suh, I assure you. Reckon Mr Prescott's got good taste in mos' things —eh, honey?" And he set Penny squealing with a pinch.

What possessed him to stick his oar in, God knows; just my luck, I suppose. I found Omohundro's eyes on me.

"That so, suh? Well, I ain't rightly buyin', like I said, but if—"

"Nothing for sale, I'm afraid." I strove to sound offhand, and he nodded,

"In that case, your servant, ladies, colonel, gentlemen," and he and Bradlee went off towards the staircase, leaving me floundering. I had to get away, so I started to my feet, saying I must fetch something from my cabin. Potter cried that we were just about to go on with the game, and Penny squeaked that without me to guide her she couldn't tell the little clover leaves from the other black things on the cards, but by that time I was striding for the staircase, cursing Potter and with panic rising in my chest.

I saw Omohundro and Bradlee disappear downwards just ahead of me, so I hung back, and then slipped down the spiral staircase in their wake. By the time I reached the main deck they were already over at the far port rail, where Bradlee's coffle lay, calling for the overseer to bring another light. It was pretty dim on the main deck, with only a few flare lamps which cast great black shadows among the bales and machinery; the various coffles of niggers were scattered about, nesting among the cargo, with my own crew up forward, away from the rest.

I lurked in the shadows, debating whether to go and warn strung gentleman might do if he thought there was danger close Randolph, and decided not to; you never knew what that high-by. It seemed best to lurk in the shadows unobserved, keeping an eye on Bradlee and Omohundro, and ready to intervene—God alone knew how—if they decided to take an interest in my coffle. The truth was I just didn't know what to do for the best, and so did nothing.

Peeping over a box I watched while Omohundro, by the light of the overseer's lantern, examined a couple of Bradlee's slaves, walking round them prodding and poking. I couldn't hear what was said, what with the churning of the great paddle wheel and the steady murmur and crooning of the slaves, but after about five minutes Omohundro shook his head, I heard Bradlee laugh, and then the three of them moved slowly amidships, where Omohundro stopped to light a cigar. From where I lurked among the bales I began to hear their voices.

"... and of course I don't blame you, pricin' high," Omohundro was saying. "Reckon your figure is about right, these days, but that wouldn't leave any margin of profit. Still, I'm right sorry; good bucks you have, suh, an' well schooled."

"Guess I can train a nigger," says Bradlee. "Yessir, I jus' about think I can. Whup seldom, but whup good, my ol' dad used to say, an' he was right. Guess I ain't laid a rawhide on a nigger o' mine this las' twelve-month; don't have to. They got a respect for me, on 'count they know if I *do* trim one of 'em up, he'll *stay* trimmed."

"That's the style with 'em," chips in the overseer. "On'y way, otherwise they git spoiled. Breaks my heart to see good niggers spoiled, too, by soft handlin', like the coffle that Englishman brung aboard."

"How's that?" says Bradlee. "I hear they's prime; so Potter sayin'."

"Oh, prime enough—just now. But he don't know how to handle 'em, an' he in a right way to ruinin' 'em, to my way o' thinkin'. Shame, it is." And then to my horror, he added: "Care to see 'em, gennelmen?"

My heart stopped beating, and then Omohundro said:

"Reckon not; he ain't sellin', so he tell me."

"No?" chuckles the overseer. "I guess he'll be glad 'nough to, come a year or so. Leastways with one of 'em—the uppitiest yaller son-of-a-bitch you ever see. First-rate nigger, too—clean, straight, smart, an' talks like a college p'fessor—oh, you know *his* sort, I reckon. All frills an' goddam' lip."

"Uh-huh," says Bradlee. "Educated, likely, an' spoiled to hell an' gone. Got no use for 'em, myself."

"That kind of fancy fetches a good price, though, once the tar's been taken out of 'em," says Omohundro. "Make valets, butlers, an' so forth—ladies in Awlins an' Mobile payin' heavy money for 'em." He paused. "Think the Englishman knows what this feller's worth?"

"How could he?" says Bradlee. "He tells me he spent all his time in Afriky slave ships, till now. He don't know the value of talkin' niggers."

Shut up, shut up about my bloody niggers, I found myself whispering. Mind your own business and get upstairs where you belong, can't you. And they would have done but for that benighted swine of an overseer.

"Talkin' niggers is right—this one of Prescott's sure can handle his gab. Highest-falutin' smart-assed buck in creation, answers back sassy as be damned. An' what you think Mist' Prescott do, gennelmen, hey? Why, he jus' pats and smooths him! Yessir. Makes a body sick to listen."

"The English is soft on niggers. Ev'yone know that," says Bradlee. "I'd like to see the buck'd talk back to *me*; I'd just about like to hear *that*."

"Well, suh, you don't have to stir more'n twenty feet to see him," cries the infernal clod. "Here, gennelman, step across this ways—I see Mist' Omohundro kinda interested anyway, that right, suh?"

I should have strode out then and there, I know, and done something, anything, to keep them away from my coffle. I might have talked them away, or damned their eyes for going near my blacks, or made some diversion. But my consternation had reached the point where I had lost my nerve altogether; I hesitated, and then the overseer was up forward, barking at my niggers to rise and let the white men have a look at them. I waited, helpless, for the blow to fall.

"Where that George?" the overseer was shouting. "Here, you George, ye black varmint, step out when I calls ye!"

It was like watching a play I had seen before, and a bloody tragedy at that. Randolph, unsuspecting, stood up among his fellows, blinking in the light.

"That one?" says Bradlee. "Well, he don't look so dam' pert, eh, Omohundro? Good clean buck, too, quadroon, I reckon—why, what's the matter with you, boy? You seen a ghost?"

Randolph was staring, with his hand to his mouth, at Omohundro, who was stooping to peer at him.

"What's that? Wait, though—hold on a minute! What's your name, boy? I seen you before somewheres, ain't I—yes! By God, I have!" His voice rose in a shout of amazement. "You're George Rand—"

In that moment Randolph was on him like a tiger, carrying the big man to the deck, and then falling himself as his shackles tripped him. He was up in an instant though, agile as a cat, smashing a fist into Bradlee's face before the overseer, swearing in astonishment, managed to close with him. They reeled against the bales, locked together, and then Randolph jerked his knees up, and the overseer staggered away yelping, clutching his groin.

"Get him!" bawls Omohundro. "He's a runaway—Randolph! Stop him, Bradlee!"

Hobbled by his irons—he hadn't time to get at his hidden key—Randolph half hopped, half ran for the rail, with Bradlee clutching at his shirt, trying to drag him back. Omohundro got a hold, too, but stumbled and fell, cursing; as they tried to grapple him Randolph broke away, and before his irons finally tripped him he had covered half a dozen yards which brought him to the big box where I was crouching. He saw me as he fell, and shouted:

"Help! Help me, Prescott! Fight them off!"

Such an appeal, addressed to Flashy, meets a prompt response. I ducked back behind cover just as Omohundro came crashing over the bales, clutching at Randolph's feet. The quadroon kicked free, scrambled on to the rail, and was trying to roll over it when he must have realised that he would fall plumb in the path of the great thirty-foot paddle wheel; he shrieked, rearing up on the rail, the overseer's pistol banged, and I saw Randolph's body arch and his face contort with agony. He fell, outwards, and the huge wheel blades came churning down on him as he hit the water.

I daresay that if I had had a few minutes for quiet reflection it would have occurred to me that the safest course would be to stand my ground, playing the innocent trader amazed at the news that there had been a runaway in his coffle, and brazen it out that way. But I hadn't those few minutes, and I'm not sure I'd have acted any differently anyway. The overwhelming feeling that I had when I saw Randolph's body fall, with Omohundro and Bradlee roaring bloody murder and the whole deck in uproar, was that here was no place for Flashy any longer. I was skipping away between the bales before the echo of the shot had died; Omohundro's bellow to me to stop merely assisted my flight. I crossed the deck in half a dozen strides, and launched myself over the starboard rail in a fine flat dive; there was no wheel on that side, I knew, and when I surfaced in the warm Mississippi water with all the breath knocked out of me the *Sultana* was already a hundred yards away upriver.

Even today I can't feel anything but irritation and dislike for George Randolph. If he had only had the sense to keep his mouth shut and act humble for once, he'd never have been confronted by Omohundro that night; the odds are he'd have reached Canada without fuss and embarked immediately on a happy life as a professor at some liberal university, or the leader of a nigger minstrel troupe, or something equally useful. Instead his pride and folly had bought him a bullet in the belly and a grave in the Mississippi mud, as far as I could see; more important, he had put me in a highly dangerous and embarrassing position.

My wits must have been cleared by the water, for I had the immediate presence of mind not to swim for the Arkansas shore, a mere hundred yards away, but to strike out instead across the stream for the Mississippi bank, which was almost three-quarters of a mile off. I'm a strong swimmer, and the water was warm, so I made it easily enough; by the time I climbed out across a mud bank and plumped down among some willows, the *Sultana* had stopped at the next bend, but after half an hour she started off again, doubtless to stop at the next landing and start the hue and cry.

I blasted Randolph bitterly at the thought that I was a hunted fugitive once more, in the middle of a strange land with only a few dollars in my pocket. The one consolation was that they would scour the Arkansas side first, and I would have time to get inland in Mississippi unmolested. And then whither? There could be no going back south, with the Navy still doubtless on the look-out for me, and it would be madness to try to continue north along the river on foot. But north I would have to go eventually, if I were to reach home again; in the meantime I must find some place to lie up undetected until all the hullaballoo had died down, and I could work cautiously upriver to the free states, and so to the Atlantic seaboard and a passage home.

It was a damned tall order and depressing prospect, and I had a grand old curse that night at my folly in being bullied into this fearful fix by Crixus. My one hope was that Mississippi was such a big place, where I assumed news travelled slowly and uncertainly, that I ought to be able to find a bolt-hole; I reasoned that itinerant strangers must be commonplace in the western states, so I might escape remark if I was careful how I went.

I slept that night among the cottonwoods, and struck due east before sunrise, as I wanted to get away from the river as quickly as possible. And so began three of the most dam' dismal days of my life, in which I skulked through woods and along by-roads, living the life of a vagrant, stopping only at the loneliest farms and places I could find to buy a meal out of the few dollars I had left. The one thing that cheered me was that none of the people I saw paid me any close attention, which confirmed my belief that they were used to all sorts of odd fellows trudging about the country; I tried to speak as American as I could, when I spoke at all, and must have made a passable job of it, for nobody appeared to take me for anything else.

However, I realised that this could not continue. Soon I would be destitute, and since I've never been any hand at petty theft or highway robbery, I came to the reluctant conclusion that I must try and find work. It's a last resort, of course, but it seemed to me if I could get some employment in an out-of-the-way spot I could lie up and save money for my eventual flight at one and the same time. I made one or two cautious inquiries, without success beyond an afternoon's labour splitting logs for my supper, and I was in despair by the fourth morning, when by sheer chance I lit on the very thing I was looking for.

I had slept in the woods, and spent my last few cents on bread and milk at a run-down store, when a burly chap on a grey horse comes cantering up, roaring for the storekeeper that he had come to settle his debt.

"What's the row then, Jim?" says the storekeeper. "Where you off to?"

"Headed west," cries Jim. "I seen my last load o' goddamned cotton, I can tell you that. It's Califorhey for me, my boy, an' a

pisspotful of gold. There's your four dollars, Jake, an' much
obliged to ye."

"Well, that beats all," says the storeman. "Californey, eh?
Wisht I could go myself, by thunder. Say, but what's Mandeville
goin' to do without a driver, in the middle o' pickin' time?"

"Do his goddamned drivin' his goddamned self," says the other
cheerfully. "I guess I'll worry about him, won't I, all the way to
the diggin's. I'm off to see the elephant! Yeh-hoo! It's Californey
or bust!" And he waved his hat and thundered away, leaving the
storeman scratching his head in wonder.

I didn't inquire at the store; the less said the better. But I met a
nigger up the road, found where Mandeville's place was, and after
a four-mile walk came to his imposing front gates. They were
made of granite, no less, and the place was called Greystones, an
impressive spread of cotton plantation with a fine white colonial
house at the head of a tree-lined drive. It looked a likely spot for
me, so I strode up and presented myself as a driver in need of work.

Mandeville was a broad, bull-necked man of about fifty with
heavy whiskers on a coarse red face.

"Who told you I needin' a driver?" says he, standing four-
square on his verandah and squinting down at me suspiciously.
I said I had met his former employee on the road.

"Huh! That fool Jim Bakewell! Ups an' off in the middle o'
pickin', cool as you please, to go to Californey. Ifn he ain't any
better at diggin' than at drivin' he'll finish up cleanin' out privies,
which is all he good for anyways. Triflin' useless bastard."
He cocked his head at me. "Reckon you kin drive?"

"Anything that moves," says I.

"Oh, my niggers *move*," says he. "They *move*, ifn someone on
hand to make 'em skip. You driven cotton-hands befo', I guess,
by the look o' you." In the surprise of realising what "driving"
meant, I overlooked the doubtful compliment. "Where you from,
an' what your name?"

"Tom Arnold," says I. "From Texas, a while back."

"Uh-huh, the Texies. Well, no denyin', gotta have a driver.
Dunno where I get one, this season, ifn I don't take ye. Ain't no
slouch of a job, min'—you be th' only white driver on the place.
Thirty dolla's a month, an' yo' keep. Satisfy ye, Tom?"

I said it would, and at that moment a nigger came round the house leading a fine white mare, and a lady came through the pillared front door, dressed for riding. Mandeville hailed her eagerly.

"Why, Annie dahlin', there you are! Fine, fine—jus' off a-ridin', I see. That's fine, fine." And then, seeing her eyes on me, he hurried to explain. "This here's Tom Arnold, honey; jus' hired him as a new driver, in room o' that no-good Bakewell. Right piece o' luck, I reckon, him turnin' up. Yes, suh."

"Is it?" said the lady, and you could see she doubted it. She was one of the tiniest women I've ever seen, somewhere under five feet, although well-shaped in a dainty doll-like way. But there was nothing doll-like about the sharp little face, with its pointed elfin chin, tight lips, and cold grey eyes that played over me with a look of bleak disdain. I became conscious of my bedraggled appearance and unshaven face; three days in the woods make a poor toilet.

"We may hope he is a better driver than Bakewell," says the lady coldly. "At the moment he looks as though he was more accustomed to being driven."

And without another word or glance at me she mounted her mare, Mandeville fussing to help her, and cantered off along the drive with the nigger groom trotting at her heels. Mandeville waved after her, his red face beaming, and then turned back to me.

"That Mrs Mandeville," says he, proudly. "She the lady o' my plantation. Yessuh, Mrs Mandeville." Then his eyes slid away and he said he would show me my quarters and instruct me in my duties.

As it turned out, these were easy enough; slave-driving is as pleasant an occupation as any, if you must work. You ride round the cotton rows on horse-back, seeing that the niggers don't let up in filling their baskets, and laying on the leather when they slack. Greystones was a fair-sized place, with about a hundred niggers working the great snowy fields that stretched away from behind the house to the river, and they were a well-drilled pack by the time I'd done with 'em, I can tell you. I vented the discontent I felt at America on them, and enjoyed myself more than I'd done since my Rugby days, when lacing fags was the prime sport.

Although I had a couple of black drivers to help me, I became quite expert with my hide—you could make a sleepy nigger jump his own height with a well-placed welt across his backside, squealing his head off, and if any of them were short-weighted at the end of the day you gave them half a dozen cuts for luck. Mandeville was delighted with the tally of cotton picked, and told me I was the best overseer he'd ever had, which didn't surprise me. It was work I could take a hearty interest in.

After the first few days he left me alone to the job, for he frequently had business in Helena, about fifty miles away on the other side of the Mississippi river, or in Memphis, over the Tennessee border, and would stay away for nights at a time. He always went alone, leaving his wife in the house, which seemed damned indiscreet to me. I didn't realise, fortunately for my self-esteem, that while a Southern planter wouldn't have dreamed of leaving his wife unchaperoned in a house while there was a white man there, he'd never think twice if that man was a hired servant living in a cottage fifty yards away. However, she kept out of my way in those early days, and I out of hers.

Knowing me, you may think that strange. But all my thoughts at this stage were on my own plight; Greystones seemed to be just the kind of out-of-the-way spot I required; it was isolated in the woodland and marsh, and was seldom visited, but even so I had my heart in my mouth every time hoofbeats sounded on the drive, and I kept well out of sight when one of Mandeville's neighbours called. It didn't seem likely that if there was a search going on for me, it would reach this far from the river, and there was nothing to connect the steamboat fugitive with Mandeville's new driver, but even so I kept a sharp eye open at first for any hint of danger. As the days passed, and none appeared, I began to feel easier.

Another reason why I kept out of Annette Mandeville's way was that I disliked her, and she me, apparently. I had guessed two things from our first brief meeting: one was that she was an unpleasant, arrogant little piece, and the other that she had her big, powerful husband on a string. He was more than twice her age, of course (she couldn't have been above two-and-twenty), and I've noticed that there are few things that a middle-aged man will go in such awe of as an imperious young wife; he'll face a wounded buffalo, or go headlong into a sabre charge, but he'll turn pale and stutter at the thought of saying, "I'd rather not, dearest." Well, I can understand it, when the wife holds the purse, or is bigger than he, or can get the law on him. But even without these things Mandeville went in awe of her.

And she knew it, and enjoyed using her power to torment him. She wasn't just spoiled and petulant—she was cruel, in a subtle way, and I say it who am a recognised authority. I saw enough of them together to judge the pleasure she took in fretting and hurting him with her ready sneers and icy disdain; the more eager he was to please her, this man who was so coarse and masterful in other things, the more she seemed to delight in making him uneasy and bewildered.

Much of this I learned from Mandeville himself—not that he dreamed he was instructing me. But he loved to talk, and there not being another white man on the place, he took to inviting me up to the house at night, after his wife had retired, for a booze and prose; he was a decent enough fellow, I suppose, in his rough way, and greatly given to foxing himself on corn toddy, and nothing pleased him more than to yarn away about his niggers and his horses, and—when he was well maudlin—about his wife. And this most often after she had set him down, which she did most days.

"Yes, suh," this infatuated idiot would say, smiling blearily at his glass, "I'm a lucky man, an' she a won'erful li'l lady. Yes suh, 'deed she is. Well, you kin see that, Tom; you a travelled man, I guess, you kin see she is. Course, she git a li'l short, time to time—like today, now—but it ain't nuthin' at all. My own fault, I guess. Y'see, the truth is, although this here's a pretty fair spread at Greystones, tain't altogether what she bin used to. No-suh. She come from one o' the best French families in N'Awlins—the Delancy's, likely you heard o' them, gotta tre-mendous big estate out to Lake Pontchartrain. Trouble is, ol' man Delancy, he a bit stretched, an' I helped him out over a couple o' deals. Five years ago, that was, when I married Annie. Here, Jonah, light a see-gar for Mist' Arnold; fill your glass, suh."

By now he would be well launched, convincing himself for the thousandth time, against all reason.

"Ye-es, five years ago. Happiest day o' my life, suh. But I'll admit—you take a gel who's bin brought up a real lady, who's got real blood, bin to convent, had a half-dozen yaller maids waitin' on her, an' who's used to livin' in the top so-ciety in N'Awlins —well, I do her pretty good here, I reckon, but it ain't the same. Not much society, even in Memphis, an' the local folks ain't 'xactly the kin' o' bucks an' belles she used to meet at home. So it's natural she gits these fits an' starts now an' then. But you 'ppreciate that, Tom. An' no denyin', either, me bein' older'n she is, a little, she get kinda bored. I don't talk quite her way, you see, an' I ain't got her—tastes, so to speak. So she get a mite res'less, like I say. An' boy, don' she dress me down then!" And he would giggle drunkenly, as though at some good joke which he thoroughly enjoyed. "Say, you oughta hear her when she got a real head o' steam. My stars! Course, tain't often."

Not more than twice a day, and three times on Sundays, I would say to myself. Serve the clown right for marrying out of his class.

"Say, but don' get me wrong! Here, have 'nuther drink. Don' get me wrong—she a real lovin' gel. Yes-suh. She the lovin'est little creatur' you ever did see. When I say she sometimes bored, don' think I mean she goin' short! Ho-ho, I guess not!" And he would nudge me, winking ponderously, with a lewd leer. "I tell you, I'm 'bout wore out pilin' inter that li'l darlin'! Fact. She cain't seem t'get enough o' me. 'Do it again, Johnny lover, do it again.' That what she say. An' don' I do it? Oh, I should say not! I should jus' 'bout reckon not. An' don' she know how to rouse a man on, hey? Why, I see some men—like Parkins, down at Helena, an' young Mackay, who got the Yellowtree place—they jus' itchin' for her, jus' at the sight of her. Why, I could see you fancy her you'self—no, don't fret you'self, don't fret. I don't mind one li'l bit. It's only natural, ain't it? I don't take no offence, cos I know she never think o' no one but me. 'Do it again, Johnny lover.' That what she say. Talk 'bout your nigger wenches—pish!'"

It was from drunken meanderings such as this that I formed my conclusions about the Mandevilles—an obvious one being that they didn't bed together, and probably never had. Well, that could explain a lot about Madame Annette's behaviour, and in other circumstances I would probably have set myself to supply her want, for she was a trim little half-pint, bar her shrew face. But she was so damned unpleasant that the thought didn't cross my mind; when we met she either looked straight through me or treated me as though I were no better than the blacks. If I hadn't needed the work I'd have taken the rough side of my tongue to her, and as it was I gave her back sneer for sneer as far as I dared, so that before long we hated each other as cordially as man and woman can. And mind you, I don't like this sort of thing; it ain't usual to find a woman who isn't prepared to be civil to me, and I'd grown my whiskers long again, and a rakish little black imperial, too.

However, I had my own affairs to attend to. I was working quietly away towards the day when I'd have enough saved to be able to move off north again. I reckoned two or three months would see me set and ready, and by that time all the haroosh caused by my flight from the *Sultana* would have died down, and I'd be able to take the road in safety.

So I laboured away, whopping niggers, mounting the occasional black wench in my quarters, and counting my dollars every fortnight, and never gave a thought to Annette Mandeville. Which was foolish of me; equally foolish was the way in which I allowed a sense of security to grow on me as the weeks passed and no hue and cry came to disturb the peace of Greystones. Picking time passed and with less to do I got restless, and impatient to be up and away for England; I suppose that made me more thoughtless and short-tempered than usual, all of which was to lead to my undoing.

It was the approach of Christmas that finally broke my patience, I think. I suppose everyone's thoughts turn home then, whether they really wish they were there or not. I had only Elspeth to miss —and the baby I'd never seen. Not that I've any use for brats, mind you, but any excuse will do for a self-pitying weep when you're alone in your quarters in a foreign land, with two inches left in the bottom of the corn bottle, and the rest gurgling in your belly and making you feel sick and miserable. I imagined Elspeth, fair and radiant, bending over a crib and shaking a rattle at its occupant, and looking adoringly across at me with that lovely pink bloom on her cheeks, and myself toasting my arse at the nursery fire with my coat tails pulled back, and a fine helping of duff and brandy inside me, quite the proud papa, while waits sang in the street outside. Instead, here I was, half-foxed and croaking to myself in a draughty shack, with no Elspeth, but a black slut snoring open-mouthed in the corner, and in place of waits the eternal caterwauling of the field hands as they sang one of their morbid chants. I sat there blubbering boozily, trying to put the home picture out of my mind, and telling myself it was all a sham —that Elspeth would be back in the saddle with one of her gallants by now, and old Morrison would ruin Christmas anyway by whining about the cost of geese and holly. It was no good; I was homesick, bloody homesick, and the thought of Morrison was an added incentive. By God, I'd make the old scoundrel skip when I got back and flourished Spring's papers under his ugly nose. The thought cheered me up, and when I had finished the bottle, been sick, and thrashed the nigger girl for snoring, I felt more like myself again.

But I was still chafing to be away, and with only two weeks of my enforced sojourn to go I was in a thoroughly ill humour and ready to take my spite out on anyone—even Annette Mandeville or her soused clown of a husband. Not that I was seeing much of either of them by now, for Mandeville was absent more and more, and Annette kept to the house. But she had her eyes open too, as I was to discover to my cost.

I mentioned a black girl in my quarters; she was the least ugly and smelly of the field women whom I had taken as a carnal cook —a bedfellow-cum-housekeeper, that is. She was little use as either, but one has to make do. Anyway, it happened that one evening, after a long day down by the river where the slaves were cutting a ditch, I came home to find her whimpering and groaning on her mattress, with a couple of nigger girls tending her and looking mighty scared.

"What's this?" says I.

"Oh, massa," says the wenches, "Hermia she pow'ful sick; she real po'ly, she is."

And she was. Someone had flogged her until her back was a livid mess of cuts and bruises.

"Who the devil's done this?" roars I in a great rage, and it was

Hermia herself who told me, between her wails.

"Oh, Massa Tom, it the Miz—Miz Annette. She done tell me I's ins'lent, en she'd trim me up good. I don' done nuthin' Massa Tom—but she git Hector to whup me, en oh I's hurtin', hurtin' suthin' awful, massa. Hector he lay on 'til I's swoondin' —en ain't done nuthin'. Oh, Massa Tom, whut ins'lent mean?"

Well, I knew Annette was hard on the niggers, who went in terror of her, and I'd no doubt this silly slut had offended her in some way. So I gave no thought to it, but turned Hermia out, since she was of no use for anything in her present state. Next day I picked another wench to take her place, and went off to the fields in due course—and when I came home there she was, beaten black and blue, just as Hermia had been, again on Miz Annette's orders.

Now I can take a hint as fast as the next man, but I confess I didn't see all the way through this one, which was foolish of me. I took it that the spiteful little harridan was bent on denying me female companionship, but it never occurred to me why. Which shows what a modest chap I am, I suppose. In any event, I had to do something about it, for I was seething with anger at her malice, and since Mandeville was away in Memphis, I went straight up to the house to have it out with the mistress.

She was obviously just back from a canter round the plantation, for she was still in her grey riding suit, issuing orders to Jonah in the hall. When he had gone, I tackled her straight.

"Two of the field girls have been flogged, on your instructions," says I. "May I be permitted to ask why?"

She didn't even look at me. "What concern is it of yours?" says she, taking off her gloves.

"As your husband's overseer, I'm responsible for his slaves."

"Under his authority—and mine," says she, and started off upstairs without another word. I wasn't having this, so I strode after her.

"By all means," says I, "but I find it strange that you undertake to discipline them yourself. Why not leave the matter to me— since it's what I'm paid for?"

We were at the head of the stairs by now, but she kept right on towards her room. I kept pace with her, fuming, and suddenly she snapped at me:

"What you are paid for is to obey orders, not to question what I do. Your place is in the fields—not in this house. Be so good as to leave, at once!"

"I'm damned if I do! You've had the tar whaled out of two of those girls, and I want to know why."

"Don't be impertinent!" She wheeled on me, her face screwed up with fury. "How dare you follow me in this way? How dare you take that tone? Get out, before I call the servants to throw you into the fields! Not another word!" And she flounced into her room—but she left the door open.

"Now listen to me, you vicious brat, you!" I was in a fine fury by now. "If you won't tell me, I'll tell you! You had them thrashed because they were *my* girls, didn't you? You thought—"

"Your girls!" She spat it at me. "Your girls! Since when could a penniless beggar like you talk of *your* girls! My slaves, do you hear? And if I choose to punish them, I shall do it—" she was fairly hissing the words "—as I choose, and you will keep your place, you mongrel!"

I think the only reason I didn't strike her was that she was so tiny, snarling up at me, that I was frightened of breaking her. And even in my anger I saw a better way of hurting her—always Flashy's forte, as Tom Hughes has testified.

"Well, now," says I, holding myself in, "I don't think the word 'mongrel' is one that comes at all well from a Creole lady." I let it sink in and added: "I don't have to worry about *my* finger-nails."

It was quite false, of course; I don't suppose she had a drop of black blood in her. But it struck her like a blow; she stood glaring, her face chalk-white, unable to speak, so I carried on, amiably:

"You whipped those girls because I was bedding them, and no doubt you'll be prepared to go on whipping until you've half-killed every wench on the plantation. Well, see if I care—they ain't my property. See if your husband cares, though; he mayn't like having his investment wasted. He'll maybe ask you why you did it. 'Because your overseer's covering 'em,' you'll say—using a lady-like term, I'm sure. 'And why not?' he'll say, 'what's that to you?' Why, he may even wonder—"

And there I stopped, for there, and only there, the light dawned.

As I say, I'm over-modest; she had been so damned uncivil to me, you see, that it honestly hadn't crossed my mind that she fancied me. Usually, of course, I'm ready to accept that every woman does —well, they do—but she was such a shrew-faced pip-squeak, and so unpleasant...

I stared at her now, and noted with interest that from white her witch-face had turned flushed, and her breathing was slow and thick. Well, well, thinks I, what have we here; let's see if our manly charms have truly captivated this unlikely creature after all. And purely by way of scientific experiment I leaned forward, picked her up with my hands at her waist—it was like lifting a puppet—and kissed her.

She didn't struggle or kick or cry out, so I kept at it, and very slowly her mouth opened, and she gave a little sob, and then she took my lip in her teeth and began to bite, harder and harder, until I pulled her free, holding her at arm's length. Her eyes were shut, and her face tight set; then she motioned me to set her down, and she stood against me. Her head touched my top weskit button.

"Wait," said she, in a little whisper, and quickly closing the door she vanished into her dressing-room. I could have laughed, but instead I began peeling off my coat, reflecting that the road to fornication is truly often paved with misunderstanding. I was sitting on the bed, removing my boots, when she re-entered, and she was a startling sight, for she was stark naked except for her riding boots. That took me aback, for it ain't usual among amateurs; something to do with her French upbringing, no doubt. But it was the rest of her that took the eye; I'd known she was well-shaped, but in the buff she was an undoubted little nymph. Scientific research be damned, says I, reaching out for her, and she came with her mouth open and her eyes shut, straining at me.

"You silly little popsy," says I. "Why didn't you let me know before?" And so to work, which proved none too bad, bar one unexpected and painful surprise. I was settling into my stride when I discovered why she had kept her boots on, for she suddenly clapped her legs round me, and so help me, those boots were spurred. Hair brushes (that was dear Lola) I was used to, but being stabbed in the buttocks is an arse of a different colour, if you'll forgive the pun, and it was fortunate the bed was a wide one or we'd have flown off it. There was no untangling her, for she clung like a limpet, and I could only wrestle away, yelping from time to time, until we were done. I was stuck like a Derby winner.

Then she pushed me away, slipped off the bed, and picked up a robe. She put it on, without looking at me, and then she said:

"Now get out."

And without another word she went into her dressing-room and bolted the door.

Well, I'm not used to this kind of treatment, and in other circumstances I'd have kicked the door in and taught her manners, but in a house full of niggers you can't conduct an affair as though you were man and wife. So I dressed, staunching my wounds and muttering curses, and presently limped away, vowing that she'd had the last of me.

But of course she hadn't. Mandeville returned next day, and I kept well clear of the house, but come the end of the week he was off to Helena again, to meet some fellows on business. With only a week of my time left I should have gone about my business, ignoring Madame Annette, but human nature being what it is, I didn't. No woman tells me to get out with impunity, especially a haughty dwarf who was no great shakes in bed anyway. This is illogical, of course, but those of us who study immoral philosophy are guided by some contrary rules. At all events, I came sniffing round the day after he left—well, she was white, and interesting, and apart from her face she was a well-set-up piece in a miniature way.

To my surprise, she didn't either rebuff me or welcome me with open arms. We discussed the piece of plantation business which I'd made my pretext for coming, and when I assailed her she fell to with a will—but never a word, or a smile, or anything but a fierce, cold passion that almost scared me. It was damned spooky, when I think of it now, and afterwards, when I tried to engage her in sociable chat, she sat moody and withdrawn, hardly saying a word. And not a stitch on, mark you—not even her boots. I'd taken good care of that.

I gave up, half-puzzled and half-annoyed; I couldn't fathom her at all, and I still can't. My experience with women has been, I dare say, considerable and varied; I've had them fighting to get at me and running for dear life to escape, all ages, shapes and colours, in beds, haylofts, thickets, drawing-rooms, palaces, hovels, snow-drifts (that was in Russia, in the cold spell), baths, billiard rooms, cellars, camps, covered wagons, and even in the library of Corpus Christi College, Cambridge, which is probably a record of some sort. I've sometimes regretted that the flying machine was invented so late in my life, but things move so fast nowadays it's difficult to keep pace.

Anyway, my point is that only three women that I can recall out of that darling multitude have refused to be sociable afterwards, provided there was time, of course. My Afghan lotus-blossom, Narreeman, was one, but she had been constrained, as they say, and wanted to murder me anyway. Queen Ranavalona was another, but apart from being as mad as a hatter she had affairs of state to attend to, which is some excuse. Annette Mandeville was the third, and I believe she was neither mad nor murderous. But who's to say? I doubt if she'd have been an entertaining talker anyway; she didn't have much education, for all her careful upbringing.

She was avid enough, however, for pleasure itself, and since Mandeville seemed to be making a protracted stay in Helena I visited her on each of the next three days. This was foolishness, of course, for it increased the chances of detection, but when I voiced my doubts, remarking that I hoped none of the niggers would guess what brought me to the house, she laughed un-pleasantly and said:

"Who cares if the whole plantation knows? Not one of these black animals would dare breathe a word—they know what would happen to them."

I didn't like to think what that would be, knowing Madame Annette, but since she seemed so unconcerned I saw no reason why I should fret, and consequently grew careless. I had been in the habit of opening one of her bedroom windows, so that we might hear if anyone approached the house from the road, but on the third day I forgot, so that we never heard the pad of hooves across the turf.

We had just finished a bout; Annette was lying face down on the bed, silent and sullen as usual, and I was trying to win some warmth out of her with my gay chat, and also by biting her on the buttocks. Suddenly she stiffened under me, and in the same instant feet were striding up the corridor towards the room, Mandeville's voice was shouting:

"Annie! Hullo, Annie honey, I'm home! I've brought—" and then the door was flung open and there he stood, the big grin on his red face changing to a stare of horror. My mouth was still open as I gazed across her rump, terror-stricken.

"My God!" he cries, "Betrayed!"

Well, I'd heard the same sort of exclamation before, and I've heard it since, and there's no doubt it's unnerving. But I doubt if there's a man living who can move faster with his pants round his ankles than I can; I was off that bed and diving for the window before the last word had left his lips, and had the sash half up before I remembered it was a cool twenty-foot drop to the ground. I turned like a cornered rat just as he came for me, swinging his horse-whip and bawling with rage; I ducked the cut and slipped past him to the door, stumbing on the threshold. I glanced back in panic, but he was heading straight on for the bed, yelling:

"Filthy strumpet!" and raising his whip again, but Annette, who had sprung up into a kneeling position, just snapped:

"Don't you dare touch me! Drop that whip!"

And he did. He fell back before that tiny, naked figure, mouthing, and then he turned and hurled himself at me, with a face of apoplexy. I was afoot again by this time, dragging up my breeches and haring for the landing, and then a man's figure loomed up at the head of the stair. I heard Mandeville shout: "Stop him!" and although I tried to dodge the upraised riding crop I wasn't quick enough. Something smashed against my forehead, knocking me backwards; the white ceiling spun dizzily above me, and then I was falling into nothing.

I can't have been unconscious more than a few minutes, but when I came to my own leather belt was round my wrists, blood was caking one of my eye-lids, and there was an unholy pain in my brow. I was lying at the foot of the staircase, and a man was bestriding me, one of his booted feet planted on my ankle. There was a tremendous hubbub of voices, with Mandeville yelling blue murder and others trying to quieten him. I turned my head; two or three men were holding him back, and when he saw me conscious he waved his arms and shouted:

"You slimy bastard! You stinkin' hound! I'll have your heart's blood for this! I'll crucify you! Let me at him, boys, an' I'll tear his dirty innards out!"

They struggled with him, and one of them sings out:

"Get that feller outa here, Luke—quick now! afore he gits done a mischief! Damn ye, Mandeville, won't ye hold still!"

"I'll murder him! I'll butcher him 'sif he was a hog! Oh, turn me loose, boys! He's dishonoured me! He's bin an' tried to ravish my wife, my dear Annie, pore defenceless little critter! You got to let me at him!"

The man above me chuckled, leaned down and grabbed me by the waistband, and with surprising strength dragged me across the hall and threw me bodily through a doorway. Then he stepped into the room, shut the door, and growled:

"Now you just lie there easy, friend, or it'll be the worse fer you."

He had a whip in one hand, and I guessed he was the fellow who had hit me. He was a tall, rangy chap, with a heavy moustache and bright grey eyes which surveyed me sardonically as he went on:

"Layin' still oughtn't to be no hardship fer you; I reckon you're a right smart hand at *layin'*. Mandeville seems to think so, anyways." And he nodded to the door, beyond which we could hear Mandeville still roaring.

I was getting my wits back, and they told me that this fellow wasn't unfriendly.

"For heaven's sake, sir!" I cried. "Cut me loose! I can explain, I promise you! Mandeville is mistaken, believe—"

"Well, now, I reckon he is. Leastways, 'bout his little lady gittin' ravished. I seen her, an' a less ravished-lookin' female I never clapped eyes on. Say, ain't she a sight when she's nekkid, though; mighty trim little tail." He laughed, and leaned down towards me. "Tell me, friend—what she like in the hay? I often fancied—"

"Cut me free! I assure you I can explain—"

"Well, can ye now? I would doubt that, I really would."

He laughed again. "An' if I was Mandeville, I wouldn't listen. I'd cut your goddamned throat here an' now, yessir. Hold on, though; sound like he's comin' to do it his own self."

I struggled on to my knees as the tumult in the hall increased; it sounded as though Mandeville's friends were still having to restrain him by main force. I knelt there, quaking, and pleading with Luke to cut me free, but he shook me off, and when I persisted he kicked me flat on my back.

"Didn't I tell ye to lay still? Any more out o' you an' I'll take this hide to ye." He laughed again, and I suddenly realised that his good humour was not at all friendly, as I'd supposed. He was just enjoying himself.

I didn't dare move after that, but lay shaking with dread, and then after what seemed an age the door opened and the others came in. Mandeville was in the lead, panting and dishevelled, but he seemed to have himself in hand for the moment. Not that that was any consolation; I hope I never see eyes glaring at me like that again.

"You!" says he, and it was like the growl of a beast. "I going to kill you! D'ye hear that now? Kill you for the sneakin' scum you are. Yes sir, I goin' to watch you die for what you done!" There was froth at the corner of his mouth; he was appalling. "But before I do, you goin' to tell these here gennelmen somethin' —you goin' to confess to 'em that you tried to rape my wife! That so, isn't it! You snuck up there, an' you tuk her unawares, an' try to ravish her." He paused, livid. "Now, then—you tell 'em it was so."

Terrified, I stared at the man, but I couldn't have spoken for the life of me, and suddenly he lost control and flung himself at me, kicking and clawing. The others hauled him back, and Luke says:

"It don't signify a damn thing, John! Hold him off, you fellows! You think you're goin' to get the truth out of him? Anyways, we *know* he tried to rape your good lady—don't we boys? We're all satisfied, I reckon."

He knew it was a lie, and so did they, but they chorused assent, and eventually it pacified Mandeville, at least to the point where his only interest lay in disposing of me.

"I ought to burn you alive!" he snarled. "I ought to nail you to a tree an' have the niggers geld you. In fact, that's just what I'll do! I'll—"

"Hold on there, John," says Luke. "This is jus' wild talk. You can't murder him thataway—"

"Why cain't I? After what he done?"

"Because word'd git out—an' it don't do to murder a man, even if he is a rapin', stinkin' skunk—"

"I'm not!" I cried. "I swear I'm not!"

"You shet up," says Luke. "Fact is, John Mandeville, while I don't deny he's got killin' comin' to him, I don't see how you can do it lessn you fight him, on the square."

"Fight him!" shouts Mandeville. "Damned if I do. He ain't deservin' anythin' but execution!"

"Well, now, ain't I a-tellin' you it cain't be done? Even ifn you hang him, or cut his throat, or shoot him—how you gonna be sure word ain't gonna git out?"

"Who's to tell, Luke Johnson? They's on'y us here—"

"An' niggers, with mighty long ears. No, sir, unless you fight him, which you ain't willin' to do, and cain't say as I blame you, for he don't deserve the consideration—well, then we got to study out some way of givin' him what's comin' to him."

They argued on, and I listened in horror as they discussed means of slaughtering me—for that was what they meant to do, not a doubt. God, the value men place on a rogered woman. I tried to intervene, pleading to be heard, but Mandeville smashed me in the face, and Luke stuck a gag in my mouth, and then they went on with their dreadful discussion. It was terrible, but all I could do was listen, until one of them motioned the others away, and they fell to talking in lowered voices, and all I could catch was snatches and words like "Alabama" and "Tombigbee river", and "very place for him", and "no, I reckon there ain't no risk—who's to know?", and then they laughed, and presently Mandeville came over to me.

"Well, Mr Arnold," says he, smiling like a hyena, "I got good news for you. Yes sir, mighty good. We ain't goin' to kill you —how you like that? No, sir, we value you a mite too high for that, I reckon. You're a sneakin' varmint that took advantage of a man's hospitality to try and steal his honour—we got suthin' better for you than jus' killin'. You like to hear about it?"

I wanted to stop my ears, but I couldn't. Mandeville smirked and went on.

"One of my friends here, he got a prime idea. His cousin a planter over to Alabama—quite a ways from here. Now my friend goin' over that way, takin' a runaway back to another place, and he ready to 'blige me by takin' you a stage farther, to his cousin's plantation. Nobody see you leave here, nobody see you git there. An' when you do, you know what goin' to happen to you?" Suddenly he spat in my face. "You goin' to be stripped an' put in the cane-fields, 'long with the niggers! You pretty dark now—I seen mustees as light as you—an' by the time you laboured in the sun a spell, you brown up pretty good I reckon. An' there you'll be, *Slave* Arnold, see? You won't be dead, but you'll wish you were! Ain't nobody ever goin' to see you, on account it a lonely place, an' no one ever go there—ifn they do, why you just a crazy mustee! Nobody know you here, nobody ever ask for you. An' you never escape—on account no nigger ever run from that plantation—swamps an' dogs always git 'em. So you safe there for life, see? You think you'll enjoy that life, *Slave* Arnold?" He stood up and kicked me savagely. "Now, ain't that a whole heap better'n jus' killin' you, quick an' easy?"

I couldn't believe my ears; I must be dreaming the whole ghastly thing. I writhed and tried to spit the gag out—tried to beg for mercy with my eyes, but it was useless. They laughed at my struggles, and then they tied my feet and threw me into a cupboard. Before they shut the door, Luke leaned over me with his friendly grin, and said softly:

"Reckon you'll count it a pretty dear ride you had, friend. Was she good? I hope for your sake she was, 'cos she's the last white woman you'll ever see, you dirty Texian bastard!"

I couldn't believe what I'd heard—I still find it incredible. That white men—civilised white men, could doom another white man to be dragged away to some vile plantation, herded with niggers, flogged to work like a beast—it couldn't be true, surely? All I'd done was rattle Mandeville's wife—well, if I ever caught a man doing the like to Elspeth, I'd want to kill him, probably, and I could understand Mandeville wanting to as well—but how could he doom me to the living hell of black slavery? It must be their ghastly idea of a joke—it couldn't be true, it just could not be!

But it was. How long I lay in that cupboard I don't know, but it was dark when the door opened and I was dragged out. They had brought my coat, and it was wrapped over my head, and then I felt the horror of fetters being clapped on my ankles. I tried to scream through my gag, and struggled, but they carried me away bodily, muttering and laughing, and presently I was flung on to the hard surface of a cart. I heard Luke say, "Take good care o' that valuable merchandise, Tom Little," and laughter, and then we were jolting away in the darkness.

I twisted in my bonds, half-crazed with the abomination of it, and then the jacket was pulled away, and in the dimness of the cart a woman's voice said:

"Lie still. There's no use struggling. Believe me, I tried struggling —once. It's no good. You must wait—wait and hope."

She pulled out the gag, but my mouth was too parched to speak. She laid her hand on my head, stroking it, and in the dark her voice kept whispering:

"Rest, don't struggle. Wait and hope. Lie still. Wait and hope."

Her name was Cassy, and I believe that without her I must have gone mad on that first night on the slave cart. The darkness, the close animal stench of the enclosed space in which we were cooped up, and most of all the horror of what lay ahead, reduced me to a croaking wreck. And while I lay shuddering and moaning to myself, she stroked my head and talked in a soft, sibilant voice—hardly a trace of nigger, more New Orleans Frenchy, like Annette's—telling me to be easy, and rest, and not to waste my breath on foolish raving. All very well, but foolish raving is a capital way of releasing one's feelings. However, she talked on, and in the end it must have soothed me, because when I opened my eyes the cart was stopped, and a little sunlight was filtering through cracks in the board roof, giving a dim illumination to the interior.

The first thing I did was to crawl about the place—it wasn't above four feet high—examining it, but it was as tight as a drum, and the doors appeared to be padlocked. I couldn't see a hope of escape. I was chained by the legs—the woman had managed to untie the cord at my wrists—and even if I had succeeded in breaking out, what could I have done against two armed men? They would doubtless be making for Alabama by back roads and trails, far from any hope of assistance, and even if, by some miracle, I got out and gave them the slip, they would easily run me down, hobbled as I was.

The horror of it overcame me again, and I just lay there and wept. There was no hope, and the woman's voice suddenly came to confirm my fears.

"It won't seem so bad after a while," she said. "Nothing ever does."

I turned to look at her, and for a moment a crazy thought struck me—that she, too, was white, and the victim of some fearful plot like my own. For she was no more like a nigger than

I was, at first glance. You have seen her head on old Egyptian carvings, both chin and forehead sloping sharply away from a thin curved nose and wide heavy lips, with great almond-shaped devil's eyes which can look strong and terrible in that delicate face. She was unusually tall, but everything about her was fine and fragile, from the high cheekbones and thin black hair bound tight behind her head to the slender ankles locked in slave fetters; even her colour was delicate, like very pale honey, and I realised she was the lightest kind of nigger, what they call a musteefino.[37] She reminded me of a Siamese cat, graceful and sinuous and probably far stronger than she looked.

Mind you, my thoughts weren't running in their usual direction; I was too powerfully occupied with my predicament for that, and I fell to groaning and cursing again. I must have babbled something about escape, because she suddenly said:

"Why do you waste your breath? Don't you know better by now—there's no escape. Not now, or ever."

"My God!" I cried. "There must be. You don't know what they're going to do to me. I'm to be enslaved on a plantation —for life!"

"Is that so strange?" said she, bitterly. "You're lucky you haven't been there before. What were you—a house slave?"

"I'm not a bloody slave!" I shouted. "I'm a white man."

She stared at me through the dimness. "Oh, come now. We stop saying that when we're ten years old."

"It's true, I tell you! I'm an Englishman! Can't you tell?"

She moved across the cart, peering at my face, frowning. Then: "Give me your hand," she says.

I let her look at my nails; she dropped my hand and sat back, staring at me with those great amber-flecked eyes. "Then what are you doing here, in God's name?"

You may be sure I told her—at length, but leaving out the juicy parts: Mandeville suspected me unjustly, I told her. She sat like a graven image until it was done, and then all she said was:

"Well, now one of you knows what it feels like." She went back to her corner. "Now you know what a filthy race you belong to."

"But, dear Christ!" I exclaimed. "I must get out of it, I must—"

"How?" Her lips writhed in a sneer. "Do you know how many times I've run? Three times! And each time they caught me, and dragged me back. Escape! Bah! You talk like a fool."

"But . . . but . . . last night . . . in the dark . . . you said something about waiting and hoping . . ."

"That was to comfort you. I thought you were . . . one of us." She gave a bitter little laugh. "Well, you are, now, and I tell you there isn't any hope. Where can you run to, in this vile country? This land of freedom! With slave-catchers everywhere, and dogs, and whipping-houses, and laws that say I'm no better than a beast in a sty!" Her eyes were blazing with a hatred that was scaring. "You try and run! See what good it does you!"

"But slave-catchers can't touch me! If only I can get out of this cursed wagon! Look," I went on, desperately, "there must be a chance—when they open the doors, to feed us—"

"How little you know of slavery!" she mocked me. "They won't open the doors—not till they get me to Forster's place, and you to wherever you're going. Feed us!—that's how they feed us, like dogs in a kennel!" And she pointed to a hatch in the door, which I hadn't noticed. "For the rest, you foul your sty— why shouldn't you? You're just a beast! Did you know that was what the Romans called us—talking beasts? Oh, yes, I learned a lot about slavery, in the fine house I was brought up in. Brought up so that I could be made the chattel of any filthy ruffian, any beggar or ignorant scum of the levees—just so he was white!" She sat glaring at me, then her shoulders drooped. "What use to talk? You don't know what it means. But you will. You will."

Well, you may guess how this raised my spirits. The very fierceness of the woman, her bitter certainty, knocked what little fight I had out of me. I sat dejected, and she silent, until after a while I heard Little and his companion talking outside, and presently the hatch was raised, and a tin dish was shoved in, and a bottle of water. I was at the hatch in a flash, shouting to them, pleading and offering money, which set them into roars of laughter.

"Say, hear that now! Ain't that bully? What about you, Cass— ain't you got a thousand dollars to spare for ifn we let you go? No? Well, ain't that a shame, though? No, my lord, I'm sorry, but truth is me an' George here, we don't need the money anyways. An' I ain't too sure we'd trust your note o' hand, either. Haw-haw!"

And the cruel brute slammed down the hatch and went off, chuckling.

Through all this Cass never said a word, and when we had tried to eat the filthy muck they had given us, and rinsed our throats from the bottle, she went back to her corner and sat there, her head against the boards, staring into vacancy. Presently the cart started up, and for the rest of the day we jolted slowly over what must have been a damned bad road, while the atmosphere in the cart grew so hot and stifling that I was sure we must suffocate before long. Once or twice I bawled out to Little, pleading with him, but all I got was oaths and obscene jokes, so I gave up, and all the time Cassy sat silent, only occasionally turning to stare at me, but making no reply to my croaks and questions. I cursed her for a black slut, but she didn't seem to hear.

Towards sunset, the cart stopped, and immediately Cassy seemed to come to life. She peered through a crack in the side of the wagon, and then crawled over to me, motioning me to talk in whispers.

"Listen," she said. "You want to escape?"

I couldn't believe my ears. "Escape? I—"

"Quiet, in heaven's name! Now, listen. If I can show you how to escape—will you make me a promise?"

"Anything! My God, anything!"

The great almond eyes stared into mine. "Don't protest too easily—I mean what I say. Will you swear, by all that you believe to be holy, that if I help you escape, you will never desert me —that you will help me, in my turn, to gain my freedom?"

I'd have sworn a good deal more than that. With hope surging through me, I whispered. "I swear—I promise! I'll do anything. No, I'll never desert you, I swear it!"

She stared at me a moment longer, and then glanced towards the door.

"Soon now they will bring our food. When they do, you will be making love to me—do you understand?"

I couldn't follow this, but I nodded, feverish with excitement.

In a whisper she went on:

"When they see us, whatever they say, defy them. Do you understand me? Taunt them, swear at them—anything! Then leave the rest to me. Whatever I do or say, do nothing further."

"What are you going to do? What can I—"

"Quiet!" She started up. "They're coming, I think. Now—over there, where they'll see us."

And as footsteps came round to the back of the cart she sprawled into the middle of the floor, dragging up her dress, and pulling me down on top of her. Trembling, and for once not for the usual reasons, I clung to the pliant body, crushing my mouth down on hers and plunging like mad—gad, as I look back, what a waste of good effort it was, in the circumstances. I heard the hatch flung open, and in that moment Cassy writhed and began to sob in simulated ecstasy, clawing at me and squealing. There was an oath and commotion at the hatch, and then a cry of:

"Tom! Tom! Come quick! That damned Texian feller, he's screwin' the wench!"

More commotion, and then Little's voice:

"What you think you're doin', blast ye? Get offa her, this minute! Get off, d'ye hear, or I'll fill yore ass with buckshot!"

I bawled an obscenity at him, and then there was a rattling at the lock, the door was flung wide, to the gathering dusk, and Little glared in, his piece levelled at me. I decided I had defied him sufficiently, and rolled away; Cassy scrambled up into a reclining position.

"Damn you!" bawls Little. "Don't you never get enough?"

I stayed mum, while he cursed at me, his pal staring pop-eyed over his shoulder. And then Cass, shrugging her shoulders petulantly and moving to display her fine long legs, remarked:

"Why can't you let us be? What's the harm in it?"

Little's piggy little eyes went over her; he licked his lips, still keeping his gun pointed at me.

"Harm in it?" His voice was thick. "You ol' Forster's wench, ain't you? Think you can rattle with everyone you please? Not while I'm around, my gel. You dirty nigger tail, you!"

She shrugged again, pouting, and spoke in a voice very unlike her own.

"Ifn massa say. Cassy don' mind none, anyways. This feller ain't bait for a gel like me—I used to real men."

Little's eyes opened wide. "Is that a fact?" His loose bearded mouth opened in a grin. "Well, think o' that, now. I didn't know you was thataway inclined, Cass—fancy yellow gel like you, with all them lady airs." He was thinking as he talked, and there was no doubting what those thoughts were. "Well, now—you just come out o' that cart this minute, d'ye hear? You—" this was to me—"keep yourself mighty still, lessn you want a belly-full o' lead. Come on, my gel, git your ass outa that wagon—smart!"

Cassy slid herself to the tail of the cart, while they watched her closely, and dropped lightly to the ground. I stayed where I was, my heart hammering. Little motioned with his gun, and the other fellow slammed and locked the door, leaving me in darkness. But I could hear their voices, plain enough.

"Now, then, Cass," says Little. "You step roun' there, lively now. So—now, you jus' shuck down, d'ye hear?" There was a pause, and then Cassy's new voice:

"Massa gwine ter be nice to Cassy?—Cassy a good gel, please massa ever so much."

"By God, an' so ye will! Look at that, George—here, you hol' the gun! An' make yourself scarce. By gosh, I'm goin' to 'tend to this li'l beauty right here an' now! What you waitin' for, George —you get outa here!"

"Don' I get none o' her, then? Don' I even get to watch?"

"Watch? Why, how you talk! Think I'm a hog, or a nigger, that I'd do my screwin' with you watchin'? Get outa here, quick! You'll get your piece when I'm done. Here, gimme back that gun—reckon I'll keep it by, case her ladyship gits up to anythin'. But you won't, honey, will you?"

I heard George's reluctant footsteps retreating, and then silence; I strained my ears, but could hear nothing through the wagon side. A minute passed, and then there was a sudden sharp gasp, and a thin whining sound half-way between a sigh and a wail, and the sound of it made the hairs rise on my neck. A moment later, and Cassy's voice in sudden alarm:

"Mas' George, Mas' George! Come quick! Suthin' happen to

Mas' Tom—he hurt himself! Come quick!"

"What's that?" George's voice sounded from a little way off, and I heard his feet running. "What you say—what happened, Tom? You all right, Tom? What—"

The gunshot crashed out with startling suddenness, near the back of the wagon; there was a scream and a choking groan, and then nothing, until I heard the padlock rattle, the door was flung back, and there was Cassy. Even in the dusk I could see she was naked; she still had the musket in her hand.

"Quickly!" she cried. "Come out! They're both done for!"

I was out, fetters and all, in a twinkling. George lay spread-eagled at my feet, the top half of his face a bloody mash—she had given him the buckshot at point-blank range. I looked round and saw Little, crouched on his knees by the camp-fire, his head down; even as I started towards him he rolled over, with a little bubbling sob, and I saw the knife hilt sticking out of the crimson soaking mess that stained his shirt. He twitched for a moment, bubbling, and then was still.

Cassy was at the wagon, holding weakly to the door, her head hanging. I hopped over to her, grabbed her round the waist and swung her off her feet.

"Oh, you wonderful nigger!" I shouted, spinning her round. "You little black beauty, you! Bravo! Two at one stroke, by George! Well done indeed!" And I kissed her gleefully.

"Set me down!" she gasped. "In God's name, set me down!"

So I put her down, and she shuddered and sank to the ground, all of a heap. For a moment I thought she'd fainted, but she was a prime girl, that one. With her teeth chattering she grabbed up her dress, pulling it down over her head, which seemed a pity, for she cut a truly splendid figure in the firelight. I patted her on the shoulder, telling her what a brave wench she was.

"Oh, God!" says she, with her eyes tight shut. "Oh, horrible! I didn't know . . . what it was like . . . when I drew the knife from his belt and . . . " She put her face in her hands and sobbed.

"Serve him right," says I. "You've done him a power of good. And the other one, too—couldn't have done better myself, by jove, no, I couldn't! You're a damned good-plucked 'un, young Cassy, and you may tell 'em that Tom Arnold said so!"

But she sat there, shivering, so I wasted no more time but searched Tom's pockets for the keys to our fetters, and soon had us both loose. Then I went through their pockets, but apart from fifteen dollars there was nothing worth a curse. I stripped George's body, because it struck me that he was about my size, and his togs might come in handy. Then I looked to their guns—one musket, two pistols, with powder and ball—saw that the wagon horse was all to rights, and all the time my heart was singing inside me. I was free again, thanks to that splendid nigger wench. By gum, I admired that girl, and still do—she'd have made a rare mate for my old Sergeant Hudson—and while I heated up some coffee and vittles left by the late unlamented, I told her what I thought of her.

She was crouched by the fire, staring straight ahead of her, but now she seemed to shake herself out of her trance, for she threw back that lovely Egyptian head and looked at me. "You remember your promise?" says she, and I assured her I did—assured her twenty times over. I can see her now, those wonderful almond eyes watching me while I prattled on, praising her resource and courage—it was a strange meal that, a runaway slave girl and I, sitting round a camp fire in Mississippi, with two dead bodies lying by. And before it was done she had thrown off her fit of the shakes—after all, when you're new to it, killing is almost as disturbing as nearly being killed—and was telling me what we must do next. My admiration increased—why, she had thought it out all beforehand, in the wagon, down to the last detail.

It had been my remark about slave-catchers not touching a white man that had set her thinking, and shown her how she could make a successful run this time, with me to help her.

"We must travel as master and slave," says she. "That way no one will give us a second thought—but we must go quickly. It may be a week before Mandeville discovers that this wagon never reached Forster's place, and that these two men"—she gave a little shudder—"are missing. It might even be longer, but we dare not count on it—we dare not! Long before then we must be out of the state, on our way north."

"In that?" says I, nodding to the cart, and she shook her head.

"It can take us no farther than the river; we must go faster than it will carry us. We must go by steamboat."

"Hold on, though—that costs money, and these two hadn't but fifteen dollars between them. We can't get a passage on that."

"Then we'll steal money!" says she, fiercely. "We have pistols —you are a strong man! We can take what we need!"

But I wasn't having that—not that I'm scrupulous, but I'm no hand as a foot-pad. It's too risky by half, and so I told her.

"Risk!" she blazed. "You talk of risk, after what I have done this night? Don't you see—we have two murders on our hands— isn't *that* a risk? Do you know what will happen if we're caught— you will be hanged, and I'll be burned alive! And you talk of robbery as a risk!"

"Holding someone up will only increase the danger," says I, "for then we *would* be hunted, whereas if we go our way quietly there'll be no hue and cry until these two are found—if they ever are."

"Whoever we robbed could go the way these went," says she. "Then there would be no added danger." By God, she was a cold-blooded one, that. When I protested, she lost her temper:

"Why should we be squeamish over white lives? D'you think I care if every one of these filthy slave-driving swine is torn to pieces tomorrow? And why should you shrink from it, after what they would have done to you? Are they your people, these?"

I tried to convince her it wasn't principle, but pure lack of nerve, and we argued on, she waxing passionate—she hated with a lust for revenge that frightened me. But I wouldn't have it, and eventually she gave up, and sat staring into the fire, her hands clenched on her knees. At last she says, very quietly:

"Well, money we must have, however we come by it. And if you will not steal for it—well, there is only one other way. It does not add greatly to the risk, but... but I would do almost anything to avoid it."

Possibly I'm a natural-born pimp, for I jumped to the conclusion that she was thinking of whoring her way upriver, with me as her protector, but it was something far grander than that.

"We must go to Memphis," says she. "It is a town on the river, not more than fifty miles from here, so far as I can judge. That would be for the day after tomorrow—perhaps another day. That in itself is no great risk, for we have to go to the river anyway, and if God is kind to us none of Mandeville's friends, or people of Forster's, who would know me, will cross our path. And when we are there . . . we can find the money. Oh, yes, we can find the money!"

And to my astonishment she began to weep—not sobbing, but just great tears rolling down her cheeks. She dashed them away, and then fumbled inside her dress, and after a moment she produced a paper, soiled but very carefully-folded, which she passed to me. Wondering, I opened it, and saw that it was a bill of sale, dated February 1843, for one Cassy, a negro girl, the property of one Angel de Marmalade (I swear that was the name) of New Orleans, now duly sold and delivered to Fitzroy Howard, of San Antonio de Bexar. There was another scrap of paper with it which fluttered down—she made a grab, but not in time to prevent me seeing the words scrawled on it in a coarse, lumpy hand:

"Wensh Cassy. Ten lashys. Wun dollar," and a signature that was illegible.

She drew away, and spoke with her head turned from me.

"That was my second bill of sale. I was fourteen. I stole it from Howard, when he was drunk and I ran from him. They caught me, but he was dead by then, and when they auctioned me with his other . . . goods, they didn't bother to look for the old bill. I kept it—to remember. Just to remember, so that when I was free, and far away, I should never forget what it was to be a slave! No one ever found it!—they never found it!" Her voice was rising, and she swung her head round to stare at me, her eyes brimming. "I never thought it might serve to win my freedom! But it will!"

"How, in heaven's name?"

"You'll carry it to Memphis—you'll be Mr Fitzroy Howard! No one knows him this far north—he died in Texas four years ago—four years he's been screaming in Hell! And you'll *sell* me in Memphis—oh, I'll fetch a fine price, you'll see! A thousand, two thousand dollars—maybe three, for a choice mustee wench, fancy-bred, only nineteen, and schooled in a New Orleans brothel! Oh, they'll buy all right!"

Well, this seemed first-rate business to me, and I said so.

"Three thousand dollars—why, woman, what were you ever thinking of highway robbery for? Half that sum will see us rolling upriver in style—but wait though! If you're sold—how'll you get away?"

"I can run. Oh, believe me, I can run! The moment you have the money, you'll buy passages on a boat north—we'll have decided which one beforehand. Leave it to me to run at the right time—we'll meet at the levee or somewhere and go aboard together. You'll be what they call a nigger-stealer then, and I a runaway slave—but they won't catch us. What, Mr and Mrs Whatever-we-choose-to-call-ourselves, first-class passengers to Louisville? Oh, no, we'll be safe enough—if you keep our bargain."

Well, it had crossed my mind, of course, in the last two seconds, from the moment she'd reminded me of the nasty stigma of nigger-stealing, that it would be a sight safer to catch a different boat, all on my own, with the three thousand dollars, and leave Miss Cassy to fend for herself. But she was as quick as I was.

"If I didn't get out of Memphis," says she, slowly and intently, leaning forward to look into my face, "I'd give myself up—and tell them how we had run together, and you had killed two men back in Mississippi, and where the bodies were, and all about you. You wouldn't get far, Mr—what is your name, anyway?"

"Er, Flash—, er, Brown, I mean. But, look here, my dear girl, I promised not to desert you—remember? D'you think I'm the kind to break his word? I must say—"

"I don't know," says she, slowly. "I only tell you what will happen if you do. It may cost me my life, but it will certainly cost you yours, Mr Flash-er-Brown."

"I wouldn't dream of leaving you," says I, seriously. "Not for a moment. But, I say, Cassy—this is a top-hole plan! Why didn't you tell me before—it's absolutely splendid!"

She gazed at me, and took a deep breath, and then turned to gaze into the fire.

"You would think so, I suppose. Perhaps it seems a little thing to you—to be placed on a block, and auctioned like a beast to the highest bidder. To be pawed over and fumbled by dirty hands—stripped even, and gloated over!" The tears were starting again, but her voice never shook. "How could you even begin to imagine it? The hideous shame—the humiliation!" She swung round on me again—a habit of hers which I confess made me damned jumpy.

"Do you know what I was, until I was thirteen? I was a little Creole girl, in a fine house in Baton Rouge, with my papa and two brothers and two sisters, all older than I. Their mother was dead—she was white—and my mother, who was a slave mustee, was mother to them as well. We were the happiest family in the world—I loved them, and they loved me, or so I thought, until my father died. And then they sold us—my loving brothers sold me, their sister, and my mother, who had been more than a mother to them. They *sold* us! My mother to a planter—me to a bawd in New Orleans!"

She was shaking with passion. Something seemed called for, so I says:

"Pretty steep work, that. Bad business."

"I was a whore—at thirteen! I ran away, back to my family—and they gave me up! They put me in a cellar until my owner came, and took me back to New Orleans. You saw that other paper, with the bill of sale. Do you know what it is? It is a receipt from a whipping-house—where slaves are sent to be corrected! I was only thirteen, so they were lenient with me—only ten lashes! Can you understand what that did to me? Can you? For they make a spectacle of it—oh, yes! I was tied up naked, and whipped before an audience of men! Can you even begin to dream what it is like—the unbelievable, frightful shame of it? But how could I make you understand!" She was beating her fist on my knee by now, crying into my face. "You are a man—what would it do to you, to be stripped and bound and flogged before a pack of leering, laughing women?"

"Oh, well," says I, "I don't really know—"

"They cheered me! Do you hear that—cheered me, because I wouldn't cry, and one of them gave me a dollar! I ran back, blind with tears, with that receipt in my hand, and the she-devil who kept that brothel said: 'Keep it to remind you of what disobedience brings'. And I kept it, with the other. So that I shall never forget!"

She buried her head on my knee, weeping, and I was at a loss for once. I could think of one good way of comforting us both, but I doubted if she'd take kindly to it. So I patted her head and said:

"Well, it's a hard life, Cassy, there's no denying. But cheer up —there's a good time coming, you know. We'll be away to Memphis in the morning, raffle you off, collect the cash, and then, hey! for the steamboat! Why, we can have a deuced good time of it, I daresay, for I'm bound for the east coast, you know, and we can travel together. Why, we can—"

"Do you swear it?" She had lifted her head and was gazing up at me, her face wasted with crying. God, she was a queer one, one minute all cold steel and killing two men, and then getting the jumps over 'em—and from that she was plotting calmly, and suddenly raging with passion, and now imploring me with the wistful eyes of a child. By George, she was a handsome piece—but it wasn't the time or place, I knew. She was too much in a taking —I'll wager she had talked more that night than she'd done for years. But women have always loved to confide in me; I think it's my bluff, honest, manly countenance—and my whiskers, of course.

"You do promise?" she begged me. "You will help me, and never desert me? Never, until I'm free?"

Well, you know what my promises are; still I gave it, and I believe I meant it at the time. She took my hand, and kissed it, which disturbed me oddly, and then she says, looking me in the eyes:

"Strange, that you should be an Englishman. I remember, years ago, on the Pierrepoint Plantation, the slaves used to talk of the underground railroad—the freedom road, they called it—and how those who could travel it in safety might win at last to Canada, and then they could never be made slaves again. There was one old man, a very old slave, who had a book that he had gotten from somewhere, and I used to read to them from it—it was called *Nore's Epitome of Navigation*, all about the sea, and ships, and none of us could understand it, but it was the only book we had, and so they loved to hear me read from it." She tried to smile, with her eyes full of tears, and her voice was trembling. "On the outside there was a picture of a ship, with a Union Jack at its mast, and the old man used to point to it and say: 'Dat's de flag o' liberty, chillun; dat de ol' flag'. And I used to remember what I had once heard someone say—I can't recall where or when, but I never forgot the words." She paused a moment, and then said in a whisper almost: " 'Whoever stands on British soil, shall be forever free'. It's true, isn't it? "

"Oh, absolutely," says I. "We're the chaps, all right. Don't hold with slavery at all, don't you know."

And, strange as it may seem, sitting there with her looking at me as though I were the Second Coming, well—I felt quite proud, you know. Not that I care a damn, but—well, it's nice, when you're far away and don't expect it, to hear the old place well spoken of.

"God bless you," says she, and she let go my hand, and I thought of making a grab at her, for the third time, but changed my mind. And we went to sleep on opposite sides of the fire, after I'd stoked it up and shoved Little's body into the bushes; deuce of a weight to move he was, too.

*　　*　　*

It took us two full days to Memphis, and the closer we got the more uneasy I became about the scheme we had undertaken. The chief risk was that we would be recognised by somebody, and if looking back I can say that it was only a chance in a thousand— well, that's still an uncomfy chance if your neck depends on it.

I was in high enough spirits when we set off from our camping place at dawn, for the glow of being free again hadn't worn off. It was with positive zest that I hauled the corpses of Little and George well into the thickets, and dumped them in a swampy pool full of reeds and frogs; then I tidied up the tracks as well as I could, and we set off. Cassy sat in the back of the cart, out of sight, while I drove, and we rolled along through the woods over the rutted road—it was more like a farm-track, really—until I came to a fork running north-west, which was the direction we wanted to go.

We followed it until noon without seeing a soul, which I now know was pretty lucky, but soon after we had cooked up a fry and moved on we came to a small village, and here something happened which damped my spirits a good deal, for it showed me what a small place even the American backwoods can be, and how difficult it is to pass through without every Tom, Dick and Harry taking an interest in you.

The village was dozing in the afternoon, with only a nigger or two kicking about, a dog nosing in a rubbish tip, and a baby wailing on a porch, but just the other side of town there was the inevitable yokel whittling on a stump, with his straw hat over his eyes and his bare feet stuck in the dust. I decided it was safe to make an inquiry, and pulled up.

"Hollo," says I, cheerily.

"Hollo, y'self," says he.

"Am I on the road to Memphis, friend?" says I.

He thought about this, chewing and polishing up one of those cracker-barrel witticisms which are Mississippi's gift to civilisation. At last he said:

"Well, if y'don't know for sartain, you're a damfool to be headin' along it, ain't you?"

"I would be, if I wasn't sure of direction from a smart man like you," says I.

He cocked an eye at me. "How come you're so sure?"

It's like talking before salt with the Arabs, or doing business with a Turk; you must go through the ritual.

"Because it's a hot day."

"That makes you sure?"

"Makes me sure you're thirsty, which makes me sure you'll take a suck at the jug I've got under my seat—and then you'll tell me the road to Memphis." I threw the jug at him, and he snapped it up like a trout taking a fly.

"Guess I might sample it, at that," says he, and sampled about a pint. "Jay-zus! That's drinkin' liquor. Ye-ah—I reckon you might be on the Memphis road, sure enough. Should git there, too, provided you don't fall in Coldwater Creek or git elected guv-nor or die afore you arrive." He threw the jug back, and I was about to whip up when he says:

"You f'm Nawth? You don't talk like ol' Miss, nor Arkinsaw, neether."

"No, I'm from Texas."

"You don't say? Long ways off, the Texies. Young Jim Noble, he went down there, 'bout two years back. Ever run across Jim?"

"I reckon not."

"No." He considered me, the sharp, sleepy little eyes peeping out under the frayed straw brim. "Would that be Tom Little's wagon your drivin'? Seems I know that broken spoke—an' the horse."

For a moment my blood ran cold, and I stopped my hand from going to the pistol in the back of my belt.

"Well, it *was* Tom Little's wagon," says I. "Still would be, if he hadn't loaned it me yesterday. When I take it back, it will be his again, I guess." If I'd stayed in that country, and learned to whittle with a Barlow knife, and chew tobacco, I'd have made president.

"That a fact," says he. "First time I heerd o' Tom lendin' anything."

"Well, I'm his cousin," says I. "So he didn't mind lending it to me." And I whipped up and made off.

"Good for him," calls the yokel after me. "He might ha' told you the road to Memphis, while he was about it."

By George, it rattled me, I can tell you. When we were out of sight I conferred with Cassy, and she agreed we must press on as hard as we could go. With every loafer in the county weighing us up, the sooner we were clear the better. So we pushed on, and might have made it next day if I hadn't had to rest the horse—spavined old bitch she was. We had to sleep another night out, and the following morning we left the cart beside a melon patch, telling a nigger to mind it for us, and walked the last mile into Memphis town.

It was a fair-sized place, even in those days, for half the cotton in the world seemed to find its way there, but to my jaundiced eye it appeared to be made entirely out of mud. It had rained from first light, and by the time we had walked through the churned-up streets, and been splashed by wagons and by dam-fools who didn't look where they were going, we were in a sorry state. But the crowded bustle of the place, and the foul weather, made me feel happier, because both lessened the chance of anyone recognising us.

Now all that remained to be done was for me to sell a runaway slave and arrange for us to get out of town without any holes in our hides. Easy enough, you may think, for a chap of Flashy's capabilities, and I'll admit your confidence wouldn't be misplaced. But I wonder how many young chaps nowadays, in this civilised twentieth century, would know how to go about it, if they were planked down, near penniless and with their boots letting in, on a foreign soil, and asked to dispose of a fine-strung mustee woman whose depression and nervousness were growing steadily as the crisis approached? It takes thought, I tell you, and a strong grip on one's own gorge to keep it from leaping out.

The first thing was to find when the next sale was, and here we were lucky, for there was one in the market that very afternoon, which meant we could do our business and, God willing, be out by nightfall. Next I must inquire about steamboats, so leaving Cassy under the shelter of a shop porch, I ploshed down to the levee to make inquiries. It was pouring fit to frighten Noah by now, with a howling wind as well, and by the time I tacked up to the steamboat office I was plastered with gumbo to the thighs and sodden from there up. To add to my difficulties, the ancient at the office window, wearing a dirty old pilot cap and a vacant expression, was both stone deaf and three parts senile; when I bawled my inquiries to him above the noise of the storm he responded with a hand to his ear and a bewildered grin.

"Is there a boat to Louisville tonight?" I roared.

"Hey?"

"Boat to Louisville?"

"Cain't hear you, mister. Speak up, cain't ye?"

I dragged my collar closer and dashed the rain out of my eyes.

"Boat to Louisville—tonight?" I yelled.

"Boat to where?"

"Oh, for pity's sake! LOUIS!—" I gathered all my lung power "—VILLE! Is there a boat tonight?"

At last he beamed and nodded.

"Shore 'nough, mister. The new *Missouri*. Leaves at ten."

I thanked him forcibly and ploughed back up town. Now all that must be done was render myself and Cassy as respectable as possible and go to work with our hands on our hearts. The first part we managed, roughly, in the back room of a cheap apartment house which I hired for the day; my good coat, which had been thrown over my head when I left Greystones—a prodigious stroke of luck that, for it had Spring's precious papers sewn in the lining —was sadly soiled, but we made the best of it, and rehearsed the final details of our plan. I was in a sweat about how Cassy would slip away from her new owner, but this she brushed aside; what made her grit her teeth to stop them chattering was the thought of mounting the slave block and being sold, which seemed strange to me, since it had happened to her before, and didn't involve any pain or danger at all.

She was to run late that evening, make her way back to the apartment house, knock at my window, which was on the ground floor, and be admitted. I would have clothes for her by then, and we'd make our way to the levee and go aboard the *Missouri* as Mr and Mrs James B. Montague, of Baton Rouge, travelling north. In the dark it should be simple enough.

"If I do not come—wait," says she. "I will come in the end. If I don't come by tomorrow, I'll be dead, and you will be able to go where you will. But until then I hold you to your word—your pledged promise, remember?"

"I remember, I remember!" says I, jittering. "But suppose you can't run—suppose he chains you up, or something. What then?"

"He won't," says she, calmly. "Be assured, I can run. There is nothing hard about running—any slave can do it. But to stay free —that is the impossible part, unless you have a refuge, a protector. I have you."

Well, I've been called a few things in my time, but these were new. If she'd known me better she'd have thought different, no doubt, but she was desperate, and I was her only hope—a hellish pickle for a girl to be in, you'll agree. I strove to calm my fluttering bowels, and presently we set out for the slave market.

If you've never seen a slave auction, I can tell you it's no different from an ordinary cattle sale. The market was a great low shed, with sawdust on the floor, a block at one end for the slaves and auctioneer, and the rest of the space taken up with the buyers and spectators—wealthy traders on seats at the front, very much at ease, casual buyers behind, and more than half the whole crew just spectators, loafers, bumarees and sightseers, spitting and gossiping and haw-hawing. The place was noisy and stank like the deuce, with clouds of baccy smoke and esprit de corps hanging under the beams.

I'd been scared stiff that when I entered Cassy for sale there would be all sorts of questions, cross-examination, and the like, which I wouldn't be able to answer convincingly, but I had been fretting unduly. I believe if you entered a Swedish albino at a Memphis sale and swore he was a nigger, they'd stick him on the block, no questions asked. That auctioneer would have sold his own grandfather, and probably had. He was a small, furious, red-bearded man with a slouch hat, a big cigar, and a quart bottle of forty-rod in his coat pocket which he sucked at in between accusing his assistants of swindling him and bawling to everyone to give him some sellin' room.

When I entered Cassy he hardly glanced at her bill of sale, but spat neatly between my feet and asked me aggressively if I was an underground railroad agent who'd thought better of convoying a nigger to Canada and decided to sell her off for private gain.

The crowd round him all haw-hawed immensely at this, and said he was a prime case, which relieved my momentary horror at his question, and the auctioneer said he didn't give a damn, anyhow, and where the hell was Eli Bowles's nigger's papers, because he hadn't got them, and they'd drive a man out of his mind in this country, what with their finickin' regulations, and would they get the hell out of his way so he could start the sale? No, he wouldn't put up Jackson's buck Perseus, because he was rotten with pox, and everyone knew it; Jackson had better put him out to stud over in Arkansas, where nobody noticed such things. No, he wouldn't take notes of hand from any but dealers he knew—he'd enough tarnation paper as it was, and his clerk just used it to confuse him and line his own pockets, and *he* knew all about it, and one of these days wouldn't he make that clerk's ass warm for him. And, strike him dumb, but his bottle was half empty and he hadn't even started the sale yet—would they git out from under his feet or did they want to be still biddin' their bollix off at two in the morning?

And more of the same, all of which was mighty reassuring. I left Cassy to be herded off with the other niggers, and got a place by the wall to watch the sale, which the little auctioneer conducted as if he was a ring-master, pattering away incessantly, and keeping up his style of irascible confusion all the time. The crowd loved it, and he was good, too, taking an occasional swill at his bottle and firing his comments at the lots while the bids came in.

"See this here old wench of Masterson's, who died last week. Masterson died, that is, not her. Not a day over forty, an' a prime cook. Well, y'only had to look at the belly Masterson had on him; that's testimony enough, I reckon. Yes sir, it was her fine cookin' that kilt him—now then, what say? Eight hunnert to start—nine, for the best vittles-slinger 'tween Evansville an' the Gulf." Or again: "This buck of Tomkins, he sired more saplin's than Methuselah—that's why they call him George, after George Washington, the father of his country. Why, 'thout this boy, the nigger pop'lation'd be only half what it is—we wouldn't hardly be havin' this sale today, but for this randy little hero. There was talk of a syndicate to send him back to Afriky to keep the numbers up—now then, who'll say a thousand?"

But there was someone there who knew more about raising prices than even he did, and that was Cassy. When she took the block, after a whispered conference with the auctioneer, he went on about how she spoke French, and could embroider and 'tend to growing children or be a lady's maid or governess and play the piano and paint—but it was all sham. He knew what she would be sold for, and the mob kept chorusing "Shuck her down! Let's get a look at her!" while she stood, very demure, with her hands folded in front of her and her head bowed. She was pale, and I could see the strain in her face, but she knew what to do, and presently when the auctioneer spoke to her she took off her shoes and then let down her hair, very carefully, so that it hung down her back almost to her waist.

That wasn't what they wanted, of course; they yelled and stamped and whistled, but the auctioneer got the bidding up to seventeen hundred before he nodded to her, and without a change of expression she shrugged her shoulders out of the dress, let it slip down, and stepped out as bare as a babe. By gad, I was proud of her as she stood there like a pale golden statue, in the dim light under the beams, with the mob goggling and roaring approval; the price ran up to twenty-five hundred dollars in less than a minute.

At that there were only two bidders left, a fancy-weskitted young dandy in a stove-pipe hat with his mouth open, and a grey-bearded planter in the front row with a red face and big panama hat, who had a little nigger boy behind his seat to fan him. I reckon Cassy got another thousand dollars out of those two, all on her own. She put one hand on her hip—twenty-seven hundred; then she put her hands behind her head—three thousand; she stirred her rump at the dandy—thirty-two hundred, and the planter shook his head, his face sweating. She looked straight down at him, grave-faced, and winked, the crowd yelled and cheered, and the dirty old goat slapped his thigh and bid thirty-four. The dandy swore and looked sulky, but that was the bottom of his poke, evidently, for he turned away, and Cassy was knocked down to the other, amidst whoops and cries of obscene advice to him; he'd better send his wife away to visit her folks in Nashville for a spell, they shouted, and when she came back she could give him a decent burial, for he'd have killed himself by then, haw-haw.

"Wish I'd a wench like that every day," says the little auctioneer, at paying-out time—you never saw such a heap of gold coin on one dirty deal table. "I'd make my fortune. Say, if you'd given me time to advertise proper, we'd ha' had four, mebbe five thousand. Where d'you git her, Mr—eh—Howard?"

"As you said, she was a lady's maid—at my academy for gentle-women," says I gravely, and the crowd in his office roared and clapped me on the back and offered me swigs from their bottles; I was a card, they said.

I had no opportunity to see what happened to Cassy after she came down from the block; her buyer was obviously a local man, so presumably she wouldn't be taken far. For the hundredth time I found myself wondering how she was going to make her escape, and what I would do if she didn't come before steamboat time. I daren't leave without her, for fear she'd split. I would just have to wait, jumping at every shadow, no doubt. But in the meantime I had plenty to occupy myself with, and I set off for town, well-weighted down with my new-found wealth.

It was the deuce of a lot of cash to be carrying—or so I thought. I didn't know America well then, or I'd have realised that they don't think twice about carrying and dealing in sums that in England would be represented by a banker's draft. Odd, in such a wild country, but they like to have their cash about 'em, and don't mind killing in its defence.

The first thing I now did was to repair to the best tailor in town and buy myself some decent gear, and from there I made for a dressmakers, to do the like for Cassy. I've never numbered meanness with cash among my many faults, and I do like my women to have the very finest clothes to take off, and all the little vanities to go with 'em. There had been just north of three thousand dollars left when the auctioneer had taken his commission—a man could do worse than be a slave-knocker, it occurred to me—and I made a fine hole in them with my purchases; I spent probably twice on Cassy what I'd spent on myself, and didn't grudge it; the Creole woman who ran the shop was in a tremendous twitter, showing every gown she had, and the deuce of it was I could see Cassy looking peachy in every one.

In any event, I had two trunks full of gear which I ordered to be delivered to the levee, labelled to go aboard the *Missouri* that evening, and took only enough clothing away with me for us to look respectable when we went aboard. While I was doing my buying, I had the dressmaker send a nigger to buy the tickets— God, the tiny things that change one's life; if I'd gone in person, all would have been different. But there—he brought them back, and I stuffed them into the pocket of my new coat, and that was that.

The business of sitting back like a sultan, buying all the silks and satins in sight and gallantly chaffing Madame Threadneedle, had put me in excellent fettle, but as the afternoon wore away I began to feel less bobbish. My worries about Cassy's escape returned, and brandy didn't drive them away; I couldn't bring myself to eat anything, and finally I went back to my mean little room and busied myself removing Spring's papers from my old coat and stitching them into the waist-band of one of my new pairs of pants. After that I sat and chewed my nails, while seven o'clock went by, and then eight, and outside the rain pattered down in the dark, and I envisaged Cassy being overtaken in some dirty alley and hauled off to a cell, or being shot climbing a fence, or pulled down by hounds—give me leisure in my fearful moments and my imaginings can outrun Dante's any day.

I was standing staring at the candle guttering on its stand, feeling the gnawing certainty that she'd come adrift, when a scratching at the window had me leaping out of my skin. I whipped up the sash, and she slipped in over the sill, but my momentary delight was quickly snuffed when I saw the state she was in. She was plastered from head to foot with mud, her dress was reduced to a torn, sodden rag, her eyes were wild, and she was panting like a spent dog.

"They're after me!" she sobbed, slithering down against the wall; there was blood oozing through the mud from a cut on her foot. "They spotted me slipping out of the pen, and like a fool I ran for it! Oh, oh! I should have waited! They'll rouse the section . . . find us . . . oh, quick, let us go now—at once, before they come!"

She might, as she said, be an experienced runner, but she wasn't up to Flashy's touch. "Steady, and listen," says I. "Keep your voice low. How far behind are they?"

She sobbed for breath. "I . . . don't know. They lost me, when I . . . doubled back. Oh, dear God! But they know I've run . . . they'll scour the town . . . take me again . . ." She lay back against the wall, exhausted.

"How long since you last heard 'em?"

"Oh, oh . . . five minutes . . . I don't know. But they have . . . dogs . . . track us here..."

"Not on a night like this, they won't, and certainly not through a town." My mind was racing, but I was thinking well. Should I bolt and leave her? No, she'd talk for certain. Could we make the boat? Yes, if I could put her in order.

"Up," says I, and hauled her to her feet. She sagged against me, weeping, and I had to hold her up. "Now, listen, Cassy. We have time; they don't know where you are, and every hunt in Rutland couldn't nose you out here. We can't run until you're clean and dressed—we'd never get aboard the boat. Haste won't serve—

when Mr and Mrs Montague step out on to that street to go to the levee, they'll go nice and sedate." As I talked I was already sponging at her with the wet cloths I had ready. "Now, rest easy while I get you shipshape."

"I can't run any longer!" she sobbed. "I can't!" She tossed her head from side to side, crying with fatigue. "I just want to lie down and die!"

I went on towelling her, cleansing away the filth, whispering urgently all the while. We would make it, I told her, the boat was waiting, we were rotten with money, if we kept calm and went ahead without flinching we were bound to win free, I had bought her a wardrobe that would take Canada by storm—yes, Canada, I told her, the freedom road—an hour from now we would be steaming upriver, safe as sleep. I was trying to convince myself as much as her, as I sponged and dried away frantically, with one ear cocked for sounds of approaching pursuit.

It was tremendous work, because even when I had got her clean she just lay there, quite played out in mind and body, moaning softly to herself. I was almost in despair as I tried to haul clothes on to her; she just lay back in the chair, her golden body heaving —gad, she was a picture, but I'd no time to enjoy it. I struggled away, coaxing, pleading, swearing—"come on, come on, you can't give up, Cassy, not a staunch girl like you, you stupid black bitch," and finally I shook her and hissed in her ear: "All you have to do is stand up and walk, confound it! Walk! We can't fail now—and you'll never have to call anyone 'massa' again!"

That was what did it, I think, for she opened her eyes and made a feeble effort to help. I egged her on, and we got her into the long coat, and adjusted the broad-brimmed bonnet and veil, and I jammed the shoes on her feet, and gloved her, and stuck the gamp in her hand—and when she managed to stand, leaning against the table, she looked as much like the outward picture of a lady as made no odds. No one would know there wasn't a stitch on her underneath.

I had to half-lead, half-drag her out of the back way, and there was a feverish ten minutes while a nigger boy went and found a trap for us, and we waited crouched on the boardwalk against the wall, with the rain slashing down. But there was no sign of her pursuers; they must have lost her utterly, and presently we were rolling down to the levee through the mud and bustle of the Memphis waterfront, and there in the glare of the wharf lamps was the good ship *Missouri*, with her twin whistles blasting the warning of departure. I lorded it with the purser at the gangplank, explaining that I would take Madame directly to our state-room, as she was much fatigued, and he yes-sirred me all over the place, and roared up boys to escort us; everyone was too occupied with crying good-bye and stand clear and all aboard to notice that I was holding up the graceful veiled lady on my arm by main strength.

When I laid her on the bed she was either in a swoon or asleep from exhaustion and fright; I was so tuckered myself that I just collapsed in a chair and didn't stir until the whistles shrieked again and the wheel began to pound and I knew we'd done it. Then I began to slop the brandy down—lord, I needed it. The last-minute scare and hurry had been the final straw; the glass was chattering against my teeth, but it was as much exultation as nervous reaction, I think.

Cassy didn't stir for three hours, and then she could hardly believe where she was; not until I had ordered up a meal and a bottle of bubbly did she understand properly that we had got away, and then she broke down and cried, swaying from side to side while I comforted her and told her what a damned fine spunky wench she was. I got some drink into her, and forced her to eat, and at last she calmed, and when I saw her hand go up, shaking, and push her hair back, I knew she was in command of herself again. When they can think of their appearance, they're over the worst.

Sure enough, she went to the mirror, pulling the coat round herself, and then she turned to me and said:

"I don't believe it. But we are here." She put her face in her hands. "God bless you—oh, God bless you! Without you, I'd be—back yonder."

"Tut-tut," says I, champing away, "not a bit of it. Without you, we'd be in queer street, instead of jingling with cash. Have some more champagne."

She didn't answer for a moment. Then she says, in a very low voice. "You kept your word. No white man ever did that to me before. No white man ever helped me before."

"Ah, well," says I, "you haven't met the right chaps, that's all." She was overlooking, of course, that I hadn't any choice in the matter, but I wasn't complaining. She was grateful, which was first-rate, and must be promptly taken advantage of. I walked over to her, and she stood looking at me gravely, with the tears brimming up in her eyes. No time like the present, thinks I, so I smiled at her and set the glass to her lips, and slipped my free hand beneath her coat; her breast was as firm as a melon, and at my touch she gave a little whimper and closed her eyes, the tears squeezing out on to her cheeks. She was trembling and crying again, and when I pushed away the coat and carried her over to the bed she was sobbing aloud as she clasped her arms round my neck.

I blame myself. If there is one thing that can make me randier than usual, it is danger safely past, and with a creature like Cassy to occupy me I don't give a thought to anything else. She, for her part, was probably still so distraught that she was ready to abandon herself altogether—she said later that she had never willingly made love to a man before, and I believed her. I suppose if you've been a good-looking female slave, used to being hauled into bed by a lot of greasy planters whether you like it or not, it sours you against men, and when you meet a fine upstanding lad like me, who knows when to tickle rather than slap—well, you're grateful for the change, and make the most of it. But whatever the reasons, the upshot was that Mr and Mrs Montague spent that night and the rest of next day in passionate indulgence, never bothering about the world outside, and that was how I came adrift yet again.

Of course, a moralist would say that this was to be expected: he would doubtless point out that I had fornicated my way almost continuously along the Mississippi valley, and draw the conclusion that all my trials arose from this. I don't know about that, as a general statement, but I'll agree that if I hadn't made such a beast of myself in Cassy's case I would have avoided a deal of trouble.

What with sleeping and dallying, it was late on the next afternoon before I tumbled out to dress myself and take a turn on the promenade; it was a splendid sunny day, the good ship *Missouri* was booming along in great style, and I was in that sleepy, well-satisfied state where you just want to lean on the rail, smoking and watching the great river roll by, with the distant bank half hidden in haze, and the lumber rafts and river craft sweeping down, their crews waving, and the whistles tooting overhead. Cassy wouldn't come out, though; she decided that the less she was seen the better, until we were up among the free states, which was sensible.

Well, thinks I, you've had some bad luck, my boy, but surely it's behind you now. Charity Spring and his foul ship, the nosey-parkering Mr Lincoln, the Yankee Navy—they were all a long way south. I could smile at the ludicrous figure of George Randolph, although he had brought me catastrophe enough at the time; the abominable Mandeville and his shrew of a wife, the terror of the slave-cart, and the anxieties of Memphis—all by and done with, Up the Ohio to Louisville and then Pittsburgh, a quick trip to New York, and then it would be England again, and not before time. And Flashy the Vampire could go to work on his father-in-law—I was looking forward to that, rather.

I wondered, as I watched the brown water swirling by, what would become of Cassy. If she'd been a woman of less character I'd have been regretful at the thought of parting soon, for she was a fine rousing gallop, all sleek hard flesh like an athlete, except for her top hamper. But she was too much the spitfire, really; her present lazy compliance didn't fool me. I'd bid her farewell around Pittsburgh, where she'd be as safe as the bank, and could travel easily to Canada if she wanted. There, with her looks and spirit, she'd have no difficulty in getting a fortune somehow, I'd no doubt. Not that I minded, but she was a game wench.

Presently I went back to the state-room, and ordered up a dinner —the first full meal we had sat down to in style, and the first Cassy had had since she was a little girl, she told me. Although we were alone in the cabin, she insisted on putting on the finest dress I had bought her; it was a very pale coffee-coloured satin, I remember, and those golden shoulders coming out of it, and that strange Egyptian head of hers, with its slanting eyes, quite kept me off my food. That night she tasted port for the first time in her life; I recall her sipping it and setting down the glass, and saying:

"This is how the rich live, is it not? Then I am going to be rich. What use is freedom to the poor?"

Well, thinks I, it doesn't take long to get ambition; yesterday all you wanted was to be free. However, all I said was:

"What you want is a rich husband. Shouldn't be difficult."

She clicked her lips in contempt. "I need no man, from now on. You are the last man I shall be indebted to—I should hate you for it, but I don't. Do you know why? It is not just because you helped me, and kept your word—but you were kind also. I shall never forget that."

Poor little simple black girl, I was thinking, to mistake absence of cruelty for kindness; just wait till it serves my interest to do you a dirty turn, and you'll form a different opinion of me. And then she took me aback by going on:

"And yet I know that you are not by nature a kind man; that there is little love in you. I know there is lust and selfishness and cruelty, because I feel it when you take me; you are just like the others. Oh, I don't mind—I prefer that. I tell myself that it levels the score I owe you. And yet, it cannot quite level it, ever, because even although you are such a man as I have always taught myself to hate and despise—still, there were moments when you were kind. Do you understand?"

"Clearly," says I. "You're maudlin. It's the port, of course." Tell the truth, I was half-amused, half-angry, at the way she told me what she thought of me. Still, if the fool wanted to think I was kind, she was welcome. She was looking at me in her odd, solemn way, and do you know, it made me somehow uncomfortable; those big eyes saw far too much. "You're a strange chit," I told her.

"Not as strange as the man who buys a dress like this one for a runaway slave girl," says she, and blast me if the tears didn't start again.

Well, there you are; understand 'em if you can. So to cheer her up, and put an end to her foolish talk I came round and took her, across the table this time, with the crockery rattling all over the place, the wine splashing on the floor, and my left knee in a bowl of fruit. It was a fine frenzied business, and pleased me tremendously. When it was over I looked down at her, with the knives and forks scattered round her sleek head, and told her she should run away more often.

She reached over an apple and began to eat it, her eyes smouldering as she looked up at me.

"I shall never have to run again," she said. "Never, never, never."

That was all she knew. Our blissful little idyll was coming to an end, for next morning I made a discovery that turned everything topsy-turvy, and drove all thoughts of philosophy out of her head. I had determined to breakfast in the saloon, and leaving her in bed I took a turn round the deck to sharpen my appetite. It seemed to me that we ought to be making Louisville sometime that day, and seeing a bluff old chap leaning at the rail I inquired of him when we might expect to arrive.

He looked at me in amazement, removed his cigar, and says: "Gawd bless mah soul, suh! Did you say Louisville?"

"Certainly," says I. "When will we get there?"

"On this boat, suh? Never, 'pon my word."

"What?" I gazed at the man, thunderstruck.

"This boat, suh, is for St Louis—not Louisville. This is the Mississippi river, suh, not the Ohio. For Louisville you should have caught the *J. M. White* at Memphis." He regarded me with some amusement. "Do I take it you have boa'ded the wrong steamer, suh?"

"My God," says I. "But they told me—" And then I remembered my shouted conversation in the rain with that drivelling buffoon at the steamboat office; the useless old bastard had caught the word "Louis" only, and given me the wrong boat. Which meant that I was some hundreds of miles from where I wanted to be—and Cassy was as far from the free states as ever.

If I was dismayed, you should have seen her; she went blazing wild and hurled a pot of powder at my head, which fortunately missed.

"You fool! You blockhead! Hadn't you the sense to look at the tickets?" So much for all my kindness that she'd been so full of.

"It wasn't my fault," says I, trying to explain, but she cut me off.

"Do you realise the danger we are in? These are *slave* states! And we should have been close to Ohio by now! Your idiocy will cost me my freedom!"

"Stuff and nonsense! We can catch a boat from St Louis back to Louisville and be there in two days; where's the danger?"

"For a runaway like me? Turning south again, towards the people who may be coming up river to look for me. Oh, dear Lord, why did I trust an ape like you?"

"Ape, you insolent black slut? Blast you, if you had taken thought yourself, instead of whoring about this last two days like a bitch in heat, you'd have seen we were on the wrong road. D'you expect me to know one river from another in this lousy country?"

Our discussion continued on these lines for a spell, and then we quieted down. There was nothing to be done except wait through an extra two days in the slave states, and while Cassy was fearful of the prolonged risk, she said she supposed we could make Louisville, and then Cincinnati and Pittsburgh, safe enough. However, the shock didn't make our voyage any happier, and we were barely on speaking terms by the time we reached St Louis, where some more bad news awaited us. Although the river was thick with steamboats, traffic was so heavy that there wasn't a state-room, or even a maindeck passage, to be had for two days, which meant that we must kick our heels in a hotel, waiting for the *Bostona*, which would carry us up the Ohio.

We kept under cover for those forty-eight hours, except for one trip that I made down to the steamship office, and to buy one of the new Army Colt revolvers, just in case. At the same time I was able to take a look at the town, which interested me, because in those days St Louis was a great swarming place that never went to bed, and was full of every species of humanity from the ends of America and beyond. There were all the Mississippi characters, steamboat people, niggers, planters, and so on, and in addition the place was choc-a-bloc with military from the Mexican war, with Easterners and Europeans on their way to the Western gold fields, with hunters and traders from the plains, men in red shirts and buckskins, bearded to the eyes and brown as nuts, salesmen and drummers, clergymen and adventurers, ladies in all the splendours of the Eastern salons shuddering delicately away from the sight of some raucous mountain savage crouched vomiting in the muddy roadway with his bare backside, tanned black as mahogany, showing through his cutaway leather leggings. There were skinners with their long whips, sharps in tall hats with paste pins in their shirts, tall hard men chewing tobacco with their long coats thrown back to show the new five- and six-shooters stuck in their belts; there was even a fellow in a kilt lounging outside a billiard saloon with a bunch of yarning loafers as they eyed the white and yellow whores, gay as peacocks, tripping by along the boardwalk.

From the levee, crammed with bales and boxes and machinery, to the narrow, mud-churned streets uptown, it was all bustle and noise and hurry, and stuck in the middle was the church St Louis was all so proud of, with its Grecian pillars and pointed fresco— just like a London club with a spire stuck on top.

And I was sauntering back to the hotel, smoking a cigar, and congratulating myself that we would be on our way tomorrow, when I chanced to stop outside an office on one of the streets, just to cast an idle eye over the official bills and notices posted there. You know the way of it; you are just gaping for gaping's sake, and then suddenly you see something that shrivels the hairs right down to your backside. There it was, a new bill, staring me full in the face:

ONE HUNDRED DOLLARS REWARD!!

I will pay the above sum to any person or persons who will capture, DEAD or ALIVE, the Murderer and Slave stealer calling himself TOM ARNOLD, who is wanted for the brutal killings of George Hiscoe and Thomas Little, in Marshall County, Mississippi, and stealing away the female slave, CASSIOPEIA, the property of Jacob Forster, of Blue Mountain Spring Plantation, Tippah County, Mississippi.

The fugitive is six feet in height, long-legged and well built, customarily wears a Black Moustache and Whiskers, and has Genteel Manners. He pretends to be a Texian, but speaks with a Foreign Accent.

Satisfactory proofs of identity will be required.

ONE HUNDRED DOLLARS REWARD!!

Offered in the name and authority of

Joseph W. Matthews,
Governor of Mississippi.

I didn't faint away dead on the spot, but I had to hold on to a rail while the full import of it sank in. They had found the bodies, and assumed I had murdered them, and the traps were in full cry. But here—hundreds of miles away? And then I remembered the telegraph. They'd be looking in every town from St Louis to Memphis by now—you'd have thought, with killings happening every day in their savage country, that they wouldn't make such a row over another two: but of course it was the slave-stealing that had really stirred them up. Here was added reason for getting to the free states quickly; in Ohio they wouldn't give a damn how many nigger-beaters' throats I'd cut, especially in such a good cause—I'd learned enough in my brief unhappy experience of the United States to know that it was two countries even then, and they hated each other like poison. Yes, up there I'd be safe, and on trembling legs I hurried back to the hotel, to break the glad news that they were after us with a vengeance.

Cassy gasped and went pale, but she didn't cry, and while I was stamping about chewing my nails and swearing she got out a map which we had bought, and began to study it. Her finger was trembling as she traced the route down from St Louis to the Cairo fork, and then north-east up the Ohio river. At Louisville she stopped.

"Well, what now?" says I. "That's only a two-day journey, and we'll be beyond their reach, won't we?"

She took her head. "You do not understand. The Ohio river is thε boundary between the slave states and the free, but even in the free states we are not safe until we have gone well upriver. See—" She traced again. "From Louisville to Cincinnati and far beyond that, we still have slave states on our right hand, first Kentucky and then Virginia. If we were to land on the Indiana or Ohio shores, we should be in free states, but I could still be retaken by the slave-catchers who are thick along the river."

"But—but—I thought the free state folk sheltered slaves, and helped them. Surely they can't take you off free state soil?"

"Of course they can!" There were tears in her eyes now. "Oh, if we could be sure of finding an abolitionist settlement, or an underground railroad station, all would be well, but how do we know? There are laws forbidding people in Ohio to aid runaways; slaves are caught and dragged back across the river daily by these bands of catchers, with their guns and dogs! And with the time we have lost here, notices of my running from Memphis will have reached the Kentucky shore—my name will have been added to the list of the other poor hunted creatures trying to escape north!"

"Well, what the blazes can we do?"

She traced on the map again. "We must stay aboard our steamboat all the way to Pittsburgh, if indeed the boats run so far in this weather.[88] If not, they will at least take us far enough up the Ohio to catch a train from one of the eastern Ohio towns into Pennsylvania. Once we are in Pittsburgh we can laugh at all the slave-catchers in the South—and you will be far beyond the reach of the Mississippi law."

Well, that was a comforting thought. "How long does it take?" says I.

"To Pittsburgh by boat? Five days." She bit her lip and began to tremble again. "Within a week from now I shall be either free or dead."

I wish she'd thought of some other way of putting it, and it crossed my mind that I might be a good deal safer parting company with her. On the other hand, a boat to Pittsburgh was the fastest way home, and if we kept to our cabin the whole way we should come through safe. They don't look for runaway slaves in state-rooms. They might look there for a murderer, though—and blast it, I hadn't even *done* the murders! Could I fob them off on her if the worst came to the worst? But it wouldn't—there must be a limit to the distance they could chase us.

It was in a fine state of the shakes that we boarded the *Bostona* the next morning, and I didn't know an easy moment until we had passed the Cairo fork that night and were steaming up the Ohio. I drank a fair amount, and Cassy sat gazing out towards the northern shore, but early on the second morning we reached Louisville without incident, and I began to breath again. Evening saw us at Cincinnati and Cassy was in a fever of anxiety for the boat to move off again; Cincinnati, although on the Ohio side, was a great place for slave-catchers, and she cried with relief when the side-wheel started at last and we churned on upriver.

But at breakfast time next day there was a rude awakening. The weather had grown colder and colder throughout our journey, and now when you looked overside there were great cakes of dirty brown and green ice riding down the current, and a powdering of snow lying on the Ohio bank. The fellows in the saloon were of opinion that the boat would go no farther than Portsmouth, if that far; the captain wouldn't risk her in this kind of weather.

And sure enough, down comes the captain presently, all gravity and grey whiskers, to announce to the saloon that he couldn't make Portsmouth this trip, on account of the ice, but would put in at Fisher's Landing, which was three miles short of the town, and set anyone ashore that wanted to go. The rest he would carry back to Cincinnati.

They raised a tremendous howl at this, waving their tickets and demanding their money back, and one tubby little chap in gold glasses cries out angrily:

"Intolerable! Fisher's Landing is on the Kentucky shore—how am I to be in Portsmouth tonight? There won't be a ferry running in this weather."

The captain said he was sorry; the Ohio side was out of the question, because the ice was thick all down the north channel.

"But I must be in Portsmouth tonight!" fumes the tubby man. "Perhaps you don't know me, captain—Congressman Smith, Albert J. Smith, at your service. It is imperative that I be in Portsmouth to support my congressional colleague, Mr Lincoln, at tonight's meeting."

"Well, I'm sorry, Congressman Smith," says the captain, "but if you were going to support the President, I couldn't land you in Ohio today."

"Infamous!" cries the little chap. "Why, I've come from Evansville for this, and Mr Lincoln has broken his journey home specially for this meeting, and is awaiting me in Portsmouth. Really, captain, when matters of such national importance as the slave question are to be discussed by eminent—"

"The slave question!" cries the captain. "Well, sir, you may land in Kentucky for me, let me tell you, and I hope they welcome you warmly!"

And off he stumped, red in the face, leaving the little chap wattling and cursing. I didn't have to be told the captain was a Southerner, but I was vastly intrigued to find my path crossing so close to Mr Lincoln's again. That seemed to me a good reason for turning back to Cincinnati, and giving Portsmouth a wide berth. He and his sharp eyes and embarrassing questions were the last things I wanted to meet just now.

But Cassy wouldn't have it; even landing in Kentucky was preferable to Cincinnati, and she pointed out that the farther I was upriver the safer I'ld be. She was sure there must be a ferry running at Portsmouth; it was only a short walk along the shore, she said, and once across we could journey inland to Columbus and from there quickly to Pittsburgh.

If she didn't mind, I didn't, because I felt we must be beyond pursuit by now, but I noticed she hesitated at the gangplank, scanning the shore at Fisher's Landing, and her steps were slow as we walked over the creaking wooden stage. Suddenly she stopped, caught my arm, and whispered:

"Let us go back! I never thought to stand on this soil again—I feel evil hanging over us. Oh, we shouldn't have landed! Please, let us go back quickly, before it's too late!"

But it was too late even then, for the steamboat, having landed about a dozen of us, including the incensed Congressman, was already backing away from the stage, her whistle whooping like a lost soul. Cassy shuddered beside me, and pulled her veil more tightly round her face. Truth to tell, I didn't care for the look of the place much myself; just the stage, and a mean little tavern, and bleak scrubby country stretching away on both sides.

However, there was nothing for it now. The other passengers crowded round the tavern, asking about a ferry, and the yokel there opined that there might be one later that day, but with the ice he couldn't be sure. The others decided to wait and see, but Cassy insisted that we should push on along the bank; we could see Portsmouth in the distance on the far shore, and it did seem there would be a better chance of a ferry there.

So we set off together, carrying our bags, along the lonely little road that wound among the trees by the river. It was a cold, grey afternoon, with a keen wind sighing among the branches, and through the trunks the brown Ohio ran by, with the massive floes grinding and booming in the brown water. There was low cloud and a threat of snow, and a dank chill in the air that was not just the weather. Cassy was silent as we walked, but her words still sounded in my ears, and although I told myself we were safe enough by this time, surely, I found myself ever glancing back along the deserted muddy track, lying drear and silent under the winter sky.

We must have walked about an hour, and although it was still early afternoon it seemed to me to be growing darker, when we saw buildings ahead, and came to a tiny village on the river bank. We were nearly opposite Portsmouth by now, and already some lights were twinkling across the water. The river here seemed to be more choked with ice than ever, stirring and heaving but moving only gently downstream.

The keeper of the tavern that served the place laughed to scorn our inquiries about a ferry; however, in his opinion the ice would freeze again overnight, and then we could walk across. He couldn't give us beds, but we were welcome to couch down for the night, and in the meantime he could give us fried ham and coffee.

"We should have stayed at Fisher's Landing," says I, but Cassy just sank down wearily on a bench without replying. I offered her some coffee but she shook her head, and when I reminded her it was only for one night, she whispered:

"It is very near us now—I can feel the dark shadow coming closer. Oh, God! Oh, God! Why did I set foot on this accursed shore again!"

"What bloody shadow?" snaps I, for she had my nerves like fiddle strings. "We're snug enough here, girl, within spitting distance of Ohio! We've come this far, in God's name; who's going to stop us now?"

And as though in answer to my question, from somewhere down the road outside, came the yelping and baying of hounds.

Cassy started, and I own that my heart took a sudden leap, although what's a dog barking, after all? And then came the sound of footsteps, and men's voices, and presently the door was shoved open, and half a dozen or so rough fellows came in and bawled for the landlord to bring them a jug of spirits and some food. I didn't like the look of them by half, big tough-looking men with pistols in their belts and two of them carrying rifles; their leader was a tall, black-bearded villain with a broken nose who gave me a hard stare and a curt good day and then strode to the door to curse the dogs leashed up outside. I felt Cassy sink shuddering against me, and just caught her whisper:

"Slave-catchers! Oh, God help us!"

I fought down my instinctive desire to make a dash for the door; I'd made too many sudden dashes on this trip already. My throat was dry and my hands trembling, but I forced myself to drink my coffee, and even asked Cassy in a loud, steady voice if she required anything more to eat. Plainly we would have to get out of here as soon as possible, but we must not rouse an instant's suspicion, or we were done for.

The newcomers were talking so much by now that our silence went unnoticed, and almost their first words confirmed what Cassy had said.

"That nigger of Thompson's'll be hidin' up in Mason's Bottom," says one. "That's whar they always run afore they try the Portsmouth ferry. Well, he ain't gettin' no ferry tonight, for sure; he can lay out an' freeze an' the dogs kin pick him up in the mornin'."

"Too bad about the ferry, though," says the leader. "Kinda had a notion to go over tonight, to th' abolitionist meetin'."

"Since when you go to abolitionist meetin's, Buck?"

"Since I heerd that son-of-a-bitch of an Illinoy lawyer goin' to be speakin', that's since when. Precious Mr Goddam Congressman Lincoln. That's a bastard I get real discontented with, that is."

"You figurin' on takin' a few bad eggs along?" says the other, laughing.

"Could be. Could be, if things had looked right, I might have taken me a picket rail, a nice big bag o' feathers, an' mustered up some hot tar to boot. I reckon that's th' only way to discourage some o' these nigger-lovin' duffers."

"Discourage 'em a dam' sight better with a rope, or a good spread of buckshot," says a third, and other suggestions followed, most of them unrepeatable.

All this time I had felt Cassy trembling beside me, but now she suddenly whispered, in a shaking gasp:

"We must leave! I can't bear it any longer! Please, let us go—anywhere away from them!"

I knew she was near breaking—this same wench who'd killed

two men on a dark country road—so I helped her to her feet, and with a muttered good day led her towards the door. Naturally they turned to look at us, and the leader, Buck, says:

"Ain't no ferry movin' tonight, mister. Where you figurin' on goin'?"

"Er ... Fisher's Landing," says I.

"No ferry there, either," says he. "You be best here tonight."

I hesitated. "I think we'll move on," says I. "Come, my dear."

And we were almost at the door when he said:

"Hold one one moment, mister." He was sitting forward on his stool, and there was a grin on his loose mouth that I didn't care for. "Pardon my askin'—but would your companion be a white lady?"

Sickened, I turned to face him. "And if she is not?" says I.

"Thought she warn't," says he, standing up. "Mighty fancy dressed, though, for a nigger."

"I like my women well dressed." I tried to keep my voice level, but it wasn't easy.

"Sure, sure," says he, hooking his thumbs in his belt. "Jus' that when I see nigger ladies, an' their wearin' veils, an' shiverin' like they had the ague—well, I get curious." He kicked his stool away and walked forward. "What's your name, wench?"

I saw Cassy's eyes flash behind her veil, and suddenly she was no longer trembling, which made up for me. "Ask my master," she said.

He gave a growl, but checked himself. "Right pert, too. All right, Mister—what's her name?"

"Belinda."

"Is it now?" Suddenly he reached forward, before I could stop him, and twitched away her veil, laughing as she started back. "Well, well, now—right pretty, as well as pert. You're a lucky feller, mister. An' what might your name be?"

"J. C. Stubbs," says I, "and I'll be damned if—"

"You'll be damned anyway, unless I'm mistaken," he snapped, his face vicious. "Belinda an' J. C. Stubbs, eh? Jus' you wait right there, then, while I have a little look here." And he pulled a handful of papers from his pocket. "I been keepin' an eye on you, this few minutes, Mr J. C. Stubbs, an' now I get a look at your little black charmer, I got me a feelin'—where is it, now?—yes, here we have it—uh, huh, Mr Stubbs, I got a suspicion you ain't Mr Stubbs at all, but that you're a Mr Fitzroy Howard, who offered a spankin' mustee gal named Cassy at Memphis a few days back, an'—"

He broke off with a shouted oath, because he was looking down the barrel of my Colt. There was nothing else for it; at the hideous realisation that we were caught I had snatched it from the back of my waist, and as he started back and his hand swept away his coat-tail I jammed the gun into his midriff with the violence of panic, and bawled in his face:

"Move, and I'll blow your guts into Ohio! You others, get your hands up—lively now, or I'll spread your friend all over you!"

I was red in the face with terror, and my hand was quivering on the butt, but to them I was probably a fearsome sight. Their hands shot up, a rifle clattered to the floor, and Buck's ugly face turned yellow. He fell back before me, his mouth trembling, and the sight of it gave me a sudden surge of courage.

"Down on the floor, damn you—all of you! Down, I say, or I'll burn your brains!"

Buck dropped to the boards, and the others followed suit. I hadn't the nerve to go among them to remove their weapons, and for the life of me I couldn't think what to do next. I stood there, swearing at them, wondering if I should shoot Buck where he lay, but I hadn't the bate for it. He raised his head to cry hoarsely:

"You ain't gonna run nowhere, mister! We'll get you before you're gone a mile—you an' that yaller slut! We'll make you pay for this—"

I snarled and mowed at them, brandishing my gun, and he cowered down, and then I backed slowly towards the door, still covering them—the Colt was shaking like a jelly. I couldn't think—there wasn't time. If we ran for it now, where would we run to? They'd overhaul us, with their filthy dogs—if only there was some way to delay them! A sudden inspiration struck me, and I glanced at Cassy; she was at my elbow, quivering like a hunted beast, and if she too was terrified at least it wasn't with the terror that is helpless.

"Cassy!" I snapped. "Can you use a gun?"

She nodded. "Take this, then," says I. "Cover them—and if one of them stirs a finger shoot the swine in the stomach! There—catch hold. Good girl, good girl—I'll be back in an instant!"

"What is it?" Her eyes were wild. "Where are you—"

"Don't ask questions! Trust me!" And with that I slipped out of the door, pulled it to, and was off like a stung whippet. I'd make quarter of a mile, maybe more, before she would twig, or they overpowered her, and that quarter mile could be the difference between life and death—but even as I was away with my first frenzied spring a dun-coloured, white-fanged horror came surging up at my side, teeth dragged at the tail of my coat, and I came down in a sprawling tangle of limbs with one of those damned hounds snarling and tearing at me.

By the grace of God I fell just beyond reach of its leash; I suppose the brute had gone for me because it knew a guilty fugitive when it saw one, and now it tore and frothed against its chain to be at me. I jumped up to resume my flight, and then I heard Cassy scream in the tavern, the Colt banged, somebody howled, and the door flew open. Cassy came out at a blind run, making for the thicket that bordered the river; I spared not a glance for the tavern door but went high-stepping after her for all I was worth, expecting a bullet between the shoulders at every stride.

As luck had it the thicket was only a dozen yards away, but by the time I had burst through it Cassy was well ahead of me. I suppose it was blind instinct that made me follow her, now that my own chance of a clear getaway had been scuppered by whatever had gone amiss in the tavern—the stupid bitch could have held them longer than two seconds, you'd have thought—and there was nothing to do but shift like blazes. It was growing dusk, but not near dark enough for concealment, and she was running for dear life along the bank eastwards. I pounded down the slope, yelling to her, at my wits' end over where we were going to run to. Could we hide—no, my God, the dogs! We couldn't outstrip them along the bank—where then? The same thoughts must have been in Cassy's mind, for as I closed on her, and heard the din of shouting rise a hundred yards behind me, she suddenly checked, and with a despairing cry leaped down the bank to the water's edge.

"No! No!" I bawled. "Not on the ice—we'll drown for certain!"
But she never heeded. There was a narrow strip of brown water
between her and the nearest floe, and she cleared it like a hunter,
slipping and falling, but scrambling up again and clambering over
the hummocks beyond. Oh, Christ, thinks I, she's mad, but then I
looked behind, and there they were, running down from the
tavern, with the dogs yelping in the background. I took a race
down the bank and jumped, my feet flew from under me on the
ice, and I came down with a sickening crash. I staggered up,
plunging over the mass of frozen cakes locked like a great raft
ahead of me, and saw Cassy steadying herself for a leap on to a
level floe beyond. She made it, and I tumbled down the hummocks
and leaped after her. Somehow I kept my footing, and slithered
and slipped across the floe, which must have been thirty yards
from side to side.

Beyond it there were great rough cakes bucking about in the
current, but so close together that we were able to scramble
across them. Once my leg went in, and I just avoided plunging
headlong; Cassy was twenty yards ahead, and I remember roaring
to her to wait for me—God knows why, but one does these things.
And then behind me came the crack of a shot, and glancing over
my shoulder I saw that our pursuers were leaving the bank and
taking the ice in our wake.

God! It was a nightmare. If I'd had a moment to think I'd have
given up the ghost, but fear sent me skipping and stumbling over
the pack, babbling prayers and curses, sprawling on the ice, cutting
my hands and knees to shreds, and staggering up to follow her
dark figure over the floes. All round the ice was grinding and
groaning fearfully; it surged beneath our feet, cracking and tilting,
and then I saw her stumble and kneel clinging to a floe; she was
sobbing and shrieking, and two more shots came banging behind
and whistled above us in the dusk.

As I overtook her she managed to regain her feet, glaring
wildly back beyond me. Her dress was in shreds, her hands were
dark with blood, her hair was trailing loose like a witch's. But she
went reeling on, jumping another channel and staggering across
the rugged floe beyond. I set myself for the jump, slipped, and
fell full length into the icy water.

It was so bitter that I screamed, and she turned back and came slithering on all fours to the edge. I grabbed her hand, and somehow I managed to scramble out. The yelping of the dogs was sounding closer, a gun banged, a frightful pain tore through my buttock, and I pitched forward on to the ice. Cassy screamed, a man's voice sounded in a distant roar of triumph, and I felt blood coursing warm down my leg.

"My God, are you hurt?" she cried, and for some idiot reason I had a vision of a tombstone bearing the legend: "Here lies Harry Flashman, late 11th Hussars, shot in the arse while crossing the Ohio River". The pain was sickening, but I managed to lurch to my feet, clutching my backside, and Cassy seized my hand, dragging me on.

"Not far! Not far!" she was crying, and through a mist of pain I could see the lights on the Ohio bank, not far away on our right. If only we could make the shore, we might hide, or stagger into Portsmouth itself and get assistance, but then my wound betrayed me, my leg wouldn't answer, and I sank down on the ice.

We weren't fifty yards from the shore, with fairly level ice ahead, but the feeling had gone from my limb. I looked round; Buck and his fellows were floundering across the ice a bare hundred yards away. Cassy's voice was crying:

"Up! Up! Only a little farther! Oh, try, try!"

"Rot you!" cries I. "I'm shot! I can't!"

She gave an inarticulate cry, and then by God, she seized my arms, stooped into me, and somehow managed to half-drag, half-carry me across the ice. There must have been amazing strength in the slim body, for I'm a great hulking fellow, and she was near exhaustion. But she got me along, until we fell in a heap close to the bank, and then we slithered and floundered through the ice-filled shallows, and dragged ourselves up the muddy slope of the Ohio bank.[89]

"Free soil" sobs Cassy. "Free soil!" And a bullet smacked into the bank between us to remind her that we were still a long way from safety. That shot must have done something to my muscular control, for I managed to hobble up the bank, with Cassy hauling at me, and then we stumbled forward towards the lights of Portsmouth. It was only half a mile away, but try running half a mile with a bullet hole in your rump. With Cassy's arm round me I could just stagger; we plunged ahead through the gloaming, and there were figures on the road ahead, people staring at us and calling out. Just before we reached them, we passed a tree, and my eye caught the lettering on a great yellow bill that had been stuck there. It read something about "Great Meeting Tonight, All Welcome", and in large letters the names "Lincoln" and "Smith". I was gasping, all in, but I remembered that the little tubby man on the steamboat had been Smith, and he had said Lincoln was speaking in Portsmouth. And I had sense enough to realise that wherever Lincoln was there would be enemies of slavery and friends to all fugitives like us. Two hours ago I'd been wanting to avoid him like the pox, but now it was life or death, and there was something else stirring in my head. I don't know why it was, but I remembered that big man, and his great hard knuckles and dark smiling eyes, and I thought, by God, get to Lincoln! Get to him; we'll be safe with him. They won't dare touch us if he's there. And as Cassy and I stumbled along the road, and I heard voices calling out in concern: "Who are they? What is it? Great snakes, he's bleeding—look, he's been shot," I managed to find the breath to cry out:

"Mr Lincoln—where can I find Mr Lincoln?"

"Great snakes, man!" A face was peering into mine. "Who are you? What's—"

"Slave-catchers!" cries Cassy. "Behind us—with guns and dogs."

"What's that, girl? Slave-catchers! My stars, get them up—here, Harry, lend a hand! John, you run to your uncle's—quick now! Tell him slave-catchers come over the river—hurry, boy, there's no time to lose!"

I could have cried out in relief, but as I turned my head I saw in the distance figures clambering the bank, and heard the yelp of those accursed dogs.

"Get me to Lincoln, for God's sake!" I shouted. "Where is he —what house?"

"Lincoln? You mean Mr Abraham Lincoln? Why, he's up to Judge Payne's, ain't he, Harry? C'mon, then, mister, it ain't that far, ifn you can manage along. Harry, help the lady, there. This way, then—best foot forward!"

Somehow I managed to raise a run, and by blessed chance the house proved to be not more than a few furlongs away. I was aware of a hubbub behind us, and gathered that Buck and his friends had run into various Ohio citizens who were disputing their progress, but only verbally, for as we turned into a wide gateway, and our helpers assisted us up a long pathway to a fine white house, I heard the barking again, and what I thought was Buck's voice raised in angry defiance.

We stumbled up the steps, and someone knocked and beat on the panels, and a scared-looking nigger put his head round the door, but I blundered ahead, pushing him back, with a man helping Cassy beside me. We were in a big, well-lit hall, and I remember the carpet was deep red, and there was a fine mural painted on the wall above the stairs. People were hurrying out of the rooms; two or three gentlemen, and a lady who gave a little shriek at the sight of us.

"Good God!" cries one of the men. "What is the meaning—? who are you—?"

"Lincoln!" I shouted, and as my leg gave way I sat down heavily. "Where's Lincoln? I want him. I've been shot in the backside—slave-catchers! Lincoln!"

At this there was a great hubbub, and women swooning by the sound of it, and I hobbled to the newell post of the stair and hung on—I couldn't sit down, you understand. Cassy, with a man supporting her, tottered past me and sank into a chair, while the nicely-dressed ladies and gentlemen gaped at us in consternation, two horrid, bleeding scarecrows leaving a muddy trail across that excellent carpet. A stout man in a white beard was confronting me, shouting:

"How dare you, sir? Who are you, and what—?"

"Lincoln," says I, pretty hoarse. "Where's Lincoln?"

"Here I am," says a voice. "What do you want with me?"

And there he was, at my shoulder, frowning in astonishment.

"I'm Fitzhoward," says I. "You remember—"

"Fitzhoward? I don't—"

"No, not Fitzhoward, blast it. Wait, though—Arnold—oh, God, no!" My mind was swimming. "No—Comber! Lieutenant

Comber—you must remember me?"

He took a pace back in bewilderment. "Comber? The English officer—how in the world—?"

"That's a slave girl," I gasped out. "I—I rescued her—from down South—the slave-catchers found us—chased us across river —still coming after us." And praise be to providence I had the sense to hit the right note. "Don't let them take her back! Save her, for God's sake!"

It must have sounded well, at least to the others, for I heard a gasp of dismay and pity, and one of the women, a little ugly battleship of a creature, bustles over to Cassy to take her hands.

"But—but, here, sir!" The stout chap was all agog. "What, a runaway girl? Septy, shut that door this minute—what's that? My God, more scarecrows! What the devil is this? Who are—?"

I looked to the door, and my heart went down to my boots. The old nigger was clinging to the handle as though to support himself, his eyes rolling, the people of the house were rustling back to the doorways off the hall, the stout man—who I guessed was Judge Payne—had fallen silent. Buck stood in the doorway, panting hard, his clothes sodden and mud-spattered, with his gun cradled in his left arm, and behind him were the bearded faces of his fellows. Buck was grinning, though, with his loose lower lip stuck out, and now he raised his free hand and pointed at Cassy.

"That's a runaway slave there, mister—an' I'm a warranted slave-catcher! That scoundrel at the stair there's the thievin' skunk that stole her!" He took a pace forward into the hall. "I'm gonna take both of 'em back where they belong!"

Payne seemed to swell up. "Good God!" says he. "What— what? This is intolerable! First these two, and now—is my house supposed to be a slave market, or what?"

"I want 'em both," Buck was beginning, and then he must have realised where he was. "Kindly sorry for intrudin' on you, mister, but this is where they run to, an' this is where I gotta follow. So— jus' you roust 'em out here to me, an' we won't be troublin' you or your ladies no further."

For a moment you could have heard a pin drop. Then Buck added defiantly:

"That's the law. I got the law on my side."

I felt Lincoln stiffen beside me. "For God's sake," I whispered. "Don't let them take us!"

He moved forward a pace, beside Judge Payne, and I heard one of the ladies begin to sob gently—the first sobs before hysterics. Then Lincoln says, very quietly:

"There's a law against forcing an entry into a private house."

"Indeed there is!" cries the judge. "Take yourself off, sir—this instant, and your bandits with you!"

Buck glared at him. "Ain't forcin' nuthin'. I'm recapturin' a slave, like I'm legally entitled to. Anyone gits in my way, is harbourin' runaways, an' that's a crime! I know the law, mister, an' I tell you, either you put them out o' doors for us, or stand aside—because if they ain't comin' out, we're comin' in!"

Judge Payne fell back at that, and the other people shrank away, some of the women bolting back to the drawing room. But not the ugly little woman who had her arm round Cassy's shoulders.

"Don't you move another step!" she cries out. "Nathan—don't permit him. They don't touch a hair of this poor creature's head in this house. Stand back, you bully!"

"But, my dear!" cries Payne in distress. "If what they say is true, we have no choice, I fear—"

"Who says it's true? There now, child, be still; they shan't harm you."

"Look, missus." Buck swaggered forward, limbering his rifle, and stood four-square, with his pals at his back. "You best 'tend to what your ol' man says. We got the law behind us." He glanced at Lincoln, who hadn't moved and was right in his path. "Step aside."

Lincoln still didn't move. He stood very easy and his drawl was steady as ever.

"On the subject of the law," says he, "you say she's a runaway, and that this man stole her. We don't know the truth about that, though, do we? Perhaps they tell a different tale. I know a little law myself, friend, and I would suggest that if you have a claim on these two persons, you should pursue it in the proper fashion, which is through a court. An Ohio court," he added. "And I'd further advise you, as a legal man, not to prejudice your case by armed house-breaking. Or, for that matter, by dirtying this good lady's carpet. If you have a just claim, go and enter it, in the proper place." He paused. "Good night, sir."

It was so cool and measured and unanswerable that I could have wept with relief to hear him—but I didn't know much about slave-catchers. Buck just grunted and sneered at him.

"Oh, yeah, I know about the courts! I guess I do—I bin to court before—"

"I'll believe that," says Lincoln.

"Yeah? You're a mighty fancy goddam legal beanpole, ain't you though? Well, I'll tell you suthin', mister—I know about courts an' writs an' all, an' there ain't one o' them worth a lick in hell to me! I'm here—them dam' runaways is here—an' if I take 'em away nice an' quiet, we don' have to trouble with no courts nor nuthin'. An' afterwards—well, I reckon I'll answer right smart for any incon-venience caused here tonight. But I ain't bein' fobbed by smart talk—they're comin' with me!"

And he pushed the barrel of his piece forward just a trifle.

"You'll just take them," says Lincoln. "By force. Is that so?"

"You bet it's so! I reckon the courts won't worry me none, neither! We'll have done justice, see?"

I quailed to listen to him. God, I thought, we're finished; he had the force behind him. If he wanted to march in and drag us out bodily, the law would support him in the end. There would be protests, no doubt, and some local public outcry, but what good would that be to us, once they had us south of the river again? I heard Cassy moan, and I sank down, done up and despairing, beside the newell. And then Lincoln laughed, shaking his head.

"So that's your case is it, Mr—?"

"Buck Robinson's my—"

"Buck will do. That's your style, is it, Buck? Brute force and talk about it afterwards. Well, it has its logic, I suppose—but, d'ye know, Buck, I don't like it. No, sir. That's not how we do things where I come from—"

"I don't give a damn how you do things where you come from, Mr Smart," Buck spat out. "Get out of my way."

"I see," says Lincoln, not moving. "Well, I've put my case to you, in fair terms, and you've answered it—admirably, after your own lights. And since you won't listen to reason, and believe that might is right—well, I'll just have to talk in your terms, won't I? So—"

"You hold your gab and stand aside, mister," shouts Buck. "Now, I'm warnin' you fair!"

"And I'm warning you, Buck!" Lincoln's voice was suddenly sharp. "Oh, I know you, I reckon. You're a real hard-barked Kentucky boy, own brother to the small-pox, weaned on snake juice and grizzly hide, aren't you? You've killed more niggers than the dysentery, and your grandma can lick any white man in Tennessee. You talk big, step high, and do what you please, and if any 'legal beanpole' in a store suit gets in your way you'll cut him right down to size, won't you just? He's not a *practical* man, is he? But you are, Buck—when you've got your gang at your back! Yes, sir, you're a practical man, all right."

Buck was mouthing at him, red-faced and furious, but Lincoln went on in the same hard voice.

"So am I, Buck. And more—for the benefit of any shirt-tail chawbacon with a big mouth, I'm a who's-yar boy from Indiana myself, and I've put down better men than you just by spitting teeth at them.[40] If you doubt it, come ahead! You want these people—you're going to take them?" He gestured towards Cassy. "All right, Buck—you try it. Just—try it."

The rest of the world decided that Abraham Lincoln was a great orator after his speech at Gettysburg. I realised it much earlier, when I heard him laying it over that gun-carrying bearded ruffian who was breathing brimstone at him. I couldn't see Lincoln's face, but I'll never forget that big gangling body in the long coat that didn't quite fit, towering in the centre of the hall, with the big hands motionless at his sides. God knows how he had the nerve, with six armed men in front of him. But when I think back to it, and hear that hard, rasping drawl sounding in my memory, and remember the force in those eyes, I wonder how Buck had the nerve to stand up in front of him, either. He did, though, for about half a minute, glaring from Lincoln to Cassy to me and back to Lincoln again. Twice he was going to speak, and twice thought better of it; he was a brawny, violent man with a gun in his hands, but speaking objectively at a safe distance now, he has my sympathy. As a fellow bully and coward, I can say that Buck behaved precisely as I should have done in his place. He glared and breathed hard, but that was his limit. And then through the open door came the distant sound of raised voices, and a hurrying of many feet on the road.

"I doubt if that's the Kentucky militia," says Lincoln. "Better be going, Buck."

Buck stood livid, still hesitating; then with a curse he swung about and stumped to the door. He turned again there, dark with passion, and pointed a shaking finger.

"I'll be back!" says he. "Don't you doubt it, mister—I'll be back, an' I'll have the law with me! We'll see about this, by thunder! I'll get the law!"

They clattered down the steps, Buck swearing at the others, and as the door closed and the exclamations started flying, Lincoln turned and looked down at me. His forehead was just a little damp.

"The ancients, in their wisdom, made a great study of rhetoric," says he. "But I wonder did they ever envisage Buck Robinson? Yes, they probably did." He pursed his lips. "He's a big fellow, though—likely big fellow, he is. I—I think I'd sooner see Cicero square up to him behind the barn than me. Yes, I rather think I would." He adjusted his coat and cracked his knuckles. "And now, Mr Comber—?"

I've been wounded several times, all of them damned painful, but you may take my word for it that a ball in the bum is the worst. By the time that ham-fisted sawbones had hauled it out I was weak and weeping, and my immediate recuperation wasn't eased by the fact that Judge Payne and Lincoln agreed that Cassy and I must be spirited out of the house without delay, in case Buck and his friends returned with an officer and a warrant. With two men to support me and my buttocks in a sling I was helped about half a mile to another establishment, where I gathered the folk were red-hot abolitionists, and put to bed face down.

Of course I had already given a rough account of what had happened, in answer to the questions they fired at me after Buck had gone. The Judge wasn't concerned with anything but the events of the last few hours, and was full of praise for my daring and endurance, while his wife, the ugly little woman, and the other females made much of Cassy, and called her a poor dear, and clucked over her cuts and bruises. They were all stout anti-slavers, of course, as I'd guessed they would be, and would you believe it, while that blasted doctor was probing and muttering over my bottom, the women downstairs actually sang "Now Israel may say and that truly", with harmonium accompaniment. This to celebrate what Judge Payne called our deliverance, and the others cried "Amen", and were furious in their wrath against these vile slave-traffickers who hounded poor innocents with dogs and guns—"and she such a sweet and refined young thing—oh, my land, the pity of her poor bruised limbs." You ought to see her with a knife sometime, thinks I, or stripping for the buyers. And for me they had nothing but blessings and commiseration for my torn arse, which the Judge called an honourable scar, taken in the defence of liberty. Lincoln stood in the background, watching under his brows.

But when they had taken us to the new house, and I had been tucked up in bed, he came along, very patient, and begged our hosts for a little time alone with me.

"I'm afraid the good people of Portsmouth will have to do without me this evening," says he. "They might find my presence in public somewhat embarrassing. Anyway, one successful speech in a day is quite enough." So they left us, and he sat down beside the bed, with his tall hat between his feet.

"Now, sir," says he, pointing that formidable head of his at me, "may I hear from you at some length? I last parted from a respectable British naval officer in Washington; tonight I meet a wounded fugitive running an escaped slave across the Ohio. I'm not only curious, you understand—I'm also a legislator of my country,[41] a maker and guardian of its laws which, on your behalf, I suspect I have broken fairly comprehensively this night. I feel I'm entitled to an explanation. Pray begin, Mr Comber."

So I did. There was no point in lying, much; I hadn't time for invention, anyway, and he would have seen through it. So from New Orleans on I told him the truth—Crixus, my escape with Randolph, what happened on the steamboat, the Mandevilles, the slave cart and Cassy, Memphis, and our eventual flight. I kept out the spicy bits, of course, and Mandeville's barbarous treatment of me I explained by pretending that Omohundro had turned up at Greystones with searchers and identified me—that was how they treated underground railroad men in the south, I said. He listened attentively, saying nothing, the bright eyes never leaving my face. When I had finished he sat silent a long while, studying. Then he said:

"Well," and then a long pause. "That's quite a story." Another pause. "Yes, sir, that is quite a story." He coughed. "Haven't heard anything to touch it since last time I was in the Liberal Club. There's—nothing you wish to add to it—at all? No detail you may have, uh, overlooked?"

"That is all, sir," says I wondering.

"I see. I see. No, no, I just thought—oh, a balloon flight over Arkansas, or perhaps an encounter with pirates and alligators in the bayous of Louisiana—you know—"

I demanded, did he not believe me?

"On the contrary, I don't doubt it for a moment—more or less, anyway. No, I believe you, sir—my expressions of astonishment are really a tribute to you. In America, as in most other places, it's only the truth that we find hard to believe. No—it's not what you've told me, but what you haven't told me that I find downright fascinating. However, I shan't press you. I would hate to force you off the path of veracity—"

"If you doubt me," says I stiffly, "you may ask the girl Cassy."

"I already have, and she confirms a great part of your story. Remarkable young woman, that; she has much character." He cracked his knuckles thoughtfully. "Very beautiful, too; very beautiful. Had you noticed? Yes, I guess the Queen of Sheba must have looked something—'black but comely', wasn't it? However —I was also going to add that your narrative of Randolph fits very well with what I read in the papers about his escape from the steamboat—"

"His escape?"

"Oh, yes, indeed. He turned up, in Vermont of all places, about two weeks ago, and is now in Canada, I understand. The liberal sheets were full of his exploits." He smiled. "I don't hold it against you that there was no mention of you in his very full relation. No mention of anyone, much, except George Randolph. But from all I've heard of him, that is consistent. Extraordinary fellow, he must be. He should be grateful to you, though—up to a point, at least."

"I doubt it," says I.

"Is that so? Well, well, I've no doubt you've noticed that even when gratitude costs nothing, folks are often reluctant to show it. They'll even pay hard money to avoid giving it where it's due. Strange, but human, I suppose." He was silent a moment. "You're sure there's nothing further you wish to tell me, Mr Comber?"

"Why, no, sir," says I. "I can think of nothing—"

"I doubt that very much," says he, drily. "I really and truly do —you've never seen the day when you couldn't think of something. But do you know what I think, Mr Comber—speaking plain, as man to man? I look at you, fine bluff British figurehead, well-spoken, easy, frank, splendid whiskers—and I can't help remembering the story they tell in Illinois about the honest South-

- 244

ern gentleman—you ever hear that one?"

I said I hadn't.

"Well, what they say about the honest Southern gentleman—he never stole the Mississippi river. No, don't take any offence. It's as I said in Washington—I don't know about you, except what my slight knowledge of humanity tells me, which is that you're a rascal. But again, I don't *know*. The trouble with people like you—and me, I guess—is that nobody ever finds us out. Just as well, maybe. But it lays a burden on us—we don't meet with regular punishments and penalties for our misdeeds, which will make it all the harder for us to achieve salvation in the long run." He frowned at the carpet. "Anyway, I'm a lawyer, not a judge. I don't really believe that I want to know all about you. It's enough for me that you brought that girl across the Ohio river today. I don't know why, for what reason, or out of what strange chance. It's sufficient that she's here, and will never wear chains again."

Well, since that was what counted most with him, I was all for it; his talk about suspecting me for a rascal had been downright unnerving. It seemed a good time to butter him a bit.

"Sir," says I eagerly, "all my efforts on that poor unfortunate girl's behalf, the hardships of the flight, the desperate stratagems to which I was forced, the wound taken in her defence—wound, did I say? Scratch, rather—why, all these things would have been without avail had you not championed us in our hour of direst need. That, sir, was the act of a Christian hero, of a sublime spirit, if I may say so."

He stood looking at me, with his head cocked on one side.

"I must have been mad," says he. "Mind you, I quite enjoyed it there, for a moment—" he laughed uncertainly—"at least, now that it's over, I think I did. Do you realise what I allowed myself to do? You, sir, are in a way to being as highly successful a slave stealer as ever I heard of—at least, Arnold Fitzroy Prescott or whatever his name is—he's one. He's also an accessory to two murders—that's what they'd call it, although I'd say it was moral self-defence, myself. But a Southern jury certainly wouldn't agree. In the eyes of the law you're a deep-dyed criminal, Mr Comber—and I, the junior Congressman from Illinois, a pillar of the community, a trusted legislator, a former holder of the United States commission, a God-fearing, respected citizen—it's all there in my election address, and the people believed it, so it must be true—I allowed myself, in a moment of derangement, moved by pity for that girl Cassy's distress—I allowed myself, sir, to aid and abet you. God knows what the penalty is in Ohio for harbouring runaway slaves, assisting slave-stealers, resisting a warranted slave-catcher, and offering to disturb the peace by assault and battery, but whatever it is, I'm not in a hurry to answer for it, I can tell you."

He scratched his head ruefully and began to fidget about the room, twitching at the curtains and tapping the furniture with his foot, his head sunk on his chest.

"Not that I regret it, you understand. I'ld do it again, and again, and again, in spite of the law. Fine thing for a lawyer—humph! But there's a higher thing than the law, and it belongs in the conscience, and it says that evils such as slavery must be fought until the dragon is dead. And in that cause I hope I'll never stand back." He stopped, frowning. "Also, if there's one thing can get my dander good and high, it's a big mouthed Kentuckian hill rooster with his belly over his britches and a sass-me-and-see-what-happens look in his eye. Yes, sir, big-chested bravos like our friend Buck Robinson seem to bring out the worst in me. Still—I don't imagine we'll hear much more from his direction, and if we do, Judge Payne is fortunately a man of considerable influence—or Mrs Payne is, I'm never sure which—and by the time the good judge has come out from under the bedclothes and scrambled into his dignity again, I don't think I'll have much to fret over. Anyway, I can look after myself and lose no sleep. But you, Mr Comber, would be better a long way from here, and as quickly as may be."

Now he was talking most excellent sense; I twisted round from my prone position to cry agreement, and gave my backside a nasty twinge.

"Indeed, sir," says I. "The sooner I can reach England—"

"I wasn't thinking of quite so far as that; not just yet awhile. I know you're all on fire to get home, which is why you say you slipped away in New Orleans in the first place. Pity you allowed yourself to be . . . uh . . . distracted along the way. However, since you did, and have broken federal laws in the process, it puts a different complexion on things. For me, you could go home now, but it's not that simple. The way I see it, my government—my country—needs you; they still want you down in New Orleans to give evidence against the crew of—the *Balliol College*, wasn't it? Your testimony, as I understand it, can put those gentlemen where they belong—"

"But, Mr Lincoln, there is evidence enough against them without me," I cried, all a-sweat again.

"Well, perhaps there may be, but a little more won't hurt, if it makes certain of them. After all, that was why you sailed with them, why you risked your hide as an agent, wasn't it?" He was smiling down at me. "To bring them to book, to strike another blow against the slave trade?"

"Oh, of course, to be sure, but . . . well . . . er . . ."

"You're perhaps reluctant to go back to New Orleans because you feel it may be unsafe for you, after . . . recent events?."

"Exactly! You're absolutely right, sir . . ."

"Have no fear of that," says he. "No one is going to connect the eminently respectable Lieutenant Comber, R.N., with all those goings on far away up the river. That was the work of some scoundrel called Arnold FitzPrescott or Prescott FitzArnold or someone. And if anyone did connect them, I can assure you there would be no lack of influence working on your behalf to keep you out of trouble—there are enough sympathetic ears in high places in the federal government to see to that at need. Provided, of course, that you are doing your duty by that same government—and, incidentally, by your own."

By George, this was desperate; I had to talk him out of it somehow, without raising more suspicions of me than he had already.

"Even so, Mr Lincoln, I'm sure it would be best if I could proceed home directly. The case against the *Balliol College* can surely be proved without my help."

"Well, I daresay, but that's not the point any longer. This is quite a delicate situation, you know. See here: I've stood up for you tonight—and for that girl—helped you both to break my country's laws, and broken 'em myself, in a just, fine cause which

I believe to be in my country's true interest. And if it ever got out—which I pray to the Lord it won't—there is enough anti-slavery sentiment in our federal government to ensure that it would all be winked at, and no more said. But they're not going to wink if I, a Congressman, help a witness in an important case to avoid his duty. That's why I'm bound to send you back to Orleans. Believe me, you have nothing to fear there—you can say your piece in the witness box, and then go home as fast as my distant influence and that of grateful friends will send you."

Aye, and wait till the *Balliol College* scoundrels denounce me as Flashman, their fellow-slaver, posing as a dead man, thinks I; we'll see how much influence is exerted on my behalf then. I made a last effort.

"Mr Lincoln," says I, "believe me that nothing would give me more satisfaction than to accede to your request—"

"Capital," says he, "because that's what you're going to do." He regarded me quizzically. "Why you should be reluctant beats me—I begin to wonder if there's an outraged husband waiting for you in Orleans, or something of that order. If so, tell him to go to blazes—I daresay you've done that before."

There was one I could cheerfully have consigned to blazes, as I lay there going hot and cold, chewing my nether lip. I have damnable luck, truly—how many poor devils have had to try and wriggle clear in arguments with folk like Lincoln and Bismarck? He had me with my short hairs fast in the mangle, and I daren't protest any longer. What the devil was I to say, with those dark caverns of eyes smiling down at me?

"I doubt if it's anything as simple as an outraged husband, though," says he. "However, you don't choose to tell me, and I don't choose to press you. I owe you that much, on behalf of Randolph and the girl Cassy—in return you owe it to me to go to Orleans." He stood beside the bed, that odd quirk to his mouth, watching me. "Come, Mr Comber, it isn't very much, after all —and it's in the cause dear to your heart, remember."

There was nothing else for it, and I tried to keep the despair out of my voice as I agreed.

"So that's settled," says he cheerily. "You can go south again, but by a safe eastern route. I'll speak to Judge Payne, and see that

- 248

a hint reaches Governor Bebb. We'll arrange for a U.S. marshal to accompany you. You'll be safe that way, and you won't run the risk of straying again." He was positively benign, the long villain; I could have sworn he was enjoying himself. "The trouble with you jolly tars is you don't seem to find your way on land any too well."

He talked a little more, and then picked up his hat, shook hands, and went over to the door.

"Good luck in New Orleans, Mr Comber—or whatever your name is. In the unlikely event that we ever meet again, try and find out for me what club-hauling is, won't you?" He pulled on his gloves. "And God bless you for what you did for that girl."

It was some consolation to think that I'd fooled Mr Lincoln some of the time, at least; he believed I had a spark of decency, apparently. So I thought it best to respond with a few modest and manly phrases about saving an innocent soul from bondage, but he interrupted me with his hand on the door.

"Keep it for the recording angel," says he. "I've a feeling you're going to need it."

And then he was gone, and I was not to see him again until that fateful night fifteen years later when, as President of the United States, he bribed and coerced me into ruining my military reputation (which mattered something) and risking my neck (which mattered a great deal) in order to save his Union from disaster (which didn't matter at all—not to me, anyway). But that's another tale, for another day.

That night in Portsmouth he left me in a fine frustrated fury. After all my struggling and running and ingenuity, I was going to be shipped back to New Orleans—and inevitably a prison cell, or worse. I couldn't even run any more, what with my behind laid open, and there would be a marshal to see that I got safe into the clutches of the American Navy, too. By George, I was angry; I could have broken Lincoln's long neck for him. You'd have thought, after all I'd done for his precious abolitionist cause —albeit against my will and better judgment—that he'd have had the decency to let me go my ways, and given me a pound or two out of the poor box to boot. But politicians are all the same; there's no trusting them whatever, not only because they're knaves, but because they're even more inconsistent than women. Selfish brutes, too.

At least, though, I was still alive, and fairly full of sin and impudence, when I might easily have been dead or chained on an Alabama plantation, or rotting at the bottom of the Mississippi or the Ohio. For the future, although it looked pretty horrid, I would just have to wait and see, and take my chance—if it came.

I was allowed up next day, and sat in state on the edge of a chair, with my wounded cheek over the edge, and various people came to see me—abolitionists, of course, who wanted to shake the hero's hand, and in the case of the older ladies of the community, to kiss his weathered brow. They came secretly, because like all towns thereabouts Portsmouth was split between pro-slavers and abolitionists, and my whereabouts was known only to a safe few. They brought me gingerbread and good wishes, and one of them said I was a saint; normally I'd have basked in it, as I'd done on other occasions, but the thought of Orleans took the fun out of it.

One of my visitors I even assailed with a thrown boot; he was a small boy, I suspect a child of the house, who came in when I was alone and asked: "Is it right you got shot up the ass, mister? Say, can I see?" I missed him, unfortunately.

Another glum thing was that Cassy left that evening. She isn't one of my prime favourites, looking back—too strong-willed and high strung—but I hate to lose a good mistress just when I'm getting the taste of her. However, they said it wasn't safe for her to remain so near the Ohio, and an underground railroad man was to take her to Canada. We didn't even have the chance of a lusty farewell, for when she came to say good-bye the ugly Mrs Payne was on hand to see fair play, with Cassy looking uncommonly demure and rather uncomfortable in a drab brown gown and poke bonnet. I gathered she hadn't realised that I'd done my level best to desert her on the far bank of the Ohio, for she thanked me very prettily for all my help, while Mrs Payne stood with her hands in her muff, nodding severe approval.

"Cassiopeia is quite recovered from her ordeal," says she, "and looks forward with the liveliest anticipation to reaching Canada. There our friends will see to it that she is provided with shelter and such employment as fits her station. I have no doubt that she will prove a credit to all of us her benefactors, and especially to you, Mr Comber."

Cassy's face was like a mask, but I saw her eyes glint in the shadow of the bonnet.

"Oh, I don't doubt it," says I. "Cassiopeia is a very biddable child, are you not, my dear?" I patted her hand. "There, there —just be a good girl, and mind what Mrs Payne and her kind friends tell you. Say your prayers each night, and remember your ... er ... station."

"There," says Mrs Payne. "I think you may kiss your deliverer's hand, child."

I wouldn't have been surprised if Cassy had burst out laughing, or in a fit of rage, but she did something that horrified Mrs Payne more than either could have done. She bent down and gave me a long, fierce kiss on the mouth, while her chaperone squawked and squeaked, and eventually bustled her away.

"Such liberties!" cries she. "These simple creatures! My child, this will *never*—"

"Good-bye," says Cassy, and that was the last I ever saw of her —or of the two thousand dollars we had had between us. I've never been able to recall for the life of me where it was stowed when we got off the steamboat at Fisher's Landing, but I know I didn't have it on my person, which was careless of me. Ah, well, I've no doubt she put it to good use—and it had been paid for her anyway.

However, money was the least of my concerns just then. Unless there was some unexpected turn of events in the next few weeks I could see the American republic would be paying my board and lodging for some time to come. I had nightmares about it, in which I was in a place like the Old Bailey, but with great stained-glass windows, and a hanging judge in scarlet on the bench, and Spring and his mates all chained up, leering, in the dock, and a voice droning out, "Call Beauchamp Comber, R.N." And I saw myself creeping into the witness box, goaded on by Lincoln and a U.S. marshal, and Spring bawling out: "That's not Comber—Comber's dead! That's the notorious Flashy, *monstrum horrendum*, come to impose on your worships like the bloody liar he is!" And then consternation, and I was dragged to the dock and chained to the others, and the judge said it would be twice as bad for me as for them, and upon conviction I would be shot in the other buttock and then hanged. At which there was great cheering, and I pleaded with them that I had been led astray and that it all came of playing vingt-et-un with D'Israeli, and they said that made it worse still, and then the faces and voices faded, and I would find myself awake, boiling with sweat and my wound aching like be-damned.

In the end, it wasn't quite like that, as you shall see. Have you noticed that things are never quite as bad or good as you expect them to be—at least, not in the way that you expect? So it was now, when my rump had healed enough for me to travel, and Judge Payne brought along the marshal, and with much hand-clasping and cheek-kissing and hallelujahs I was despatched on my way to continue God's work, as Payne put it.

I won't bother you with the journey, which was by coach and rail through Columbus, Pittsburgh and Baltimore, and then by packet down to Orleans. Sufficient to say that the marshal, a decent enough fellow called Cottrell, watched over me like a mother over a chick, very friendly, very careful, and that no official notice of our passage seemed to be taken, until we came to New Orleans.

There I was delivered into the care of Captain Bailey, U.S.N., a very bluff gentleman who shook me cordially by the hand, and said they were glad to see me, hey, and a fine commotion there had been when Captain Fairbrother had lost me, by thunder, yes, but here I was, safe and sound, so all was well that ended well.

"Mind you, Mr Comber, in these days I don't ask too many questions," says he. "I'm a sailor; like you, I do my duty. The past few months are a closed account to me, sir—one hears all about outlandish things like underground railroads and what not, but that's nothing to the point. What I know is that facing me now is a brother officer in the service of a friendly power, who is going to give evidence on behalf of the U.S. Navy against slave-runners. Capital work." And he rubbed his hands. "More than that—not my concern, sir. Not my concern at all. If anyone has been working for the underground railroad—which is an illegal organisation, of course—well, that's not our province, is it?

That's for Washington, or state governments, to worry about."
He grew confidential. "You see, Mr Comber, we're a strangely
divided country here—some for slave-holding, others against.
Now the government recognises it, officially, as you know, but a
lot of very important people—some in the government itself—
are against it. We have the strange position where federal government people, who may detest slavery, nevertheless are bound to
enforce the law against things like underground railroading. So,
often as not, a great many people frequently have to follow the
example of your good Lord Nelson, and turn a blind eye to a great
many things. Such as what you've been doing between your . . . er
. . . departure from Captain Fairbrother and this moment, sir." He
frowned at me. "Do I make myself clear, sir?"

"I think so, sir," says I.

"Ye-es," says he. Then suddenly: "Look here, Comber, between
these four walls, I heard from circles in Washington that you've
been slave-stealing. Well, fine. I approve of that; so does half the
government. But it couldn't approve officially—my God, no!
Officially, it should arrest you and heaven knows what besides.
But we can't, even if we wanted to. We need your evidence in this
case, you're a damned important agent, by all Washington
accounts, and we can't, for the love of mercy, have an international
incident with the British." He shook his head. "I could wish you
had let well alone, young man—and yet, by God, from what I hear
from the friends of a certain Northern Congressman, you did a
capital piece of work, sir!" He beamed at me, winking. "So—there
it is. Washington is concerned at all costs to keep your name
and . . . er . . . recent activities quiet. You just make your statement
in court, put on your hat, and take the first packet out from this
port. You take me?"

If only it could be that simple, thinks I. But I made one last
effort to wriggle free.

"Is my evidence so necessary, sir?" says I. "Surely these
Balliol College people can be convicted . . ."

"Convicted?" says he. "Why, we're a long way short of that at
the moment. You know the procedure, sir—when a slave-trading
ship is captured, she must first of all be *adjudged* to be a slaver.
You know how it is in your own mixed commission courts at

Surinam and Havana and so forth—they hear evidence and pronounce themselves satisfied that she *was* carrying slaves. You must have seen it a score of times. And *then*—when the ship has been confiscated and condemned—then her master and crew may be charged with slave-trading, and on conviction, they can be hanged—although they seldom are. Jail terms sometimes, fines, etc. But with us it's not quite the same, as you'll see."

I was hanging on every word, hoping and praying that he would point out some loophole to me.

"Here, in New Orleans, a court of adjudication will pronounce on the *Balliol College*, and according to that, her master and crew may be charged with slave-trading, and possibly—since Spring fought against ships of the U.S. Navy—with piracy. But none of these charges can even be brought, sir, unless the court of adjudication finds that the *Balliol College* was indeed a slaver. So far, then, we follow the same course as the mixed courts at Havana and elsewhere. But here, sir, there are much more powerful interests involved—this is New Orleans, remember, a long way from Washington, and New Orleans holds no grudge against slave-traders like Spring. To secure the confiscation and condemnation of the *Balliol College* as a slave ship, the case must be proved to the hilt and beyond. Now do you see why your evidence is vital?" He tapped his desk. "This is not just a criminal—a legal case, Mr Comber. It's a political one, sir. See here," he grew confidential again. "This man Spring. No ordinary blackbirder, that. Why, when he was brought in by Fairbrother's people—what happened? The fellow was wounded—I tell you, sir, there was a bail bond posted faster than you could sneeze, a surgeon in attendance, more lawyers running about than you'd think existed. Why, sir? Because there's money, and power, and political influence behind this damned trade—that's why! There's his ship—how many hundreds of thousands of dollars investment d'you think she represents—and not just dollars, either, but pounds sterling and pesos and francs? They couldn't find any papers on her, because that damned wife of Spring's heaved them all overside—so what happens now, but Spring's counsel enter papers to show she's registered in Vera Cruz, Mexico, of all places, and her owner is some bloody Dago with a name as long as your leg—Mendoza y

Cascara, or something. Mexico, Lord save us! If there's one place we don't need complications with, it's Mexico—and they know it. But they can prove she's Mexican-owned—for all she's Baltimore built, with an English skipper."

I could make little of this, but one thing seemed clear.

"But if she was carrying slaves when they took her—and had slave gear aboard—"

"Slave gear doesn't matter—the equipment treaty doesn't hold up in New Orleans, sir. Mixed commission trials, yes, but not here. The slaves, sir—they're the thing!"

"Well, then—"

"Precisely. That's where we've got them. There were slaves aboard, and for all the treasure and effort that will be poured in on their side, I don't see how they can get round it. Mind you, sir, the shifting and lying and trickery that goes on at a slave ship adjudication is something you must see to believe. It wouldn't surprise me if Spring claimed they were all his sons and daughters, wearing chains because they're perverted creatures. I've seen excuses just as wild. And in New Orleans—well, you can't tell. I would to God," he added, "that Fairbrother had had the sense to take the *Balliol College* to Havana—she'd have been nailed there, fast enough, and we'd have been spared all this. But with your evidence, Mr Comber, I don't see how we can go wrong. Oh, they'll fight; they've got Anderson, who's as sharp a mind as ever took a brief—or bribed a witness. He'll try every trick and dodge going, and the adjudicator will be leaning his way, remember. But when you take the stand—well, sir, where will they be then?"

Where *they* would be was of small interest to me; where was Flashy going to be? I gulped and asked:

"Do they ... er ... do they know about ... that I'll be giving evidence?"

"Not yet," says he, smiling happily. "You see, an adjudication isn't a trial—we don't have to come and go with the other side much beforehand, officially, although I can tell you that the politicking that's been done in this case—offers of settlement, God knows what—has been amazing. Whoever is behind Spring, they're people who matter. They want him and his ship clear —probably frightened of what he'll divulge if he's ever brought to trial. Oh, it's a fine, dirty business, Mr Comber—the slime and corruption doesn't end on the slave deck, I can tell you. No, they don't know about you, yet—but I'll be surprised if a little bird doesn't tell 'em pretty soon. Lucky, in a way, that you didn't turn up until now—court sits the day after tomorrow, and if you hadn't been here we'd have had to go in without our best witness."

Lucky, I thought—just another few days lost up north and they might have started and got it over, and I'd have been spared my appearance and inevitable unmasking. I couldn't see anything for it, now—unless I got the chance to run again, but Bailey, for all his amiability, was no less watchful than the marshal had been. Even at the Navy office there was a damned little American snotty keeping me company wherever I went, and on the following day, when I was taken down to the building where the adjudication court sat, and was introduced to the counsel representing the U.S. Navy, the snotty and a petty officer were trailing at my heels.

The counsel was a lordly man from Washington with a fine aristocratic beak and silver hair falling to his shoulders. His name was Clitheroe, and he talked to the air a yard above my head; to hear him, the business would be over in a couple of hours at most, and then he would be able to get back to Washington and direct his talents to something worth while. He talked briskly for a moment or two about my part in the proceedings—"decisive corroboration" was the expression he used—and then consigned me to the care of his junior, a quiet, dark little fellow called Dunne, who had said very little, and now took me apart into a side room, instructing my escort to wait while he had a private word with me.

Now what followed is gospel true, and you will just have to believe me. If it runs counter to your notions of how justice is done in the civilised world, I can't help it; nothing in my experience leads me to believe that things are any different in England or France, even today. This is what happened.

Dunne talked to me for about five minutes, around and about the case, but all very vague, and then begged to be excused for a moment. He went out, leaving me alone, and then the door opened and in comes a prodigious fat man, with a round face and spectacles, for all the world like some Friar Tuck in a high collar. He closed the door carefully, beamed at me, and says:

"Mr Comber? Delighted to meet you, sir. My name is Anderson —Marcellus Anderson, sir, very much at your service. You may have heard of me—I represent the defendants in the case in which you are to be a distinguished witness."

My jaw dropped, and I must have glanced at the door through which I had come from Clitheroe's office, for he gave a fat man's chuckle and slid into a chair, observing:

"Have no fears, sir; I shall not detain you above a moment. The admirable Clitheroe, and your, ha-ha, watchdog, Captain Bailey, would grudge me even that long, no doubt, but Mr Dunne is a safe man, sir—he and I understand each other." He regarded me happily over his spectacles; Mr Pickwick as ever was.

"Now, very briefly, Mr—er—Comber, when we heard that you were to testify, my client, Captain Spring, was mystified. Indeed, sir—do you know, he even seemed to doubt your existence? However, you will know why, I dare say. I made rapid inquiry, obtained a description of you, and when this was conveyed to my client—why, sir, a great light dawned upon him. Oh, he was thunderstruck, and I needn't go into distressing detail about what he said—but he understood your, ha-ha, position, and the steps you had taken to safeguard yourself when the *Balliol College* was arrested some months ago."

He took off his glasses and polished them, regarding me benignly.

"Rash, sir, very rash—if you'll forgive me for saying so. However, it's done. Now Captain Spring was incensed at what he considered—justifiably, I think—to be a disloyalty on your part. Yes, indeed, and it was his first instinct to denounce you the moment you took the stand. However, sir, it occurred to me— it's what I'm paid for—that there might even be advantage to my client in having Lieutenant—" he paused— "Beauchamp Millward Comber as a witness for the plaintiff. If his evidence was—oh, shall we say, inconclusive, it might do the defendant more good than harm. Do you take me, sir?"

I took him all right, but without giving me a chance to reply he went on.

"It amounts to this, sir. If my client is cleared, as I feel bound to tell you I believe he will be—for we have more shots in our locker than friend Clitheroe dreams of—then we have no interest in directing attention to the antecedents of Lieutenant Comber. If Captain Spring is *not* cleared—" he shook his head solemnly "—then when the crew of the *Balliol College* are arraigned for slave-trading and so forth, their number will be greater by one than it is at present."

He stood up quickly. "Now, sir, Mr Dunne will be impatient to speak to you again. When we meet again, at the hearing, it will be as strangers. Until then, I have the honour to bid you a very good day."

"Wait . . . wait, for God's sake!" I was on my feet, my mind in a turmoil. "Sir . . . what am I to do?"

"Do, sir?" says he, pausing at the door. "Why, it is not for me to tell a witness how he shall give evidence. I leave that to your own judgment, Mr . . . er . . . Comber." He beamed at me again. "Your servant, sir."

And then he was away, and two shakes later Dunne was back, aloof and business-like, describing to me the form and procedure of an adjudication court, all of which went straight by me. Well, I've been in some fearful dilemmas, but this beat everything. The Navy expected my evidence to follow the lines of the statements I'd made in Washington, months back. If it did, Spring would cut me down in open court and I'd be for the dock myself. If it didn't—if I lied myself hoarse—Spring would keep his mouth shut, but the Navy . . . my God, what would they do to me? What could they do? They couldn't arrest me, surely . . . no, but they could investigate and question, and God alone knew what might come of that. The tangle was so terrible that I couldn't think straight at all—there was nothing for it but to be carried along on the tide, and do what seemed safest at the time. I wondered if I should confess to Bailey, telling him who I really was and admitting my imposture, but I daren't; I'd have been putting a rope round my own neck for certain.

There aren't many blank periods in my memory, but the rest of that terrible day is one; I cannot remember the night that followed, but I recall that on the next morning, the day of the adjudication, a strange recklessness had come over me. I was beyond caring, I suppose, but I remember I stood muttering to myself before a mirror as I brushed my hair: "Come on,

Flashy, my boy, they haven't got you yet. Remember Gul Shah's dungeon; remember Rudi's point at your throat in the Jotunberg cellar; remember the Ghazis coming at you on the road above Jugdulluk; remember the slave cart in Mississippi; remember de Gautet drawing a bead on you. Well, you're still here, ain't you? Your backside is better enough for you to run again, if need be—bristle up the courage of the cornered rat, put on a bold front, and to hell with them. Bluff, my boy—bluff, shift and lie for the sake of your neck and the honour of Old England."

And with these thoughts in my head and a freezing void in my bowels I was escorted to the adjudication court.

It was held in a great white room with brown panelling, like a lecture theatre, with tiers of crescent-shaped benches to one end for the spectators, a little rostrum and desk for the adjudicator and his two assessors at the other, and in between, right beneath the rostrum, were three great tables. At one sat Clitheroe and Dunne, and on a bench behind were just myself and—to my astonishment—two of the prettiest yellow girls you ever saw, all in New Orleans finery, with an old female in charge of them. They were giggling to each other under the broad brims of their bonnets, and when I sat down they looked slantendicular and giggled more than ever, whispering in each other's ears until the old biddy told them to leave off. My escort left me and went to sit on the first of the public benches, beside Captain Bailey, who was in full fig; he nodded to me and smiled confidently, and I gave him back a terrified grin.

At the centre table were a few clerks, but the far table was empty until just before the proceedings began. By that time the public benches were crowded with folk—nearly all men, and consequential people at that, talking and taking snuff and calling out to each other; I felt plenty of eyes on me, although most were directed at the two yellow girls, who preened and simpered and played with their gloves and parasols. Who the blazes they might be, I couldn't imagine, or what they were doing here.

And then a door behind the far table opened, in rolls Anderson, and to a rising buzz of chatter and comment, John Charity Spring entered and took his seat, with Anderson puffing at his elbow. The last time I had seen him he had been rolling on his own deck with Looney's bullet in his back; he looked a trifle paler now, but the beard and tight-buttoned jacket were as trim as ever, and when the pale eyes looked across directly into my own, I saw his lips twitch and the scar on his forehead began to darken. He stared at me fixedly for a full minute, with his hands clenched on the table before him, and then Anderson whispered in his ear, and he sat back, looking slowly about the court. He didn't look like a prisoner, I'll say that for him; if anyone looked guilty you may have three guesses who it was.

Then the adjudicator came in and we all stood up; he was a little, sharp-faced man, who smiled briefly to Clitheroe and Anderson, shot quick, accusing glances at everyone else, and told the nigger boy behind his chair to mind what he was about, and fetch some lime juice directly. Everyone fell silent, the two assessors sat either side of the adjudicator, and the clerk called out the case for hearing of the barque *Balliol College*, reputedly owned and registered in Mexico, master John Charity Spring, a British citizen; the said barque taken by U.S. brig *Cormorant*, in latitude 85 west 22.30 north or thereabouts, on such and such a day, and then carrying aboard her certain slaves and slaving equipment, in contravention of United States law—

Anderson was on his feet at once. "May the adjudicator take note that the *Balliol College* was not and is not an American vessel, and that her master is not an American citizen."

"Nevertheless," says Clitheroe, rising, "may the adjudicator note that the ownership is disputed, and recall the case of the ship *Butterfly*, condemned in similar circumstances.[42] Further, it will appear that the *Balliol College* was carrying slaves intended for trans-shipment to the United States, which is a clear violation of American law, and that when challenged by a United States ship of war, such challenge being proper and lawful, the *Balliol College* fired upon her challenger, which is piracy under American law."

"If these things are proved, sir," says Anderson, beaming.

"As they will be manifestly proved," says Clitheroe.

"Proceed," says the adjudicator.

The clerk read on that the *Balliol College* had resisted arrest, that an attempt had been made to dispose of the slaves aboard her by drowning them, and that the plaintiff, Abraham Fairbrother, U.S. Navy—it was news to me that the case was undertaken in his name—sought the confiscation and condemnation of the *Balliol College* as a slave-trading vessel.

That done, Clitheroe and Anderson and the adjudicator went into a great wrangle about procedure which lasted most of the morning, and had everyone yawning and trooping out and in, and fidgetting, until they had it settled. It was beyond me, but the result was that the business was conducted in a most informal way —more like a discussion than a court. But this, apparently, was the case with these adjudications; they had evolved a strange procedure that was all their own.[48]

For example, when they were at last ready to begin, it was Anderson who got up and addressed the adjudicator, not Clitheroe. I didn't know that it was common for the defendant to show his innocence, rather than the other way about. And for the life of me I couldn't see that Spring had a leg to stand on, but Anderson went ahead, quite unruffled.

The plaintiff's case, he said, such as it was, rested on the hope that he might show the *Balliol College* to be, de facto, American-owned, or part American-owned. Secondly, that it was carrying slaves for America in contravention of American law. Thirdly, that in such illicit carriage, it resisted arrest by an American ship of war, such resistance amounting to piracy.

"Unless I mistake the plaintiff's case," says he, easily, "everything rests on the second point. If the *Balliol College* was *not* carrying slaves for the United States, and so breaching American law, it is immaterial whether she is American-owned or no: further, if she was *not* carrying slaves, her arrest was illegal, and such resistance as she showed cannot be held against her master or crew. The plaintiff must show that she was a slave-trading ship, carrying slaves illegally." He beamed across the court. "May I hear counsel on the point?"

Clitheroe rose, frowning slightly, very austere. "That is the essence of the plaintiff's case, sir," says he. "We shall so demonstrate." He picked up a paper. "I have here the sworn deposition of Captain Abraham Fairbrother, U.S. Navy, commander of the brig *Cormorant*, who effected the capture."

"Deposition?" cries Anderson. "Where is the gentleman himself?"

"He is at sea, sir, as you well know. I have already had a word to say—" and he looked hard at Anderson "—on the point of delays engineered, in my opinion, by the defendant's counsel, in the knowledge that the witness would be compelled to resume his duties afloat, and would therefore be unable to appear in person."

Anderson was up like a shot, protesting innocence to heaven, with Clitheroe sneering across at him, until the adjudicator banged his desk and told them sharply to mind their manners. When the hubbub and laughter on the public benches had subsided, Clitheroe went ahead with Fairbrother's statement.

It was a fair, truthful tale, so far as I could see. He had challenged the *Balliol College*, which had been flying no flag, she had sheered off, he had fired a warning shot, which had been replied to, an action had been fought, and he had boarded. A dozen or so slaves had been found aboard, recently released from their shackles—as he understood it this had been done by Lieutenant Comber, R.N., who was aboard the ship ostensibly as one of the crew, although in fact he was a British naval officer. Lieutenant Comber would testify that it had been the intention of the master of the *Balliol College* to drown these slaves, and so remove all evidence.

There was a great humming in the court at this, and many glances in my direction, including a genial smile from Anderson and a glare from Spring. The adjudicator banged his desk for quiet, and Clitheroe went on to describe how the *Balliol College* crew had been arrested, and the ship brought into New Orleans for adjudication. He sat down, and Anderson got up.

"An interesting statement," says he. "A pity that we cannot cross-examine the deponent, since he isn't here. However, may I point out that the statement takes us no further so far as the status of the coloured people on board the *Balliol College* is concerned. Negroes were found—"

"And slave shackles, sir," says Clitheroe.

"Granted, sir, but the precise relation of one to the other is not determined by the statement. No doubt my friend, having delivered the statement which is the basis of his case, will call witnesses in due course. May I now enter my client's answer to the statement?"

Clitheroe nodded, the adjudicator snapped: "Proceed," and at Anderson's request one of the clerks swore Spring in to testify. Then Anderson said:

"Tell us, Captain Spring, of your voyage in the *Balliol College* prior to and including the events in question."

Spring glanced at the adjudicator, came to his feet, and leaned his hands on the table. The harsh grating voice took me back at once—I could smell the *Balliol College* again, and feel the hot sun beating down on my head.

"I sailed from Brest, in France, with a cargo of trade goods for the Dahomey coast," says he. "There we exchanged them for a general cargo of native produce, largely palm oil, which I conveyed to Roatan, in the Bay Islands. Thence I was proceeding in ballast for Havana, when I was intercepted by an American brig and sloop, who without justification that I could see, ordered me to heave to and fired upon me. I resisted, and my ship was presently boarded by these Navy pirates, who seized my ship, my person, and my crew!" His voice was rising, and the red scar burning. "We were carried in chains to New Orleans—I myself had been grievously wounded in defence of my ship, and I have since been held here, my ship confined, and myself and my owners deprived of its use, with subsequent loss to ourselves. I have protested in the strongest terms at this illegal detention, for which an accounting will be demanded not only of the person involved, but of his government." And in true Spring fashion he growled: "*Qui facit per alium facit per se** holds as good in American law as in any other, I dare say. That I was carrying slaves in contravention of this country's enactments I emphatically deny—"

"My dear sir, my dear captain." This was Anderson. "May I anticipate my friend's question: if this is so, why did you not heave to when required, and permit a search of your vessel? Then all might have been easily resolved."

Spring made noises in his throat. "Do I have to tell an American court, of all places? I responded to a signal to heave to, from an American vessel, in precisely the manner in which an American captain would have replied to a similar demand from a British naval ship. In short, sir, I defied it."

There was a great shout of laughter from the public benches, and feet drummed on the floor in applause. The little adjudicator hammered his desk, and when all was fairly quiet Anderson asked:

*What a man does through another, he does himself.

"As the British captain of a Mexican vessel you saw no reason to heave to—quite so. You know, Captain Spring, it has been suggested that your vessel is not Mexican owned. I believe my friend may wish to pursue the matter?" And he invited Clitheroe with a cocked eyebrow.

So Clitheroe set about Spring—he threw names at him, American, British and French; he pointed out that the *Balliol College* was Baltimore-built and originally Yankee-owned; he put it to Spring that the papers now set before the adjudicator, showing Mexican ownership, were forgeries and makeshift. Why, he demanded, if Spring were an honest merchantman, had his wife thrown the ship's papers overboard?

"When I am attacked by pirates, sir," says Spring, "I do not permit my papers to fall into their hands. How do I know that they might not be falsified and tampered with to be used against me? Here is a whole trumped-up business anyway—to suggest that I am a slaver, without a rag of proof, and to badger me with nonsense about my papers!" He pointed to the adjudicator's desk. "My papers are there, sir—certified, vouched copies! Look at them, sir, *litera scripta manet*,* and get on to the point of your inquisition, if it has one!"

It seemed to me he was playing the bulldog British skipper a thought too hard for safety, but the public were with him, crying, "hear, hear" until the adjudicator had to call them to order. Clitheroe shrugged and smiled.

"By all means, captain, since you desire it. I pass from the matter of ownership, which is secondary, to the heart of the matter. Since you are fond of tags, let's see if you remain quite so *rectus in curia*† when I ask—"

The adjudicator hammered his desk again. "I'll be obliged if you'll both speak English," cries he. "Most of us are familiar with the classics, but not on that account will I permit this adjudication to be conducted in Latin. Proceed."

Clitheroe bowed. "Captain Spring, you say you brought palm oil from Dahomey to Roatan—an unusual cargo. Why then was your ship rigged with slave shelves?"

*The written letter remains (as evidence).
†Upright in the court.

"Slave shelves, as you call them, are a convenient way of stowing palm oil panniers," says Spring. "Ask any merchant skipper."

"And they're also convenient for stowing slaves?"

"Are they?" says Spring. "May I point out that the shelves were not rigged when my ship was seized—when you say I was running slaves."

"I shall come to those same slaves, if you please," says Clitheroe. "There were, according to the affidavit we have heard, negroes aboard your ship—about a dozen women. They were found on deck, with slave shackles beside them. Evidence will be given that they had been chained, and that you had been preparing to cast them overboard, to destroy the evidence of your crime." He paused, and there wasn't a sound in court. "You are on oath, Captain Spring. Who were those women?"

Spring stuck out his jaw, considering. Then he answered, and the words hit the court like a thunderclap.

"Those women," says he deliberately, "were slaves."

Clitheroe gaped at him. There was a gasp from the public benches and then a great tumult, hushed at last by the adjudicator, who now turned to Spring.

"You admit you were carrying slaves?"

"I've never denied it." Spring was quite composed.

"Well—" The adjudicator looked about him. "Permit me, sir, but I have been in error. I thought that was what your counsel had been vigorously denying on your behalf."

Anderson got to his feet. "Not precisely, sir. May I suggest that my client be allowed to stand down for the moment, while the court digests his statement and reflects upon it? In the meantime, perhaps my friend will continue with his case."

"Frankly, sir," says Clitheroe, "it seems my case is made, I move for an order of confiscation and condemnation against the *Balliol College*, proved to be a slave-trader on her own master's word."

"Not quite proved," says Anderson. "If I may invite my friend to provide the corroboration which he doubtless has at command?"

Clitheroe looked at the adjudicator, and the adjudicator shrugged, and Clitheroe shuffled his papers and muttered to Dunne. For the life of me I couldn't fathom it; Spring appeared to have thrown away, with those words, his case, his ship, his liberty—

perhaps even his neck. It made no sense—not to the public or the adjudicator or to me. The one thing I prayed for now was that my evidence wouldn't be needed.

Clitheroe didn't like it; you could see, by the way he shot looks across at Anderson, that he smelled a rat. But Anderson sat smug and smiling, and presently Clitheroe shrugged ill-humouredly and picked up his papers.

"If the adjudicator wishes, I shall continue," says he. "But I confess I don't see the point of it."

The adjudicator peered at Anderson, thoughtfully. "Perhaps it would be as well, Mr Clitheroe."

"Very well." Clitheroe looked at his papers. "I shall call and examine the former slaves Drusilla and Messalina."

At this the yellow girls popped up, with little squeaks of surprise—and I realised that these tarts must be two of the women we had been shipping to Havana. Well, here were the two final nails for Spring's coffin, but he never batted an eyelid as they were brought forward, fluttering nervously, to the table, and sworn in by the clerk. The fellows on the public benches were showing great interest now, nudging and muttering as the little beauties took their stand, like two butterflies, one pink and one yellow, and Clitheroe turned to the adjudicator.

"With permission I shall examine them together, and so save the court's valuable time," says he. "As I understand it, both you young ladies speak English?"

The young ladies giggled, and the pink one says: "Yassuh, we both speak English, Drusilla'n' me."

"Very good. Now, if you will answer for both, Messalina. I believe you were in a place called Roatan—the Bay Islands, you might call it, a few months ago. What were you doing there?"

Messalina simpered. "We wuz in a who'-house, suh."

"A what?"

"A who'-house—a knockin'-shop, suh." She put her gloved hand up to her mouth, and tittered, and the public slapped their thighs and guffawed. The adjudicator snapped for silence, and Clitheroe, looking uncomfortable, went on:

"You were both—employed in a . . . whore-house. I see. Now then, you were taken on a ship, were you not?" They both nodded, suppressing their giggles. "Do you see here any of the men who were on that ship?"

They looked round, nervously, at the adjudicator, and then further afield. A voice near the back of the public benches called out: "Not me, honey. I was at home," and a great hoot of mirth broke out and had to be quieted, the adjudicator threatening to clear the room if there was unseemly behaviour. Then Messalina timidly pointed to Spring, and then they both looked round at me, and giggled, and whispered, and Messalina finally said:

"That one, too—with the nice whiskers. He was awful kind to us."

"I'll bet he was," says the voice again, and the adjudicator got so angry he swore, and said that was the last warning. Clitheroe gave me a look, and said:

"I see—these two men. Captain Spring and Mr Comber. They and others took you on a ship—where to, do you know?"

"Oh, to Havana, ev'yone said. An' then we was goin' on to here, by 'nother ship, to Awlins, right here."

"I see. Did you know where you were going to, in New Orleans?"

They giggled and conferred. "Miz Rivers' who'-house, so ev'yone reckon."

"I see, first to Havana, and then to Mrs Rivers' . . . er, establishment, in New Orleans." Clitheroe paused. "There is, I am told, such an establishment."

There was some haw-hawing from the public, and a cry of "He ain't foolin' ', but the adjudicator let it go.

"Now, girls," says Clitheroe, "when you were in Roatan, what were you?"

"Please, suh, we wuz whores," giggled Drusilla.

"Yes, yes, but what else? Were you free?"

"Oh, no, suh, we wuz slaves. Warn't we, Drusie? Yassuh, we'z slaves a'right."

"Thank you. And as slaves you were sent aboard the ship, to be taken to Havana, and thence sold to Mrs Rivers' . . . ah . . . whorehouse in New Orleans. But by the favour and mercy of God, the ship was captured by the United States Navy and—" Clitheroe leaned forward impressively "—you were brought to New Orleans and *there set free*. Is this not so?"

"Oh, yassuh. We's set free, sho' nuff." Messalina smiled winningly at him.

"Fine. Splendid. You were liberated from that unspeakable servitude, and you are now free women." Clitheroe was enjoying himself. "Since when I don't doubt you have been happy in your new-found land of adoption and blessed free estate. You are both safe in New Orleans?"

"Oh, yassuh. We's fine, at Miz' Rivers' who'-house."

Even the adjudicator didn't try to stop the peal of laughter and applause that this provoked, and Drusilla and Messalina smiled around happily and preened themselves under all this male attention. But Clitheroe just sat down, red in the face, and Anderson got up and waited for the noise to subside.

"A very moving story," says he, and everyone roared again. "Tell me, Drusilla and Messalina—I don't doubt for a moment that every word you have told us is true, and I accept it as true—but tell me, you first, Messalina dear: where were you born?"

"Why . . . Baton Rouge, suh."

"And you, Drusilla?"

"N'Awlins, suh."

"Indeed. Very interesting. And how did you come to be at Roatan?"

Messalina had been taken by a wealthy planter visiting Cuba; she had been his mistress, but he had tired of her and sold her. ("Silly bastard," says the unseen voice.) Drusilla had been one of a party taken on a cruise by wealthy degenerates, who had sold their doxies at various places in the Caribbean.

"So you are both American-born? I see—and both born slaves?"

"Yassuh."

"The other girls on the ship with you—were they also American-born? You don't know—of course not. And they have not been cited as witnesses in this case, and can't be called now, accordingly." Anderson glanced knowingly across the court at Clitheroe, who was looking like a man who sees a ghost. "May I refresh the court's memory by referring to the enactment of 1820"
—he rattled off a string of numbers while he leafed through a large

tome. "Here we have it. Briefly it defines as piracy and illegal slave-trading—" he paused impressively "—the transportation for enslavement of any coloured person *who is not already a slave under American law.*"

In the hush that followed Anderson closed the book with a snap like a pistol shot.

"There we have it, sir. Captain Spring, as he has admitted, freely and openly, was carrying slaves—American slaves, born slaves, and in so doing he was in no way contravening any United States law. No more than a man breaks the law when he carries a slave across the Mississippi River. He was not *running* slaves, or slave-trading in the illicit sense, or—"

Clitheroe was on his feet, raging. "This is an outrageous twisting of the truth—why, just because these two happen to be American-born—why, they were only chosen to testify because they spoke English well—half of their fellow-captives on the *Balliol College*, I am certain, were not American-born, and were therefore—"

"Then it's a pity you didn't bring them here today," says Anderson. "You should choose your witnesses more carefully."

"Sir, this is monstrous!" cries Clitheroe. "In the name of justice, I demand to be allowed to call another—"

"In the name of justice you'll keep us here till kingdom come!" cries Anderson. "Really, sir, are we to be detained while this distinguished counsel rakes the whole of Louisiana for some witness who will suit his book? He has entered his witnesses before this court—let him abide by what they say. If they let him down, so much the worse for him, and so much the better for justice!"

There was no doubt whose side the spectators were on. They cheered and stamped and drowned out everyone until the little adjudicator had to shout for silence. And after several minutes, when all was quiet, he remarked:

"You had ample time to consider who you should call, sir. I'll hear the witnesses you have named."

"I protest!" cries Clitheroe, his white hair flung back. "I protest—but very well, sir—you shall hear my last witness, who will prove my case for me!" And as my heart shot into my mouth he turned and boomed:

"Beauchamp Millward Comber, Royal Navy!"

I suppose I took the oath, but I don't remember it. Then Clitheroe was taking me through my antecedents, my commissioning by the Board of Trade, my shipping aboard the *Balliol College* —all of which I had to invent, on the spur of the moment, and it wasn't made any easier by the unseen voice growling: "Goddam' limey spy!"—and so to the business he wanted to get his teeth into.

"You can, I think, testify, that when the *Balliol College* reached Dahomey, she took aboard not palm oil, as the defendant claims— but a human cargo. Slaves! Is this not so?"

But Anderson, bless his honest fat face, was on his feet. "This is quite improper, sir! I demand that the witness be instructed to ignore the question. We are not here concerned with what the British master of a Mexican ship was doing many thousands of miles from our shore. Such a case, if any there were, would be for a British or Mexican court, or a mixed commission of the type to which the United States does not subscribe. I demand—nay, insist—that no irrelevant observations, such as might prejudice my client's position, be permitted. We are here to determine the status of the *Balliol College* at the time of her seizure—" and he went bounding on to cite a great string of precedents—*Bright Despatch, Rosalinda, Ladies' Delight*, heaven knows what.

It sounded a near thing to me; I stood there with my palms sweating, and if that adjudicator had been an honest man I'd have been sunk. But someone had been to work, I've no doubt, for he shook his head, and snapped:

"I take the point of defendant's counsel. We are not concerned with the Captain's past history—"

"Or his ship's?" bawls Clitheroe. "What about *Mendon, Uncas*, any number I could name, sir—why, slavers have been condemned before ever they had taken a black on board, simply on a question of intent! This—"

"May I make a point, sir?" says Anderson. "I respectfully suggest that it would ill become an American court to deny to a British master the very rights which we insist upon for our own captains where British justice is concerned. We demand that our captains be not interfered with unless they expressly break British law; it cannot be argued that what Captain Spring was doing thousands of miles away, in a Mexican ship, is any concern of ours."

"Humbug—" Clitheroe was beginning, but Anderson added quickly:

"The court would hardly wish to set a precedent of which foreign governments, particularly the British, might take note."

That clinched it. The adjudicator glanced at me: "You will ignore that question, sir. Mr Clitheroe, I must ask you to confine yourself to the matter in hand. Proceed, sir."

"I protest again, most emphatically," says Clitheroe. "Very well, then—Mr Comber, were these negroes who were carried from Roatan for Havana—were they chained, sir?"

"Most of the time, not," says I, which was true.

"But chains were placed upon them when the American brig challenged the *Balliol College*?"

"Yes." I tried not to catch Spring's eye.

"Why were they chained, sir?"

"To prevent their possible escape, I imagine. I was below decks at the time."

He gave me an odd look. "Was there not another reason? Was it not so that a length of anchor chain could be rove through their shackles, so that they could be brutally hurled into the deep and drowned?" He looked at his papers. "I quote from your own statement to the Navy Department."

Up came Anderson. "May I point out that this ... statement, supposedly made by the witness, is not in itself evidence. We are concerned with what he says now, not what he said then."

I could feel the sweat starting out on my brow. How to balance the tightrope? Talk for your life, Flash, thinks I, so I looked perplexed, and said, addressing the adjudicator:

"Sir, I have reflected much on this matter in the past few months. That the slaves were shackled, and the anchor chain passed between those shackles, is true—I myself released them later. But in strict justice I must add that the shackling was performed by the late Mr Sullivan, mate of the *Balliol College*, and it was followed by a most violent altercation between Sullivan and Captain Spring."

Clitheroe's eyes narrowed, and I saw Bailey, who was behind him, sit up suddenly.

"Are you saying," says Clitheroe, "that Spring was objecting to this shackling?"

"I can't say, sir." God, I was treading warily. "What was the cause of their altercation, I do not know." I took a deep breath. "But I do know that Mr Sullivan had served aboard slave ships in the past—and I don't believe he was quite right in the head, sir."

Clitheroe was staring at me in frank disbelief. "But this is totally out of accord with your earlier statement, sir. What?—" he scrabbled over a page "—here we have you referring to Spring as 'an unhuman beast', a 'callous murderer', a —"

"This is infamous!" roars Anderson. "I have protested already —sir!" He swung on Clitheroe. "Is that statement, that rubbish you hold in your hand, and read out to vilify my client—is it signed, sir!"

"It is not signed, sir, but—"

"Then take it away, sir! Remove it! It is a scandal, a disgrace! I appeal to the adjudicator!"

"We will hear the witness," says the adjudicator. "Not what you say he once said, Mr Clitheroe. You must not lead the witness, sir—as you should know." Someone had greased his palm, right enough.

Clitheroe was in a quandary; Bailey, I could tell from his face, was in a fury. Clitheroe turned back to me, and his face was ugly.

"Very well," says he. "I now put the matter to you in different terms. Can you say, from your own knowledge, that there were slaves being carried on board the *Balliol College* in contravention of American law—that is to say, non-American slaves, and that an attempt was made to dispose of them by casting them overside— whoever gave the order."

I was ready enough for that. "Two hours ago, sir, I would have been able positively to answer your question as to the slaves. However, you must see, in the light of what we have heard from the last two witnesses, that I cannot in conscience answer positively now. The distinction about American-born slaves is new to me, sir; I cannot say whether the others were also American or not."

He gave a snort of impatience. "Was there not, on the *Balliol College*, an African woman—brought from Africa, sir, and carried to Baltimore with the others by Captain Fairbrother. A woman named—" he looked at his paper "—Lady Caroline Lamb, who spoke no English, and had been carried from Dahomey as a slave? Who could not possibly have been American, whatever the others were."

"I remember the woman perfectly," says I. "As to her status, I confess I am reluctant—now—to be too definite, since she was certainly not among those shackled by Mr Sullivan." (That was true, too; how had he overlooked her? She must have been in my cabin. Ah well, it's an ill wind.)

"Reluctant?" Clitheroe threw down his papers in disgust. Behind him I could see Bailey muttering with rage. "Reluctant? On my word, Mr Comber—I find this most extraordinary. Are you here, sir, to testify against that man—" and he flung out a hand at Spring "—or are you not? Damme, sir—I beg the adjudicator's pardon—what does this mean? Your whole tone, your attitude, the burden of your evidence, is so far from what you led us to believe it would be, that I could almost wonder—" His glance flickered to Anderson, but he thought better of it. Before he could go on, I plucked up my courage and got in first.

"I have answered your questions to the best of my ability, sir," says I. "If I am scrupulous, I must say I find it hard that I should be blamed for that."

He looked as though he would burst. "Scrupulous, by all that's holy! I don't ask you to be scrupulous—I ask for the truth! What did you sail aboard this damned slaver for, if not to bring him to justice, eh? Answer me that, sir?"

When in difficulty, bluster; it was the only weapon I had left, and I seized it, now that his loss of composure had given me the chance.

"I sailed in the performance of my duty to my chiefs, sir, as you well know. That duty I have done—or will do, as soon as I am permitted. If you look in my statement, sir, you will see that I was reluctant from the first to appear in this case, and that I appeared only because your Navy Department assured me it was necessary. I had assumed, wrongly, I fear—" and I took my whole courage in my hands, and tried to sound furious "—that such a simple case would be easily concluded without my intervention being called for."

He went white, and then red, and his breath came out in a great shudder. He looked at me with pure hate, and when he spoke, it was with great care.

"Indeed, sir? Very high-minded, and high-handed, are we not? Very well, Mr Comber, let us examine this, if you please. Your duty, sir, you have told us, is to your chiefs—you are an agent against the slave trade—although one would hardly suspect it from your conduct today. As such, I understand you obtained possession, during this voyage, of papers belonging to the master of the *Balliol College*—" out of the tail of my eye I saw Spring stiffen in his seat. "Will you tell us, sir, whether or not there was evidence in those papers—as to the ownership of the vessel, for example—to prove that she was engaged illegally in the slave trade, in contravention of American law? You are on oath, sir— remember that!"

My heart lurched, because I had seen the way out. I held my breath a moment, to make my face red, and let it out slowly. I drew myself up, and glared at him with all the venom I could muster.

"This, sir," says I, "is intolerable. It is precisely why I did not wish to appear. You are well aware, sir, that there are facts which I am in duty bound not to disclose—facts of the highest import— it is all explained in that statement, sir—which I cannot in honour convey to anyone except to my chiefs at home. I was promised immunity from this—" brazening it for all I was worth, I rounded on Bailey. "Captain Bailey, I appeal to you. This is entirely unworthy—I am badgered, sir, on the very grounds which it was promised to me would be inviolate. I will not endure it, sir! The counsel's questions must lead inevitably to the point which I was assured would not be touched. I...I..." There's nothing like a good stammer for conviction. "I was a fool to be coerced into this! I should have known . . . incompetence! . . . harm done!"

There was tumult in the court; even Bailey was looking bewildered now; the adjudicator was at a loss. Anderson, clever man, had the good sense to look amazed; Spring was looking worried. Clitheroe, stuck between rage and astonishment, looked to Bailey, and then to me.

"On my word!" This was the adjudicator, darting his nose at me. "What is this, sir? This outburst is quite—"

"Sir," says I, "I most humbly beg your pardon. I intended no disrespect to you, or to this august court." I hesitated. "I found myself placed in an intolerable position, sir—if an explanation is necessary, I beg that you will ask counsel for the plaintiff."

There was a moment's silence, in which the adjudicator looked at Clitheroe, and Clitheroe stood with his face white and his mouth set. Then he shook his head.

"I see no advantage to the court in . . . examining this witness further," says he, and he sat down.

Anderson jumped up, and began to address the adjudicator, but I was too bemused by my own eloquence to listen. The next thing I knew there was an adjournment, and I was hustled off to Bailey's office, with Clitheroe and Dunne, and the first two rounded on me like bears. But I snatched the ball from their hands, and laced into them for all I was worth—it was my only chance, I knew, to play the mystery as I had done in the Washington Navy Department, and play it as furiously as I could.

"If you so mishandle your case, sir, that you can't get a condemnation order that a child could obtain, is that my fault? The wrong slaves called as witnesses—this fellow Anderson permitted to shut me up on the very point where I could have given conclusive testimony! And then—the impudence to break the solemn assurance I was given in Washington, by questioning me in a way which, if I'd been fool enough to answer, must have elicited the names I am duty bound to conceal! And you dare to raise your voice to me, sir? Do you think I'll see my work ruined—two years of it—" Well, why not lay it on hard? "—simply because some fool of a lawyer can't win a case which in itself is nothing—nothing, sir, I tell you—compared with what I and my people are trying to do? Oh, this is too much!"

How I managed to lose my temper so badly for so long, when my innards were quaking, I am far from sure. They didn't take it lying down, either—especially Bailey, who was half-convinced my indignation was sham. But he couldn't be sure, you see; there was just enough mystery, as a result of all the bloody lies I'd told in Washington, to make him wonder.

"Your conduct, sir, gives me the gravest suspicions," says he. "I don't know—this is a deplorable affair! But we'll go into this, sir, believe you me; we'll get to the bottom—"

"Then you'll do it in your own good time, sir!" says I, looking him in the eye. "Not in mine. I'm sick and tired of this whole sorry business. I was promised protection, sir—"

"Protection?" cries he, looking ugly. "You have forfeited all claim to that. My department's protection is withdrawn, you may take that as read—"

"Thank God!" I exclaimed. "For all the good it's been to me, I'm better without it. I intend to place myself, at once, under the protection of my ambassador in Washington. At once, do you hear? And whoever tries to hinder me will do so at his peril!"

For a moment he looked as though he was believing me, and then we were summoned back to the court, and I sat red-faced, squeezing myself to keep it up, while Clitheroe and Anderson bandied away at each other, and finally Anderson challenged him on some point or other, and Clitheroe made a speech, and concluded it by moving for the confiscation and condemnation of the *Balliol College*. There was much palaver over the matter of Spring's resisting arrest, and Anderson stuck to the point about an innocent merchantman being entitled to protect himself, etc., and finally the adjudicator took off his spectacles and asked did their cases rest? They nodded, and he put his spectacles back on, and everyone stood up.

The adjudicator talked for about half an hour, while our legs creaked, and I couldn't for the life of me stop my hands trembling, for there was no telling which way he was going. He reviewed the evidence, Spring's and the girls and my own, and then came to his peroration. It was short, and decisive.

"It rests with the plaintiff, Abraham Fairbrother, to show that the *Balliol College* was carrying slaves in contravention of United States law. There are grounds for believing that she was, in view of her equipment and other circumstances related in evidence. It may also appear that grounds could exist for charges to be brought in connection with damage done to United States property by Captain Spring. On the other hand, it may be that, after the conclusion of this court, the owners of the *Balliol College* may hold that an action lies against the United States government for unlawful detention.⁴⁴ These are matters outside the scope of this adjudication. The activities of the *Balliol College*, prior to her arrest, may also be matters for a mixed commission court of the British or other governments.

"It is precisely for the attention of such court, if it be called, that I have mentioned the conclusion of this adjudication that grounds exist for believing that the *Balliol College* was carrying slaves in contravention of United States law. But I cannot hold that the grounds have been proved conclusively to the satisfaction of this adjudication. The motion for confiscation fails."

I pulled myself together and shot Clitheroe as baleful a look as I could manage, for Bailey's benefit. The adjudicator turned to Spring.

"You are free to go. As I understand it, your vessel is in the river, is it not, under a prize crew? Hear our order that this prize crew be withdrawn forthwith, and that such stores, water and wood as may be required in reason for your departure shall be left aboard, and in accordance with custom, clearance be granted for your departure this very day, or such date thereafter as you find fitting."

"Thank you, sir," says Spring. "I thank the court. I shall leave anchorage today."

The adjudicator banged his desk and scuttled out, and at once there was a great rush from the public benches to Spring's table, and he was being clapped on the back, and fellows were shaking Anderson's hand and hurrah-ing. Clitheroe walked out of the court without a word, and Bailey, after a lowering look at me, followed him. The two yellow girls, giggling and ogling, tripped away with their chaperone or bawd or whatever she was.

And suddenly I was standing alone. But I doubted, somehow, if this happy state would endure for long. My escort had gone with Bailey, but in spite of our violent exchanges, they would be expecting me at his office, or at least back at the Navy place where he had housed me. And then, for all my fine talk, they would keep a tight grip on me—for what? Interrogation, no doubt, and at best a convoy to Washington and my embassy, and God knew what would come of that. My buttock ached at the thought of sliding out again, but I knew I daren't stay. For one thing, the longer I was in this blasted country the greater the chance of my activities on the Mississippi being brought home to roost.

I looked about me. The spectators were all streaming out now, by the entrances at the back of the room. Half a dozen steps and I was among them—once outside, I could easily find my way to Susie's brothel, and this time, surely, she would be able to see me safe away; at least she could hide me until I grew a beard, or—.

And then it struck me, all in a moment, the dazzling thought. It was fearful, at first, but as I considered it, on the steps leading down to the street, it seemed the only safe way. It was the answer, surely—and I found my legs taking me off to one side, behind a pillar, where I thought some more, and then I stepped out into the busy street, and walked across to the far side, and took refuge beneath a tree, waiting.

It was ten minutes before I saw what I wanted, and my heart was in my mouth in case Bailey or my escort would come on the scene, but they didn't. And then I was rewarded, and I set off, walking quickly, along the street, and into another, and there I overtook the figure ahead of me.

"Captain Spring," says I. "Captain Spring—it's me."

He swung round as if stung, as near startled as I'd ever seen him.

"The devil!" he exclaimed. "You!"

"Captain," says I, "in God's name, will you give me a passage out of here? You're leaving, on the *College*, aren't you? For pity's sake, take me with you—out of this blasted—"

"What?" cries he, his scar beginning to jump like St Vitus dance. "Take you? Why the devil should I? You—"

"Listen, please, captain," says I. "Look, I played up today, didn't I? I could have sworn you to kingdom come, couldn't I? But I didn't—I didn't! I got you off—"

"You got me off!" He tilted back his hat and glared at me. "You saved your own dirty little neck, you Judas, you! And you've the nerve to come crawling to me?"

"I'll buy my passage!" I pleaded. "Look, I'm not just begging —I can buy it with something you want."

"And what would that be?" But he stepped aside with me into a doorway, the pale eyes fixed on me.

"You heard in court—I got Comber's papers—the things he'd filched from you. Well—" I forced myself not to notice the darkening scar on his brow. "—I've still got 'em. Are they price enough?"

His face was like flint. "Where are they?" he growled.

"In a safe place—a very safe place. Not on me," I lied, praying he'd believe it. "But I know where they are, and unless I say the word—well, they could get into the wrong hands, couldn't they? You'd be clear and away before that, of course, but your owners wouldn't like it. Morrison, for one."

"Where are they?" he demanded, and his hands came up, as though to seize me. But I shook my head.

"I'll tell you," says I, "in Liverpool or Bristol—not before. They'll be safe until then, on my word."

"Your word!" he sneered. "We know what that's worth! You perjured rascal. Look at you!" He laughed softly. "*Post equitem sedet atra cura.** Your friends in the American Navy are looking for you, I don't doubt."

"If they find me, they find those papers," says I. "But if you take me with you, I swear you'll have 'em." And welcome, I thought privately. Even when I'd handed them over, the knowledge of what was in 'em would still be in my head, and I'd use it to squeeze old Morrison dry. "You'll have them, captain," I repeated. "I promise."

"By God I will," says Spring. "I'll see to that." He stood considering me, "What a worthless creature you are—what shreds of loyalty have you, you object?"

"Plenty—to myself," says I. "Just as you have, Captain Spring."

His scar went pink; then he laughed again. "Well, well. You've picked up some Yankee sauce over here, I believe. Perhaps you're right, though. Horace reminds me, why should I sneer at you?

* Dark care sits behind the horseman (A guilty man cannot escape himself).

Mutato nomine de te fabula narratur."* He looked up and down the street. "I'll take you. But you tell me those papers are safe, do you? For if they're not—by God, I'll drop you overside with a bag of coal on your feet, if we're within ten feet of the Mersey. Or Brest, which is where I'm going. Well?"

"You have my word," says I.

"No," says he. "But I've got your carcase, and I'll settle for that. Now, then—are these damned Yankees close behind you? Then step lively, Mr Flashman!"

Strange, I thought, how long it was since anyone had called me by my proper name. For the first time in months I felt I was almost home again. With Elspeth, and the youngster, too. Aye, and my dear papa-in-law—I was looking forward to presenting my account to him.

* Change the name, and the story is told of yourself.

[EDITOR'S POSTSCRIPT. On this optimistic note the third packet of the Flashman Papers comes to an end. How far the optimism was justified may be judged from the fact that, instead of describing his return in gloating detail, Flashman concluded this portion of his memoirs by attaching to the last page of manuscript a clipping, cracked and faded with age, from a newspaper (probably, from its type face and extreme column width, the *Glasgow Herald*) dated January 26, 1849. The news it contains was, of course, unknown to him when he left New Orleans homeward bound. It reads, in part:

"It is with deep regret that we impart to our readers news of the death of Lord Paisley. This untimely event occurred last week at the home of his daughter, Mrs Harry Flashman, in London, where he had been residing for some time past. Those who knew him, either as John Morrison of Paisley and this city, where he was formerly Deacon of Weavers in the Trades' House of Glasgow, or by the title to which he was raised by a gracious sovereign only in November last, will be united in mourning his sudden melancholy demise . . ."]

NOTES

1. The great Chartist Demonstration of Monday, April 10, 1848, was, as Flashman says, a frost. Following the numerous continental revolutions, there were those who feared that civil strife would break out in Britain, and in addition to extra troops brought to the capital, the authorities enlisted 170,000 special constables between April 6 and 10 to deal with disturbances. Peel, Gladstone, Prince Louis Napoleon (later Napoleon III), about half the House of Lords and an immense number of middle-class volunteers were among the "specials". In the event, only about twenty to thirty thousand Chartists demonstrated, instead of the half million expected, and there was little violence apart from the fight between the butcher's boy and the French agitator, which happened as Flashman describes it. (Foreign agitators and hooligan elements were a frequent embarrassment to the Chartists, since they discredited the movement). Of the two (not five) million signatures to the great petition, about one-fifth are said to have been bogus—"Punch" noted caustically that if they had all been genuine, the Chartist procession should have been headed by the Queen and seventeen Dukes of Wellington. (See Halevy's *History of the English People in the Nineteenth Century*, vol. 4, pp. 242–6.)

2. From this and other allusions it is obvious that Flashman spent at least part of the 1843–47 period (the "missing years" so far untouched by his memoirs) in Madagascar and Borneo. He is known to have been both military adviser to Queen Ranavalona and chief of staff to Rajah Brooke of Sarawak; it now seems probable that he held these appointments between 1843 and 1847. Other evidence suggests that he may also have taken part in the First Sikh War of 1845–6.

3. Lord John Russell was then Prime Minister; Lansdowne was Lord President of the Council.

4. Berlins: articles, particularly gloves, knitted of Berlin wool.

5. Attendance money. A charge introduced on the railway about this time, which amounted to a kind of cover or service charge. It appears to have been levied for as small a service as asking a railway servant the time of day. Flashman's memory may be playing him false when he speaks of a railway book-stall; it was more probably a railway library.

6. Frances Isabella Locke (1829–1903) was to become famous in later years as Mrs Fanny Duberly, Victorian heroine, campaigner, and "army wife" extraordinary. She left celebrated journals of her service in the Crimea and the Indian Mutiny. (See E.E.P. Tisdall's *Mrs Duberly's Campaigns.*)

7. Lord George Bentinck (1802–48), one of the foremost sporting figures of his day, and leader of the Protectionist Tory opposition in the Commons. Handsome, arrogant, and viciously aggressive in political argument, Bentinck was widely respected as a guardian of the purity of the turf, although after his death his former friend Greville alleged

that he was guilty of "fraud, falsehood, and selfishness" and "a mass of roguery" in his racing conduct. Bentinck resigned his leadership of the opposition early in 1848, but was still the power in his party at the time of his meeting with Flashman at Cleeve. He died suddenly only a few months later, on September 21, 1848.

Disraeli, who then succeeded him as Tory leader in the Commons, was not to become Prime Minister for another twenty years. Flashman's view of him in 1848 fairly reflects the feeling of many Tories—"they detest D'Israeli, the only man of talent", wrote Greville in that year. His extravagances of dress and speech, his success as a novelist, and his Jewish antecedents combined to render him unpopular—Flashman, like Greville, insists on spelling him D'Israeli, although Disraeli himself had dropped the apostrophe ten years earlier. The nickname Codlingsby is a pun on *Coningsby*, perhaps his best novel, published in 1844. (See Charles Greville's *Memoirs*, January 7–September 28, 1848.)

8. Surplice had just beaten Shylock in the Derby, and on the following day the Jewish Disabilities Bill failed in the House of Lords.

9. With revolution everywhere on the Continent in 1848, it was confidently expected that Ireland would erupt, and there was a small abortive rising in the summer. John Mitchel, a leading agitator, was sentenced in May to fourteen years' transportation.

10. *Jane Eyre* by Charlotte Brontë was published in the autumn of 1847. *Varney the Vampire, or The Feast of Blood* by Malcolm Rymer was an outstanding horror story even in a decade which was unusually rich in novels of ghouls, vampires, and gothic spine-chilling.

11. Miss Fanny's excuse was not very flattering to her fiancé, whose position with the Eighth Hussars was that of paymaster.

12. The *Black Joke* schooner had a career befitting its romantic name, being in turn a slaver, a Royal Navy tender, and an opium smuggler in the China Seas.

13. Under the Anglo–Dutch treaty of 1822 a ship fitted out for slaving (with shackles, slave shelves, unusually large cooking facilities, etc.,) could be condemned as a slaver even if she was not carrying slaves. (See W. E. F. Ward's *The Royal Navy and the Slavers*.)

14. What Flashman says of the background to the slave trade in the 1840s is accurate enough, but obviously he does not give more than a hint of the complicated system of treaties and anti-slavery laws by which the civilised nations fought the traffic. (See Ward). Virtually all were prepared to pay at least lip service to the anti-slave trade cause, but only Britain mounted a continuous major campaign against the slaving vessels on the high seas and along the African coast, although at the time of Flashman's voyage the United States Navy was also lending its assistance. But there was no consistency about the various national laws against the trade, and the slavers were quick to take advantage of the numerous loopholes. What is sometimes not appreciated is the distinction that was drawn by governments between slavery and actual slave trading: for example, Britain prohibited the *trade* as early as 1807, but did not abolish *slavery* within the Empire until 1833; the United States prohibited the trade in 1808, but continued to practise slavery in her slave states until the Civil War. In this topsy-turvy situation, with huge private interests involved in the traffic, slave trading flourished into the second half of the century.

15. Pedro Blanco was a leading slave-broker who specialised in collecting Africans for sale to slaving ships. His usual scene of operations was farther north, on the Sierra Leone coast. Flashman's description of Whydah and the Kroos corresponds very closely with contemporary accounts.

16. With epidemics an ever-present danger on the Middle Passage, slaver captains took every precaution against shipping diseased or weakly slaves However, they had no scruples about marketing those who fell ill on the voyage, and were at pains to disguise their disabilities. Spring is here referring to a particularly revolting means of hiding the symptoms of dysentery.

17. Spring was giving considerably less space to his slaves than that allowed by the Wilberforce Committee in 1788, when the famous plan of the slaving ship *Brookes* gave the following figures: Males, six feet by sixteen inches; females, five feet by sixteen inches; boys, five feet by fourteen inches; girls, four feet six by twelve inches. This, as F. George Kay points out in *The Shameful Trade*, meant that five men were packed into a space equivalent to two modern single beds, and lay there for perhaps twenty hours a day over a period of several weeks. Parliament was prepared to accept a death rate of two per cent.

18. *The Genius of Universal Emancipation*, a newspaper published from 1821 to 1839 by Benjamin Lundy, an early American abolitionist. William Lloyd Garrison, perhaps the greatest of anti-slavery journalists, worked with Lundy before founding his own paper, *The Liberator*, in 1831 which ran until the end of the Civil War. Arthur and Lewis Tappan were dedicated New York abolitionists.

19. The revolvers, by Flashman's description, were probably early Colt Patersons of 1836 (single-action muzzle-loaders, five-shot, .40 calibre), although it is not impossible that they were Colt Walkers of the type produced for the Mexican War (six-shot, .44). The needle guns must be the Prussian Dreyse single-shot breech-loaders of 1840, which were the first bolt-action military weapons.

20. The Dahomeyans believed that human sacrifices were messengers to the gods, and despatched about 500 each year, about a tenth of whom were killed at the "annual custom", as the great ritual slaughter festival was called. The "grand custom", held only when a king died, involved much greater bloodshed.

21. King Gezo, a liberal ruler by Dahomeyan standards, made £60,000 a year from the slave trade, according to Royal Navy intelligence estimates, and also reorganised the army of Amazons, which had previously been composed of female criminals, unfaithful wives, etc. Gezo, by recruiting from all the unmarried girls of his kingdom, raised a force of about 4,000 fighting women, and there is ample evidence of their ferocity and discipline. Flashman's description of them is accurate. Gezo ruled Dahomey for 40 years, dying of small-pox in 1858.

22. Quite apart from Harriet Beecher Stowe's famous villain, there was a Southern slave trader called Legree in Spring's time.

23. Methods of slave-packing varied according to a ship's accommodation, but Flashman's account gives a vivid impression of what a hideous business it was. His details of branding, sizing, and dancing are accurate; even so, it appears that Spring, despite his insistence on close packing, was a more humane skipper than most on the Middle Passage. Conditions on the *Balliol College* compare favourably with those on other slave ships of which contemporary records exist, and which tell appalling tales of human cargoes thrown overboard, epidemics, mutinies, and unspeakable cruelties. Even the sailors' stories which Flashman retells give only a pale impression of the reality. Figures compiled by Warren S. Howard in his *American Slavers and the Federal Law* indicate that on average one-sixth of slaves shipped died on the Middle Passage. The *Balliol College's* low mortality rate was not unique, however, in 1847 only three slaves died out of 530 aboard the barque *Fame*, running to Brazil.

24. Captain Robert Waterman of the *Sea Witch*, one of the great Yankee tea clippers. His passages from China to New York broke all records in the mid-1840s.
25. Blackwall fashion: competent but leisurely sea-faring, as opposed to the tough life aboard the packets.
26. One of the slaver's common ruses was to fly whatever colours seemed safest, according to their position at sea. In fact American colours were most common on the Middle Passage.
27. Although Spain had banned the slave trade, Cuba continued to operate a large unofficial slave market, and cargoes were smuggled in as circumstances permitted. Possibly these did not appear favourable to Spring, and he determined to run to Roatan, a popular clearing house.
28. On January 24, 1848, James W. Marshall found gold at Coloma, California. News of his discovery led to the great rushes of '48 and '49.
29. Prices varied enormously from year to year, but the figures quoted generally by Flashman are above average. Possibly 1848 was a good year from the seller's point of view.
30. Slaves certainly were thrown overboard on the approach of patrol vessels (see the case of the *Regulo* which drowned over 200 in the Bight of Biafra, and the reported case of the clipper captain who was said to have murdered over 500 by dropping them with his anchor chain, both quoted in Kay).
31. Abraham Lincoln was 39 at this time, and the physical description tallies closely with his first known photograph, taken in 1846. When he met Flashman he was in the middle of his only term as a U.S. Congressman, although he already had a successful career in local politics and as a lawyer behind him. As a Congressman he was not especially distinguished, and his bill to abolish slavery in the District of Columbia was never brought in.
32. Cassius Clay (1810–1903), a fighting Kentuckian and fervent abolitionist, who later became President Lincoln's minister to Russia.
33. The underground railroad was a truly heroic organisation which ran more than 70,000 slaves to freedom. Founded in the early 1840s by a clergyman, its agents included the famous John Brown of the popular song, and the extraordinary little negress, Harriet Tubman, herself a runaway. She guided no fewer than nineteen convoys of escaped negroes out of the slave states, including infants who had to be drugged to escape detection, and is reputed never to have lost any of her many hundred "passengers".
34. The true identity of "Mr Crixus" can only be guessed at. Obviously he had adopted the name from the Gaulish slave who was a chief lieutenant to Spartacus in the Roman gladiators' rebellion of 73 B.C.
35. The *Sultana's* record for the trip was five days and twelve hours exactly, set in 1844. Although often exaggerated, the performance of the Mississippi steamboats was extraordinary, and reached a peak with the run of Captain Cannon in the "good ship *Robert E. Lee*" in 1870, when the 1218 miles from New Orleans to St Louis was covered in three days eighteen hours fourteen minutes. Normally a big side-wheeler could easily maintain an average of over 12 m.p.h. upstream.
36. Mr Bixby was later head pilot of the Union forces in the Civil War. His other claim to fame is that he taught the craft of steamboat piloting to Mark Twain.
37. Mustee, a shortened form of musteefino or musterfino: loosely, a half-caste, but particularly one who was very pale skinned. Strictly speaking, the child of one black and one white parent is a mulatto; the child of a mulatto and a white is a quadroon (one quarter black); the child of a quadroon and a white is a mustee (one eighth black). It is

a curious feature of colour prejudice that *any* admixture of coloured blood, however small, is deemed sufficient to make the owner a negro.

38. Thanks to Flashman's vagueness about dates, it is impossible to say in exactly which week he and Cassy were contemplating their journey up the Ohio. It must surely have been early spring in 1849, in which case Flashman must have spent longer on the Mandeville plantation than his narrative suggests; he was there for cotton-picking, which normally takes place in September and October, but can extend into early December.

39. There can be little doubt that Harriet Beecher Stowe, who was living in Cincinnati at the time, must have heard of Cassy and Flashman crossing the Ohio ice pursued by slave-catchers, and decided to incorporate the incident in her best-selling *Uncle Tom's Cabin*, which was published two years later. She, of course, attributed the feat to the slave girl Eliza; it can be no more than an interesting coincidence that the burden Eliza carried in her flight was a "real handsome boy" named Harry. But it seems quite likely that Mrs Stowe met the real Cassy, and used her, name and all, in that part of the book which describes life on Simon Legree's plantation.

Incidentally, Mrs Stowe timed Eliza's fictitious crossing for late February (which she calls "early spring"); this provides a further clue to the time of Flashman's crossing in similar weather conditions.

40. A "who's-yar" (usually spelled hoosier): an Indianan, supposedly deriving from the rustic dialect for "who's there?", although this is much disputed. In fact, although Lincoln spent most of his youth in Indiana, he himself was a Kentuckian by birth.

41. But not for much longer. Lincoln's term in Congress ended on March 4, 1849, which can only have been a few days after his meeting with Flashman in Portsmouth; it is curious that their conversation contains no mention of his impending retirement.

42. The *Butterfly*, a newly-built slave ship, was captured before she had even reached Africa, let alone taken on slaves. After a fierce legal battle she was condemned.

43. From Flashman's account of the adjudication, it is obvious that he has greatly simplified the procedure of the court; no doubt after half a century only the highlights remained in his mind. Procedure in slave-ship cases varied greatly from country to country, and did not remain consistent, and many such cases were never even printed. So bearing in mind that what he is describing was a form of preliminary hearing, and not a slave-ship trial proper, one can only take his word for what happened in the *Balliol College* adjudication.

As to Flashman's allegations of corruption and pressure exerted in slave-ship cases, one cannot do better than quote the words of a contemporary skipper, Captain C. E. Driscoll (see Howard), who boasted flatly: "I can get any man off in New York for a thousand dollars."

44. The owners of a ship arrested as a slaver, but subsequently acquitted, might well be in a strong position to claim damages from the arresting party. For this reason there was some reluctance in the late 1840s, especially among American Navy officers, to capture suspected slaveships, for fear of being sued.

A NOTE ON THE TYPE

The text of this book was set on the Linotype in Juliana, a type face designed by the eminent Dutch typographer and engraver Sem L. Hartz. A new face, introduced in 1958, Juliana has gained growing popularity as a text type. The design is reminiscent of sixteenth-century Italian forms with a pronounced calligraphic italic, yet entirely original.